CERTAIN THINGS LAST

CERTAIN THINGS

LAST

The Selected
Short Stories of
SHERWOOD ANDERSON

Edited and Introduced by

Charles E. Modlin

FOUR WALLS EIGHT WINDOWS

Published by
Four Walls Eight Windows
PO Box 548
Village Station
New York, N.Y. 10014
First Edition
First Printing October 1992
Library of Congress Cataloging-in-Publication Data:
Anderson, Sherwood, 1876-1941
Certain things last: the selected short stories of Sherwood Anderson:
edited and introduced by Charles E. Modlin
p. cm.
ISBN 0-941423-85-9 $24.95
I. Modlin, Charles E. II. Title.
PS3501, N4C45 1992
813.52—dc20
Design by Martin Moskof
Printed in the U.S.A.

CONTENTS

Introduction   vii
Notes   xxiii
Stories
    Certain Things Last   1
    I Want to Know Why   8
    The Other Woman   18
    The Egg   27
    Brothers   39
    I'm a Fool   48
    The Man Who Became a Woman   60
    Milk Bottles   93
    The Man's Story   102
    An Ohio Pagan   122
    Death in the Woods   147
    The Return   161
    There She Is—She Is Taking Her Bath   179
    In a Strange Town   192
    These Mountaineers   203
    A Meeting South   210

The Flood	222
Brother Death	231
In a Field	248
A Criminal's Christmas	252
Virginia Justice	258
The Corn Planting	265
Mrs. Wife	271
Pastoral	288
Not Sixteen	297
Nobody Laughed	307
For What?	318
The Masterpiece	327
Fred	337
The Red Dog	344
Editorial Notes	350
Early Publications of Stories	356
About Sherwood Anderson	358

INTRODUCTION

WHEN KATE SWIFT ADVISES THE YOUNG ASPIRING AUTHOR GEORGE Willard in *Winesburg, Ohio* that "You will have to know life,"[1] she speaks as well for Sherwood Anderson. The need for a heightened sensitivity to life was central to his whole approach to writing. He wrote that "what I wanted for myself most of all, rather than so-called success, acclaim, to be praised by publishers and editors, was to try to develop, to the top of my bent, my own capacity to feel, see, taste, smell, hear."[2] Anderson's own experience in life was rich, and he drew heavily upon it in his writing, bringing, in both style and subject matter, a distinctive new realism to early twentieth century fiction.

His narrative style derived largely from the oral stories that he heard first as a child from his own father and relished throughout his life. Old-time storytellers, he explained, were actors. "As they talked they modulated their voices, made gestures with their hands. Often they carried conviction simply by the power of their own conviction. All of our modern fussing with style in writing is an attempt to do the same thing."[3] He freely acknowledged his indebtedness over the years to such storytellers—"feeders" he called them—who masterfully rendered oral narratives but left to him the task of turning them into fiction. Often his manner of writing his stories was itself akin to the oral tradition. Many of them developed through a long process of reshaping. A woman who knew him in 1919 recalled his revising stories such as "I Want to Know Why" by "telling them and re-telling them to friends, adding a phrase here and dropping one out there."[4]

Anderson criticized the writers of popular fiction that pandered to the public's desire for adventure, romance, or moral uplift. They relied on the trickery of the "Poison Plot," which, he wrote in *A Story Teller's Story*, had nothing in common with "any life I had known anything about."[5] He maintained instead that fiction should take on a natural form that, instead of distorting life, captures it honestly. While art is distinct from real life, "the imagination must constantly feed upon reality or starve."[6]

This is the essential point in "Certain Things Last," a story that Anderson probably wrote in the early 1920s but never published. When the narrator, who is moved to write a "certain book," pursues his colorful, freefloating imagination, the results are unsatisfactory. He must instead get closer to the experience that gave him the impulse to write, which is, he hints, his haltingly acknowledged love for the woman. Playing, as he does throughout his narration, on the word "certain," he turns away from fantasy and realizes: "At a certain hour of a certain day and in a certain place, something happened that has changed the whole current of my life." If he is to write his book truly, he must tell "the adventures of that certain moment," which, commonplace though it may be, holds the true mystery and challenge for the writer.

"Milk Bottles" is based on a similar premise. The allegorical intent of the story is indicated by its title when it first appeared in 1921: "Why There Must Be a Midwestern Literature." The need for writers to address the reality around them is expressed through Ed, whose job is to extol the virtues of condensed milk but whose ambition is to write the equally exaggerated epic of Chicago. Yet the story that he writes in anger and throws away is the real one, having in its honesty and feeling a "lovely singing quality."

The storyteller's conversion of observed reality into art is also the subject of "In a Field." The narrator is witness to a whole drama of love, conflict, and resolution taking place before him.

He could intervene but decides he is "a recorder of things, a teller of tales" rather than "a man of action." To a great extent he does simply record what he observes and, from his fixed position in the field, is able to gather the pieces of the story that give it body. Yet what brings it to life is the additional factor of the narrator's own imagination as he vicariously joins in the drama and at one point even becomes the fleeing lover.

Anderson's ability to get close to ordinary life and to convert it into art became stunningly realized with the publication in 1919 of his *Winesburg, Ohio* stories, which are justly recognized today as a landmark in modern American fiction. But in the perspective of Anderson's total career, they were just the culmination of his early work in short fiction, which would be followed by the middle and late stages when he wrote some of his finest but mostly overlooked stories. It is from these post-*Winesburg* periods that the present collection is drawn.

I

The stories from the middle years are those of the early 1920s. They continue many of the *Winesburg* themes—such as young people's initiation into adulthood, the alienation of the artist, the breakdown of human relationships, and the loss of love—but venture far beyond the confines of a small midwestern town and display a greater technical skill. While the narrative voice in *Winesburg* was omniscient and tightly controlled, the best stories of the middle period are typically told by characters who use their narration as a way of coming to grips with their own problems and thus approximate the oral storytelling style that Anderson so admired.

The stories of adolescent initiation—"I Want to Know Why," "I'm a Fool," "The Man Who Became a Woman," and "An Ohio Pagan"—are based on Anderson's memories of his own youth. One of his many boyhood jobs was as a groom or "swipe" in a livery stable in Clyde, and, in the summer and fall of 1895, he travelled on the racing circuit in the area tending to the horses of a local farmer, Tom Whitehead, who appears in "I'm a Fool" and

"An Ohio Pagan" as Harry Whitehead.

The most popular of the horse racing stories, "I'm a Fool," was written, Anderson recalled, when he was at his desk at the advertising agency supposedly "writing copy for a gas engine company."[7] First published in 1922, it was praised by William Faulkner in 1925 as "the best short story in America."[8] While Anderson was pleased with the story, its many subsequent reprintings (he called it "more reproductive than a rabbit"[9]) became an annoyance to him in that he felt himself stereotyped as the writer of yarns about the vagaries of young love. Nevertheless, its lively narration and sensitive characterization still retain their appeal.

Anderson said that he got the impulse to write "I Want to Know Why" on a visit to the Saratoga races with David Bohon, an advertising client from Kentucky (hence the reference in the story to Banker Bohon).[10] But it had a long background. Noting that a psychiatrist once told him that it must have been written after a passionate love affair with a woman who turned out to be a prostitute, Anderson instead associated the story with an experience from his early days in Chicago. During a period of loneliness, he imagined and wrote long letters to an ideal woman named Cecelia. He later met a prostitute and convinced himself, in accepting her proposition, that she was Cecelia. At her apartment as she undressed, one of her two young children on the other side of a curtain began to cry, and Anderson, brought back to reality, gave her five dollars and left. He concludes: "And so I imagine myself, walking again in the street, still on the same day, and thinking of the theme of the story "I Want to Know Why." I would simply have been questioning the two sides of myself, being, in myself, both the boy who was a horse lover and the trainer who went off to the whore."[11]

The boy's idealized attitude towards horses may be traced to an unpleasant series of incidents that Anderson remembered from his days of working at the livery stable. A fellow workman, who constantly bragged to him about his sexual conquests, was particularly offensive one night, inviting him to take a turn with a prostitute he had brought back to the stable. On another occasion Anderson was tricked into getting drunk and, when he passed out, was thrown in a stall strewn with manure. He left the job, he writes, with "the conviction that the animals that are the servants of man are infinitely finer and better than many men a boy would have to deal with in living his life."[12]

The idea recurs in "The Man Who Became a Woman," in which the natural world of thoroughbred horses is juxtaposed to man-made horrors. In this complex story, young Herman Dudley temporarily leaves respectable society, having had his fill of its conventional standards of material success and pretentious morality, to become a swipe. But, in his loneliness after the departure of his friend Tom Means, he struggles with his identity and his relationships with others. He likes his black co-worker Burt but feels distanced from him by social barriers. He is attracted to women but is too inhibited to approach them. The progressively bizarre experiences that follow still haunt Herman years later, and thus the narration itself becomes the means of finally putting the experience to rest: "Sometimes I even screamed out at night and so I said to myself, 'I'll write the dang story....'"

"An Ohio Pagan" is another startlingly imaginative story of a boy's growing up. Originally a part of a promising but abandoned novel, "Ohio Pagans," it was first published in *Horses and Men.* Anderson was drawing from his own work experience—not only as a swipe but also as a thresher in the summer of 1899 following his return from the Spanish-American War and prior to his enrollment at Wittenberg Academy. The scenes of Tom's religious and sexual awakenings include some of the most lyrical descriptions of nature that Anderson ever wrote. Although some critics as well as Anderson himself have commented on the inconclusiveness of the ending, it has effectively understated poignancy as the young pagan looks expectantly toward the city.

"The Egg" is one of Anderson's own favorite stories and generally acknowledged to be one of his finest. Originally published in 1920 as "The Triumph of the Egg," it, like "An Ohio Pagan," takes place in and around Bidwell, Ohio, the setting of Anderson's novel *Poor White,* where it is the scene of industrial growth and capitalistic greed. This association is borne out in "The Egg" when the father quits his job on Tom Butterworth's farm and gets caught up in the entrepreneurial spirit of the times (as does Butterworth in *Poor White).* Particularly effective is the role of the narrator, who interprets the experience of growing up under such conditions with humor, sympathy, and insight. As the child of his father, he knows intuitively just what went on downstairs with Joe Kane, and as a storyteller he can recreate it. Moreover, his ability to enclose the whole history of his father in the simple but all-pervasive symbolism of the egg is itself a triumph.

In two subtly humorous stories, "The Other Woman" and "There She Is–She Is Taking Her Bath," ambivalent narrators use their storytelling as a way to work through, if not to solve, problems with their spouses. "The Other Woman," written, Anderson said, "partly with my tongue in my cheek—bad little boy stuff,"[13] is a subtle portrait of an idealistic but self-deceived poet basking in the successes of his government appointment, a poetry prize, and an opportune marriage to an "awakening" wife. In "There She Is—She Is Taking Her Bath," John Smith is torn between his desire to know the truth and his inability to face it. Years after he wrote the story, Anderson referred to the "timid and absurdly jealous" husband and his "quite innocent" wife, "[a]s a detective he hired to watch her assured him...."[14] The circumstances are more complex, however, because Smith has paid a second detective to assure a favorable report. While at times his jealousy may cloud his perceptions, he cites evidence that is hard to dismiss, as is his conclusion that, having come too close to the truth of the matter, he is better off settling for illusion. The wife, meanwhile, takes her bath—whether immersed in innocence or cleansing her impurities, we cannot be sure.

In 1921 Anderson made his first trip to Europe, published *The Triumph of the Egg,* and became the first recipient of the *Dial* prize for outstanding contributions to American literature. Feeling increasingly trapped in Chicago, he lamented to his friend Paul

Rosenfeld in late October that "I have accepted my own Mid-America as a walled-in place" and that "Artists have to be strangers to the body of the people now in Chicago, in Ohio, in all this empire of Mid-America."[15] This theme of alienation carries over in some of his most powerful writing during this period.

"Brothers," first published in April 1921, eloquently depicts both the barriers between people—especially the "muddle" of relations between men and women—and the impulse to escape, through romantic fantasy or the artistic imagination. The man who, distracted by his romanticized image of the woman at work, murders his pregnant wife is interpreted, as well as paralleled, by the old man who, obscured by the heavy fog in the remarkable last scene, swings "back and forth like a body hanging on the gallows" as he tells "The whole story of mankind's loneliness, of the effort to reach out to unattainable beauty."

"The Man's Story," which Anderson calls "one of the very great and beautiful short stories of the world,"[16] presents a similar case of detachment in which the poet builds "the wall between himself and all us others constantly higher and higher." The narrator, a newspaperman and amateur poet, is made "woozy" by Wilson's poems about walls and wells but feels, like the murdered woman and the hunchback, strangely drawn to him. Anderson associated with the story a strange romantic interlude of his own one night in Chicago when he was nineteen. After carrying groceries for a woman to her drab apartment, he stayed to become her lover. While he had no interest in any commitment to her, she was, he wrote, "a woman in the darkness" who provided "warm life that I so wanted to come to me, for the breaking up of my own isolation in life."[17] Her apartment was the model for that of Wilson and the woman, and surely another part of the association with this memory was the theme of isolation. The shooting scene is taken from an unfinished novel, "Talbot Whittingham," written in 1914-15, where, Anderson's biographer Kim Townsend suggests, it plays out both Anderson's artistic ambition and his destructive feelings toward his first wife, Cornelia.[18] After many attempts to write "The Man's Story" over the years, Anderson finally succeeded in 1922. He finished it with a flourish, borrowing the apartment of fellow author Stark Young to write all day. Having consumed most of a quart of whiskey by the time Young returned in the evening, Anderson told him: "I am drunk now but, before I got drunk, I wrote oh such a beautiful story."[19]

II

In 1922 Anderson made the break from his job and an unhappy marriage and left Chicago. Following his marriage to Elizabeth Prall, he moved to New Orleans. Over the next few years he had some dark periods to go through as he experienced the breakup of another marriage as well as a declining literary reputation. While the publication of his novel *Dark Laughter* was a financial success, some critics and fellow authors like Ernest Hemingway and F. Scott Fitzgerald concluded from it that Anderson was finished as a writer. Subsequent works such as *Sherwood Anderson's Notebook, Tar,* and *A New Testament*—products of a troublesome arrangement he had entered into with Horace Liveright, his new publisher, to produce a book a year for five years—did little to revive his reputation. But when a critic complained in 1927 that "The author of 'Winesburg, Ohio,' is dying before our eyes," Anderson replied, "Well, let him die," and looked forward to "another Sherwood Anderson coming slowly to life."[20]

Anderson was in fact making a new beginning. In 1926 he moved to southwestern Virginia and built his only permanent home, Ripshin, there. He tried his hand at publishing and editing two newspapers in Marion, travelled extensively, and enjoyed at last an exceptionally stable and fulfilling marriage to Eleanor Copenhaver. He continued to write fiction, including an excellent collection of short stories, *Death in the Woods.* Over the later years, despite occasional bouts with illness and some despondency over the difficulty of making a living from his writing, he was reasonably content with his life and developed a mellowed outlook that carries over into the stories of this period. The literary critic Maxwell Geismar has aptly called their style "simple, easy, almost conversational, and 'artlessly' translucent...."[21] They tend to be shorter and to reflect a generally milder view of life than the earlier stories. Lacking the brooding narrators of the middle period, they are sometimes tinged with humor and generally end happily or at least serenely.

In the fall of 1924, during Anderson's residence in New Orleans, he met and befriended a young William Faulkner, and the two explored the city together. One evening they visited a retired madame there, Aunt Rose Arnold; Anderson's fictional-ized account of that occasion is "A Meeting South," first published in 1925. The details of David's war wounds, which cause pain that only whiskey can relieve, correspond to the fabricated stories that Faulkner frequently told about himself at the time,[22] which Anderson may or may not have believed.

Perhaps the most celebrated of Anderson's short stories, "Death in the Woods" is an account of a childhood experience working on the mind of the narrator. Piecing together information and impressions from a variety of sources, including his direct obser-vations, hearsay in the town, and later his own similar experiences, the narrator only eventually, with the aid of his imagination, is able to turn a haunting incident into "the real story." Its devel-opment in Anderson's own imagination was similar. He recalls having seen in his youth an old woman frozen in the snow whose clothes had been torn off by a pack of dogs, and he attempted to write a version of the story as early as 1916. He also describes in his *Memoirs* a later (around 1921) personal experience on a snowy night during a walk in a forest near Palos Park, Illinois, when he was followed by a pack of dogs. While he rested on a log, they ran in a "mysterious circle," occasionally breaking away to come over to stare at him. It was this incident, he wrote, in which he had the feeling of being "transported suddenly to a primitive world," that gave him the impulse to write the story as it would eventually, after many versions, take shape.[23]

Anderson's travels over the years occasionally brought him back to his hometown of Clyde, Ohio, and "The Return," first published in 1925, was influenced by his own stir of emotions during the visits. On one such occasion in 1916 he commented on the ugly build-up of houses where once "Romance dwelt," the "dull, heavy faces" of women passing by his hotel, and his sense of sadness and loneliness.[24] John Holden's homecoming a year after his wife's death is similarly difficult as he copes with both change and introspection.

The narrator of "In a Strange Town," a philosophy professor, seeks therapy in travel, as he has done periodically since the sudden death of the female student whose visits to his office had been so rejuvenating. With a stark, almost incantatory style, the narrator finds relief in the new sensations of the strange town. In his *Memoirs* Anderson states that he wrote the story "to tell what wandering in some new and strange town did to me."[25] More specifically, however, it marks a crux in his personal life. He wrote it in the summer of 1929 while staying in Danbury, Connecticut with Mary Vernon Greer, a woman who had done secretarial work for him in Marion and with whom he was carrying on a sporadic affair. During the previous spring he had become attracted to Eleanor Copenhaver but left Marion in late June, annoyed at her resistance to his physical advances. He traveled north to visit a young artist Charles Bockler and his wife Katharine, Greer's sister, who were renting a farm near Dykemans, New York, and from there made the short trip to Danbury. The whole summer venture turned out to be a disappointment because Katharine, who was pregnant, complained constantly and prevented him from writing. But more importantly, after visiting with Greer "in a strange town," he decided to end his relationship with her and returned to Marion with a fresh appreciation of Eleanor and a determination to win her over.

Another philosophy professor, the "old stick" in "The Flood," has to deal with his loneliness after the death of his wife and his tendency to search for values in his head rather than in the life around him. Again the story grows out of Anderson's own experience. In 1927 Anderson had bought the Marion newspapers with a $5,000 loan from Burton Emmett, a retired advertising executive, who, being a collector of literary artifacts, offered to take manuscripts as in-kind payments on the loan. Anderson agreed and began to send them. But by the spring of 1930 he became sensitive to the process of determining the market—as opposed to artistic—values of such items. One of the manuscripts he sent Emmett was a novel that he abandoned late in 1929. While he worked on it, he told Emmett, Horace Liveright kept insisting that it would make him rich and famous. The intrusion of monetary considerations upon his work, Anderson claimed, had much to do with its failure. As for the appraisal of the manuscripts, he accepted Emmett's estimate of $3,000 but wrote on May 25, 1930: "I'll never get any sense of values at all in these scrawled pieces of paper...."[26] A month later he reported to Emmett that he had written "The Flood." The story loosely parallels Anderson's own life at the time. He had gone through severe depression at the end of 1929 brought on by his discouragement with the aborted novel and the suicide of Tennessee Mitchell, his second wife. In early 1930, with the support of Eleanor Copenhaver, he began his tours of the South and a whole new direction for his writing. In the spring he and Eleanor became lovers, and this time period was an unusually happy one for him. Exultantly he asked: "How can people live without love?"[27]

When Anderson built his country home in Grayson County, Virginia, in 1926, he also set about the task of meeting and being accepted by the mountain people around him. By the time the house was finished, he wrote, the period of assimilation with his neighbors was also complete: "They were John and Will and Pete and Frank to me and I was Sherwood to them."[28] "These Mountaineers" and "Virginia Justice" indirectly depict Anderson's own adjustment to the culture of southwestern Virginia.

In writing "These Mountaineers" in the fall of 1929, Anderson said he was "more objective" than usual in his presentation of the pregnant girl: "I tried to make her stand alone, without relation to anyone, a portrait."[29] In the story, the writer from the North is "possessed" by her wild yet aristocratic face but, despite his good intentions, leaves the hollow still very much an outsider. Fred in

"Virginia Justice" is much more successful in bridging the cultural gap. Felix, the story-telling neighbor is modeled after Felix Sullivan, who built Anderson's wall at Ripshin and told him endless stories of both the mountain people and his own Sergeant York-like adventures in World War One. The story was first published in 1934, but when it was prepared for inclusion in *The Sherwood Anderson Reader,* the title was changed to "Justice" at the suggestion of Roger Sergel, an old friend of Anderson's, who preferred the universal designation. But Anderson's title is here restored; he clearly intended it to refer to the *ad hoc* country justice meted out by the Virginia squires, who "don't pretend to know much law."

In 1933 Anderson made a late addition to his *Death in the Woods* volume, extracting a story, which he called "Brother Death," from a novel, "Thanksgiving," that he had abandoned. He was pleased with the result, calling it "one of the finest stories I've done, and I even dare say one of the finest and most significant anyone has ever done."[30] It is set in Rich Valley, a farming area located a few miles northwest of Marion. The tree stumps, on which the story effectively centers, represent an opposition within the family between practical and human values that Mary senses as a child but only fully understands as she looks back years later.

"The Corn Planting," first published in 1934, presents a more positive attachment to the land. While the Grey farm in "Brother Death" is big business with cattle as commodities, the Hutchensons live on a humble farm on Scratch Gravel Road (the actual name of a road leading out of Marion that Anderson liked), with close ties to their milk cows and the soil. The story validates their attitude toward human life and death as shaped and expressed through their participation in the cycles of nature.

"Nobody Laughed" tells the story of a sordid side of small-town life. Anderson had considerable difficulty with it, putting it through numerous drafts, with Laura Lu Copenhaver helping with revisions. An early version entitled "Playthings" (later "The Town's Playthings") was, his agent reported, "too grim" to sell.[31] Anderson then tried to avoid indicting the whole town by changing the title to "Nobody Laughed" and writing a new ending that places most of the responsibility on a few ringleaders whose enthusiasm for practical jokes gets out of hand during a hot summer with no baseball. But it still found no publisher in Anderson's lifetime and appeared in print only after Paul Rosenfeld made a few changes of his own and included it in *The Sherwood Anderson Reader.*

On a much lighter note, Anderson returns in "A Criminal's Christmas" and "Not Sixteen" to stories about young people. It is appropriate that he should write about a young thief who hides out from the law at Christmas, since Anderson himself called it "a horrid day really, so much fakiness clustered about it,"[32] and frequently associated it with his family's poverty and his mother's illness. Yet "A Criminal's Christmas" has real charm in its adult narrator's recounting of his guilt, which he wryly extends into the spring when his ill-gotten gain comes finally to naught. "Not Sixteen" in its earliest form was an autobiographical account of Anderson's threshing experience in the summer of 1899. As it began to take on a fictional life of its own, he rewrote it in November 1937 as a short story, updating it to post-World War One and creating in John, the frustrated but ambitious veteran, one of his most enjoyable characters.

An occupational group that attracted Anderson's interest throughout his writing career are the quirky small-town physicians such as Dr. Reefy and Dr. Parcival in *Winesburg,* Dr. Cochran in "Unlighted Lamps" (1921), and, in the present collection, the unnamed doctors in "Pastoral" and "Mrs. Wife." Anderson claimed to have served as a stable boy and companion to an old physician and commented once that he always wanted to be a doctor with the opportunity "to touch people's lives."[33] He admired the Russian author Anton Chekhov, who combined medicine with writing, and, like the narrator in "Mrs. Wife," envied "country doctors the opportunity they have to enter houses, hear stories, stand with people in times of trouble."

"Pastoral" was begun on August 5, 1938 at Ripshin during a visit by Eleanor's sister, Katharine, and brother-in-law, Henry Van Meier, a physician from Minnesota. In April 1939, Anderson worked on the story again and, at the suggestion of the *Reader's Digest*, sent it to them as a contribution to their "Most Unforgettable Character" series (thus the opening sentence). It was rejected, however, and after further revisions, it appeared in *Redbook* in January 1940. The story draws on Anderson's own interest in nature, especially mushrooms, as well as his compulsive letter writing—including perhaps the old letters to Cecelia. In 1932 he had in fact written a whole year's worth of letters and notes which he put away for Eleanor to read—a "letter-a-day" for a year after his death.[34]

"Mrs. Wife" is one of the best of Anderson's later stories. Its leisurely paced and richly textured narration is particularly well framed by the fishing scenes. The "inner laughter" of both the husband and wife as a sign of their maturity is a concept Anderson developed in late 1935 when at the age of 59 he described with admiration the serenity that follows from "knowing that the ultimate perfect thing we want cannot be attained.[35] "Mrs. Wife" was published in *Redbook* as "A Moonlight Walk" in a version that was the result of much editing and rewriting by Laura Lu Copenhaver. Her title was later changed by Paul Rosenfeld in *The Sherwood Anderson Reader* to "A Walk in the Moonlight." The text in the present collection is that of the latest manuscript prepared by Anderson himself, including his own title, "Mrs. Wife."

In the last years of his life, Anderson was keenly aware of the frustrations and disappointments of his writing career. His letters and diaries during this period record the cycle of hope and disappointment as so many of his projects fell short of his own expectations or those of publishers. Even modest successes could be heartbreaking; in the fall of 1938 he sold "His Chest of Drawers" to *Household Magazine* for $75, which he said "made me very blue."[36] And yet, he never stopped writing. "I'm trying again," he wrote in May 1939; "a man has to begin over and over."[37] A final group of four stories from this period deal with struggling or disappointed artists and their connections with the world of reality.

In 1937 Anderson wrote a reminiscence of the period around 1912-13, when he was living with other writers and artists in Chicago, that he called "We Little Children of the Arts." In November 1939 he prepared a story from this material, "For What?" which the *Yale Review* accepted but failed to publish until June 1941, three months after Anderson's death. The attempt referred to in the title, to achieve "something beyond money to be made, fame got, a big name," results in frustration for the narrator, who cannot write his story, and the art students, especially Jerry, who feels but cannot adequately express his vision of America. As Anderson was completing the story, he wrote to Laura Lu Copenhaver, who had apparently misinterpreted the ending, that Jerry

> didn't surrender when he found his dreams were fading. He searched about to find his brushes again. What I had in mind was something I have always felt in farmers. They work hard, often, at the end of the year, get nothing for a whole year's work, but in the spring you see them out again, plowing soil. It has always been to me something heroic, not in a big showy way but in a kind of heroic patience with failure.[38]

As the narrator comes to this understanding, his account of the day and its meaning substitutes for the story he was unable to write.

"The Masterpiece" also deals with the connections between art and reality. In a whimsical and deceptively simple style, it explores the complex relationship between Harold's idealized but conventional painting and the narrator's joyful but ultimately disappointing collaboration with Mildred. Anderson never completed a final draft of the story. It was first published by Eleanor Anderson in *Mademoiselle* a year after Anderson's death as "The Yellow Gown," a title assigned by Laura Lu Copenhaver prior to her death in 1940.

Two final stories, "Fred" and "The Red Dog," have not previously been published. Although a note by Eleanor Anderson on the manuscript of "Fred" dates it as before 1928, it may have been written two or three years later, referring obliquely to

Anderson's courtship of her to the dismay of her school superintendent father. Fred, the painter-turned-illustrator, has found in
his relations with women a substitute for his disappointed artistic
aspirations. "The Red Dog" exists only in manuscript with notes
by Eleanor Anderson attached indicating that the idea for the story
originated with one that Anderson's artist brother Karl had told
him concerning a painter doing a portrait of a rich woman with
an "aristocratic looking" dog. Sherwood reverses the meaning of
the dog, connecting it to the poor man with the gold tooth. The
disillusioned artist prizes the man's family and considers his
painting of them his masterpiece, but no one will buy it and he is
reduced to doing portraits of rich women.

It is noteworthy that in each story of this group the disappointed
artist has achieved a human gain, small and personal though it may
be. Anderson had his own share of personal satisfactions in later
years and perhaps partially attained that state of inner laughter he
wrote about. But he was never really content with falling short of
his goals and, with the persistence of spirit that he admired in
farmers and artists, kept on working, hoping to be, he wrote to
Eleanor, "like Johnny Appleseed, walking through the wilderness,
planting here and there an apple tree to bloom and bear fruit
maybe after he is dead."[39] More than a half-century after his death,
Anderson's short stories are still full of life.

For their help in the planning and preparation of this book, I
would like to thank the following: William Aiken, Hilbert H.
Campbell, Becky Cox, Karen Coates, Diana Haskell, Chris
Holbrook, John Keeling, Margaret Kulis, Marjorie Modlin, Fritz
Oehlschlaeger, Patricia Powell, Walter B. Rideout, Dan Simon,
Judy Jo Small, Welford D. Taylor, and Ray Lewis White. I am also
grateful to the English Department of Virginia Polytechnic Institute
and State University for many forms of assistance, and to the
Newberry Library and the Sherwood Anderson Literary Estate
Trust for permission to use Anderson's previously unpublished
writings.

—*Charles E. Modlin*

NOTES

1. "The Teacher," *Winesburg, Ohio* (New York: Huebsch, 1919), 192.

2. *Letters of Sherwood Anderson,* ed. Howard Mumford Jones and Walter B. Rideout (Boston: Little, Brown, 1953), 404.

3. "A Chicago Hamlet," *Horses and Men* (New York: Huebsch, 1923), 177.

4. Letter from Karen Hollis to Harry Hansen, March 12, 1941, (Newberry Library).

5. *A Story Teller's Story* (New York: Huebsch, 1924), 352, 362.

6. "Man and His Imagination," *The Intent of the Artist,* ed. Augusto Centeno (Princeton: University of Princeton Press, 1941), 67.

7. *Sherwood Anderson: Centennial Studies,* ed. Hilbert H. Campbell and Charles E. Modlin (Troy, N.Y.: Whitston Publishing Co., 1976), 10.

8. *Dallas Morning News,* April 26, 1925, part 3, p. 7.

9. *Sherwood Anderson: Selected Letters,* ed. Charles E. Modlin (Knoxville: University of Tennessee Press, 1984), 91.

10. *Sherwood Anderson's Secret Love Letters,* ed. Ray Lewis White (Baton Rouge: Louisiana State University Press, 1991), 39.

11. *The "Writer's Book" by Sherwood Anderson,* ed. Martha Mulroy Curry (Metuchen, N.J.: Scarecrow Press, 1975), 9-21, 113-14.

12. *Sherwood Anderson's Memoirs,* ed. Ray Lewis White (Chapel Hill: University of North Carolina Press, 1969), 114.

13. *Selected Letters,* 52.

14. "The Sound of the Stream," *The Triumph of the Egg* (New York: Four Walls Eight Windows, 1988), 285.

15. *Letters,* 80.

16. *Memoirs,* 278.

17. *Memoirs,* 161.

18. Kim Townsend, *Sherwood Anderson* (Boston: Houghton Mifflin, 1987), 101-03.

19. *Memoirs,* 435.

20. *Selected Letters,* 95, 96.

21. Introduction, *Sherwood Anderson: Short Stories,* ed. Maxwell Geismar (New York: Hill and Wang, 1962), xx.

22. Joseph Blotner, *Faulkner: A Biography,* vol. 1 (New York: Random House, 1974), 410.

23. *Memoirs,* 426.

24. *Letters to Bab,* ed. William A. Sutton (Urbana: University of Illinois Press, 1985), 23, 25.

25. *Memoirs,* 435.

26. *Selected Letters,* 120.

27. *Love Letters,* 95.

28. *Memoirs,* 504.

29. *Love Letters,* 27.

30. *Letters,* 278.

31. *The Sherwood Anderson Diaries,* ed. Hilbert H. Campbell (Athens: University of Georgia Press, 1987), 124.

32. *Love Letters,* 33.

33. *Story Teller's Story,* 149; *Selected Letters,* 66.

34. Published in *Sherwood Anderson's Secret Love Letters.*

35. *Love Letters,* 305.

36. Letter to Laura Lu Copenhaver (Newberry Library).

37. *Selected Letters,* 233.

38. Letter to Laura Lu Copenhaver (Newberry Library).

39. *Love Letters,* 180.

CERTAIN THINGS
LAST

FOR A YEAR NOW I HAVE BEEN THINKING OF WRITING A CERTAIN BOOK.
"Well, tomorrow I'll get at it," I've been saying to myself. Every
night when I get into bed I think about the book. The people
that are to be put between its covers dance before my eyes. I live
in the city of Chicago and at night motor trucks go rumbling
along the roadway outside my house. Not so very far away there
is an elevated railroad and after twelve o'clock at night trains pass
at pretty long intervals. Before it began I went to sleep during
one of the quieter intervals but now that the idea of writing this
book has got into me I lie awake and think.

For one thing it is hard to get the whole idea of the book fixed
in the setting of the city I live in now. I wonder if you, who do
not try to write books, perhaps will understand what I mean.
Maybe you will, maybe you won't. It is a little hard to explain.
You see, it's something like this. You as a reader will, some evening
or some afternoon, be reading in my book and then you will
grow tired of reading and put it down. You will go out of your
house and into the street. The sun is shining and you meet people
you know. There are certain facts of your life just the same as of
mine. If you are a man, you go from your house to an office and
sit at a desk where you pick up a telephone and begin to talk
about some matter of business with a client or a customer of your

house. If you are an honest housewife, the ice man has come or there drifts into your mind the thought that yesterday you forgot to remember some detail concerned with running your house. Little outside thoughts come and go in your mind, and it is so with me too. For example when I have written the above sentence, I wonder why I have written the words "honest housewife." A housewife I suppose can be as dishonest as I can. What I am trying to make clear is that, as a writer, I am up against the same things that confront you, as a reader.

What I want to do is to express in my book a sense of the strangeness that has gradually, since I was a boy, been creeping more and more into my feeling about everyday life. It would all be very simple if I could write of life in an interior city of China or in an African forest. A man I know has recently told me of another man who, wanting to write a book about Parisian life and having no money to go to Paris to study the life there, went instead to the city of New Orleans. He had heard that many people lived in New Orleans whose ancestors were French. "They will have retained enough of the flavor of Parisian life for me to get the feeling," he said to himself. The man told me that the book turned out to be very successful and that the city of Paris read with delight a translation of his work as a study of French life, and I am only sorry I can't find as simple a way out of my own job.

The whole point with me is that my wish to write this book springs from a somewhat different notion. "If I can write everything out plainly, perhaps I will myself understand better what has happened," I say to myself and smile. During these days I spend a good deal of time smiling at nothing. It bothers people. "What are you smiling about now?" they ask, and I am up against as hard a job trying to answer as I am trying to get underway with my book.

Sometimes in the morning I sit down at my desk and begin writing, taking as my subject a scene from my own boyhood. Very well, I am coming home from school. The town in which I was born and raised was a dreary, lonely little place in the far western section of the state of Nebraska, and I imagine myself walking along one of its streets. Sitting upon a curbing before a store is a sheep herder who has left his flock many miles away in the foothills at the base of the western mountains and has come into our town, for what purpose he himself does not seem to know. He is a bearded man without a hat and sits with his mouth slightly open, staring up and down the street. There is a half-wild uncertain look in his eyes and his eyes have awakened a creepy feeling in me. I hurry away with a kind of dread of some unknown thing eating at my vital organs. Old men are great talkers. It may be that only kids know the real terror of loneliness.

I have tried, you see, to start my book at that particular point in my own life. "If I can catch exactly the feeling of that afternoon of my boyhood, I can give the reader the key to my character," I tell myself.

The plan won't work. When I have written five, ten, fifteen hundred words, I stop writing and look out at my window. A man is driving a team of horses hitched to a wagon-load of coal along my street and is swearing at another man who drives a Ford. They have both stopped and are cursing each other. The coal wagon driver's face is black with coal dust but anger has reddened his cheeks and the red and black have produced a dusky brown like the skin of a Negro.

I have got up from my typewriter and walk up and down in my room smoking cigarettes. My fingers pick up little things on my desk and then put them down.

I am nervous like the race horses I used to be with at one period of my boyhood. Before a race and when they had been brought out on the tracks before all the people and before the race started, their legs quivered. Sometimes there was a horse got into such a state that when the race started he would do nothing. "Look at him. He can't untrack himself," we said.

Right now I am in that state about my book. I run to the typewriter, write for a time, and then walk nervously about. I smoke a whole package of cigarettes during the morning.

And then suddenly I have again torn up all I have written. "It won't do," I have told myself.

In this book I am not intending to try to give you the story of my life. "What of life, any man's life?—forked radishes running about, writing declarations of independence, telling themselves little lies, having dreams, getting puffed up now and then with what is called greatness. Life begins, runs its course and ends," a man I once knew told me one evening, and it is true. Even as I write these words a hearse is going through my street. Two young girls, who are going off with two young men to walk I suppose in the fields where the city ends, stop laughing for a moment and look up at the hearse. It will be a moment before they forget the passing hearse and begin laughing again.

"A life is like that, it passes like that," I say to myself as I tear up my sheets and begin again walking and smoking the cigarettes.

If you think I am sad, having these thoughts about the brevity and insignificance of a life, you are mistaken. In the state I am in such things do not matter. "Certain things last," I say to myself. "One might make things a little clear. One might even imagine a man, say a Negro, going along a city street and humming a song. It catches the ear of another man who repeats it on the next day. A thin strand of song, like a tiny stream far up in some hill, begins to flow down into the wide plains. It waters the fields. It freshens the air above a hot stuffy city."

Now I have got myself worked up into a state. I am always doing that these days. I write again and again tear up my words.

I go out of my room and walk about.

I have been with a woman I have found and who loves me. It has happened that I am a man who has not been loved by women and have all my life been awkward and a little mixed up when in their presence. Perhaps I have had too much respect for them, have wanted them too much. That may be. Anyway I am not so rattled in her presence.

She, I think, has a certain control over herself and that is helpful to me. When I am with her I keep smiling to myself and thinking, "It would be rather a joke all around if she found me out."

When she is looking in another direction I study her a little. That she should seem to like me so much surprises me and I am sore at my own surprise. I grow humble and do not like my humbleness either. "What is she up to? She is very lovely. Why is she wasting her time with me?"

I shall remember always certain hours when I have been with her. Late on a certain Sunday afternoon I remember I sat in a chair in a room in her apartment. I sat with my hand against my cheek, leaning a little forward. I had dressed myself carefully because I was going to see her, had put on my best suit of clothes. My hair was carefully combed and my glasses carefully balanced on my rather large nose.

And there I was, in her apartment in a certain city, in a chair in a rather dark corner, with my hand against my cheek, looking as solemn as an old owl. We had been walking about and had come into the house and she had gone away leaving me sitting there, as I have said. The apartment was in a part of the city where many foreign people live and from my chair I could, by turning my head a little, look down into a street filled with Italians.

It was growing dark outside and I could just see the people in the street. If I cannot remember facts about my own and other people's lives, I can always remember every feeling that has gone through me, or that I have thought went through anyone about me.

The men going along the street below the window all had dark swarthy faces and nearly all of them wore, somewhere about them, a spot of color. The younger men, who walked with a certain swagger, all had on flaming red ties. The street was dark but far down the street there was a spot where a streak of sunlight still managed to find its way in between two tall buildings and fell sharp against the face of a smaller red-brick building. It pleased my fancy to imagine the street had also put on a red necktie, perhaps because there would be lovemaking along the street before Monday morning.

Anyway I sat there looking and thinking such thoughts as came to me. The women who went along the street nearly all had dark

colored shawls drawn up about their faces. The roadway was filled
with children whose voices made a sharp tinkling sound.

My fancy went out of my body in a way of speaking, I suppose,
and I began thinking of myself as being at that moment in a city
in Italy. Americans like myself who have not traveled are always
doing that. I suppose the people of another nation would not
understand how doing it is almost necessity in our lives, but any
American will understand. The American, particularly a middle-
American, sits as I was doing at that moment, dreaming you understand, and suddenly he is in Italy or in a Spanish town where a
dark-looking man is riding a bony horse along a street, or he is
being driven over the Russian steppes in a sled by a man whose
face is all covered with whiskers. It is an idea of the Russians got
from looking at cartoons in newspapers but it answers the purpose. In the distance a pack of wolves are following the sled. A
fellow I once knew told me that Americans are always up to such
tricks because all of our old stories and dreams have come to us
from over the sea and because we have no old stories and dreams
of our own.

Of that I can't say. I am not putting myself forward as a thinker
on the subject of the causes of the characteristics of the American
people or any other monstrous or important matter of that kind.

But anyway, there I was, sitting, as I have told you, in the
Italian section of an American city and dreaming of myself being
in Italy.

To be sure I wasn't alone. Such a fellow as myself never is alone
in his dreams. And as I sat having my dream, the woman with
whom I had been spending the afternoon, and with whom I am
no doubt what is called "in love," passed between me and the
window through which I had been looking. She had on a dress of
some soft clinging stuff and her slender figure made a very lovely
line across the light. Well, she was like a young tree you might see
on a hill, in a windstorm perhaps.

What I did, as you may have supposed, was to take her with
me into Italy.

The woman became at once, and in my dream, a very beautiful princess in a strange land I have never visited. It may be that when I was a boy in my western town some traveler came there to lecture on life in Italian cities before a club that met at the Presbyterian church and to which my mother belonged, or perhaps later I read some novel the name of which I can't remember.

And so my princess had come down to me along a path out of a green wooded hill where her castle was located. She had walked under blossoming trees in the uncertain evening light and some blossoms had fallen on her black hair. The perfume of Italian nights was in her hair. That notion came into my head. That's what I mean.

What really happened was that she saw me sitting there lost in my dream and, coming to me, rumpled my hair and upset the glasses perched on my big nose and, having done that, went laughing out of the room.

I speak of all this because later, on that same evening, I lost all notion of the book I am now writing and sat until three in the morning writing on another book, making the woman the central figure. "It will be a story of old times, filled with moons and stars and the fragrance of half-decayed trees in an old land," I told myself, but when I had written many pages I tore them up too.

"Something has happened to me or I should not be filled with the idea of writing this book at all," I told myself going to my window to look out at the night. "At a certain hour of a certain day and in a certain place, something happened that has changed the whole current of my life.

"The thing to be done," I then told myself, "is to begin writing my book by telling as clearly as I can the adventures of that certain moment."

I WANT
TO KNOW WHY

WE GOT UP AT FOUR IN THE MORNING, THAT FIRST DAY IN THE EAST. On the evening before we had climbed off a freight train at the edge of town, and with the true instinct of Kentucky boys had found our way across town and to the race track and the stables at once. Then we knew we were all right. Hanley Turner right away found a nigger we knew. It was Bildad Johnson who in the winter works at Ed Becker's livery barn in our home town, Beckersville. Bildad is a good cook as almost all our niggers are and of course he, like everyone in our part of Kentucky who is anyone at all, likes the horses. In the spring Bildad begins to scratch around. A nigger from our country can flatter and wheedle anyone into letting him do most anything he wants. Bildad wheedles the stable men and the trainers from the horse farms in our country around Lexington. The trainers come into town in the evening to stand around and talk and maybe get into a poker game. Bildad gets in with them. He is always doing little favors and telling about things to eat, chicken browned in a pan, and how is the best way to cook sweet potatoes and corn bread. It makes your mouth water to hear him.

When the racing season comes on and the horses go to the races and there is all the talk on the streets in the evenings about the new colts, and everyone says when they are going over to

Lexington or to the spring meeting at Churchill Downs or to
Latonia, and the horsemen that have been down to New Orleans
or maybe at the winter meeting at Havana in Cuba come home
to spend a week before they start out again, at such a time when
everything talked about in Beckersville is just horses and nothing
else and the outfits start out and horse racing is in every breath of
air you breathe, Bildad shows up with a job as cook for some
outfit. Often when I think about it, his always going all season to
the races and working in the livery barn in the winter where horses
are and where men like to come and talk about horses, I wish I
was a nigger. It's a foolish thing to say, but that's the way I am
about being around horses, just crazy. I can't help it.

Well, I must tell you about what we did and let you in on what
I'm talking about. Four of us boys from Beckersville, all whites
and sons of men who live in Beckersville regular, made up our
minds we were going to the races, not just to Lexington or Louisville,
I don't mean, but to the big eastern track we were always hearing
our Beckersville men talk about, to Saratoga. We were all pretty
young then. I was just turned fifteen and I was the oldest of the
four. It was my scheme. I admit that and I talked the others into
trying it. There was Hanley Turner and Henry Rieback and Tom
Tumberton and myself. I had thirty-seven dollars I had earned
during the winter working nights and Saturdays in Enoch Myer's
grocery. Henry Rieback had eleven dollars and the others, Hanley
and Tom, had only a dollar or two each. We fixed it all up and
laid low until the Kentucky spring meetings were over and some
of our men, the sportiest ones, the ones we envied the most, had
cut out—then we cut out too.

I won't tell you the trouble we had beating our way on freights
and all. We went through Cleveland and Buffalo and other cities
and saw Niagara Falls. We bought things there, souvenirs and
spoons and cards and shells with pictures of the falls on them for
our sisters and mothers, but thought we had better not send any
of the things home. We didn't want to put the folks on our trail
and maybe be nabbed.

We got into Saratoga as I said at night and went to the track.

Bildad fed us up. He showed us a place to sleep in hay over a shed and promised to keep still. Niggers are all right about things like that. They won't squeal on you. Often a white man you might meet, when you had run away from home like that, might appear to be all right and give you a quarter or a half dollar or something, and then go right and give you away. White men will do that, but not a nigger. You can trust them. They are squarer with kids. I don't know why.

At the Saratoga meeting that year there were a lot of men from home. Dave Williams and Arthur Mulford and Jerry Myers and others. Then there was a lot from Louisville and Lexington Henry Rieback knew but I didn't. They were professional gamblers and Henry Rieback's father is one too. He is what is called a sheet writer and goes away most of the year to tracks. In the winter when he is home in Beckersville he don't stay there much but goes away to cities and deals faro. He is a nice man and generous, is always sending Henry presents, a bicycle and a gold watch and a boy scout suit of clothes and things like that.

My own father is a lawyer. He's all right, but don't make much money and can't buy me things and anyway I'm getting so old now I don't expect it. He never said nothing to me against Henry, but Hanley Turner and Tom Tumberton's fathers did. They said to their boys that money so come by is no good and they didn't want their boys brought up to hear gamblers' talk and be thinking about such things and maybe embrace them.

That's all right and I guess the men know what they are talking about, but I don't see what it's got to do with Henry or with horses either. That's what I'm writing this story about. I'm puzzled. I'm getting to be a man and want to think straight and be O.K., and there's something I saw at the race meeting at the eastern track I can't figure out.

I can't help it, I'm crazy about thoroughbred horses. I've always been that way. When I was ten years old and saw I was growing to be big and couldn't be a rider I was so sorry I nearly died. Harry Hellinfinger in Beckersville, whose father is Postmaster, is grown up and too lazy to work, but likes to stand around in the street and get up jokes on boys like sending them to a hardware store for a gimlet to bore square holes and other jokes like that. He played one on me. He told me that if I would eat a half a cigar I would be stunted and not grow anymore and maybe could be a rider. I did it. When father wasn't looking I took a cigar out of his pocket and gagged it down some way. It made me awful sick and the doctor had to be sent for, and then it did no good. I kept right on growing. It was a joke. When I told what I had done and why, most fathers would have whipped me but mine didn't.

Well, I didn't get stunted and didn't die. It serves Harry Hellinfinger right. Then I made up my mind I would like to be a stable boy, but had to give that up too. Mostly niggers do that work and I knew father wouldn't let me go into it. No use to ask him.

If you've never been crazy about thoroughbreds it's because you've never been around where they are much and don't know any better. They're beautiful. There isn't anything so lovely and clean and full of spunk and honest and everything as some race horses. On the big horse farms that are all around our town Beckersville there are tracks and the horses run in the early morning. More than a thousand times I've got out of bed before daylight and walked two or three miles to the tracks. Mother wouldn't of let me go but father always says, "Let him alone," So I got some bread out of the bread box and some butter and jam, gobbled it and lit out.

At the tracks you sit on the fence with men, whites and niggers, and they chew tobacco and talk, and then the colts are brought out. It's early and the grass is covered with shiny dew and in another field a man is plowing and they are frying things in a shed where the track niggers sleep, and you know how a nigger can giggle and laugh and say things that make you laugh. A white man can't do it and some niggers can't but a track nigger can every time.

And so the colts are brought out and some are just galloped by stable boys, but almost every morning on a big track owned by a rich man who lives maybe in New York, there are always, nearly every morning, a few colts and some of the old race horses and geldings and mares that are cut loose.

It brings a lump up into my throat when a horse runs. I don't mean all horses but some. I can pick them nearly every time. It's in my blood like in the blood of race track niggers and trainers. Even when they just go slop-jogging along with a little nigger on their backs I can tell a winner. If my throat hurts and it's hard for me to swallow, that's him. He'll run like Sam Hill when you let him out. If he don't win every time it'll be a wonder and because they've got him in a pocket behind other horses or he was pulled or got off bad at the post or something. If I wanted to be a gambler like Henry Rieback's father I could get rich. I know I could and Henry says so too. All I would have to do is to wait till that hurt comes when I see a horse and then bet every cent. That's what I would do if I wanted to be a gambler, but I don't.

When you're at the tracks in the morning—not the race tracks but the training tracks around Beckersville—you don't see a horse, the kind I've been talking about, very often, but it's nice anyway. Any thoroughbred, that is sired right and out of a good mare and trained by a man that knows how, can run. If he couldn't what would he be there for and not pulling a plow?

Well, out of the stables they come and the boys are on their backs and it's lovely to be there. You hunch down on top of the fence and itch inside you. Over in the sheds the niggers giggle and sing. Bacon is being fried and coffee made. Everything smells lovely. Nothing smells better than coffee and manure and horses and niggers and bacon frying and pipes being smoked out of doors on a morning like that. It just gets you, that's what it does.

But about Saratoga. We was there six days and not a soul from home seen us and everything came off just as we wanted it to, fine weather and horses and races and all. We beat our way home and Bildad gave us a basket with fried chicken and bread and other eatables in, and I had eighteen dollars when we got back to Beckersville. Mother jawed and cried but Pop didn't say much. I told everything we done except one thing. I did and saw that alone. That's what I'm writing about. It got me upset. I think about it at night. Here it is.

At Saratoga we laid up nights in the hay in the shed Bildad had showed us and ate with the niggers early and at night when the race people had all gone away. The men from home stayed mostly in the grandstand and betting field, and didn't come out around the places where the horses are kept except to the paddocks just before a race when the horses are saddled. At Saratoga they don't have paddocks under an open shed as at Lexington and Churchill Downs and other tracks down in our country, but saddle the horses right out in an open place under trees on a lawn as smooth and nice as Banker Bohon's front yard here in Beckersville. It's lovely. The horses are sweaty and nervous and shine and the men come out and smoke cigars and look at them and the trainers are there and the owners, and your heart thumps so you can hardly breathe.

Then the bugle blows for post and the boys that ride come running out with their silk clothes on and you run to get a place by the fence with the niggers.

I always am wanting to be a trainer or owner, and at the risk of being seen and caught and sent home I went to the paddocks before every race. The other boys didn't but I did.

We got to Saratoga on a Friday and on Wednesday the next week the big Mullford Handicap was to be run. Middlestride was in it and Sunstreak. The weather was fine and the track fast. I couldn't sleep the night before.

What had happened was that both these horses are the kind it makes my throat hurt to see. Middlestride is long and looks awkward and is a gelding. He belongs to Joe Thompson, a little owner from home who only has a half-dozen horses. The Mullford Handicap is for a mile and Middlestride can't untrack fast. He goes away slow and is always way back at the half, then he begins to run and if the race is a mile and a quarter he'll just eat up everything and get there.

Sunstreak is different. He is a stallion and nervous and belongs on the biggest farm we've got in our country, the Van Riddle place that belongs to Mr. Van Riddle of New York. Sunstreak is like a girl you think about sometimes but never see. He is hard all over and lovely too. When you look at his head you want to kiss him. He is trained by Jerry Tillford who knows me and has been good to me lots of times, lets me walk into a horse's stall to look at him close and other things. There isn't anything as sweet as that horse. He stands at the post quiet and not letting on, but he is just burning up inside. Then when the barrier goes up he is off like his name, Sunstreak. It makes you ache to see him. It hurts you. He just lays down and runs like a bird dog. There can't anything I ever see run like him except Middlestride when he gets untracked and stretches himself.

Gee, I ached to see that race and those two horses run, ached and dreaded it too. I didn't want to see either of our horses beaten. We had never sent a pair like that to the races before. Old men in Beckersville said so and the niggers said so. It was a fact.

Before the race I went over to the paddocks to see. I looked a last look at Middlestride, who isn't such a much standing in a paddock that way, then I went to see Sunstreak.

It was his day. I knew when I see him. I forgot all about being seen myself and walked right up. All the men from Beckersville were there and no one noticed me except Jerry Tillford. He saw me and something happened. I'll tell you about that.

I was standing looking at that horse and aching. In some way, I can't tell how, I knew just how Sunstreak felt inside. He was quiet and letting the niggers rub his legs and Mr. Van Riddle himself put the saddle on, but he was just a raging torrent inside. He was like the water in the river at Niagara Falls just before it goes plunk down. That horse wasn't thinking about running. He don't have to think about that. He was just thinking about holding himself back till the time for the running came. I knew that. I could just in a way see right inside him. He was going to do some awful running and I knew it. He wasn't bragging or letting on much or prancing or making a fuss, but just waiting. I knew it and Jerry Tillford his trainer knew. I looked up and then that man and I looked into each other's eyes. Something happened to me. I guess I loved the man as much as I did the horse because he knew what I knew. Seemed to me there wasn't anything in the world but that man and the horse and me. I cried and Jerry Tillford had a shine in his eyes. Then I came away to the fence to wait for the race. The horse was better than me, more steadier, and now I know better than Jerry. He was the quietest and he had to do the running.

Sunstreak ran first of course and he busted the world's record for a mile. I've seen that if I never see anything more. Everything came out just as I expected. Middlestride got left at the post and was way back and closed up to be second, just as I knew he would. He'll get a world's record too some day. They can't skin the Beckersville country on horses.

I watched the race calm because I knew what would happen. I was sure. Hanley Turner and Henry Rieback and Tom Tumberton were all more excited than me.

A funny thing had happened to me. I was thinking about Jerry Tillford the trainer and how happy he was all through the race. I liked him that afternoon even more than I ever liked my own father. I almost forgot the horses thinking that way about him. It was because of what I had seen in his eyes as he stood in the paddocks beside Sunstreak before the race started. I knew he had been watching and working with Sunstreak since the horse was a baby colt, had taught him to run and be patient and when to let himself out and not to quit, never. I knew that for him it was like a mother seeing her child do something brave or wonderful. It was the first time I ever felt for a man like that.

After the race that night I cut out from Tom and Hanley and Henry. I wanted to be by myself and I wanted to be near Jerry Tillford if I could work it. Here is what happened.

The track in Saratoga is near the edge of town. It is all polished up and trees around, the evergreen kind, and grass and everything painted and nice. If you go past the track you get to a hard road made of asphalt for automobiles, and if you go along this for a few miles there is a road turns off to a little rummy-looking farmhouse set in a yard.

That night after the race I went along that road because I had seen Jerry and some other men go that way in an automobile. I

didn't expect to find them. I walked for a ways and then sat down
by a fence to think. It was the direction they went in. I wanted to
be as near Jerry as I could. I felt close to him. Pretty soon I went
up the side road—I don't know why—and came to the rummy
farmhouse. I was just lonesome to see Jerry, like wanting to see
your father at night when you are a young kid. Just then an automobile came along and turned in. Jerry was in it and Henry Rieback's
father, and Arthur Bedford from home, and Dave Williams and
two other men I didn't know. They got out of the car and went
into the house, all but Henry Rieback's father who quarreled with
them and said he wouldn't go. It was only about nine o'clock, but
they were all drunk and the rummy-looking farmhouse was a
place for bad women to stay in. That's what it was. I crept up
along a fence and looked through a window and saw.

It's what give me the fantods. I can't make it out. The women
in the house were all ugly mean-looking women, not nice to look
at or be near. They were homely too, except one who was tall and
looked a little like the gelding Middlestride, but not clean like
him, but with a hard ugly mouth. She had red hair. I saw everything
plain. I got up by an old rose bush by an open window and looked.
The women had on loose dresses and sat around in chairs. The
men came in and some sat on the women's laps. The place smelled
rotten and there was rotten talk, the kind a kid hears around a
livery stable in a town like Beckersville in the winter but don't
ever expect to hear talked when there are women around. It was
rotten. A nigger wouldn't go into such a place.

I looked at Jerry Tillford. I've told you how I had been feeling
about him on account of his knowing what was going on inside
of Sunstreak in the minute before he went to the post for the race
in which he made a world's record.

Jerry bragged in that bad woman house as I know Sunstreak
wouldn't never have bragged. He said that he made that horse,
that it was him that won the race and made the record. He lied
and bragged like a fool. I never heard such silly talk.

And then what do you suppose he did? He looked at the woman
in there, the one that was lean and hard-mouthed and looked a

little like the gelding Middlestride, but not clean like him, and his eyes began to shine just as they did when he looked at me and at Sunstreak in the paddocks at the track in the afternoon. I stood there by the window—gee, but I wished I hadn't gone away from the tracks but had stayed with the boys and the niggers and the horses. The tall rotten-looking woman was between us just as Sunstreak was in the paddocks in the afternoon.

Then, all of a sudden, I began to hate that man. I wanted to scream and rush in the room and kill him. I never had such a feeling before. I was so mad clean through that I cried and my fists were doubled up so my fingernails cut my hands.

And Jerry's eyes kept shining and he weaved back and forth, and then he went and kissed that woman and I crept away and went back to the tracks and to bed and didn't sleep hardly any, and then next day I got the other kids to start home with me and never told them anything I seen.

I been thinking about it ever since. I can't make it out. Spring has come again and I'm nearly sixteen and go to the tracks mornings same as always, and I see Sunstreak and Middlestride and a new colt named Strident I'll bet will lay them all out, but no one thinks so but me and two or three niggers.

But things are different. At the tracks the air don't taste as good or smell as good. It's because a man like Jerry Tillford, who knows what he does, could see a horse like Sunstreak run, and kiss a woman like that the same day. I can't make it out. Darn him, what did he want to do like that for? I keep thinking about it and it spoils looking at horses and smelling things and hearing niggers laugh and everything. Sometimes I'm so mad about it I want to fight someone. It gives me the fantods. What did he do it for? I want to know why.

THE OTHER WOMAN

"I AM IN LOVE WITH MY WIFE," HE SAID—A SUPERFLUOUS REMARK, AS I had not questioned his attachment to the woman he had married. We walked for ten minutes and then he said it again. I turned to look at him. He began to talk and told me the tale I am now about to set down.

The thing he had on his mind happened during what must have been the most eventful week of his life. He was to be married on Friday afternoon. On Friday of the week before he got a telegram announcing his appointment to a government position. Something else happened that made him very proud and glad. In secret he was in the habit of writing verses and during the year before several of them had been printed in poetry magazines. One of the societies that give prizes for what they think the best poems published during the year put his name at the head of its list. The story of his triumph was printed in the newspapers of his home city and one of them also printed his picture.

As might have been expected he was excited and in a rather highly strung nervous state all during that week. Almost every evening he went to call on his fiancée, the daughter of a judge. When he got there the house was filled with people and many letters, telegrams and packages were being received. He stood a little to one side and men and women kept coming up to speak to him. They congratulated him upon his success in getting the government position and on his achievement as a poet. Everyone seemed to be praising him and when he went home and to bed he could not sleep. On Wednesday evening he went to the theatre and it seemed to him that people all over the house recognized him. Everyone nodded and smiled. After the first act five or six men and two women left their seats to gather about him. A little group was formed. Strangers sitting along the same row of seats stretched their necks and looked. He had never received so much attention before, and now a fever of expectancy took possession of him.

As he explained when he told me of his experience, it was for him an altogether abnormal time. He felt like one floating in air. When he got into bed after seeing so many people and hearing so many words of praise his head whirled round and round. When he closed his eyes a crowd of people invaded his room. It seemed as though the minds of all the people of his city were centered on himself. The most absurd fancies took possession of him. He imagined himself riding in a carriage through the streets of a city. Windows were thrown open and people ran out at the doors of houses. "There he is. That's him," they shouted, and at the words a glad cry arose. The carriage drove into a street blocked with people. A hundred thousand pairs of eyes looked up at him. "There you are! What a fellow you have managed to make of yourself!" the eyes seemed to be saying.

My friend could not explain whether the excitement of the people was due to the fact that he had written a new poem or whether, in his new government position, he had performed some notable act. The apartment where he lived at that time was on a street perched along the top of a cliff far out at the edge of his city, and from his bedroom window he could look down over trees and factory roofs to a river. As he could not sleep and as the fancies that kept crowding in upon him only made him more excited, he got out of bed and tried to think.

As would be natural under such circumstances, he tried to control his thoughts, but when he sat by the window and was wide awake a most unexpected and humiliating thing happened. The night was clear and fine. There was a moon. He wanted to dream of the woman who was to be his wife, to think out lines for noble poems or make plans that would affect his career. Much to his surprise his mind refused to do anything of the sort.

At a corner of the street where he lived there was a small cigar store and newspaper stand run by a fat man of forty and his wife, a small active woman with bright grey eyes. In the morning he stopped there to buy a paper before going down to the city. Sometimes he saw only the fat man, but often the man had disappeared and the woman waited on him. She was, as he assured me at least twenty times in telling me his tale, a very ordinary person with nothing special or notable about her, but for some reason he could not explain, being in her presence stirred him profoundly. During that week in the midst of his distraction she was the only person he knew who stood out clear and distinct in his mind. When he wanted so much to think noble thoughts he could think only of her. Before he knew what was happening his imagination had taken hold of the notion of having a love affair with the woman.

"I could not understand myself," he declared, in telling me the story. "At night, when the city was quiet and when I should have been asleep, I thought about her all the time. After two or three days of that sort of thing the consciousness of her got into my daytime thoughts. I was terribly muddled. When I went to see the woman who is now my wife I found that my love for her was in no way affected by my vagrant thoughts. There was but one woman in the world I wanted to live with and to be my comrade in undertaking to improve my own character and my position in the world, but for the moment, you see, I wanted this other woman to be in my arms. She had worked her way into my being. On all sides people were saying I was a big man who would do big things, and there I was. That evening when I went to the theatre I walked home because I knew I would be unable to sleep, and to satisfy the annoying impulse in myself I went and stood on the sidewalk before the tobacco shop. It was a two-story building, and I knew the woman lived upstairs with her husband. For a long time I stood in the darkness with my body pressed against the wall of the building, and then I thought of the two of them up there and no doubt in bed together. That made me furious.

"Then I grew more furious with myself. I went home and got into bed, shaken with anger. There are certain books of verse and some prose writings that have always moved me deeply, and so I put several books on a table by my bed.

"The voices in the books were like the voices of the dead. I did not hear them. The printed words would not penetrate into my consciousness. I tried to think of the woman I loved, but her figure had also become something far away, something with which I for the moment seemed to have nothing to do. I rolled and tumbled about in the bed. It was a miserable experience.

"On Thursday morning I went into the store. There stood the woman alone. I think she knew how I felt. Perhaps she had been thinking of me as I had been thinking of her. A doubtful hesitating smile played about the corners of her mouth. She had on a dress made of cheap cloth and there was a tear on the shoulder. She must have been ten years older than myself. When I tried to put my pennies on the glass counter behind which she stood, my hand trembled so that the pennies made a sharp rattling noise. When I spoke the voice that came out of my throat did not sound like anything that had ever belonged to me. It barely arose above a thick whisper. 'I want you,' I said. 'I want you very much. Can't you run away from your husband? Come to me at my apartment at seven tonight.'

"The woman did come to my apartment at seven. That morning she didn't say anything at all. For a minute perhaps we stood looking at each other. I had forgotten everything in the world but just her. Then she nodded her head and I went away. Now that I think of it I cannot remember a word I ever heard her say. She came to my apartment at seven and it was dark. You must understand this was in the month of October. I had not lighted a light and I had sent my servant away.

"During that day I was no good at all. Several men came to

see me at my office, but I got all muddled up in trying to talk
with them. They attributed my rattle-headedness to my approaching
marriage and went away laughing.

"It was on that morning, just the day before my marriage,
that I got a long and very beautiful letter from my fiancée. During the night before she also had been unable to sleep and had
got out of bed to write the letter. Everything she said in it was
very sharp and real, but she herself, as a living thing, seemed to
have receded into the distance. It seemed to me that she was like
a bird flying far away in distant skies, and that I was like a per-
plexed barefooted boy standing in the dusty road before a farmhouse
and looking at her receding figure. I wonder if you will understand what I mean?

"In regard to the letter. In it she, the awakening woman, poured
out her heart. She of course knew nothing of life, but she was a
woman. She lay, I suppose, in her bed feeling nervous and wrought
up as I had been doing. She realized that a great change was about
to take place in her life and was glad and afraid too. There she lay
thinking of it all. Then she got out of bed and began talking to
me on the bit of paper. She told me how afraid she was and how
glad too. Like most young women she had heard things whispered.
In the letter she was very sweet and fine. 'For a long time, after
we are married, we will forget we are a man and woman,' she
wrote. 'We will be human beings. You must remember that I am
ignorant and often I will be very stupid. You must love me and be
very patient and kind. When I know more, when after a long
time you have taught me the way of life, I will try to repay you. I
will love you tenderly and passionately. The possibility of that is
in me or I would not want to marry at all. I am afraid but I am
also happy. O, I am so glad our marriage time is near at hand!'

"Now you see clearly enough what a mess I was in. In my
office, after I had read my fiancée's letter, I became at once very
resolute and strong. I remember that I got out of my chair and
walked about, proud of the fact that I was to be the husband of
so noble a woman. Right away I felt concerning her as I had been
feeling about myself before I found out what a weak thing I was.

To be sure I took a strong resolution that I would not be weak. At nine that evening I had planned to run in to see my fiancée. 'I'm all right now,' I said to myself. 'The beauty of her character has saved me from myself. I will go home now and send the other woman away.' In the morning I had telephoned to my servant and told him that I did not want him to be at the apartment that evening and I now picked up the telephone to tell him to stay at home.

"Then a thought came to me. 'I will not want him there in any event,' I told myself. 'What will he think when he sees a woman coming in my place on the evening before the day I am to be married?' I put the telephone down and prepared to go home. 'If I want my servant out of the apartment it is because I do not want him to hear me talk with the woman. I cannot be rude to her. I will have to make some kind of an explanation,' I said to myself.

"The woman came at seven o'clock, and, as you may have guessed, I let her in and forgot the resolution I had made. It is likely I never had any intention of doing anything else. There was a bell on my door, but she did not ring, but knocked very softly. It seems to me that everything she did that evening was soft and quiet, but very determined and quick. Do I make myself clear? When she came I was standing just within the door where I had been standing and waiting for a half hour. My hands were trembling as they had trembled in the morning when her eyes looked at me and when I tried to put the pennies on the counter in the store. When I opened the door she stepped quickly in and I took her into my arms. We stood together in the darkness. My hands no longer trembled. I felt very happy and strong.

"Although I have tried to make everything clear I have not told you what the woman I married is like. I have emphasized, you see, the other woman. I make the blind statement that I love my wife, and to a man of your shrewdness that means nothing at all. To tell the truth, had I not started to speak of this matter I would feel more comfortable. It is inevitable that I give you the impression that I am in love with the tobacconist's wife. That's not true. To be sure I was very conscious of her all during the week before my marriage, but after she had come to me at my apartment she went entirely out of my mind.

"Am I telling the truth? I am trying very hard to tell what happened to me. I am saying that I have not since that evening thought of the woman who came to my apartment. Now, to tell the facts of the case, that is not true. On that evening I went to my fiancée at nine, as she had asked me to do in her letter. In a kind of way I cannot explain the other woman went with me. This is what I mean—you see I had been thinking that if anything happened between me and the tobacconist's wife I would not be able to go through with my marriage. 'It is one thing or the other with me,' I had said to myself.

"As a matter of fact I went to see my beloved on that evening filled with a new faith in the outcome of our life together. I am afraid I muddle this matter in trying to tell it. A moment ago I said the other woman, the tobacconist's wife, went with me. I do not mean she went in fact. What I am trying to say is that something of her faith in her own desires and her courage in seeing things through went with me. Is that clear to you? When I got to my fiancée's house there was a crowd of people standing about. Some were relatives from distant places I had not seen before. She looked up quickly when I came into the room. My face must have been radiant. I never saw her so moved. She thought her letter had affected me deeply, and of course it had. Up she jumped and ran to meet me. She was like a glad child. Right before the people who turned and looked inquiringly at us, she said the thing that was in her mind. 'O, I am so happy,' she cried. 'You have understood. We will be two human beings. We will not have to be husband and wife.'

"As you may suppose everyone laughed, but I did not laugh. The tears came into my eyes. I was so happy I wanted to shout. Perhaps you understand what I mean. In the office that day when I read the letter my fiancée had written I had said to myself, 'I will take care of the dear little woman.' There was something smug, you see, about that. In her house when she cried out in that way, and when everyone laughed, what I said to myself was something like this: 'We will take care of ourselves.' I whispered something of the sort into her ears. To tell you the truth I had come down off my perch. The spirit of the other woman did that to me. Before all the people gathered about I held my fiancée close and we kissed. They thought it very sweet of us to be so affected at the sight of each other. What they would have thought had they known the truth about me God only knows!

"Twice now I have said that after that evening I never thought of the other woman at all. That is partially true but, sometimes in the evening when I am walking alone in the street or in the park as we are walking now, and when evening comes softly and quickly as it has come tonight, the feeling of her comes sharply into my body and mind. After that one meeting I never saw her again. On the next day I was married and I have never gone back into her street. Often however as I am walking along as I am doing now, a quick sharp earthy feeling takes possession of me. It is as though I were a seed in the ground and the warm rains of the spring had come. It is as though I were not a man but a tree.

"And now you see I am married and everything is all right. My marriage is to me a very beautiful fact. If you were to say that my marriage is not a happy one I could call you a liar and be speaking the absolute truth. I have tried to tell you about this other woman. There is a kind of relief in speaking of her. I have never done it before. I wonder why I was so silly as to be afraid that I would give you the impression I am not in love with my wife. If I did not instinctively trust your understanding I would not have spoken. As the matter stands I have a little stirred myself up. Tonight I shall think of the other woman. That sometimes occurs. It will happen after I have gone to bed. My wife sleeps in the next room to mine and the door is always left open. There will be a moon tonight, and when there is a moon long streaks of light fall on her bed. I shall awake at midnight tonight. She will be lying asleep with one arm thrown over her head.

"What is it that I am now talking about? A man does not speak of his wife lying in bed. What I am trying to say is that, because of this talk, I shall think of the other woman tonight. My thoughts will not take the form they did during the week before I was married. I will wonder what has become of the woman. For a moment I will again feel myself holding her close. I will think that for an hour I was closer to her than I have ever been to anyone else. Then I will think of the time when I will be as close as that to my wife. She is still, you see, an awakening woman. For a moment I will close my eyes and the quick, shrewd, determined eyes of that other woman will look into mine. My head will swim and then I will quickly open my eyes and see again the dear woman with whom I have undertaken to live out my life. Then I will sleep and when I awake in the morning it will be as it was that evening when I walked out of my dark apartment after having had the most notable experience of my life. What I mean to say, you understand, is that, for me, when I awake, the other woman will be utterly gone."

THE EGG

My father was, I am sure, intended by nature to be a cheerful, kindly man. Until he was thirty-four years old he worked as a farmhand for a man named Thomas Butterworth whose place lay near the town of Bidwell, Ohio. He had then a horse of his own and on Saturday evenings drove into town to spend a few hours in social intercourse with other farmhands. In town he drank several glasses of beer and stood about in Ben Head's saloon—crowded on Saturday evenings with visiting farmhands. Songs were sung and glasses thumped on the bar. At ten o'clock father drove home along a lonely country road, made his horse comfortable for the night and himself went to bed, quite happy in his position in life. He had at that time no notion of trying to rise in the world.

It was in the spring of his thirty-fifth year that father married my mother, then a country schoolteacher, and in the following spring I came wriggling and crying into the world. Something happened to the two people. They became ambitious. The American passion for getting up in the world took possession of them.

It may have been that mother was responsible. Being a schoolteacher she had no doubt read books and magazines. She had, I presume, read of how Garfield, Lincoln, and other Americans rose from poverty to fame and greatness and as I lay beside her—in the days of her lying-in—she may have dreamed that I would someday rule men and cities. At any rate she induced father to give up his place as a farmhand, sell his horse and embark on an independent enterprise of his own. She was a tall silent woman with a long nose and troubled grey eyes. For herself she wanted nothing. For father and myself she was incurably ambitious.

The first venture into which the two people went turned out badly. They rented ten acres of poor stony land on Griggs's Road, eight miles from Bidwell, and launched into chicken raising. I grew into boyhood on the place and got my first impressions of life there. From the beginning they were impressions of disaster and if, in my turn, I am a gloomy man inclined to see the darker side of life, I attribute it to the fact that what should have been for me the happy joyous days of childhood were spent on a chicken farm.

One unversed in such matters can have no notion of the many and tragic things that can happen to a chicken. It is born out of an egg, lives for a few weeks as a tiny fluffy thing such as you will see pictured on Easter cards, then becomes hideously naked, eats quantities of corn and meal bought by the sweat of your father's brow, gets diseases called pip, cholera, and other names, stands looking with stupid eyes at the sun, becomes sick and dies. A few hens and now and then a rooster, intended to serve God's mysterious ends, struggle through to maturity. The hens lay eggs out of which come other chickens and the dreadful cycle is thus made complete. It is all unbelievably complex. Most philosophers must have been raised on chicken farms. One hopes for so much from a chicken and is so dreadfully disillusioned. Small chickens, just setting out on the journey of life, look so bright and alert and they are in fact so dreadfully stupid. They are so much like people they mix one up in one's judgments of life. If disease does not kill them they wait until your expectations are thoroughly aroused and then walk under the wheels of a wagon—to go squashed and dead back to their maker. Vermin infest their youth, and fortunes must be spent for curative powders. In later life I have seen how a literature has been built up on the subject of fortunes to be made out of the raising of chickens. It is intended to be read by the gods who have just eaten of the tree of the knowledge of good and evil. It is a hopeful literature and declares that much may be done by simple ambitious people who own a few hens. Do not be led astray by it. It was not written for you. Go hunt for gold on the frozen hills of Alaska, put your faith in the honesty of a politician, believe if you will that the world is daily growing better and that good will triumph over evil, but do not read and believe the literature that is written concerning the hen. It was not written for you.

I, however, digress. My tale does not primarily concern itself with the hen. If correctly told it will center on the egg. For ten years my father and mother struggled to make our chicken farm pay and then they gave up that struggle and began another. They moved into the town of Bidwell, Ohio and embarked in the restaurant business. After ten years of worry with incubators that did not hatch, and with tiny—and in their own way lovely—balls of fluff that passed on into semi-naked pullethood and from that into dead henhood, we threw all aside and packing our belongings on a wagon drove down Griggs's Road toward Bidwell, a tiny caravan of hope looking for a new place from which to start on our upward journey through life.

We must have been a sad looking lot, not, I fancy, unlike refugees fleeing from a battlefield. Mother and I walked in the road. The wagon that contained our goods had been borrowed for the day from Mr. Albert Griggs, a neighbor. Out of its sides stuck the legs of cheap chairs and at the back of the pile of beds, tables, and boxes filled with kitchen utensils was a crate of live chickens, and on top of that the baby carriage in which I had been wheeled about in my infancy. Why we stuck to the baby carriage I don't know. It was unlikely other children would be born and the wheels were broken. People who have few possessions cling tightly to those they have. That is one of the facts that make life so discouraging.

Father rode on top of the wagon. He was then a bald-headed man of forty-five, a little fat and from long association with mother and the chickens he had become habitually silent and discouraged.

All during our ten years on the chicken farm he had worked as a laborer on neighboring farms and most of the money he had earned had been spent for remedies to cure chicken diseases, on Wilmer's White Wonder Cholera Cure or Professor Bidlow's Egg Producer or some other preparations that mother found advertised in the poultry papers. There were two little patches of hair on father's head just above his ears. I remember that as a child I used to sit looking at him when he had gone to sleep in a chair before the stove on Sunday afternoons in the winter. I had at that time already begun to read books and have notions of my own and the bald path that led over the top of his head was, I fancied, something like a broad road, such a road as Caesar might have made on which to lead his legions out of Rome and into the wonders of an unknown world. The tufts of hair that grew above father's ears were, I thought, like forests. I fell into a half-sleeping, half-waking state and dreamed I was a tiny thing going along the road into a far beautiful place where there were no chicken farms and where life was a happy eggless affair.

One might write a book concerning our flight from the chicken farm into town. Mother and I walked the entire eight miles—she to be sure that nothing fell from the wagon and I to see the wonders of the world. On the seat of the wagon beside father was his greatest treasure. I will tell you of that.

On a chicken farm where hundreds and even thousands of chickens come out of eggs, surprising things sometimes happen. Grotesques are born out of eggs as out of people. The accident does not often occur—perhaps once in a thousand births. A chicken is, you see, born that has four legs, two pairs of wings, two heads or what not. The things do not live. They go quickly back to the hand of their maker that has for a moment trembled. The fact that the poor little things could not live was one of the tragedies of life to father. He had some sort of notion that if he could but bring into henhood or roosterhood a five-legged hen or a two-headed rooster his fortune would be made. He dreamed of taking the wonder about to county fairs and of growing rich by exhibiting it to other farmhands.

At any rate he saved all the little monstrous things that had been born on our chicken farm. They were preserved in alcohol and put each in its own glass bottle. These he had carefully put into a box and on our journey into town it was carried on the wagon seat beside him. He drove the horses with one hand and with the other clung to the box. When we got to our destination the box was taken down at once and the bottles removed. All during our days as keepers of a restaurant in the town of Bidwell, Ohio, the grotesques in their little glass bottles sat on a shelf back of the counter. Mother sometimes protested but father was a rock on the subject of his treasure. The grotesques were, he declared, valuable. People, he said, liked to look at strange and wonderful things.

Did I say that we embarked in the restaurant business in the town of Bidwell, Ohio? I exaggerated a little. The town itself lay at the foot of a low hill and on the shore of a small river. The railroad did not run through the town and the station was a mile away to the north at a place called Pickleville. There had been a cider mill and pickle factory at the station, but before the time of our coming they had both gone out of business. In the morning and in the evening busses came down to the station along a road called Turner's Pike from the hotel on the main street of Bidwell. Our going to the out-of-the-way place to embark in the restaurant business was mother's idea. She talked of it for a year and then one day went off and rented an empty store building opposite the railroad station. It was her idea that the restaurant would be profitable. Travelling men, she said, would be always waiting around to take trains out of town and town people would come to the station to await incoming trains. They would come to the restaurant to buy pieces of pie and drink coffee. Now that I am older I know that she had another motive in going. She was ambitious for me. She wanted me to rise in the world, to get into a town school and become a man of the towns.

At Pickleville father and mother worked hard as they always had done. At first there was the necessity of putting our place into shape to be a restaurant. That took a month. Father built a shelf on which he put tins of vegetables. He painted a sign on which he put his name in large red letters. Below his name was the sharp command—"EAT HERE"—that was so seldom obeyed. A showcase was bought and filled with cigars and tobacco. Mother scrubbed the floor and the walls of the room. I went to school in the town and was glad to be away from the farm and from the presence of the discouraged, sad-looking chickens. Still I was not very joyous. In the evening I walked home from school along Turner's Pike and remembered the children I had seen playing in the town school yard. A troop of little girls had gone hopping about and singing. I tried that. Down along the frozen road I went hopping solemnly on one leg. "Hippity hop to the barber shop," I sang shrilly. Then I stopped and looked doubtfully about. I was afraid of being seen in my gay mood. It must have seemed to me that I was doing a thing that should not be done by one who, like myself, had been raised on a chicken farm where death was a daily visitor.

Mother decided that our restaurant should remain open at night. At ten in the evening a passenger train went north past our door followed by a local freight. The freight crew had switching to do in Pickleville and when the work was done they came to our restaurant for hot coffee and food. Sometimes one of them ordered a fried egg. In the morning at four they returned northbound and again visited us. A little trade began to grow up. Mother slept at night and during the day tended the restaurant and fed our boarders while father slept. He slept in the same bed mother had occupied during the night and I went off to the town of Bidwell and to school. During the long nights, while mother and I slept, father cooked meats that were to go into sandwiches for the lunch baskets of our boarders. Then an idea in regard to getting up in the world came into his head. The American spirit took hold of him. He also became ambitious.

In the long nights when there was little to do father had time to think. That was his undoing. He decided that he had in the past been an unsuccessful man because he had not been cheerful enough and that in the future he would adopt a cheerful outlook on life. In the early morning he came upstairs and got into bed with mother. She woke and the two talked. From my bed in the corner I listened.

It was father's idea that both he and mother should try to entertain the people who came to eat at our restaurant. I cannot now remember his words, but he gave the impression of one about to become in some obscure way a kind of public entertainer. When people, particularly young people from the town of Bidwell, came into our place, as on very rare occasions they did, bright entertaining conversation was to be made. From father's words I gathered that something of the jolly innkeeper effect was to be sought. Mother must have been doubtful from the first, but she said nothing discouraging. It was father's notion that a passion for the company of himself and mother would spring up in the breasts of the younger people of the town of Bidwell. In the evening bright happy groups would come singing down Turner's Pike. They would troop shouting with joy and laughter into our place. There would be song and festivity. I do not mean to give the impression that father spoke so elaborately of the matter. He was as I have said an uncommunicative man. "They want some place to go. I tell you they want some place to go," he said over and over. That was as far as he got. My own imagination has filled in the blanks.

For two or three weeks this notion of father's invaded our house. We did not talk much but in our daily lives tried earnestly to make smiles take the place of glum looks. Mother smiled at the boarders and I, catching the infection, smiled at our cat. Father became a little feverish in his anxiety to please. There was no doubt lurking somewhere in him a touch of the spirit of the showman. He did not waste much of his ammunition on the railroad men he served at night but seemed to be waiting for a young man or woman from Bidwell to come in to show what he could do. On the counter in the restaurant there was a wire basket kept always filled with eggs, and it must have been before his eyes when the idea of being entertaining was born in his brain. There was something pre-natal about the way eggs kept themselves connected with the development of his idea. At any rate an egg

ruined his new impulse in life. Late one night I was awakened by
a roar of anger coming from father's throat. Both mother and I
sat upright in our beds. With trembling hands she lighted a lamp
that stood on a table by her head. Downstairs the front door of
our restaurant went shut with a bang and in a few minutes father
tramped up the stairs. He held an egg in his hand and his hand
trembled as though he were having a chill. There was a half insane
light in his eyes. As he stood glaring at us I was sure he intended
throwing the egg at either mother or me. Then he laid it gently
on the table beside the lamp and dropped on his knees beside
mother's bed. He began to cry like a boy and I, carried away by
his grief, cried with him. The two of us filled the little upstairs
room with our wailing voices. It is ridiculous, but of the picture
we made I can remember only the fact that mother's hand continually
stroked the bald path that ran across the top of his head. I have
forgotten what mother said to him and how she induced him to
tell her of what had happened downstairs. His explanation also
has gone out of my mind. I remember only my own grief and
fright and the shiny path over father's head glowing in the lamplight
as he knelt by the bed.

As to what happened downstairs. For some unexplainable reason
I know the story as well as though I had been a witness to my
father's discomfiture. One in time gets to know many unexplainable
things. On that evening young Joe Kane, son of a merchant of
Bidwell, came to Pickleville to meet his father, who was expected
on the ten o'clock evening train from the south. The train was
three hours late and Joe came into our place to loaf about and to
wait for its arrival. The local freight train came in and the freight
crew were fed. Joe was left alone in the restaurant with father.

From the moment he came into our place the Bidwell young
man must have been puzzled by my father's actions. It was his
notion that father was angry at him for hanging around. He noticed
that the restaurant keeper was apparently disturbed by his presence
and he thought of going out. However, it began to rain and he
did not fancy the long walk to town and back. He bought a five-
cent cigar and ordered a cup of coffee. He had a newspaper in his

pocket and took it out and began to read. "I'm waiting for the evening train. It's late," he said apologetically.

For a long time father, whom Joe Kane had never seen before, remained silently gazing at his visitor. He was no doubt suffering from an attack of stage fright. As so often happens in life he had thought so much and so often of the situation that now confronted him that he was somewhat nervous in its presence.

For one thing, he did not know what to do with his hands. He thrust one of them nervously over the counter and shook hands with Joe Kane. "How-de-do," he said. Joe Kane put his newspaper down and stared at him. Father's eye lighted on the basket of eggs that sat on the counter and he began to talk. "Well," he began hesitatingly, "well, you have heard of Christopher Columbus, eh?" He seemed to be angry. "That Christopher Columbus was a cheat," he declared emphatically. "He talked of making an egg stand on its end. He talked, he did, and then he went and broke the end of the egg."

My father seemed to his visitor to be beside himself at the duplicity of Christopher Columbus. He muttered and swore. He declared it was wrong to teach children that Christopher Columbus was a great man when, after all, he cheated at the critical moment. He had declared he would make an egg stand on end and then when his bluff had been called he had done a trick. Still grumbling at Columbus, father took an egg from the basket on the counter and began to walk up and down. He rolled the egg between the palms of his hands. He smiled genially. He began to mumble words regarding the effect to be produced on an egg by the electricity that comes out of the human body. He declared that without breaking its shell and by virtue of rolling it back and forth in his hands he could stand the egg on its end. He explained that the warmth of his hands and the gentle rolling movement he gave the egg created a new center of gravity, and Joe Kane was mildly interested. "I have handled thousands of eggs," father said. "No one knows more about eggs than I do."

He stood the egg on the counter and it fell on its side. He tried the trick again and again, each time rolling the egg between the palms of his hands and saying the words regarding the wonders of electricity and the laws of gravity. When after a half hour's effort he did succeed in making the egg stand for a moment, he looked up to find that his visitor was no longer watching. By the time he had succeeded in calling Joe Kane's attention to the success of his effort, the egg had again rolled over and lay on its side.

Afire with the showman's passion and at the same time a good deal disconcerted by the failure of his first effort, father now took the bottles containing the poultry monstrosities down from their place on the shelf and began to show them to his visitor. "How would you like to have seven legs and two heads like this fellow?" he asked, exhibiting the most remarkable of his treasures. A cheerful smile played over his face. He reached over the counter and tried to slap Joe Kane on the shoulder as he had seen men do in Ben Head's saloon when he was a young farmhand and drove to town on Saturday evenings. His visitor was made a little ill by the sight of the body of the terribly deformed bird floating in the alcohol in the bottle and got up to go. Coming from behind the counter, father took hold of the young man's arm and led him back to his seat. He grew a little angry and for a moment had to turn his face away and force himself to smile. Then he put the bottles back on the shelf. In an outburst of generosity he fairly compelled Joe Kane to have a fresh cup of coffee and another cigar at his expense. Then he took a pan and filling it with vinegar, taken from a jug that sat beneath the counter, he declared himself about to do a new trick. "I will heat this egg in this pan of vinegar," he said. "Then I will put it through the neck of a bottle without breaking the shell. When the egg is inside the bottle it will resume its normal shape and the shell will become hard again. Then I will give the bottle with the egg in it to you. You can take it about with you wherever you go. People will want to know how you got the egg in the bottle. Don't tell them. Keep them guessing. That is the way to have fun with this trick."

Father grinned and winked at his visitor. Joe Kane decided that the man who confronted him was mildly insane but harmless. He drank the cup of coffee that had been given him and began to read his paper again. When the egg had been heated in vinegar, father carried it on a spoon to the counter and going into a back room got an empty bottle. He was angry because his visitor did not watch him as he began to do his trick, but nevertheless went cheerfully to work. For a long time he struggled, trying to get the egg to go through the neck of the bottle. He put the pan of vinegar back on the stove, intending to reheat the egg, then picked it up and burned his fingers. After a second bath in the hot vinegar, the shell of the egg had been softened a little but not enough for his purpose. He worked and worked and a spirit of desperate determination took possession of him. When he thought that at last the trick was about to be consummated, the delayed train came in at the station and Joe Kane started to go nonchalantly out at the door. Father made a last desperate effort to conquer the egg and make it do the thing that would establish his reputation as one who knew how to entertain guests who came into his restaurant. He worried the egg. He attempted to be somewhat rough with it. He swore and the sweat stood out on his forehead. The egg broke under his hand. When the contents spurted over his clothes, Joe Kane, who had stopped at the door, turned and laughed.

A roar of anger rose from my father's throat. He danced and shouted a string of inarticulate words. Grabbing another egg from the basket on the counter, he threw it, just missing the head of the young man as he dodged through the door and escaped.

Father came upstairs to mother and me with an egg in his hand. I do not know what he intended to do. I imagine he had some idea of destroying it, of destroying all eggs, and that he intended to let mother and me see him begin. When, however, he got into the presence of mother something happened to him. He laid the egg gently on the table and dropped on his knees by the bed as I have already explained. He later decided to close the restaurant for the night and to come upstairs and get into bed. When he did so he blew out the light and after much muttered conversation both he and mother went to sleep. I suppose I went to sleep also, but my sleep was troubled. I awoke at dawn and for a long time looked at the egg that lay on the table. I wondered why eggs had to be and why from the egg came the hen who again laid the egg. The question got into my blood. It has stayed there, I imagine, because I am the son of my father. At any rate, the problem remains unsolved in my mind. And that, I conclude, is but another evidence of the complete and final triumph of the egg—at least as far as my family is concerned.

BROTHERS

I AM AT MY HOUSE IN THE COUNTRY AND IT IS LATE OCTOBER. IT rains. Back of my house is a forest and in front there is a road and beyond that open fields. The country is one of low hills, flattening suddenly into plains. Some twenty miles away, across the flat country, lies the huge city Chicago.

On this rainy day the leaves of the trees that line the road before my window are falling like rain—the yellow, red and golden leaves fall straight down, heavily. The rain beats them brutally down. They are denied a last golden flash across the sky. In October leaves should be carried away, out over the plains, in a wind. They should go dancing away.

Yesterday morning I arose at daybreak and went for a walk. There was a heavy fog and I lost myself in it. I went down into the plains and returned to the hills, and everywhere the fog was as a wall before me. Out of it trees sprang suddenly, grotesquely, as in a city street late at night people come suddenly out of the darkness into the circle of light under a street lamp. Above there was the light of day forcing itself slowly into the fog. The fog moved slowly. The tops of trees moved slowly. Under the trees the fog was dense, purple. It was like smoke lying in the streets of a factory town.

An old man came up to me in the fog. I know him well. The

people here call him insane. "He is a little cracked," they say. He lives alone in a little house buried deep in the forest and has a small dog he carries always in his arms. On many mornings I have met him walking on the road and he has told me of men and women who are his brothers and sisters, his cousins, aunts, uncles, brothers-in-law. It is confusing. He cannot draw close to people near at hand so he gets hold of a name out of a newspaper and his mind plays with it. On one morning he told me he was a cousin to the man named Cox who at the time when I write is a candidate for the presidency. On another morning he told me that Caruso the singer had married a woman who was his sister-in-law. "She is my wife's sister," he said, holding the little dog close. His grey watery eyes looked appealing up to me. He wanted me to believe. "My wife was a sweet slim girl," he declared. "We lived together in a big house and in the morning walked about arm in arm. Now her sister has married Caruso the singer. He is of my family now."

As someone had told me the old man had never married, I went away wondering. One morning in early September I came upon him sitting under a tree beside a path near his house. The dog barked at me and then ran and crept into his arms. At that time the Chicago newspapers were filled with the story of a millionaire who had got into trouble with his wife because of an intimacy with an actress. The old man told me that the actress was his sister. He is sixty years old and the actress whose story appeared in the newspapers is twenty but he spoke of their childhood together. "You would not realize it to see us now but we were poor then," he said. "It's true. We lived in a little house on the side of a hill. Once when there was a storm, the wind nearly swept our house away. How the wind blew! Our father was a carpenter and he built strong houses for other people but our own house he did not build very strong!" He shook his head sorrowfully. "My sister the actress has got into trouble. Our house is not built very strongly," he said as I went away along the path.

For a month, two months, the Chicago newspapers, that are

delivered every morning in our village, have been filled with the story of a murder. A man there has murdered his wife and there seems no reason for the deed. The tale runs something like this—

The man, who is now on trial in the courts and will no doubt be hanged, worked in a bicycle factory where he was a foreman and lived with his wife and his wife's mother in an apartment in Thirty-second Street. He loved a girl who worked in the office of the factory where he was employed. She came from a town in Iowa and when she first came to the city lived with her aunt who has since died. To the foreman, a heavy stolid looking man with grey eyes, she seemed the most beautiful woman in the world. Her desk was by a window at an angle of the factory, a sort of wing of the building, and the foreman down in the shop had a desk by another window. He sat at his desk making out sheets containing the record of the work done by each man in his department. When he looked up he could see the girl sitting at work at her desk. The notion got into his head that she was peculiarly lovely. He did not think of trying to draw close to her or of winning her love. He looked at her as one might look at a star or across a country of low hills in October when the leaves of the trees are all red and yellow gold. "She is a pure, virginal thing," he thought vaguely. "What can she be thinking about as she sits there by the window at work?"

In fancy the foreman took the girl from Iowa home with him to his apartment in Thirty-second Street and into the presence of his wife and his mother-in-law. All day in the shop and during the evening at home he carried her figure about with him in his mind. As he stood by a window in his apartment and looked out toward the Illinois Central railroad tracks and beyond the tracks to the lake, the girl was there beside him. Down below women walked in the street and in every woman he saw there was something of the Iowa girl. One woman walked as she did, another made a gesture with her hand that reminded of her. All the women he saw except his wife and his mother-in-law were like the girl he had taken inside himself.

The two women in his own house puzzled and confused him.

They became suddenly unlovely and commonplace. His wife in particular was like some strange unlovely growth that had attached itself to his body.

In the evening after the day at the factory he went home to his own place and had dinner. He had always been a silent man and when he did not talk no one minded. After dinner he with his wife went to a picture show. When they came home his wife's mother sat under an electric light reading. There were two children and his wife expected another. They came into the apartment and sat down. The climb up two flights of stairs had wearied his wife. She sat in a chair beside her mother groaning with weariness.

The mother-in-law was the soul of goodness. She took the place of a servant in the home and got no pay. When her daughter wanted to go to a picture show she waved her hand and smiled. "Go on," she said. "I don't want to go. I'd rather sit here." She got a book and sat reading. The little boy of nine awoke and cried. He wanted to sit on the po-po. The mother-in-law attended to that.

After the man and his wife came home the three people sat in silence for an hour or two before bedtime. The man pretended to read a newspaper. He looked at his hands. Although he had washed them carefully, grease from the bicycle frames left dark stains under the nails. He thought of the Iowa girl and of her white quick hands playing over the keys of a typewriter. He felt dirty and uncomfortable.

The girl at the factory knew the foreman had fallen in love with her and the thought excited her a little. Since her aunt's death she had gone to live in a rooming house and had nothing to do in the evening. Although the foreman meant nothing to her she could in a way use him. To her he became a symbol. Sometimes he came into the office and stood for a moment by the door. His large hands were covered with black grease. She looked at him without seeing. In his place in her imagination stood a tall slender young man. Of the foreman she saw only the grey eyes that began to burn with a strange fire. The eyes expressed eagerness, a humble and devout eagerness. In the presence of a man with such eyes she felt she need not be afraid.

She wanted a lover who would come to her with such a look in his eyes. Occasionally, perhaps once in two weeks, she stayed a little late at the office, pretending to have work that must be finished. Through the window she could see the foreman waiting. When everyone had gone she closed her desk and went into the street. At the same moment the foreman came out at the factory door.

They walked together along the street a half dozen blocks to where she got aboard her car. The factory was in a place called South Chicago and as they went along evening was coming on. The streets were lined with small unpainted frame houses and dirty-faced children ran screaming in the dusty roadway. They crossed over a bridge. Two abandoned coal barges lay rotting in the stream.

He went by her side walking heavily and striving to conceal his hands. He had scrubbed them carefully before leaving the factory but they seemed to him like heavy dirty pieces of waste matter hanging at his side. Their walking together happened but a few times and during one summer. "It's hot," he said. He never spoke to her of anything but the weather. "It's hot," he said. "I think it may rain."

She dreamed of the lover who would some time come, a tall fair young man, a rich man owning houses and lands. The workingman who walked beside her had nothing to do with her conception of love. She walked with him, stayed at the office until the others had gone to walk unobserved with him because of his eyes, because of the eager thing in his eyes that was at the same time humble, that bowed down to her. In his presence there was no danger, could be no danger. He would never attempt to approach too closely, to touch her with his hands. She was safe with him.

In his apartment in the evening the man sat under the electric light with his wife and his mother-in-law. In the next room his two children were asleep. In a short time his wife would have another child. He had been with her to a picture show and in a short time they would get into bed together.

He would lie awake thinking, would hear the creaking of the springs of a bed where, in another room, his mother-in-law was crawling between the sheets. Life was too intimate. He would lie awake eager, expectant—expecting what?

Nothing. Presently one of the children would cry. It wanted to get out of bed and sit on the po-po. Nothing strange or unusual or lovely would or could happen. Life was too close, intimate. Nothing that could happen in the apartment could in any way stir him; the things his wife might say, her occasional half-hearted outbursts of passion, the goodness of his mother-in-law who did the work of a servant without pay—

He sat in the apartment under the electric light pretending to read a newspaper—thinking. He looked at his hands. They were large, shapeless, a workingman's hands.

The figure of the girl from Iowa walked about the room. With her he went out of the apartment and walked in silence through miles of streets. It was not necessary to say words. He walked with her by a sea, along the crest of a mountain. The night was clear and silent and the stars shone. She also was a star. It was not necessary to say words.

Her eyes were like stars and her lips were like soft hills rising out of dim, starlit plains. "She is unattainable, she is far off like the stars," he thought. "She is unattainable like the stars but unlike the stars she breathes, she lives, like myself she has being."

One evening, some six weeks ago, the man who worked as foreman in the bicycle factory killed his wife and he is now in the courts being tried for murder. Every day the newspapers are filled with the story. On the evening of the murder he had taken his wife as usual to a picture show and they started home at nine. In Thirty-second Street, at a corner near their apartment building, the figure of a man darted suddenly out of an alleyway and then darted back again. The incident may have put the idea of killing his wife into the man's head.

They got to the entrance to the apartment building and stepped into a dark hallway. Then quite suddenly and apparently without thought the man took a knife out of his pocket. "Suppose that man who darted into the alleyway had intended to kill us," he thought. Opening the knife he whirled about and struck at his wife. He struck twice, a dozen times—madly. There was a scream and his wife's body fell.

The janitor had neglected to light the gas in the lower hallway. Afterwards, the foreman decided, that was the reason he did it, that and the fact that the dark slinking figure of a man darted out of an alleyway and then darted back again. "Surely," he told himself, "I could never have done it had the gas been lighted."

He stood in the hallway thinking. His wife was dead and with her had died her unborn child. There was a sound of doors opening in the apartments above. For several minutes nothing happened. His wife and her unborn child were dead—that was all.

He ran upstairs thinking quickly. In the darkness on the lower stairway he had put the knife back into his pocket and, as it turned out later, there was no blood on his hands or on his clothes. The knife he later washed carefully in the bathroom, when the excitement had died down a little. He told everyone the same story. "There has been a holdup," he explained. "A man came slinking out of an alleyway and followed me and my wife home. He followed us into the hallway of the building and there was no light. The janitor had neglected to light the gas." Well—there had been a struggle and in the darkness his wife had been killed. He could not tell how it had happened. "There was no light. The janitor had neglected to light the gas," he kept saying.

For a day or two they did not question him specially and he had time to get rid of the knife. He took a long walk and threw it away into the river in South Chicago where the two abandoned coal barges lay rotting under the bridge, the bridge he had crossed when on the summer evenings he walked to the street car with the girl who was virginal and pure, who was far off and unattainable, like a star and yet not like a star.

And then he was arrested and right away he confessed—told everything. He said he did not know why he killed his wife and was careful to say nothing of the girl at the office. The newspapers tried to discover the motive for the crime. They are still trying.

Someone had seen him on the few evenings when he walked with the girl and she was dragged into the affair and had her picture printed in the papers. That has been annoying for her, as of course she has been able to prove she had nothing to do with the man.

Yesterday morning a heavy fog lay over our village here at the edge of the city and I went for a long walk in the early morning. As I returned out of the lowlands into our hill country I met the old man whose family has so many and such strange ramifications. For a time he walked beside me holding the little dog in his arms. It was cold and the dog whined and shivered. In the fog the old man's face was indistinct. It moved slowly back and forth with the fog banks of the upper air and with the tops of trees. He spoke of the man who has killed his wife and whose name is being shouted in the pages of the city newspapers that come to our village each morning. As he walked beside me he launched into a long tale concerning a life he and his brother, who has now become a murderer, once lived together. "He is my brother," he said over and over, shaking his head. He seemed afraid I would not believe. There was a fact that must be established. "We were boys together that man and I," he began again. "You see we played together in a barn back of our father's house. Our father went away to sea in a ship. That is the way our names became confused. You understand that. We have different names, but we are brothers. We had the same father. We played together in a barn back of our father's house. For hours we lay together in the hay in the barn and it was warm there."

In the fog the slender body of the old man became like a little gnarled tree. Then it became a thing suspended in air. It swung back and forth like a body hanging on the gallows. The face beseeched me to believe the story the lips were trying to tell. In my mind everything concerning the relationship of men and women became confused, a muddle. The spirit of the man who had killed his wife came into the body of the little old man there by the roadside. It was striving to tell me the story it would never be able to tell in the courtroom in the city, in the presence of the judge. The whole story of mankind's loneliness, of the effort to reach out to unattainable beauty, tried to get itself expressed from the lips of a mumbling old man, crazed with loneliness, who stood by the side of a country road on a foggy morning holding a little dog in his arms.

The arms of the old man held the dog so closely that it began to whine with pain. A sort of convulsion shook his body. The soul seemed striving to wrench itself out of the body, to fly away through the fog, down across the plain to the city, to the singer, the politician, the millionaire, the murderer, to its brothers, cousins, sisters, down in the city. The intensity of the old man's desire was terrible and in sympathy my body began to tremble. His arms tightened about the body of the little dog so that it cried with pain. I stepped forward and tore the arms away and the dog fell to the ground and lay whining. No doubt it had been injured. Perhaps ribs had been crushed. The old man stared at the dog lying at his feet as in the hallway of the apartment building the worker from the bicycle factory had stared at his dead wife. "We are brothers," he said again. "We have different names but we are brothers. Our father you understand went off to sea."

I am sitting in my house in the country and it rains. Before my eyes the hills fall suddenly away and there are the flat plains and beyond the plains the city. An hour ago the old man of the house in the forest went past my door and the little dog was not with him. It may be that as we talked in the fog he crushed the life out of his companion. It may be that the dog like the workman's wife and her unborn child is now dead. The leaves of the trees that line the road before my window are falling like rain—the yellow, red and golden leaves fall straight down, heavily. The rain beats them brutally down. They are denied a last golden flash across the sky. In October leaves should be carried away, out over the plains, in a wind. They should go dancing away.

I'M A FOOL

It was a hard jolt for me, one of the most bitterest I ever had to face. And it all came about through my own foolishness too. Even yet sometimes, when I think of it, I want to cry or swear or kick myself. Perhaps, even now, after all this time, there will be a kind of satisfaction in making myself look cheap by telling of it.

It began at three o'clock one October afternoon as I sat in the grandstand at the fall trotting and pacing meet at Sandusky, Ohio.

To tell the truth, I felt a little foolish that I should be sitting in the grandstand at all. During the summer before I had left my home town with Harry Whitehead and, with a nigger named Burt, had taken a job as swipe with one of the two horses Harry was campaigning through the fall race meets that year. Mother cried and my sister Mildred, who wanted to get a job as a school teacher in our town that fall, stormed and scolded about the house all during the week before I left. They both thought it something disgraceful that one of our family should take a place as a swipe with race horses. I've an idea Mildred thought my taking the place would stand in the way of her getting the job she'd been working so long for.

But after all I had to work, and there was no other work to be got. A big lumbering fellow of nineteen couldn't just hang around the house and I had got too big to mow people's lawns and sell newspapers. Little chaps who could get next to people's sympa-

thies by their sizes were always getting jobs away from me. There
was one fellow who kept saying to everyone who wanted a lawn
mowed or a cistern cleaned, that he was saving money to work
his way through college, and I used to lay awake nights thinking
up ways to injure him without being found out. I kept thinking
of wagons running over him and bricks falling on his head as he
walked along the street. But never mind him.

I got the place with Harry and I liked Burt fine. We got along
splendid together. He was a big nigger with a lazy sprawling body
and soft, kind eyes, and when it came to a fight he could hit like
Jack Johnson. He had Bucephalus, a big black pacing stallion
that could do 2.09 or 2.10, if he had to, and I had a little gelding
named Doctor Fritz that never lost a race all fall when Harry
wanted him to win.

We set out from home late in July in a box car with the two
horses and after that, until late November, we kept moving along
to the race meets and the fairs. It was a peachy time for me, I'll
say that. Sometimes now I think that boys who are raised regular
in houses, and never have a fine nigger like Burt for best friend,
and go to high schools and college, and never steal anything, or
get drunk a little, or learn to swear from fellows who know how,
or come walking up in front of a grandstand in their shirt sleeves
and with dirty horsey pants on when the races are going on and
the grandstand is full of people all dressed up—what's the use of
talking about it? Such fellows don't know nothing at all. They've
never had no opportunity.

But I did. Burt taught me how to rub down a horse and put
the bandages on after a race and steam a horse out and a lot of
valuable things for any man to know. He could wrap a bandage
on a horse's leg so smooth that if it had been the same color you
would think it was his skin, and I guess he'd have been a big
driver too and got to the top like Murphy and Walter Cox and
the others if he hadn't been black.

Gee whizz, it was fun. You got to a county seat town, maybe
say on a Saturday or Sunday, and the fair began the next Tuesday
and lasted until Friday afternoon. Doctor Fritz would be, say in
the 2.25 trot on Tuesday afternoon and on Thursday afternoon

Bucephalus would knock 'em cold in the "free-for-all" pace. It left you a lot of time to hang around and listen to horse talk, and see Burt knock some yap cold that got too gay, and you'd find out about horses and men and pick up a lot of stuff you could use all the rest of your life, if you had some sense and salted down what you heard and felt and saw.

And then at the end of the week when the race meet was over, and Harry had run home to tend up to his livery stable business, you and Burt hitched the two horses to carts and drove slow and steady across country to the place for the next meeting, so as to not over-heat the horses, etc., etc., you know.

Gee whizz, gosh amighty, the nice hickorynut and beechnut and oaks and other kinds of trees along the roads, all brown and red, and the good smells, and Burt singing a song that was called Deep River, and the country girls at the windows of houses and everything. You can stick your colleges up your nose for all me. I guess I know where I got my education.

Why, one of those little burgs of towns you come to on the way, say now on a Saturday afternoon, and Burt says, "Let's lay up here." And you did.

And you took the horses to a livery stable and fed them, and you got your good clothes out of a box and put them on.

And the town was full of farmers gaping, because they could see you were race horse people, and the kids maybe never see a nigger before and was afraid and run away when the two of us walked down their main street.

And that was before prohibition and all that foolishness, and so you went into a saloon, the two of you, and all the yaps come and stood around, and there was always someone pretended he was horsey and knew things and spoke up and began asking questions, and all you did was to lie and lie all you could about what horses you had, and I said I owned them, and then some fellow said "will you have a drink of whiskey" and Burt knocked his eye out the way he could say, offhand like, "Oh well, all right, I'm agreeable to a little nip. I'll split a quart with you." Gee whizz.

But that isn't what I want to tell my story about. We got home late in November and I promised mother I'd quit the race horses for good. There's a lot of things you've got to promise a mother because she don't know any better.

And so, there not being any work in our town any more than when I left there to go to the races, I went off to Sandusky and got a pretty good place taking care of horses for a man who owned a teaming and delivery and storage and coal and real estate business there. It was a pretty good place with good eats, and a day off each week, and sleeping on a cot in a big barn, and mostly just shovelling in hay and oats to a lot of big good-enough skates of horses, that couldn't have trotted a race with a toad. I wasn't dissatisfied and I could send money home.

And then, as I started to tell you, the fall races come to Sandusky and I got the day off and I went. I left the job at noon and had on my good clothes and my new brown derby hat, I'd just bought the Saturday before, and a stand-up collar.

First of all I went downtown and walked about with the dudes. I've always thought to myself, "Put up a good front" and so I did it. I had forty dollars in my pocket and so I went into the West House, a big hotel, and walked up to the cigar stand. "Give me three twenty-five cent cigars," I said. There was a lot of horsemen and strangers and dressed-up people from other towns standing around in the lobby and in the bar, and I mingled amongst them. In the bar there was a fellow with a cane and a Windsor tie on, that it made me sick to look at him. I like a man to be a man and dress up, but not to go put on that kind of airs. So I pushed him aside, kind of rough, and had me a drink of whiskey. And then he looked at me, as though he thought maybe he'd get gay, but he changed his mind and didn't say anything. And then I had another drink of whiskey, just to show him something, and went out and had a hack out to the races, all to myself, and when I got there I bought myself the best seat I could get up in the grandstand, but didn't go in for any of these boxes. That's putting on too many airs.

And so there I was, sitting up in the grandstand as gay as you

please and looking down on the swipes coming out with their
horses, and with their dirty horsey pants on and the horse blankets swung over their shoulders, same as I had been doing all the
year before. I liked one thing about the same as the other, sitting
up there and feeling grand and being down there and looking up
at the yaps and feeling grander and more important too. One
thing's about as good as another, if you take it just right. I've
often said that.

Well, right in front of me, in the grandstand that day, there
was a fellow with a couple of girls and they was about my age.
The young fellow was a nice guy all right. He was the kind maybe
that goes to college and then comes to be a lawyer or maybe a
newspaper editor or something like that, but he wasn't stuck on
himself. There are some of that kind are all right and he was one
of the ones.

He had his sister with him and another girl and the sister looked
around over his shoulder, accidental at first, not intending to start
anything—she wasn't that kind—and her eyes and mine happened
to meet.

You know how it is. Gee, she was a peach! She had on a soft
dress, kind of a blue stuff and it looked carelessly made, but was
well sewed and made and everything. I knew that much. I blushed
when she looked right at me and so did she. She was the nicest
girl I've ever seen in my life. She wasn't stuck on herself and she
could talk proper grammar without being like a school teacher or
something like that. What I mean is, she was O.K. I think maybe
her father was well-to-do, but not rich to make her chesty because
she was his daughter, as some are. Maybe he owned a drug store
or a drygoods store in their home town, or something like that.
She never told me and I never asked.

My own people are all O.K. too when you come to that. My
grandfather was Welsh and over in the old country, in Wales he
was— but never mind that.

The first heat of the first race come off and the young fellow
setting there with the two girls left them and went down to make

a bet. I knew what he was up to, but he didn't talk big and noisy and let everyone around know he was a sport as some do. He wasn't that kind. Well, he come back and I heard him tell the two girls what horse he'd bet on, and when the heat was trotted they all half got to their feet and acted in the excited, sweaty way people do when they've got money down on a race, and the horse they bet on is up there pretty close at the end, and they think maybe he'll come on with a rush, but he never does because he hasn't got the old juice in him, come right down to it.

And then, pretty soon, the horses came out for the 2.18 pace and there was a horse in it I knew. He was a horse Bob French had in his string but Bob didn't own him. He was a horse owned by a Mr. Mathers down at Marietta, Ohio.

This Mr. Mathers had a lot of money and owned some coal mines or something, and he had a swell place out in the country, and he was stuck on race horses, but was a Presbyterian or something, and I think more than likely his wife was one too, maybe a stiffer one than himself. So he never raced his horses hisself, and the story round the Ohio race tracks was that when one of his horses got ready to go to the races he turned him over to Bob French and pretended to his wife he was sold.

So Bob had the horses and he did pretty much as he pleased and you can't blame Bob, at least I never did. Sometimes he was out to win and sometimes he wasn't. I never cared much about that when I was swiping a horse. What I did want to know was that my horse had the speed and could go out in front if you wanted him to.

And, as I'm telling you, there was Bob in this race with one of Mr. Mathers' horses, was named About Ben Ahem or something like that, and was fast as a streak. He was a gelding and had a mark of 2.21, but could step in .08 or .09.

Because when Burt and I were out, as I've told you, the year before, there was a nigger Burt knew, worked for Mr. Mathers, and we went out there one day when we didn't have no race on at the Marietta Fair and our boss Harry was gone home.

And so everyone was gone to the fair but just this one nigger

and he took us all through Mr. Mathers' swell house and he and
Burt tapped a bottle of wine Mr. Mathers had hid in his bedroom, back in a closet, without his wife knowing, and he showed
us this Ahem horse. Burt was always stuck on being a driver but
didn't have much chance to get to the top, being a nigger, and he
and the other nigger gulped that whole bottle of wine and Burt
got a little lit up.

So the nigger let Burt take this About Ben Ahem and step him
a mile in a track Mr. Mathers had all to himself, right there on
the farm. And Mr. Mathers had one child, a daughter, kinda sick
and not very good looking, and she came home and we had to
hustle and get About Ben Ahem stuck back in the barn.

I'm only telling you to get everything straight. At Sandusky,
that afternoon I was at the fair, this young fellow with the two
girls was fussed, being with the girls and losing his bet. You know
how a fellow is that way. One of them was his girl and the other
his sister. I had figured that out.

"Gee whizz," I says to myself, "I'm going to give him the dope."

He was mighty nice when I touched him on the shoulder. He
and the girls were nice to me right from the start and clear to the
end. I'm not blaming them.

And so he leaned back and I give him the dope on About Ben
Ahem. "Don't bet a cent on this first heat because he'll go like an
oxen hitched to a plow, but when the first heat is over go right
down and lay on your pile." That's what I told him.

Well, I never saw a fellow treat any one sweller. There was a fat
man sitting beside the little girl, that had looked at me twice by
this time, and I at her, and both blushing, and what did he do
but have the nerve to turn and ask the fat man to get up and
change places with me so I could set with his crowd.

Gee whizz, craps amighty. There I was. What a chump I was
to go and get gay up there in the West House bar, and just because
that dude was standing there with a cane and that kind of a necktie
on, to go and get all balled up and drink that whiskey, just to
show off.

Of course she would know, me setting right beside her and
letting her smell of my breath. I could have kicked myself right
down out of that grandstand and all around that race track and
made a faster record than most of the skates of horses they had
there that year.

Because that girl wasn't any mutt of a girl. What wouldn't I
have give right then for a stick of chewing gum to chew, or a
lozenger, or some liquorice, or most anything. I was glad I had
those twenty-five cent cigars in my pocket and right away I give
that fellow one and lit one myself. Then that fat man got up and
we changed places and there I was, plunked right down beside
her.

They introduced themselves and the fellow's best girl he had
with him was named Miss Elinor Woodbury, and her father was
a manufacturer of barrels from a place called Tiffin, Ohio. And
the fellow himelf was named Wilbur Wessen and his sister was
Miss Lucy Wessen.

I suppose it was their having such swell names got me off my
trolley. A fellow, just because he has been a swipe with a race
horse and works taking care of horses for a man in the teaming,
delivery, and storage business, isn't any better or worse than anyone else. I've often thought that, and said it too.

But you know how a fellow is. There's something in that kind
of nice clothes, and the kind of nice eyes she had, and the way she
had looked at me, awhile before, over her brother's shoulder, and
me looking back at her, and both of us blushing.

I couldn't show her up for a boob, could I?

I made a fool of myself, that's what I did. I said my name was
Walter Mathers from Marietta, Ohio, and then I told all three of
them the smashingest lie you ever heard. What I said was that my
father owned the horse About Ben Ahem and that he had let him
out to this Bob French for racing purposes, because our family
was proud and had never gone into racing that way, in our own
name, I mean. Then I had got started and they were all leaning
over and listening, and Miss Lucy Wessen's eyes were shining,
and I went the whole hog.

I told about our place down at Marietta, and about the big stables and the grand brick house we had on a hill, up above the Ohio River, but I knew enough not to do it in no bragging way. What I did was to start things and then let them drag the rest out of me. I acted just as reluctant to tell as I could. Our family hasn't got any barrel factory, and, since I've known us, we've always been pretty poor, but not asking anything of anyone at that, and my grandfather, over in Wales—but never mind that.

We set there talking like we had known each other for years and years, and I went and told them that my father had been expecting maybe this Bob French wasn't on the square, and had sent me up to Sandusky on the sly to find out what I could.

And I bluffed it through I had found out all about the 2.18 pace, in which About Ben Ahem was to start.

I said he would lose the first heat by pacing like a lame cow and then he would come back and skin 'em alive after that. And to back up what I said I took thirty dollars out of my pocket and handed it to Mr. Wilbur Wessen and asked him, would he mind, after the first heat, to go down and place it on About Ben Ahem for whatever odds he could get. What I said was that I didn't want Bob French to see me and none of the swipes.

Sure enough the first heat come off and About Ben Ahem went off his stride up the back stretch and looked like a wooden horse or a sick one and come in to be last. Then this Wilbur Wessen went down to the betting place under the grandstand and there I was with the two girls, and when that Miss Woodbury was looking the other way once, Lucy Wessen kinda, with her shoulder you know, kinda touched me. Not just tucking down, I don't mean. You know how a woman can do. They get close, but not getting gay either. You know what they do. Gee whizz.

And then they give me a jolt. What they had done, when I didn't know, was to get together, and they had decided Wilbur Wessen would bet fifty dollars, and the two girls had gone and put in ten dollars each, of their own money too. I was sick then, but I was sicker later.

About the gelding, About Ben Ahem, and their winning their money, I wasn't worried a lot about that. It come out O.K. Ahem stepped the next three heats like a bushel of spoiled eggs going to market before they could be found out, and Wilbur Wessen had got nine to two for the money. There was something else eating at me.

Because Wilbur come back after he had bet the money, and after that he spent most of his time talking to that Miss Woodbury, and Lucy Wessen and I was left alone together like on a desert island. Gee, if I'd only been on the square or if there had been any way of getting myself on the square. There ain't any Walter Mathers, like I said to her and them, and there hasn't ever been one, but if there was, I bet I'd go to Marietta, Ohio, and shoot him tomorrow.

There I was, big boob that I am. Pretty soon the race was over, and Wilbur had gone down and collected our money, and we had a hack downtown, and he stood us a swell supper at the West House, and a bottle of champagne beside.

And I was with that girl and she wasn't saying much, and I wasn't saying much either. One thing I know. She wasn't stuck on me because of the lie about my father being rich and all that. There's a way you know . . . Craps amighty. There's a kind of girl you see just once in your life, and if you don't get busy and make hay, then you're gone for good and all, and might as well go jump off a bridge. They give you a look from inside of them somewhere, and it ain't no vamping, and what it means is—you want that girl to be your wife, and you want nice things around her like flowers and swell clothes, and you want her to have the kids you're going to have, and you want good music played and no rag time. Gee whizz.

There's a place over near Sandusky, across a kind of bay, and it's called Cedar Point. And after we had supper we went over to it in a launch, all by ourselves. Wilbur and Miss Lucy and that Miss Woodbury had to catch a ten o'clock train back to Tiffin, Ohio, because, when you're out with girls like that, you can't get careless and miss any trains and stay out all night, like you can with some kinds of Janes.

And Wilbur blowed himself to the launch and it cost him fifteen cold plunks, but I wouldn't never have knew if I hadn't listened. He wasn't no tin horn kind of a sport.

Over at the Cedar Point place, we didn't stay around where there was a gang of common kind of cattle at all.

There was big dance halls and dining places for yaps, and there was a beach you could walk along and get where it was dark, and we went there.

She didn't talk hardly at all and neither did I, and I was thinking how glad I was my mother was all right, and always made us kids learn to eat with a fork at table, and not swill soup, and not be noisy and rough like a gang you see around a race track that way.

Then Wilbur and his girl went away up the beach and Lucy and I sat down in a dark place, where there was some roots of old trees the water had washed up, and after that the time, till we had to go back in the launch and they had to catch their trains, wasn't nothing at all. It went like winking your eye.

Here's how it was. The place we were setting in was dark, like I said, and there was the roots from that old stump sticking up like arms, and there was a watery smell, and the night was like—as if you could put your hand out and feel it—so warm and soft and dark and sweet like an orange.

I most cried and I most swore and I most jumped up and danced, I was so mad and happy and sad.

When Wilbur come back from being alone with his girl, and she saw him coming, Lucy she says, "We got to go to the train now," and she was most crying too, but she never knew nothing I knew, and she couldn't be so all busted up. And then, before Wilbur and Miss Woodbury got up to where we was, she put her face up and kissed me quick and put her head up against me and she was all quivering and—gee whizz.

Sometimes I hope I have cancer and die. I guess you know what I mean. We went in the launch across the bay to the train like that, and it was dark too. She whispered and said it was like she and I could get out of the boat and walk on the water, and it sounded foolish, but I knew what she meant.

And then quick we were right at the depot, and there was a big gang of yaps, the kind that goes to the fairs, and crowded and milling around like cattle, and how could I tell her? "It won't be long because you'll write and I'll write to you." That's all she said.

I got a chance like a hay barn afire. A swell chance I got.

And maybe she would write me, down at Marietta that way, and the letter would come back, and stamped on the front of it by the U.S.A. "there ain't any such guy," or something like that, whatever they stamp on a letter that way.

And me trying to pass myself off for a bigbug and a swell—to her, as decent a little body as God ever made. Craps amighty—a swell chance I got!

And then the train come in, and she got on it, and Wilbur Wessen he come and shook hands with me, and that Miss Woodbury was nice too and bowed to me, and I at her, and the train went and I busted out and cried like a kid.

Gee, I could have run after that train and made Dan Patch look like a freight train after a wreck but, socks amighty, what was the use? Did you ever see such a fool?

I'll bet you what—if I had an arm broke right now or a train had run over my foot—I wouldn't go to no doctor at all. I'd go set down and let her hurt and hurt—that's what I'd do.

I'll bet you what—if I hadn't a drunk that booze I'd a never been such a boob as to go tell such a lie—that couldn't never be made straight to a lady like her.

I wish I had that fellow right here that had on a Windsor tie and carried a cane. I'd smash him for fair. Gosh darn his eyes. He's a big fool—that's what he is.

And if I'm not another you just go find me one and I'll quit working and be a bum and give him my job. I don't care nothing for working, and earning money, and saving it for no such boob as myself.

THE MAN WHO
BECAME A WOMAN

MY FATHER WAS A RETAIL DRUGGIST IN OUR TOWN, OUT IN NEBRASKA, which was so much like a thousand other towns I've been in since that there's no use fooling around and taking up your time and mine trying to describe it.

Anyway I became a drug clerk and after father's death the store was sold and mother took the money and went west, to her sister in California, giving me four hundred dollars with which to make my start in the world. I was only nineteen years old then.

I came to Chicago, where I worked as a drug clerk for a time, and then, as my health suddenly went back on me, perhaps because I was so sick of my lonely life in the city and of the sight and smell of the drug store, I decided to set out on what seemed to me then the great adventure and became for a time a tramp, working now and then, when I had no money, but spending all the time I could loafing around out of doors or riding up and down the land on freight trains and trying to see the world. I even did some stealing in lonely towns at night—once a pretty good suit of clothes that someone had left hanging out on a clothesline, and once some shoes out of a box in a freight car—but I was in constant terror of being caught and put into jail so realized that success as a thief was not for me.

The most delightful experience of that period of my life was when I once worked as a groom, or swipe, with race horses and it was during that time I met a young fellow of about my own age who has since become a writer of some prominence.

The young man of whom I now speak had gone into race track work as a groom, to bring a kind of flourish, a high spot, he used to say, into his life.

He was then unmarried and had not been successful as a writer. What I mean is he was free and I guess, with him as with me, there was something he liked about the people who hang about a race track, the touts, swipes, drivers, niggers and gamblers. You know what a gaudy undependable lot they are—if you've ever been around the tracks much—about the best liars I've ever seen, and not saving money or thinking about morals, like most drug-gists, dry-goods merchants and the others who used to be my father's friends in our Nebraska town—and not bending the knee much either, or kowtowing to people they thought must be grander or richer or more powerful than themselves.

What I mean is, they were an independent, go-to-the-devil, come-have-a-drink-of-whisky, kind of a crew and when one of them won a bet, "knocked 'em off," we called it, his money was just dirt to him while it lasted. No king or president or soap manufacturer—gone on a trip with his family to Europe—could throw on more dog than one of them, with his big diamond rings and the diamond horse-shoe stuck in his necktie and all.

I liked the whole blamed lot pretty well and he did too.

He was groom temporarily for a pacing gelding named Lumpy Joe owned by a tall black-mustached man named Alfred Kreymborg and trying the best he could to make the bluff to himself he was a real one. It happened that we were on the same circuit, doing the West Pennsylvania county fairs all that fall, and on fine evenings we spent a good deal of time walking and talking together.

Let us suppose it to be a Monday or Tuesday evening and our horses had been put away for the night. The racing didn't start until later in the week, maybe Wednesday, usually. There was always a little place called a dining-hall, run mostly by the Woman's Christian Temperance Associations of the towns, and we would go there to eat where we could get a pretty good meal for twenty-five cents. At least then we thought it pretty good.

I would manage it so that I sat beside this fellow, whose name was Tom Means, and when we had got through eating we would go look at our two horses again and when we got there Lumpy Joe would be eating his hay in his box stall and Alfred Kreymborg would be standing there, pulling his mustache and looking as sad as a sick crane.

But he wasn't really sad. "You two boys want to go downtown to see the girls. I'm an old duffer and way past that myself. You go on along. I'll be setting here anyway, and I'll keep an eye on both the horses for you," he would say.

So we would set off, going, not into the town to try to get in with some of the town girls, who might have taken up with us because we were strangers and race track fellows, but out into the country. Sometimes we got into a hilly country and there was a moon. The leaves were falling off the trees and lay in the road so that we kicked them up with the dust as we went along.

To tell the truth I suppose I got to love Tom Means, who was five years older than me, although I wouldn't have dared say so then. Americans are shy and timid about saying things like that and a man here don't dare own up he loves another man, I've found out, and they are afraid to admit such feelings to themselves even. I guess they're afraid it may be taken to mean something it don't need to at all.

Anyway we walked along and some of the trees were already bare and looked like people standing solemnly beside the road and listening to what we had to say. Only I didn't say much. Tom Means did most of the talking.

Sometimes we came back to the race track and it was late and the moon had gone down and it was dark. Then we often walked round and round the track, sometimes a dozen times, before we crawled into the hay to go to bed.

Tom talked always on two subjects, writing and race horses, but mostly about race horses. The quiet sounds about the race tracks and the smells of horses, and the things that go with horses, seemed to get him all excited. "Oh, hell, Herman Dudley," he would burst out suddenly, "don't go talking to me. I know what I think. I've been around more than you have and I've seen a world of people. There isn't any man or woman, not even a fellow's own mother, as fine as a horse, that is to say a thoroughbred horse."

Sometimes he would go on like that a long time, speaking of people he had seen and their characteristics. He wanted to be a writer later and what he said was that when he came to be one he wanted to write the way a well-bred horse runs or trots or paces. Whether he ever did it or not I can't say. He has written a lot, but I'm not too good a judge of such things. Anyway I don't think he has.

But when he got on the subject of horses he certainly was a darby. I would never have felt the way I finally got to feel about horses or enjoyed my stay among them half so much if it hadn't been for him. Often he would go on talking for an hour maybe, speaking of horses' bodies and of their minds and wills as though they were human beings. "Lord help us, Herman," he would say, grabbing hold of my arm, "don't it get you up in the throat? I say now, when a good one, like that Lumpy Joe I'm swiping, flattens himself at the head of the stretch and he's coming, and you know he's coming, and you know his heart's sound, and he's game, and you know he isn't going to let himself get licked—don't it get you Herman, don't it get you like the old Harry?"

That's the way he would talk, and then later, sometimes, he'd talk about writing and get himself all het up about that too. He had some notions about writing I've never got myself around to thinking much about but just the same maybe his talk, working in me, has led me to want to begin to write this story myself.

There was one experience of that time on the tracks that I am forced, by some feeling inside myself, to tell.

Well, I don't know why but I've just got to. It will be kind of like confession is, I suppose, to a good Catholic, or maybe, better yet, like cleaning up the room you live in, if you are a bachelor, like I was for so long. The room gets pretty mussy and the bed not made some days and clothes and things thrown on the closet floor and maybe under the bed. And then you clean all up and put on new sheets, and then you take off all your clothes and get down on your hands and knees, and scrub the floor so clean you could eat bread off it, and then take a walk and come home after a while and your room smells sweet and you feel sweetened-up and better inside yourself too.

What I mean is, this story has been on my chest, and I've often dreamed about the happenings in it, even after I married Jessie and was happy. Sometimes I even screamed out at night and so I said to myself, "I'll write the dang story," and here goes.

Fall had come on and in the mornings now when we crept out of our blankets, spread out on the hay in the tiny lofts above the horse stalls, and put our heads out to look around, there was a white rime of frost on the ground. When we woke the horses woke too. You know how it is at the tracks—the little barn-like stalls with the tiny lofts above are all set along in a row and there are two doors to each stall, one coming up to a horse's breast and then a top one that is only closed at night and in bad weather.

In the mornings the upper door is swung open and fastened back and the horses put their heads out. There is the white rime on the grass over inside the grey oval the track makes. Usually there is some outfit that has six, ten or even twelve horses, and perhaps they have a Negro cook who does his cooking at an open fire in the clear space before the row of stalls and he is at work now and the horses with their big fine eyes are looking about and whinnying, and a stallion looks out at the door of one of the stalls and sees a sweet-eyed mare looking at him and sends up his trumpet-call, and a man's voice laughs, and there are no women anywhere in sight or no sign of one anywhere, and everyone feels like laughing and usually does.

It's pretty fine but I didn't know how fine it was until I got to know Tom Means and heard him talk about it all.

At the time the thing happened of which I am trying to tell now Tom was no longer with me. A week before his owner, Alfred Kreymborg, had taken his horse Lumpy Joe over into the Ohio

Fair Circuit and I saw no more of Tom at the tracks.

There was a story going about the stalls that Lumpy Joe, a big rangy brown gelding, wasn't really named Lumpy Joe at all, that he was a ringer who had made a fast record out in Iowa and up through the northwest country the year before, and that Kreymborg had picked him up and had kept him under wraps all winter and had brought him over into the Pennsylvania country under this new name and made a clean-up in the books.

I know nothing about that and never talked to Tom about it but anyway he, Lumpy Joe and Kreymborg were all gone now.

I suppose I'll always remember those days, and Tom's talk at night, and before that in the early September evenings how we sat around in front of the stalls, and Kreymborg sitting on an upturned feed box and pulling at his long black mustache and sometimes humming a little ditty one couldn't catch the words of. It was something about a deep well and a little grey squirrel crawling up the sides of it, and he never laughed or smiled much but there was something in his solemn grey eyes, not quite a twinkle, something more delicate than that.

The others talked in low tones and Tom and I sat in silence. He never did his best talking except when he and I were alone.

For his sake—if he ever sees my story—I should mention that at the only big track we ever visited, at Readville, Pennsylvania, we saw old Pop Geers, the great racing driver, himself. His horses were at a place far away across the tracks from where we were stabled. I suppose a man like him was likely to get the choice of all the good places for his horses.

We went over there one evening and stood about and there was Geers himself, sitting before one of the stalls on a box tapping the ground with a riding whip. They called him, around the tracks, "the silent man from Tennessee" and he was silent—that night anyway. All we did was to stand and look at him for maybe a half hour and then we went away and that night Tom talked better than I had ever heard him. He said that the ambition of his life was to wait until Pop Geers died and then write a book about him, and to show in the book that there was at least one American who never went nutty about getting rich or owning a big factory or being any other kind of a hell of a fellow. "He's satisfied I think to sit around like that and wait until the big moments of his life come, when he heads a fast one into the stretch and then, darn his soul, he can give all of himself to the thing right in front of him," Tom said, and then he was so worked up he began to blubber. We were walking along the fence on the inside of the tracks and it was dusk and, in some trees nearby, some birds, just sparrows maybe, were making a chirping sound, and you could hear insects singing and, where there was a little light, off to the west between some trees, motes were dancing in the air. Tom said that about Pop Geers, although I think he was thinking most about something he wanted to be himself and wasn't, and then he went and stood by the fence and sort of blubbered and I began to blubber too, although I didn't know what about.

But perhaps I did know, after all. I suppose Tom wanted to feel, when he became a writer, like he thought old Pop must feel when his horse swung around the upper turn, and there lay the stretch before him, and if he was going to get his horse home in front he had to do it right then. What Tom said was that any man had something in him that understands about a thing like that but that no woman ever did except up in her brain. He often got off things like that about women but I notice he later married one of them just the same.

But to get back to my knitting. After Tom had left, the stable I was with kept drifting along through nice little Pennsylvania county seat towns. My owner, a strange excitable kind of a man from over in Ohio, who had lost a lot of money on horses but was always thinking he would maybe get it all back in some big killing, had been playing in pretty good luck that year. The horse I had, a tough little gelding, a five year old, had been getting home in front pretty regular and so he took some of his winnings and bought a three years old black pacing stallion named O, My Man. My gelding was called Pick-it-boy because when he was in a race and had got into the stretch my owner always got half wild with excitement and shouted so you could hear him a mile and a half.

"Go, pick it boy, pick it boy, pick it boy," he kept shouting and so when he had got hold of this good little gelding he had named him that.

The gelding was a fast one, all right. As the boys at the tracks used to say, he "picked 'em up sharp and set 'em down clean," and he was what we called a natural race horse, right up to all the speed he had, and didn't require much training. "All you got to do is to drop him down on the track and he'll go," was what my owner was always saying to other men, when he was bragging about his horse.

And so you see, after Tom left, I hadn't much to do evenings and then the new stallion, the three year old, came on with a Negro swipe named Burt.

I liked him fine and he liked me but not the same as Tom and me. We got to be friends all right and I suppose Burt would have done things for me, and maybe me for him, that Tom and me wouldn't have done for each other.

But with a Negro you couldn't be close friends like you can with another white man. There's some reason you can't understand but it's true. There's been too much talk about the difference between whites and blacks and you're both shy, and anyway no use trying and I suppose Burt and I both knew it and so I was pretty lonesome.

Something happened to me that happened several times, when I was a young fellow, that I have never exactly understood. Sometimes now I think it was all because I had got to be almost a man and had never been with a woman. I don't know what's the matter with me. I can't ask a woman. I've tried it a good many times in my life but every time I've tried the same thing happened.

Of course, with Jessie now, it's different, but at the time of which I'm speaking Jessie was a long ways off and a good many things were to happen to me before I got to her.

Around a race track, as you may suppose, the fellows who are swipes and drivers and strangers in the towns do not go without women. They don't have to. In any town there are always some fly girls will come around a place like that. I suppose they think they are fooling with men who lead romantic lives. Such girls will come along by the front of the stalls where the race horses are and, if you look all right to them, they will stop and make a fuss over your horse. They rub their little hands over the horse's nose and then is the time for you—if you aren't a fellow like me who can't get up the nerve—then is the time for you to smile and say, "Hello, kid," and make a date with one of them for that evening up town after supper. I couldn't do that, although the Lord knows I tried hard enough, often enough. A girl would come along alone, and she would be a little thing and give me the eye, and I would try and try but couldn't say anything. Both Tom, and Burt afterwards, used to laugh at me about it sometimes but what I think is that, had I been able to speak up to one of them and had managed to make a date with her, nothing would have come of it. We would probably have walked around the town and got off together in the dark somewhere, where the town came to an end, and then she would have had to knock me over with a club before it got any further.

And so there I was, having got used to Tom and our talks together, and Burt of course had his own friends among the black men. I got lazy and mopey and had a hard time doing my work.

It was like this. Sometimes I would be sitting, perhaps under a tree in the late afternoon when the races were over for the day and the crowds had gone away. There were always a lot of other men and boys who hadn't any horses in the races that day and they would be standing or sitting about in front of the stalls and talking.

I would listen for a time to their talk and then their voices would seem to go far away. The things I was looking at would go far away too. Perhaps there would be a tree, not more than a hundred yards away, and it would just come out of the ground and float away like a thistle. It would get smaller and smaller, away off there in the sky, and then suddenly—bang, it would be back where it belonged, in the ground, and I would begin hearing the voices of the men talking again.

When Tom was with me that summer the nights were splendid.

We usually walked about and talked until pretty late and then I crawled up into my hole and went to sleep. Always out of Tom's talk I got something that stayed in my mind, after I was off by myself, curled up in my blanket. I suppose he had a way of making pictures as he talked and the pictures stayed by me as Burt was always saying pork chops did by him. "Give me the old pork chops, they stick to the ribs," Burt was always saying and with the imagination it was always that way about Tom's talks. He started something inside you that went on and on, and your mind played with it like walking about in a strange town and seeing the sights, and you slipped off to sleep and had splendid dreams and woke up in the morning feeling fine.

And then he was gone and it wasn't that way any more and I got into the fix I have described. At night I kept seeing women's bodies and women's lips and things in my dreams, and woke up in the morning feeling like the old Harry.

Burt was pretty good to me. He always helped me cool Pick-it-boy out after a race and he did the things himself that take the most skill and quickness, like getting the bandages on a horse's leg smooth, and seeing that every strap is setting just right, and every buckle drawn up to just the right hole, before your horse goes out on the track for a heat.

Burt knew there was something wrong with me and put himself out not to let the boss know. When the boss was around he was always bragging about me. "The brightest kid I've ever worked with around the tracks," he would say and grin, and that at a time when I wasn't worth my salt.

When you go out with the horses there is one job that always takes a lot of time. In the late afternoon, after your horse has been in a race and after you have washed him and rubbed him out, he has to be walked slowly, sometimes for hours and hours, so he'll cool out slowly and won't get muscle-bound. I got so I did that job for both our horses and Burt did the more important things. It left him free to go talk or shoot dice with the other niggers and I didn't mind. I rather liked it and after a hard race even the stallion, O My Man, was tame enough, even when there were mares about.

You walk and walk and walk, around a little circle, and your horse's head is right by your shoulder, and all around you the life of the place you are in is going on, and in a queer way you get so you aren't really a part of it at all. Perhaps no one ever gets as I was then, except boys that aren't quite men yet and who like me have never been with girls or women—to really be with them, up to the hilt, I mean. I used to wonder if young girls got that way too before they married or did what we used to call "go on the town."

If I remember it right though, I didn't do much thinking then. Often I would have forgotten supper if Burt hadn't shouted at me and reminded me, and sometimes he forgot and went off to town with one of the other niggers and I did forget.

There I was with the horse, going slow slow slow, around a circle that way. The people were leaving the fairgrounds now, some afoot, some driving away to the farms in wagons and Fords. Clouds of dust floated in the air and over to the west, where the town was, maybe the sun was going down, a red ball of fire through the dust. Only a few hours before the crowd had been all filled with excitement and everyone shouting. Let us suppose my horse had been in a race that afternoon and I had stood in front of the grandstand with my horse blanket over my shoulder, alongside of Burt perhaps, and when they came into the stretch my owner began to call, in that queer high voice of his that seemed to float over the top of all the shouting up in the grandstand. And his voice was saying over and over, "Go, pick it boy, pick it boy, pick it boy," the way he always did, and my heart was thumping so I could hardly breathe, and Burt was leaning over and snapping his fingers and muttering, "Come, little sweet. Come on home. Your mama wants you. Come get your 'lasses and bread, little Pick-it-boy."

Well, all that was over now and the voices of the people left around were all low. And Pick-it-boy—I was leading him slowly around the little ring, to cool him out slowly, as I've said—he was different too. Maybe he had pretty nearly broken his heart trying to get down to the wire in front, or getting down there in front, and now everything inside him was quiet and tired, as it was nearly all the time those days in me, except in me tired but not quiet.

You remember I've told you we always walked in a circle, round and round and round. I guess something inside me got to going round and round and round too. The sun did sometimes and the trees and the clouds of dust. I had to think sometimes about putting down my feet so they went down in the right place and I didn't get to staggering like a drunken man.

And a funny feeling came that it is going to be hard to describe. It had something to do with the life in the horse and in me. Sometimes, these late years, I've thought maybe Negroes would understand what I'm trying to talk about now better than any white man ever will. I mean something about men and animals, something between them, something that can perhaps only happen to a white man when he has slipped off his base a little, as I suppose I had then. I think maybe a lot of horsey people feel it sometimes though. It's something like this, maybe—do you suppose it could be that something we whites have got, and think such a lot of, and are so proud about, isn't much of any good after all?

It's something in us that wants to be big and grand and important maybe and won't let us just be, like a horse or a dog or a bird can. Let's say Pick-it-boy had won his race that day. He did that pretty often that summer. Well, he was neither proud, like I would have been in his place, or mean in one part of the inside of him either. He was just himself, doing something with a kind of simplicity. That's what Pick-it-boy was like and I got to feeling it in him as I walked with him slowly in the gathering darkness. I got inside him in some way I can't explain and he got inside me. Often we would stop walking for no cause and he would put his nose up against my face.

I wished he was a girl sometimes or that I was a girl and he was a man. It's an odd thing to say but it's a fact. Being with him that way so long, and in such a quiet way, cured something in me a little. Often after an evening like that I slept all right and did not have the kind of dreams I've spoken about.

But I wasn't cured for very long and couldn't get cured. My body seemed all right and just as good as ever but there wasn't no pep in me.

Then the fall got later and later and we came to the last town we were going to make before my owner laid his horses up for the winter in his home town over across the state line in Ohio, and the track was up on a hill, or rather in a kind of high plain above the town.

It wasn't much of a place and the sheds were rather rickety and the track bad, especially at the turns. As soon as we got to the place and got stabled it began to rain and kept it up all week so the fair had to be put off.

As the purses weren't very large a lot of the owners shipped right out but our owner stayed. The fair owners guaranteed expenses whether the races were held the next week or not.

And all week there wasn't much of anything for Burt and me to do but clean manure out of the stalls in the morning, watch for a chance when the rain let up a little to jog the horses around the track in the mud and then clean them off, blanket them and stick them back in their stalls.

It was the hardest time of all for me. Burt wasn't so bad off as there were a dozen or two blacks around and in the evening they went off to town, got liquored up a little and came home late, singing and talking even in the cold rain.

And then one night I got mixed up in the thing I'm trying to tell you about.

It was a Saturday evening and when I look back at it now it seems to me everyone had left the tracks but just me. In the early evening swipe after swipe came over to my stall and asked me if I was going to stick around. When I said I was he would ask me to keep an eye out for him, that nothing happened to his horse. "Just take a stroll down that way now and then, eh, kid," one of them would say, "I just want to run up to town for an hour or two."

I would say "yes" to be sure, and so pretty soon it was dark as
pitch up there in that little ruined fairground and nothing living
anywhere around but the horses and me.

I stood it as long as I could, walking here and there in the mud
and rain, and thinking all the time I wished I was someone else
and not myself. "If I were someone else," I thought, "I wouldn't
be here but down there in town with the others." I saw myself
going into saloons and having drinks and later going off to a
house maybe and getting myself a woman.

I got to thinking so much that, as I went stumbling around up
there in the darkness, it was as though what was in my mind was
actually happening.

Only I wasn't with some cheap woman, such as I would have
found had I had the nerve to do what I wanted but with such a
woman as I thought then I should never find in this world. She
was slender and like a flower and with something in her like a
race horse too, something in her like Pick-it-boy in the stretch, I
guess.

And I thought about her and thought about her until I couldn't
stand thinking any more. "I'll do something anyway," I said to
myself.

So, although I had told all the swipes I would stay and watch
their horses, I went out of the fairgrounds and down the hill a
ways. I went down until I came to a little low saloon, not in the
main part of the town itself but half way up the hillside. The
saloon had once been a residence, a farmhouse perhaps, but if it
was ever a farmhouse I'm sure the farmer who lived there and
worked the land on that hillside hadn't made out very well. The
country didn't look like a farming country, such as one sees all
about the other county-seat towns we had been visiting all through
the late summer and fall. Everywhere you looked there were stones
sticking out of the ground and the trees mostly of the stubby,
stunted kind. It looked wild and untidy and ragged, that's what I
mean. On the flat plain, up above, where the fairground was,
there were a few fields and pastures, and there were some sheep
raised and in the field right next to the tracks, on the furtherest

side from town, on the back stretch side, there had once been a
slaughter-house, the ruins of which were still standing. It hadn't
been used for quite some time but there were bones of animals
lying all about in the field, and there was a smell coming out of
the old building that would curl your hair.

The horses hated the place, just as we swipes did, and in the
morning when we were jogging them around the track in the
mud, to keep them in racing condition, Pick-it-boy and O My
Man both raised old Ned every time we headed them up the
back stretch and got near to where the old slaughter-house stood.
They would rear and fight at the bit, and go off their stride and
run until they got clear of the rotten smells, and neither Burt nor
I could make them stop it. "It's a hell of a town down there and
this is a hell of a track for racing," Burt kept saying. "If they ever
have their danged old fair someone's going to get spilled and maybe
killed back here." Whether they did or not I don't know as I
didn't stay for the fair, for reasons I'll tell you pretty soon, but
Burt was speaking sense all right. A race horse isn't like a human
being. He won't stand for it to have to do his work in any rotten
ugly kind of a dump the way a man will, and he won't stand for
the smells a man will either.

But to get back to my story again. There I was, going down
the hillside in the darkness and the cold soaking rain and breaking
my word to all the others about staying up above and watching
the horses. When I got to the little saloon I decided to stop and
have a drink or two. I'd found out long before that about two
drinks upset me so I was two-thirds piped and couldn't walk straight,
but on that night I didn't care a tinker's dam.

So I went up a kind of path, out of the road, toward the front
door of the saloon. It was in what must have been the parlor of
the place when it was a farmhouse and there was a little front
porch.

I stopped before I opened the door and looked about a little.
From where I stood I could look right down into the main street
of the town, like being in a big city, like New York or Chicago,
and looking down out of the fifteenth floor of an office building

into the street.

The hillside was mighty steep and the road up had to wind and wind or no one could ever have come up out of the town to their plagued old fair at all.

It wasn't much of a town I saw—a main street with a lot of saloons and a few stores, one or two dinky moving-picture places, a few Fords, hardly any women or girls in sight and a raft of men. I tried to think of the girl I had been dreaming about as I walked around in the mud and darkness up at the fairground, living in the place, but I couldn't make it. It was like trying to think of Pick-it-boy getting himself worked up to the state I was in then and going into the ugly dump I was going into. It couldn't be done.

All the same I knew the town wasn't all right there in sight. There must have been a good many of the kinds of houses Pennsylvania miners live in back in the hills, or around a turn in the valley in which the main street stood.

What I suppose is that, it being Saturday night and raining, the women and kids had all stayed at home and only the men were out, intending to get themselves liquored up. I've been in some other mining towns since and if I was a miner and had to live in one of them, or in one of the houses they live in with their women and kids, I'd get out and liquor myself up too.

So there I stood looking, and as sick as a dog inside myself, and as wet and cold as a rat in a sewer pipe. I could see the mass of dark figures moving about down below, and beyond the main street there was a river that made a sound you could hear distinctly, even up where I was, and over beyond the river were some railroad tracks with switch engines going up and down. I suppose they had something to do with the mines in which the men of the town worked. Anyway, as I stood watching and listening there was, now and then, a sound like thunder rolling down the sky, and I suppose that was a lot of coal, maybe a whole carload, being let down plunk into a coal car.

And then besides there was, on the side of a hill far away, a long row of coke ovens. They had little doors, through which the light from the fire within leaked out and as they were set closely, side by side, they looked like the teeth of some big man-eating giant lying and waiting over there in the hills.

The sight of it all, even the sight of the kind of hell-holes men are satisfied to go on living in, gave me the fantods and the shivers right down in my liver, and on that night I guess I had in me a kind of contempt for all men, including myself, that I've never had so thoroughly since. Come right down to it, I suppose women aren't so much to blame as men. They aren't running the show.

Then I pushed open the door and went into the saloon. There were about a dozen men, miners I suppose, playing cards at tables in a little long dirty room, with a bar at one side of it, and with a big red-faced man with a mustache standing back of the bar.

The place smelled as such places do where men hang around who have worked and sweated in their clothes and perhaps slept in them too and have never had them washed but have just kept on wearing them. I guess you know what I mean if you've ever been in a city. You smell that smell in a city, in street cars on rainy nights when a lot of factory hands get on. I got pretty used to that smell when I was a tramp and pretty sick of it too.

And so I was in the place now with a glass of whisky in my hand, and I thought all the miners were staring at me, which they weren't at all, but I thought they were and so I felt just the same as though they had been. And then I looked up and saw my own face in the old cracked looking glass back of the bar. If the miners had been staring or laughing at me, I wouldn't have wondered when I saw what I looked like.

It—I mean my own face—was white and pasty-looking, and for some reason, I can't tell exactly why, it wasn't my own face at all. It's a funny business I'm trying to tell you about and I know what you may be thinking of me as well as you do, so you needn't suppose I'm innocent or ashamed. I'm only wondering. I've thought about it a lot since and I can't make it out. I know I was never that way before that night and I know I've never been that way since. Maybe it was lonesomeness, just lonesomeness, gone on in me too long. I've often wondered if women generally are lonesomer than men.

The point is that the face I saw in the looking glass back of that bar, when I looked up from my glass of whisky that evening, wasn't my own face at all but the face of a woman. It was a girl's face, that's what I mean. That's what it was. It was a girl's face, and a lonesome and scared girl too. She was just a kid at that.

When I saw that the glass of whisky came pretty near falling out of my hand but I gulped it down, put a dollar on the bar, and called for another. "I've got to be careful here—I'm up against something new," I said to myself. "If any of these men in here get on to me there's going to be trouble." When I had got the second drink in me I called for a third and I thought, "When I get this third drink down I'll get out of here and back up the hill to the fairground before I make a fool of myself and begin to get drunk."

And then, while I was thinking and drinking my third glass of whisky, the men in the room began to laugh and of course I thought they were laughing at me. But they weren't. No one in the place had really paid any attention to me.

What they were laughing at was a man who had just come in at the door. I'd never seen such a fellow. He was a huge big man with red hair that stuck straight up like bristles out of his head, and he had a red-haired kid in his arms. The kid was just like himself, big, I mean, for his age, and with the same kind of stiff red hair.

He came and set the kid up on the bar, close beside me, and called for a glass of whisky for himself and all the men in the room began to shout and laugh at him and his kid. Only they didn't shout and laugh when he was looking, so he could tell which ones did it, but did all their shouting and laughing when his head was turned the other way. They kept calling him "cracked." "The crack is getting wider in the old tin pan," someone sang and then they all laughed.

I'm puzzled you see, just how to make you feel as I felt that night. I suppose, having undertaken to write this story, that's what I'm up against, trying to do that. I'm not claiming to be able to inform you or to do you any good. I'm just trying to make you understand some things about me, as I would like to understand some things about you, or anyone, if I had the chance. Anyway the whole blamed thing, the thing that went on I mean in that little saloon on that rainy Saturday night, wasn't like anything quite real. I've already told you how I had looked into the glass back of the bar and had seen there, not my own face, but the face of a scared young girl. Well, the men, the miners, sitting at the tables in the half-dark room, the red-faced bartender, the unholy looking big man who had come in and his queer-looking kid, now sitting on the bar—all of them were like characters in some play, not like real people at all.

There was myself, that wasn't myself—and I'm not any fairy. Anyone who has ever known me knows better than that.

And then there was the man who had come in. There was a feeling came out of him that wasn't like the feeling you get from a man at all. It was more like the feeling you get maybe from a horse, only his eyes weren't like a horse's eyes. Horses' eyes have a kind of calm something in them and his hadn't. If you've ever carried a lantern through a wood at night, going along a path, and then suddenly you felt something funny in the air and stopped, and there ahead of you somewhere were the eyes of some little animal, gleaming out at you from a dead wall of darkness —the eyes shine big and quiet but there is a point right in the center of each, where there is something dancing and wavering. You aren't afraid the little animal will jump at you, you are afraid the little eyes will jump at you—that's what's the matter with you.

Only of course a horse, when you go into his stall at night, or a little animal you had disturbed in a wood that way, wouldn't be talking and the big man who had come in there with his kid was talking. He kept talking all the time, saying something under his breath, as they say, and I could only understand now and then a few words. It was his talking made him kind of terrible. His eyes said one thing and his lips another. They didn't seem to get together, as though they belonged to the same person.

For one thing the man was too big. There was about him an

unnatural bigness. It was in his hands, his arms, his shoulders, his body, his head, a bigness like you might see in trees and bushes in a tropical country perhaps. I've never been in a tropical country but I've seen pictures. Only his eyes were small. In his big head they looked like the eyes of a bird. And I remember that his lips were thick, like Negroes' lips

He paid no attention to me or to the others in the room but kept on muttering to himself, or to the kid sitting on the bar—I couldn't tell to which.

First he had one drink and then, quick, another. I stood staring at him and thinking—a jumble of thoughts, I suppose.

What I must have been thinking was something like this. "Well he's one of the kind you are always seeing about towns," I thought. I meant he was one of the cracked kind. In almost any small town you go to you will find one and sometimes two or three cracked people walking around. They go through the street muttering to themselves and people generally are cruel to them. Their own folks make a bluff at being kind, but they aren't really, and the others in the town, men and boys, like to tease them. They send such a fellow, the mild silly kind, on some fool errand after a round square or a dozen post-holes or tie cards on his back saying "Kick me," or something like that, and then carry on and laugh as though they had done something funny.

And so there was this cracked one in that saloon and I could see the men in there wanted to have some fun putting up some kind of horseplay on him, but they didn't quite dare. He wasn't one of the mild kind, that was a cinch. I kept looking at the man and at his kid, and then up at that strange unreal reflection of myself in the cracked looking glass back of the bar. "Rats, rats, digging in the ground—miners are rats, little jack-rabbit," I heard him say to his solemn-faced kid. I guess, after all, maybe he wasn't so cracked.

The kid sitting on the bar kept blinking at his father, like an owl caught out in the daylight, and now the father was having another glass of whisky. He drank six glasses, one right after the other, and it was cheap ten-cent stuff. He must have had cast-iron insides all right.

Of the men in the room there were two or three (maybe they were really more scared than the others so had to put up a bluff of bravery by showing off) who kept laughing and making funny cracks about the big man and his kid and there was one fellow was the worst of the bunch. I'll never forget that fellow because of his looks and what happened to him afterwards.

He was one of the showing-off kind all right, and he was the one that had started the song about the crack getting bigger in the old tin pan. He sang it two or three times, and then he grew bolder and got up and began walking up and down the room singing it over and over. He was a showy kind of man with a fancy vest, on which there were brown tobacco spots, and he wore glasses. Every time he made some crack he thought was funny, he winked at the others as though to say, "You see me. I'm not afraid of this big fellow," and then the others laughed.

The proprietor of the place must have known what was going on, and the danger in it, because he kept leaning over the bar and saying, "Shush, now quit it," to the showy-off man, but it didn't do any good. The fellow kept prancing like a turkey-cock and he put his hat on one side of his head and stopped right back of the big man and sang that song about the crack in the old tin pan. He was one of the kind you can't shush until they get their blocks knocked off, and it didn't take him long to come to it that time anyhow.

Because the big fellow just kept on muttering to his kid and drinking his whisky, as though he hadn't heard anything, and then suddenly he turned and his big hand flashed out and he grabbed, not the fellow who had been showing off, but me. With just a sweep of his arm he brought me up against his big body. Then he shoved me over with my breast jammed against the bar and looking right into his kid's face and he said, "Now you watch him, and if you let him fall I'll kill you," in just quiet ordinary tones as though he was saying "good morning" to some neighbor.

Then the kid leaned over and threw his arms around my head, and in spite of that I did manage to screw my head around enough to see what happened.

It was a sight I'll never forget. The big fellow had whirled around, and he had the showy-off man by the shoulder now, and the fellow's face was a sight. The big man must have had some reputation as a bad man in the town, even though he was cracked, for the man with the fancy vest had his mouth open now, and his hat had fallen off his head, and he was silent and scared. Once, when I was a tramp, I saw a kid killed by a train. The kid was walking on the rail and showing off before some other kids by letting them see how close he could let an engine come to him before he got out of the way. And the engine was whistling and a woman, over on the porch of a house nearby, was jumping up and down and screaming, and the kid let the engine get nearer and nearer, wanting more and more to show off, and then he stumbled and fell. God, I'll never forget the look on his face, in just the second before he got hit and killed, and now, there in that saloon, was the same terrible look on another face.

I closed my eyes for a moment and was sick all through me and then, when I opened my eyes, the big man's fist was just coming down in the other man's face. The one blow knocked him cold and he fell down like a beast hit with an axe.

And then the most terrible thing of all happened. The big man had on heavy boots, and he raised one of them and brought it down on the other man's shoulder, as he lay white and groaning on the floor. I could hear the bones crunch and it made me so sick I could hardly stand up, but I had to stand up and hold on to that kid or I knew it would be my turn next.

Because the big fellow didn't seem excited or anything, but kept on muttering to himself as he had been doing when he was standing peacefully by the bar drinking his whisky, and now he had raised his foot again, and maybe this time he would bring it down in the other man's face and "just eliminate his map for keeps," as sports and prize-fighters sometimes say. I trembled, like I was having a chill, but thank God at that moment the kid, who had his arms around me and one hand clinging to my nose, so that there were the marks of his finger-nails on it the next morning, at that moment the kid, thank God, began to howl, and his father didn't bother any more with the man on the floor but turned around, knocked me aside, and taking the kid in his arms tramped out of that place, muttering to himself as he had been doing ever since he came in.

I went out too but I didn't prance out with any dignity, I'll tell you that. I slunk out like a thief or a coward, which perhaps I am, partly anyhow.

And so there I was, outside there in the darkness, and it was as cold and wet and black and God-forsaken a night as any man ever saw. I was so sick at the thought of human beings that night I could have vomited to think of them at all. For a while I just stumbled along in the mud of the road, going up the hill, back to the fairground, and then, almost before I knew where I was, I found myself in the stall with Pick-it-boy.

That was one of the best and sweetest feelings I've ever had in my whole life, being in that warm stall alone with that horse that night. I had told the other swipes that I would go up and down the row of stalls now and then and have an eye on the other horses, but I had altogether forgotten my promise now. I went and stood with my back against the side of the stall, thinking how mean and low and all balled-up and twisted-up human beings can become, and how the best of them are likely to get that way any time, just because they are human beings and not simple and clear in their minds, and inside themselves, as animals are, maybe.

Perhaps you know how a person feels at such a moment. There are things you think of, odd little things you had thought you had forgotten. Once, when you were a kid, you were with your father, and he was all dressed up, as for a funeral or Fourth of July, and was walking along a street holding your hand. And you were going past a railroad station, and there was a woman standing. She was a stranger in your town and was dressed as you had never seen a woman dressed before, and never thought you would see one, looking so nice. Long afterwards you knew that was because she had lovely taste in clothes, such as so few women have really, but then you thought she must be a queen. You had read about queens in fairy stories and the thoughts of them thrilled you. What lovely eyes the strange lady had and what beautiful rings she wore on her fingers.

Then your father came out, from being in the railroad station, maybe to set his watch by the station clock, and took you by the hand and he and the woman smiled at each other, in an embarrassed kind of way, and you kept looking longingly back at her, and when you were out of her hearing you asked your father if she really were a queen. And it may be that your father was one who wasn't so very hot on democracy and a free country and talked-up bunk about a free citizenry, and he said he hoped she was a queen, and maybe, for all he knew, she was.

Or maybe, when you get jammed up as I was that night, and can't get things clear about yourself or other people and why you are alive, or for that matter why anyone you can think about is alive, you think, not of people at all but of other things you have seen and felt—like walking along a road in the snow in the winter, perhaps out in Iowa, and hearing soft warm sounds in a barn close to the road, or of another time when you were on a hill and the sun was going down and the sky suddenly became a great soft-colored bowl, all glowing like a jewel-handled bowl, a great queen in some far away mighty kingdom might have put on a vast table out under the tree, once a year, when she invited all her loyal and loving subjects to come and dine with her.

I can't, of course, figure out what you try to think about when you are as desolate as I was that night. Maybe you are like me and inclined to think of women, and maybe you are like a man I met once, on the road, who told me that when he was up against it he never thought of anything but grub and a big nice clean warm bed to sleep in. "I don't care about anything else and I don't ever let myself think of anything else," he said. "If I was like you and went to thinking about women sometime I'd find myself hooked up to some skirt, and she'd have the old double cross on me, and the rest of my life maybe I'd be working in some factory for her and her kids."

As I say, there I was anyway, up there alone with that horse in that warm stall in that dark lonesome fairground and I had that feeling about being sick at the thought of human beings and what they could be like.

Well, suddenly I got again the queer feeling I'd had about him once or twice before, I mean the feeling about our understanding each other in some way I can't explain.

So having it again I went over to where he stood and began running my hands all over his body, just because I loved the feel of him and as sometimes, to tell the plain truth, I've felt about touching with my hands the body of a woman I've seen and who I thought was lovely too. I ran my hands over his head and neck and then down over his hard firm round body and then over his flanks and down his legs. His flanks quivered a little I remember and once he turned his head and stuck his cold nose down along my neck and nipped my shoulder a little, in a soft playful way. It hurt a little but I didn't care.

So then I crawled up through a hole into the loft above thinking that night was over anyway and glad of it, but it wasn't, not by a long sight.

As my clothes were all soaking wet and as we race track swipes didn't own any such things as nightgowns or pajamas I had to go to bed naked, of course.

But we had plenty of horse blankets and so I tucked myself in between a pile of them and tried not to think anymore that night. The being with Pick-it-boy and having him close right under me that way made me feel a little better.

Then I was sound asleep and dreaming and—bang like being hit with a club by someone who has sneaked up behind you—I got another wallop.

What I suppose is that, being upset the way I was, I had forgotten to bolt the door to Pick-it-boy's stall down below and two Negro men had come in there, thinking they were in their own place, and had climbed up through the hole where I was. They were half lit up but not what you might call dead drunk, and I suppose they were up against something a couple of white swipes, who had some money in their pockets, wouldn't have been up against.

What I mean is that a couple of white swipes, having liquored themselves up and being down there in the town on a bat, if they wanted a woman or a couple of women would have been able to find them. There is always a few women of that kind can be found around any town I've ever seen or heard of, and of course a bartender would have given them the tip where to go.

But a Negro, up there in that country, where there aren't any, or anyway mighty few Negro women, wouldn't know what to do when he felt that way and would be up against it.

It's so always. Burt and several other Negroes I've known pretty well have talked to me about it, lots of times. You take now a young Negro man—not a race track swipe or a tramp or any other low-down kind of a fellow—but, let us say, one who has been to college, and has behaved himself and tried to be a good man the best he could, and be clean, as they say. He isn't any better off, is he? If he has made himself some money and wants to go sit in a swell restaurant, or go to hear some good music, or see a good play at the theatre, he gets what we used to call on the tracks, "the messy end of the dung fork," doesn't he?

And even in such a low-down place as what people call a "bad house" it's the same way. The white swipes and others can go into a place where they have Negro women fast enough, and they do it too, but you let a Negro swipe try it the other way around and see how he comes out.

You see, I can think this whole thing out fairly now, sitting here in my own house and writing, and with my wife Jessie in the kitchen making a pie or something, and I can show just how the two Negro men who came into that loft, where I was asleep, were justified in what they did, and I can preach about how the Negroes are up against it in this country, like a daisy, but I tell you what, I didn't think things out that way that night.

For, you understand, what they thought, they being half liquored-up, and when one of them had jerked the blankets off me, was that I was a woman. One of them carried a lantern but it was smoky and dirty and didn't give out much light. So they must have figured it out—my body being pretty white and slender then, like a young girl's body I suppose—that some white swipe had brought me up there. The kind of girls around a town that will come with a swipe to a race track on a rainy night aren't very fancy females but you'll find that kind in the towns all right. I've seen many a one in my day.

And so, I figure, these two big buck niggers, being piped that way, just made up their minds they would snatch me away from the white swipe who had brought me out there, and who had left me lying carelessly around.

"Jes' you lie still honey. We ain't gwine hurt you none," one of them said, with a little chuckling laugh that had something in it besides a laugh too. It was the kind of laugh that gives you the shivers.

The devil of it was I couldn't say anything, not even a word. Why I couldn't yell out and say "What the hell," and just kid them a little and shoo them out of there I don't know, but I couldn't. I tried and tried so that my throat hurt but I didn't say a word. I just lay there staring at them.

It was a mixed-up night. I've never gone through another night like it.

Was I scared? Lord Almighty, I'll tell you what, I was scared. Because the two big black faces were leaning right over me now, and I could feel their liquored-up breaths on my cheeks, and their eyes were shining in the dim light from that smoky lantern, and right in the center of their eyes was that dancing flickering light I've told you about your seeing in the eyes of wild animals, when you were carrying a lantern through the woods at night.

It was a puzzler! All my life, you see—me never having had any sisters, and at that time never having had a sweetheart either— I had been dreaming and thinking about women, and I suppose I'd always been dreaming about a pure innocent one, for myself, made for me by God, maybe. Men are that way. No matter how big they talk about "let the women go hang," they've always got that notion tucked away inside themselves, somewhere. It's a kind of chesty man's notion, I suppose, but they've got it and the kind

of up-and-coming women we have nowdays who are always saying, "I'm as good as a man and will do what the men do," are on
the wrong trail if they really ever want to, what you might say
"hog-tie" a fellow of their own.

So I had invented a kind of princess, with black hair and a
slender willowy body to dream about. And I thought of her as
being shy and afraid to ever tell anything she really felt to anyone
but just me. I suppose I fancied that if I ever found such a woman
in the flesh I would be the strong sure one and she the timid
shrinking one.

And now I was that woman, or something like her, myself.

I gave a kind of wriggle, like a fish you have just taken off the
hook. What I did next wasn't a thought-out thing. I was caught
and I squirmed, that's all.

The two niggers both jumped at me but somehow—the lantern
having been kicked over and having gone out the first move they
made—well, in some way, when they both lunged at me they
missed.

As good luck would have it, my feet found the hole where you
put hay down to the horse in the stall below, and through which
we crawled up when it was time to go to bed in our blankets up
in the hay, and down I slid, not bothering to try to find the ladder
with my feet but just letting myself go.

In less than a second I was out of doors in the dark and the
rain and the two blacks were down the hole and out the door of
the stall after me.

How long or how far they really followed me I suppose I'll
never know. It was black dark and raining hard now and a roaring
wind had begun to blow. Of course, my body being white, it
must have made some kind of a faint streak in the darkness as I
ran, and anyway I thought they could see me and I knew I couldn't
see them and that made my terror ten times worse. Every minute
I thought they would grab me.

You know how it is when a person is all upset and full of terror
as I was. I suppose maybe the two niggers followed me for a while,
running across the muddy race track and into the grove of trees

that grew in the oval inside the track, but likely enough, after just a few minutes, they gave up the chase and went back, found their own place and went to sleep. They were liquored-up, as I've said, and maybe partly funning too.

But I didn't know that, if they were. As I ran I kept hearing sounds, sounds made by the rain coming down through the dead old leaves left on the trees and by the wind blowing, and it may be that the sound that scared me most of all was my own bare feet stepping on a dead branch and breaking it or something like that.

There was something strange and scary, a steady sound, like a heavy man running and breathing hard, right at my shoulder. It may have been my own breath, coming quick and fast. And I thought I heard that chuckling laugh I'd heard up in the loft, the laugh that sent the shivers right down through me. Of course every tree I came close to looked like a man standing there, ready to grab me, and I kept dodging and going—bang—into other trees. My shoulders kept knocking against trees in that way and the skin was all knocked off, and every time it happened I thought a big black hand had come down and clutched at me and was tearing my flesh.

How long it went on I don't know, maybe an hour, maybe five minutes. But anyway the darkness didn't let up, and the terror didn't let up, and I couldn't, to save my life, scream or make any sound.

Just why I couldn't I don't know. Could it be because at the time I was a woman, while at the same time I wasn't a woman? It may be that I was too ashamed of having turned into a girl and being afraid of a man to make any sound. I don't know about that. It's over my head.

But anyway I couldn't make a sound. I tried and tried and my throat hurt from trying and no sound came.

And then, after a long time, or what seemed like a long time, I got out from among the trees inside the track and was on the track itself again. I thought the two black men were still after me, you understand, and I ran like a madman.

Of course, running along the track that way, it must have been up the back stretch, I came after a time to where the old slaughter-house stood, in that field beside the track. I knew it by its ungodly smell, scared as I was. Then, in some way, I managed to get over the high old fairground fence and was in the field, where the slaughter-house was.

All the time I was trying to yell or scream, or be sensible and tell those two black men that I was a man and not a woman, but I couldn't make it. And then I heard a sound like a board cracking or breaking in the fence and thought they were still after me.

So I kept on running like a crazy man in the field, and just then I stumbled and fell over something. I've told you how the old slaughter-house field was filled with bones that had been lying there a long time and had all been washed white. There were heads of sheep and cows and all kinds of things.

And when I fell and pitched forward I fell right into the midst of something, still and cold and white.

It was probably the skeleton of a horse lying there. In small towns like that, they take an old worn-out horse that has died and haul him off to some field outside of town and skin him for the hide, that they can sell for a dollar or two. It doesn't make any difference what the horse has been, that's the way he usually ends up. Maybe even Pick-it-boy, or O My Man, or a lot of other good fast ones I've seen and known have ended that way by this time.

And so I think it was the bones of a horse lying there and he must have been lying on his back. The birds and wild animals had picked all his flesh away and the rain had washed his bones clean.

Anyway I fell and pitched forward and my side got cut pretty deep and my hands clutched at something. I had fallen right in between the ribs of the horse and they seemed to wrap themselves around me close. And my hands, clutching upwards, had got hold of the cheeks of that dead horse and the bones of his cheeks were cold as ice with the rain washing over them. White bones wrapped around me and white bones in my hands.

There was a new terror now that seemed to go down to the

very bottom of me, to the bottom of the inside of me, I mean. It shook me like I have seen a rat in a barn shaken by a dog. It was a terror like a big wave that hits you when you are walking on a seashore, maybe. You see it coming and you try to run and get away but when you start to run inshore there is a stone cliff you can't climb. So the wave comes high as a mountain, and there it is, right in front of you and nothing in all this world can stop it. And now it had knocked you down and rolled and tumbled you over and over and washed you clean, clean, but dead maybe.

And that's the way I felt—I seemed to myself dead with blind terror. It was a feeling like the finger of God running down your back and burning you clean, I mean.

It burned all that silly nonsense about being a girl right out of me.

I screamed at last and the spell that was on me was broken. I'll bet the scream I let out of me could have been heard a mile and a half.

Right away I felt better and crawled out from among the pile of bones, and then I stood on my own feet again and I wasn't a woman or a young girl any more but a man and my own self, and as far as I know I've been that way ever since. Even the black night seemed warm and alive now, like a mother might be to a kid in the dark.

Only I couldn't go back to the race track because I was blubbering and crying and was ashamed of myself and of what a fool I had made of myself. Someone might see me and I couldn't stand that, not at that moment.

So I went across the field, walking now, not running like a crazy man, and pretty soon I came to a fence and crawled over and got into another field, in which there was a straw stack I just happened to find in the pitch darkness.

The straw stack had been there a long time and some sheep had nibbled away at it until they had made a pretty deep hole, like a cave, in the side of it. I found the hole and crawled in and there were some sheep in there, about a dozen of them.

When I came in, creeping on my hands and knees, they didn't

make much fuss, just stirred around a little and then settled down.
So I settled down amongst them too. They were warm and
gentle and kind, like Pick-it-boy, and being in there with them
made me feel better than I would have felt being with any human
person I knew at that time.

So I settled down and slept after a while, and when I woke up
it was daylight and not very cold and the rain was over. The clouds
were breaking away from the sky now and maybe there would be
a fair the next week but if there was I knew I wouldn't be there to
see it.

Because what I expected to happen did happen. I had to go
back across the fields and the fairground to the place where my
clothes were, right in the broad daylight, and me stark naked,
and of course I knew someone would be up and would raise a
shout, and every swipe and every driver would stick his head out
and would whoop with laughter.

And there would be a thousand questions asked, and I would
be too mad and too ashamed to answer, and would perhaps begin
to blubber, and that would make me more ashamed than ever.

It all turned out just as I expected, except that when the noise
and the shouts of laughter were going it the loudest, Burt came
out of the stall where O My Man was kept, and when he saw me
he didn't know what was the matter but he knew something was
up that wasn't on the square and for which I wasn't to blame.

So he got so all-fired mad he couldn't speak for a minute, and
then he grabbed a pitchfork and began prancing up and down
before the other stalls, giving that gang of swipes and drivers such
a royal old dressing-down as you never heard. You should have
heard him sling language. It was grand to hear.

And while he was doing it I sneaked up into the loft, blubbering because I was so pleased and happy to hear him swear that
way, and I got my wet clothes on quick and got down, and gave
Pick-it-boy a good-bye kiss on the cheek and lit out.

The last I saw of all that part of my life was Burt, still going it,
and yelling out for the man who had put up a trick on me to
come out and get what was coming to him. He had the pitchfork

in his hand and was swinging it around, and every now and then he would make a kind of lunge at a tree or something, he was so mad through, and there was no one else in sight at all. And Burt didn't even see me cutting out along the fence through a gate and down the hill and out of the race-horse and the tramp life for the rest of my days.

MILK BOTTLES

I LIVED, DURING THAT SUMMER, IN A LARGE ROOM ON THE TOP FLOOR of an old house on the North Side in Chicago. It was August and the night was hot. Until after midnight I sat—the sweat trickling down my back—under a lamp, laboring to feel my way into the lives of the fanciful people who were trying also to live in the tale on which I was at work.

It was a hopeless affair.

I became involved in the efforts of the shadowy people and they in turn became involved in the fact of the hot uncomfortable room, in the fact that, although it was what the farmers of the Middle West call "good corn-growing weather," it was plain hell to be alive in Chicago. Hand in hand the shadowy people of my fanciful world and myself groped our way through a forest in which the leaves had all been burned off the trees. The hot ground burned the shoes off our feet. We were striving to make our way through the forest and into some cool beautiful city. The fact is, as you will clearly understand, I was a little off my head.

When I gave up the struggle and got to my feet the chairs in the room danced about. They also were running aimlessly through a burning land and striving to reach some mythical city. "I'd better get out of here and go for a walk or go jump into the lake and cool myself off," I thought.

I went down out of my room and into the street. On a lower floor of the house lived two burlesque actresses who had just come in from their evening's work and who now sat in their room talking. As I reached the street something heavy whirled past my head and broke on the stone pavement. A white liquid spurted over my clothes and the voice of one of the actresses could be heard coming from the one lighted room of the house. "Oh, hell! We live such damned lives, we do, and we work in such a town! A dog is better off! And now they are going to take booze away from us too! I come home from working in that hot theatre on a hot night like this and what do I see—a half-filled bottle of spoiled milk standing on a window sill!

"I won't stand it! I got to smash everything!" she cried.

I walked eastward from my house. From the northwestern end of the city great hordes of men, women and children had come to spend the night out of doors, by the shore of the lake. It was stifling hot there too and the air was heavy with a sense of struggle. On a few hundred acres of flat land, that had formerly been a swamp, some two million people were fighting for the peace and quiet of sleep and not getting it. Out of the half darkness, beyond the little strip of park land at the water's edge, the huge empty houses of Chicago's fashionable folk made a greyish-blue blot against the sky. "Thank the gods," I thought, "there are some people who can get out of here, who can go to the mountains or the seashore or to Europe." I stumbled in the half darkness over the legs of a woman who was lying and trying to sleep on the grass. A baby lay beside her and when she sat up it began to cry. I muttered an apology and stepped aside and as I did so my foot struck a half-filled milk bottle and I knocked it over, the milk running out on the grass. "Oh, I'm sorry. Please forgive me," I cried. "Never mind," the woman answered, "the milk is sour."

He is a tall stoop-shouldered man with prematurely greyed hair and works as a copywriter in an advertising agency in Chicago—an agency where I also have sometimes been employed—and on that night in August I met him, walking with quick eager strides along the shore of the lake and past the tired petulant people. He did not see me at first and I wondered at the evidence of life in him when everyone else seemed half dead; but a street lamp hanging over a nearby roadway threw its light down upon my face and he pounced. "Here you, come up to my place," he cried sharply. "I've got something to show you. I was on my way down to see you. That's where I was going," he lied as he hurried me along.

We went to his apartment on a street leading back from the lake and the park. German, Polish, Italian and Jewish families, equipped with soiled blankets and the ever-present half-filled bottles of milk, had come prepared to spend the night out of doors; but the American families in the crowd were giving up the struggle to find a cool spot, and a little stream of them trickled along the sidewalks, going back to hot beds in the hot houses.

It was past one o'clock and my friend's apartment was disorderly as well as hot. He explained that his wife, with their two children, had gone home to visit her mother on a farm near Springfield, Illinois.

We took off our coats and sat down. My friend's thin cheeks were flushed and his eyes shone. "You know—well—you see," he began and then hesitated and laughed like an embarrassed schoolboy. "Well now," he began again, "I've long been wanting to write something real, something besides advertisements. I suppose I'm silly but that's the way I am. It's been my dream to write something stirring and big. I suppose it's the dream of a lot of advertising writers, eh? Now look here—don't you go laughing. I think I've done it."

He explained that he had written something concerning Chicago, the capital and heart, as he said, of the whole Central West. He grew angry. "People come here from the East or from farms, or from little holes of towns like I came from, and they think it smart to run Chicago into the ground," he declared. "I thought I'd show 'em up," he added, jumping up and walking nervously about the room.

He handed me many sheets of paper covered with hastily scrawled words, but I protested and asked him to read it aloud. He did, standing with his face turned away from me. There was a quiver in his voice. The thing he had written concerned some mythical town I had never seen. He called it Chicago, but in the same breath spoke of great streets flaming with color, ghostlike buildings flung up into night skies and a river, running down a path of gold into the boundless West. It was the city, I told myself, I and the people of my story had been trying to find earlier on that same evening, when because of the heat I went a little off my head and could not work anymore. The people of the city he had written about were a cool-headed, brave people, marching forward to some spiritual triumph, the promise of which was inherent in the physical aspects of the town.

Now I am one who, by the careful cultivation of certain traits in my character, have succeeded in building up the more brutal side of my nature, but I cannot knock women and children down in order to get aboard Chicago streetcars, nor can I tell an author to his face that I think his work is rotten.

"You're all right, Ed. You're great. You've knocked out a regular sock-dolager of a masterpiece here. Why, you sound as good as Henry Mencken writing about Chicago as the literary center of America, and you've lived in Chicago and he never did. The only thing I can see you've missed is a little something about the stockyards, and you can put that in later," I added and prepared to depart.

"What's this?" I asked, picking up a half-dozen sheets of paper that lay on the floor by my chair. I read it eagerly. And when I had finished reading it he stammered and apologized and then, stepping across the room, jerked the sheets out of my hand and threw them out at an open window. "I wish you hadn't seen that. It's something else I wrote about Chicago," he explained. He was flustered.

"You see, the night was so hot, and, down at the office, I had to write a condensed-milk advertisement just as I was sneaking away to come home and work on this other thing, and the streetcar was so crowded and the people stank so, and when I finally got home here—the wife being gone—the place was a mess. Well, I couldn't write and I was sore. It's been my chance, you see, the wife and kids being gone and the house being quiet. I went for a walk. I think I went a little off my head. Then I came home and wrote that stuff I've just thrown out of the window."

He grew cheerful again. "Oh, well—it's all right. Writing that fool thing stirred me up and enabled me to write this other stuff, this real stuff I showed you first, about Chicago."

And so I went home and to bed, having in this odd way stumbled upon another bit of the kind of writing that is—for better or worse—really presenting the lives of the people of these towns and cities—sometimes in prose, sometimes in stirring, colorful song. It was the kind of thing Mr. Sandburg or Mr. Masters might have done after an evening's walk on a hot night in, say, West Congress Street in Chicago.

The thing I had read of Ed's centered about a half-filled bottle of spoiled milk standing dim in the moonlight on a window sill. There had been a moon earlier on that August evening, a new moon, a thin crescent golden streak in the sky. What had happened to my friend, the advertising writer, was something like this—I figured it all out as I lay sleepless in bed after our talk.

I am sure I do not know whether or not it is true that all advertising writers and newspapermen want to do other kinds of writing, but Ed did all right. The August day that had preceded the hot night had been a hard one for him to get through. All day he had been wanting to be at home in his quiet apartment producing literature, rather than sitting in an office and writing advertisements. In the late afternoon, when he had thought his desk cleared for the day, the boss of the copywriters came and ordered him to write a page advertisement for the magazines on the subject of condensed milk. "We got a chance to get a new account if we can knock out some crackerjack stuff in a hurry," he said. "I'm sorry to have to put it up to you on such a rotten hot day, Ed, but we're up against it. Let's see if you've got some of the old pep in you. Get down to hardpan now and knock out something snappy and unusual before you go home."

Ed had tried. He put away the thoughts he had been having

about the city beautiful—the glowing city of the plains—and got right down to business. He thought about milk, milk for little children, the Chicagoans of the future, milk that would produce a little cream to put in the coffee of advertising writers in the morning, sweet fresh milk to keep all his brother and sister Chicagoans robust and strong. What Ed really wanted was a long cool drink of something with a kick in it, but he tried to make himself think he wanted a drink of milk. He gave himself over to thoughts of milk, milk condensed and yellow, milk warm from the cows his father owned when he was a boy—his mind launched a little boat and he set out on a sea of milk.

Out of it all he got what is called an original advertisement. The sea of milk on which he sailed became a mountain of cans of condensed milk, and out of that fancy he got his idea. He made a crude sketch for a picture showing wide rolling green fields with white farmhouses. Cows grazed on the green hills and at one side of the picture a barefooted boy was driving a herd of Jersey cows out of the sweet fair land and down a lane into a kind of funnel at the small end of which was a tin of the condensed milk. Over the picture he put a heading: "The health and freshness of a whole countryside is condensed into one can of Whitney-Wells Condensed Milk." The head copywriter said it was a humdinger.

And then Ed went home. He wanted to begin writing about the city beautiful at once and so didn't go out to dinner, but fished about in the ice chest and found some cold meat out of which he made himself a sandwich. Also, he poured himself a glass of milk, but it was sour. "Oh, damn!" he said and poured it into the kitchen sink.

As Ed explained to me later, he sat down and tried to begin writing his real stuff at once, but he couldn't seem to get into it. The last hour in the office, the trip home in the hot smelly car, and the taste of the sour milk in his mouth had jangled his nerves. The truth is that Ed has a rather sensitive, finely balanced nature, and it had got mussed up.

He took a walk and tried to think, but his mind wouldn't stay where he wanted it to. Ed is now a man of nearly forty and on

that night his mind ran back to his young manhood in the city—
and stayed there. Like other boys who had become grown men in
Chicago, he had come to the city from a farm at the edge of a
prairie town, and like all such town and farm boys, he had come
filled with vague dreams.

What things he had hungered to do and be in Chicago! What
he had done you can fancy. For one thing he had got himself
married and now lived in the apartment on the North Side. To
give a real picture of his life during the twelve or fifteen years that
had slipped away since he was a young man would involve writing
a novel, and that is not my purpose.

Anyway, there he was in his room—come home from his walk—
and it was hot and quiet and he could not manage to get into his
masterpiece. How still it was in the apartment with the wife and
children away! His mind stayed on the subject of his youth in the
city.

He remembered a night of his young manhood when he had
gone out to walk, just as he did on that August evening. Then his
life wasn't complicated by the fact of the wife and children and he
lived alone in his room; but something had got on his nerves
then too. On that evening long ago he grew restless in his room
and went out to walk. It was summer and first he went down by
the river where ships were being loaded and then to a crowded
park where girls and young fellows walked about.

He grew bold and spoke to a woman who sat alone on a park
bench. She let him sit beside her and, because it was dark and she
was silent, he began to talk. The night had made him sentimental.
"Human beings are such hard things to get at. I wish I could get
close to someone," he said. "Oh, you go on! What you doing?
You ain't trying to kid someone?" asked the woman.

Ed jumped up and walked away. He went into a long street
lined with dark silent buildings and then stopped and looked
about. What he wanted was to believe that in the apartment
buildings were people who lived intense eager lives, who had great
dreams, who were capable of great adventures. "They are really
only separated from me by the brick walls," was what he told

himself on that night.

It was then that the milk bottle theme first got hold of him. He went into an alleyway to look at the backs of the apartment buildings and, on that evening also, there was a moon. Its light fell upon a long row of half-filled bottles standing on window sills.

Something within him went a little sick and he hurried out of the alleyway and into the street. A man and woman walked past him and stopped before the entrance to one of the buildings. Hoping they might be lovers, he concealed himself in the entrance to another building to listen to their conversation.

The couple turned out to be a man and wife and they were quarreling. Ed heard the woman's voice saying: "You come in here. You can't put that over on me. You say you just want to take a walk, but I know you. You want to go out and blow in some money. What I'd like to know is why you don't loosen up a little for me."

That is the story of what happened to Ed when, as a young man, he went to walk in the city in the evening, and when he had become a man of forty and went out of his house wanting to dream and to think of a city beautiful, much the same sort of thing happened again. Perhaps the writing of the condensed milk advertisement and the taste of the sour milk he had got out of the ice box had something to do with his mood; but, anyway, milk bottles, like a refrain in a song, got into his brain. They seemed to sit and mock at him from the windows of all the buildings in all the streets, and when he turned to look at people, he met the crowds from the West and the Northwest Sides going to the park and the lake. At the head of each little group of people marched a woman who carried a milk bottle in her hand.

And so, on that August night, Ed went home angry and disturbed, and in anger wrote of his city. Like the burlesque actress in my own house he wanted to smash something, and, as milk bottles were in his mind, he wanted to smash milk bottles. "I could grasp the neck of a milk bottle. It fits the hand so neatly. I could kill a man or woman with such a thing," he thought desperately.

He wrote, you see, the five or six sheets I had read in that mood and then felt better. And after that he wrote about the ghostlike buildings flung into the sky by the hands of a brave adventurous people and about the river that runs down a path of gold, and into the boundless West.

As you have already concluded, the city he described in his masterpiece was lifeless, but the city he, in a queer way, expressed in what he wrote about the milk bottle could not be forgotten. It frightened you a little but there it was and, in spite of his anger or perhaps because of it, a lovely singing quality had got into the thing. In those few scrawled pages the miracle had been worked. I was a fool not to have put the sheets into my pocket. When I went down out of his apartment that evening I did look for them in a dark alleyway, but they had become lost in a sea of rubbish that had leaked over the tops of a long row of tin ash cans that stood at the foot of a stairway leading from the back doors of the apartments above.

THE MAN'S STORY

DURING HIS TRIAL FOR MURDER AND LATER, AFTER HE HAD BEEN cleared through the confession of that queer little bald chap with the nervous hands, I watched him, fascinated by his continued effort to make something understood.

He was persistently interested in something having nothing to do with the charge that he had murdered the woman. The matter of whether or not, and by due process of law, he was to be convicted of murder and hanged by the neck until he was dead didn't seem to interest him. The law was something outside his life and he declined to have anything to do with the killing as one might decline a cigarette. "I thank you, I am not smoking at present. I made a bet with a fellow that I could go along without smoking cigarettes for a month."

That is the sort of thing I mean. It was puzzling. Really, had he been guilty and trying to save his neck he couldn't have taken a better line. You see, at first, everyone thought he had done the killing; we were all convinced of it, and then, just because of that magnificent air of indifference, everyone began wanting to save him. When news came of the confession of the crazy little stage-hand everyone broke out into cheers.

He was clear of the law after that but his manner in no way changed. There was, somewhere, a man or a woman who would understand just what he understood and it was important to find that person and talk things over. There was a time, during the trial and immediately afterward, when I saw a good deal of him, and I had this sharp sense of him feeling about in the darkness trying to find something like a needle or a pin lost on the floor. Well, he was like an old man who cannot find his glasses. He feels in all his pockets and looks helplessly about.

There was a question in my own mind too, in everyone's mind— "Can a man be wholly casual and brutal in every outward way, at a moment when the one nearest and dearest to him is dying, and at the same time, and with quite another part of himself, be altogether tender and sensitive?"

Anyway it's a story, and once in a while a man likes to tell a story straight out, without putting in any newspaper jargon about beautiful heiresses, cold-blooded murderers and all that sort of tommyrot.

As I picked the story up the sense of it was something like this—

The man's name was Wilson—Edgar Wilson—and he had come to Chicago from some place to the westward, perhaps from the mountains. He might once have been a sheep herder or something of the sort in the far west, as he had the peculiar abstract air acquired only by being a good deal alone. About himself and his past he told a good many conflicting stories and so, after being with him for a time, one instinctively discarded the past.

"The devil—it doesn't matter—the man can't tell the truth in that direction. Let it go," one said to oneself. What was known was that he had come to Chicago from a town in Kansas and that he had run away from the Kansas town with another man's wife.

As to her story, I knew little enough of it. She had been at one time, I imagine, a rather handsome thing, in a big strong upstanding sort of way, but her life, until she met Wilson, had been rather messy. In those dead flat Kansas towns lives have a way of getting ugly and messy without anything very definite having happened to make them so. One can't imagine the reasons. Let it go. It just is so and one can't at all believe the writers of Western tales about the life out there.

To be a little more definite about this particular woman—in her young girlhood her father had got into trouble. He had been some sort of a small official, a travelling agent or something of the sort for an express company, and got arrested in connection with the disappearance of some money. And then, when he was in jail and before his trial, he shot and killed himself. The girl's mother was already dead.

Within a year or two she married a man, an honest enough fellow but from all accounts rather uninteresting. He was a drug clerk and a frugal man and after a short time managed to buy a drug store of his own.

The woman, as I have said, had been strong and well built but now grew thin and nervous. Still she carried herself well with a sort of air, as it were, and there was something about her that appealed strongly to men. Several men of the seedy little town were smitten by her and wrote her letters, trying to get her to creep out with them at night. You know how such things are done. The letters were unsigned. "You go to such and such a place on Friday evening. If you are willing to talk things over with me carry a book in your hand."

Then the woman made a mistake and told her husband about the receipt of one of the letters and he grew angry and tramped off to the trysting place at night with a shotgun in his hand. When no one appeared he came home and fussed about. He said little mean tentative things. "You must have looked in a certain way at the man when he passed you on the street. A man don't grow so bold with a married woman unless an opening has been given him."

The man talked and talked after that, and life in the house must have been gay. She grew habitually silent, and when she was silent the house was silent. They had no children.

Then the man Edgar Wilson came along, going eastward, and stopped over in the town for two or three days. He had at that time a little money and stayed at a small workingmen's boardinghouse, near the railroad station. One day he saw the woman walking in the street and followed her to her home and the neighbors saw them standing and talking together for an hour by the front gate and on the next day he came again.

That time they talked for two hours and then she went into the house, got a few belongings and walked to the railroad station with him. They took a train for Chicago and lived there together, apparently very happy, until she died—in a way I am about to try to tell you about. They of course could not be married and during the three years they lived in Chicago he did nothing toward earning their common living. As he had a very small amount of money when they came, barely enough to get them here from the Kansas town, they were miserably poor.

They lived, when I knew about them, over on the North Side, in that section of old three- and four-story brick residences that were once the homes of what we call our nice people, but that had afterward gone to the bad. The section is having a kind of rebirth now but for a good many years it rather went to seed. There were these old residences, made into boardinghouses, and with unbelievably dirty lace curtains at the windows, and now and then an utterly disreputable old tumble-down frame house— in one of which Wilson lived with his woman.

The place is a sight! Someone owns it, I suppose, who is shrewd enough to know that in a big city like Chicago no section gets neglected always. Such a fellow must have said to himself, "Well, I'll let the place go. The ground on which the house stands will some day be very valuable but the house is worth nothing. I'll let it go at a low rental and do nothing to fix it up. Perhaps I will get enough out of it to pay my taxes until prices come up."

And so the house had stood there unpainted for years and the windows were out of line and the shingles nearly all off the roof. The second floor was reached by an outside stairway with a handrail that had become just the peculiar grey greasy black that wood can become in a soft-coal-burning city like Chicago or Pittsburgh. One's hand became black when the railing was touched; and the rooms above were altogether cold and cheerless.

At the front there was a large room with a fireplace, from which many bricks had fallen, and back of that were two small sleeping rooms.

Wilson and his woman lived in the place at the time when the thing happened I am to tell you about, and as they had taken it in May I presume they did not too much mind the cold barrenness of the large front room in which they lived. There was a sagging wooden bed with a leg broken off—the woman had tried to repair it with sticks from a packing box—a kitchen table that was also used by Wilson as a writing desk, and two or three cheap kitchen chairs.

The woman had managed to get a place as wardrobe woman in a theatre in Randolph Street and they lived on her earnings. It was said she had got the job because some man connected with the theatre, or a company playing there, had a passion for her, but one can always pick up stories of that sort about any woman who works about the theatre—from the scrubwoman to the star.

Anyway she worked there and had a reputation in the theatre of being quiet and efficient.

As for Wilson, he wrote poetry of a sort I've never seen before, although, like most newspapermen, I've taken a turn at verse making myself now and then—both of the rhymed kind and the newfangled vers libre sort. I rather go in for the classical stuff myself.

About Wilson's verse—it was Greek to me. Well now, to get right down to hardpan in this matter, it was and it wasn't.

The stuff made me feel just a little bit woozy when I took a whole sheaf of it and sat alone in my room reading it at night. It was all about walls and deep wells and great bowls with young trees standing erect in them and trying to find their way to the light and air over the rim of the bowl.

Queer crazy stuff, every line of it, but fascinating too in a way. One got into a new world with new values, which after all is I suppose what poetry is all about. There was the world of fact we all know—or think we know—the world of flat buildings and middle-western farms with wire fences about the fields and Fordson tractors running up and down, and towns with high schools and advertising billboards, and everything that makes up life—or that we think makes up life.

There was this world we all walk about in, and then there was this other world that I have come to think of as Wilson's world— a dim place to me at least—of faraway near places—things taking new and strange shapes, the insides of people coming out, the eyes seeing new things, the fingers feeling new and strange things.

It was a place of walls mainly. I got hold of the whole lot of Wilson's verse by a piece of luck. It happened that I was the first newspaperman who got into the place on the night when the woman's body was found, and there was all his stuff, carefully written out in a sort of child's copybook, and two or three stupid policemen standing about. I just shoved the book under my coat when they weren't looking, and later, during Wilson's trial, we published some of the more intelligible ones in the paper. It made pretty good newspaper stuff—the poet who killed his mistress,

> *"He did not wear his purple coat,*
> *For blood and wine are red"—*

and all that. Chicago loved it.

To get back to the poetry itself for a moment. I just wanted to explain that all through the book there ran this notion that men had erected walls about themselves and that all men were per- haps destined to stand forever behind the walls—on which they constantly beat with their fists, or with whatever tools they could get hold of. Wanted to break through to something, you under- stand. One couldn't quite make out whether there was just one great wall or many little individual walls. Sometimes Wilson put it one way, sometimes another. Men had themselves built the walls and now stood behind them, knowing dimly that beyond the walls there was warmth, light, air, beauty, life in fact—while at the same time, and because of a kind of madness in themselves, the walls were constantly being built higher and stronger.

The notion gives you the fantods a little, doesn't it? Anyway it does me.

And then there was that notion about deep wells, men every-where constantly digging and digging themselves down deeper and deeper into deep wells. They not wanting to do it, you un-derstand, and no one wanting them to do it, but all the time the thing going on just the same, that is to say the wells getting constantly deeper and deeper, and the voices growing dimmer and dimmer in the distance—and again the light and the warmth of life going away and going away, because of a kind of blind refusal of people to try to understand each other, I suppose.

It was all very strange to me—Wilson's poetry, I mean—when I came to it. Here is one of his things. It is not directly concerned with the walls, the bowl or the deep well theme, as you will see, but it is one we ran in the paper during the trial and a lot of folks rather liked it—as I'll admit I do myself. Maybe putting it in here will give a kind of point to my story by giving you some sense of the strangeness of the man who is the story's hero. In the book it was called merely number ninety-seven, and it went as follows:

The firm grip of my fingers on the thin paper of this cigarette is a sign that I am very quiet now. Sometimes it is not so. When I am unquiet I am weak but when I am quiet, as I am now, I am very strong.

Just now I went along one of the streets of my city and in at a door and came up here, where I am now, lying on a bed and looking out at a window. Very suddenly and completely the knowledge has come to me that I could grip the sides of tall buildings as freely and as easily as I now grip this cigarette. I could hold the building between my fingers, put it to my lips and blow smoke through it. I could blow confusion away. I could blow a thousand people out through the roof of one tall building into the sky, into the unknown. Building after building I could consume as I consume the cigarettes in this box. I could throw the burning ends of cities over my shoulder and out through a window.

It is not often I get in the state I am now in—so quiet and sure of myself. When the feeling comes over me there is a directness and simplicity in me that makes me love myself. To myself at such times I say strong sweet words.

I am on a couch by this window and I could ask a woman to come here to lie with me, or a man either for that matter.

I could take a row of houses standing on a street, tip them over, empty the people out of them, squeeze and compress all the people into one person and love that person.

Do you see this hand? Suppose it held a knife that could cut down through all the falseness in you. Suppose it could cut down through the sides of buildings and houses where thousands of people now lie asleep.

It would be something worth thinking about if the fingers of this hand gripped a knife that could cut and rip through all the ugly husks in which millions of lives are enclosed.

Well, there is the idea you see, a kind of power that could be tender too. I will quote you just one more of his things, a more gentle one. It is called in the book number eighty-three.

I am a tree that grows beside the wall. I have been thrusting up and up. My body is covered with scars. My body is old but still I thrust upward, creeping toward the top of the wall.

It is my desire to drop blossoms and fruit over the wall.

I would moisten dry lips.

I would drop blossoms on the heads of children, over the top of the wall.

I would caress with falling blossoms the bodies of those who live on the further side of the wall.

My branches are creeping upward and new sap comes into me out of the dark ground under the wall.

My fruit shall not be my fruit until it drops from my arms into the arms of the others over the top of the wall.

And now as to the life led by the man and woman in the large upper room in that old frame house. By a stroke of luck I have recently got rather a line on that by a discovery I have made.

After they had moved into the house—it was only last spring—the theatre in which the woman was employed was dark for a long time and they were more than usually hard up, so the woman tried to pick up a little extra money—to help pay the rent I suppose—by subletting the two little back rooms of that place of theirs.

Various people lived in the dark tiny holes, just how I can't make out as there was no furniture. Still there are places in Chicago called "flops" where one may sleep on the floor for five or ten cents and they are more patronized than respectable people know anything about.

What I did discover was a little woman—she wasn't so young but she was hunchbacked and small and it is hard not to think of her as a girl—who once lived in one of the rooms for several weeks. She had a job as ironer in a small hand laundry in the neighborhood and someone had given her a cheap folding cot. She was a curiously sentimental creature, with the kind of hurt eyes deformed people often have, and I have a fancy she had herself a romantic attachment of a sort for the man Wilson. Anyway I managed to find out a lot from her.

After the other woman's death and after Wilson had been cleared on the murder charge by the confession of the stagehand, I used to go over to the house where he had lived sometimes in the late afternoon after our paper had been put to bed for the day. Ours is an afternoon paper and after two o'clock most of us are free.

I found the hunchback girl standing in front of the house one day and began talking with her. She was a gold mine.

There was that look in her eyes I've told you of, the hurt sensitive look. I just spoke to her and we began talking of Wilson. She had lived in one of the rooms at the back. She told me of that at once.

On some days she found herself unable to work at the laundry because her strength suddenly gave out, and so on such days she stayed in the room lying on the cot. Blinding headaches came

that lasted for hours during which she was almost entirely un-
conscious of everything going on about her. Then afterward she
was quite conscious but for a long time very weak. She wasn't one
who is destined to live very long I suppose and I presume she
didn't much care.

Anyway, there she was in the room, in that weak state after the
times of illness, and she grew curious about the two people in the
front room, so she used to get off her couch and go softly in her
stockinged feet to the door between the rooms and peek through
the keyhole. She had to kneel on the dusty floor to do it.

The life in the room fascinated her from the beginning.
Sometimes the man was in there alone, sitting at the kitchen table
and writing the stuff he afterward put into the book I collared
and from which I have quoted; sometimes the woman was with
him, and again sometimes he was in there alone but wasn't writing.
Then he was always walking and walking up and down.

When both people were in the room, and when the man was
writing, the woman seldom moved but sat in a chair by one of
the windows with her hands crossed. He would write a few lines
and then walk up and down talking to himself or to her. When
he spoke she did not answer except with her eyes, the crippled
girl said. What I gathered of all this from her talk with me and
what is the product of my own imaginings, I confess I do not
quite know.

Anyway what I got and what I am trying in my own way to
transmit to you is a sense of a kind of strangeness in the relationship of the two. It wasn't just a domestic household, a little down
on its luck, by any means. He was trying to do something very
difficult—with his poetry I presume—and she in her own way
was trying to help him.

And of course, as I have no doubt you have gathered from
what I have quoted of Wilson's verse, the matter had something
to do with the relationships between people—not necessarily between the particular man and woman who happened to be there
in that room, but between all people.

The fellow had some half-mystic conception of all such things and, before he found his own woman, had been going aimlessly about the world looking for a mate. Then he had found the woman in the Kansas town and—he at least thought—things had cleared for him.

Well, he had the notion that no one in the world could think or feel anything alone, and that people only got into trouble and walled themselves in by trying it, or something of the sort. There was a discord. Things were jangled. Someone, it seems, had to strike a pitch that all voices could take up before the real song of life could begin. Mind you I'm not putting forth any notions of my own. What I am trying to do is to give you a sense of something I got from having read Wilson's stuff, from having known him a little, and from having seen something of the effect of his personality upon others.

He felt quite definitely that no one in the world could feel or even think alone. And then there was the notion that, if one tried to think with the mind without taking the body into account, one got all balled up. True conscious life built itself up like a pyramid. First the body and mind of a beloved one must come into one's thinking and feeling and then, in some mystic way, the bodies and minds of all the other people in the world must come in, must come sweeping in like a great wind—or something of the sort.

Is all this a little tangled up to you who read my story of Wilson? It may not be. It may be that your minds are more clear than my own and that what I take to be so difficult will be very simple to you.

However, I have to bring up to you just what I can find after diving down into this sea of motives and impulses I admit I don't rightly understand.

The hunchback girl felt (or is it my own fancy coloring what she said?)—it doesn't really matter. The thing to get at is what the man Edgar Wilson felt.

He felt, I fancy, that in the field of poetry he had something to express that could never be expressed until he had found a woman who could, in a peculiar and absolute way, give herself in the world of the flesh—and that then there was to be a marriage out of which beauty would come for all people. He had to find the woman who had that power, and the power had to be untainted by self-interest, I fancy. A profound egotist, you see, and he thought he had found what he needed in the wife of the Kansas druggist.

He had found her and had done something to her. What it was I can't quite make out, except that she was absolutely and wholly happy with him in a strangely inexpressive sort of way.

Trying to speak of him and his influence on others is rather like trying to walk on a tightrope stretched between two tall buildings above a crowded street. A cry from below, a laugh, the honk of an automobile horn, and down one goes into nothingness. One simply becomes ridiculous.

He wanted, it seems, to condense the flesh and the spirit of himself and his woman into his poems. You will remember that in one of the things of his I have quoted he speaks of condensing, of squeezing, all the people of a city into one person and of loving that person.

One might think of him as a powerful person, almost hideously powerful. You will see, as you read, how he has got me in his power and is making me serve his purpose.

And he had caught and was holding the woman in his grip. He had wanted her quite absolutely and had taken her, as all men perhaps want to do with their women and don't quite dare. Perhaps too she was in her own way greedy and he was making actual love to her always day and night, when they were together and when they were apart.

I'll admit I am confused about the whole matter myself. I am trying to express something I have felt, not in myself, nor in the words that came to me from the lips of the hunchback girl whom, you will remember, I left kneeling on the floor in that back room and peeking through a keyhole.

There she was, you see, the hunchback, and in the room before her were the man and woman, and the hunchback girl also had fallen under the power of the man Wilson. She also was in love with him—there can be no doubt of that. The room in which

she knelt was dark and dusty. There must have been a thick accumulation of dust on the floor.

What she said—or if she did not say the words, what she made
me feel was that the man Wilson worked in the room, or walked
up and down in there before his woman, and that, while he did
that, his woman sat in the chair, and that there was in her face, in
her eyes, a look—

He was all the time making love to her, and his making love to
her in just that abstract way was a kind of love-making with all
people, and that was possible because the woman was as purely
physical as he was something else. If all this is meaningless to
you, at least it wasn't to the hunchback girl—who certainly was
uneducated and never would have set herself up as having any
special powers of understanding. She knelt in the dust, listening
and looking in at the keyhole, and in the end she came to feel
that the man, in whose presence she had never been and whose
person had never in any way touched her person, had made love
to her also.

She had felt that and it had gratified her entire nature. One
might say it had satisfied her. She was what she was and it had
made life worth living for her.

Minor things happened in the room and one may speak of
them.

For example, there was a day in June, a dark warm rainy day.
The hunchback girl was in her room, kneeling on the floor, and
Wilson and his woman were in their room.

Wilson's woman had been doing a family washing, and as it
could not be dried outdoors she had stretched ropes across the
room and had hung the clothes inside.

When the clothes were all hung Wilson came from walking
outside in the rain and going to the desk sat down and began to
write.

He wrote for a few minutes and then got up and went about
the room, and in walking a wet garment brushed against his face.

He kept right on walking and talking to the woman but as he

walked and talked he gathered all the clothes in his arms and, going to the little landing at the head of the stairs outside, threw them down into the muddy yard below. He did that and the woman sat without moving or saying anything until he had gone back to his desk, then she went down the stairs, got the clothes and washed them again—and it was only after she had done that and when she was again hanging them in the room above that he appeared to know what he had done.

While the clothes were being rewashed he went for another walk and when she heard his footsteps on the stairs the hunchback girl ran to the keyhole. As she knelt there, and as he came into the room, she could look directly into his face. "He was like a puzzled child for a moment and then, although he said nothing, the tears began to run down his cheeks," she said. That happened and then the woman, who was at the moment rehanging the clothes, turned and saw him. She had her arm filled with clothes but dropped them on the floor and ran to him. She half knelt, the hunchback girl said, and putting her arms about his body and looking up into his face pleaded with him. "Don't. Don't be hurt. Believe me I know everything. Please don't be hurt," was what she said.

And now as to the story of the woman's death. It happened in the fall of that year.

In the place where she was sometimes employed—that is to say in the theatre—there was this other man, the little half-crazed stagehand who shot her.

He had fallen in love with her and, like the men in the Kansas town from which she came, had written her several silly notes of which she said nothing to Wilson. The letters weren't very nice and some of them, the most unpleasant ones, were, by some twist of the fellow's mind, signed with Wilson's name. Two of them were afterwards found on her person and were brought in as evidence against Wilson during his trial.

And so the woman worked in the theatre and the summer had passed and on an evening in the fall there was to be a dress rehearsal at the theatre and the woman went there, taking Wilson with her. It was a fall day such as we sometimes have in Chicago, cold and wet and with a heavy fog lying over the city.

The dress rehearsal did not come off. The star was ill, or something of the sort happened, and Wilson and his woman sat about in the cold empty theatre for an hour or two and then the woman was told she could go for the night.

She and Wilson walked across the city, stopping to get something to eat at a small restaurant. He was in one of the abstract silent moods common to him. No doubt he was thinking of the things he wanted to express in the poetry I have tried to tell you about. He went along, not seeing the woman beside him, not seeing the people drifting up to them and passing them in the streets. He went along in that way and she—

She was no doubt then as she always was in his presence— silent and satisfied with the fact that she was with him. There was nothing he could think or feel that did not take her into account. The very blood flowing up through his body was her blood too. He had made her feel that, and she was silent and satisfied as he went along, his body walking beside her but his fancy groping its way through the land of high walls and deep wells.

They had walked from the restaurant, in the Loop district, over a bridge to the North Side, and still no words passed between them.

When they had almost reached their own place the stagehand, the small man with the nervous hands who had written the notes, appeared out of the fog, as though out of nowhere, and shot the woman.

That was all there was to it. It was as simple as that.

They were walking, as I have described them, when a head flashed up before the woman in the midst of the fog, a hand shot out, there was the quick abrupt sound of a pistol shot and then the absurd little stagehand, he with the wrinkled impotent little old woman's face—then he turned and ran away.

All that happened just as I have written it and it made no impression at all on the mind of Wilson. He walked along as though nothing had happened, and the woman, after half falling, gathered herself together and managed to continue walking beside him, still saying nothing.

They went thus for perhaps two blocks and had reached the foot of the outer stairs that led up to their place when a policeman came running, and the woman told him a lie. She told him some story about a struggle between two drunken men, and after a moment of talk the policeman went away, sent away by the woman in a direction opposite to the one taken by the fleeing stagehand.

They were in the darkness and the fog now and the woman took her man's arm while they climbed the stairs. He was as yet— as far as I will ever be able to explain logically—unaware of the shot, and of the fact that she was dying, although he had seen and heard everything. What the doctors said, who were put on the case afterwards, was that a cord or muscle, or something of the sort that controls the action of the heart, had been practically severed by the shot.

She was dead and alive at the same time, I should say.

Anyway the two people marched up the stairs and into the room above, and then a really dramatic and lovely thing happened. One wishes that the scene, with just all its connotations, could be played out on a stage instead of having to be put down in words.

The two came into the room, the one dead but not ready to acknowledge death without a flash of something individual and lovely, that is to say, the one dead while still alive and the other alive but at the moment dead to what was going on.

The room into which they went was dark but, with the sure instinct of an animal, the woman walked across the room to the fireplace, while the man stopped and stood some ten feet from the door—thinking and thinking in his peculiarly abstract way. The fireplace was filled with an accumulation of waste matter, cigarette ends—the man was a hard smoker—bits of paper on which he had scribbled—the rubbishy accumulation that gathers about all such fellows as Wilson. There was all of this quickly combustible material stuffed into the fireplace on this, the first cold evening of the fall.

And so the woman went to it and found a match somewhere in the darkness and touched the pile off.

There is a picture that will remain with me always—just that—the barren room and the blind unseeing man standing there, and the woman kneeling and making a little flare of beauty at the last. Little flames leaped up. Lights crept and danced over the walls. Below, on the floor of the room, there was a deep well of darkness in which the man, blind with his own purpose, was standing.

The pile of burning papers must have made for a moment quite a glare of light in the room and the woman stood for a moment beside the fireplace, just outside the glare of light.

And then, pale and wavering, she walked across the light as across a lighted stage, going softly and silently toward him. Had she also something to say? No one will ever know. What happened was that she said nothing.

She walked across to him and, at the moment she reached him, fell down on the floor and died at his feet, and at the same moment the little fire of papers died. If she struggled before she died, there on the floor, she struggled in silence. There was no sound. She had fallen and lay between him and the door that led out to the stairway and to the street.

It was then Wilson became altogether inhuman—too much so for my understanding.

The fire had died and the woman he had loved had died.

And there he stood looking into nothingness, thinking—God knows—perhaps of nothingness.

He stood a minute, five minutes, perhaps ten. He was a man who, before he found the woman, had been sunk far down into a deep sea of doubt and questioning. Before he found the woman no expression had ever come from him. He had perhaps just wandered from place to place, looking at people's faces, wondering about people, wanting to come close to others and not knowing how. The woman had been able to lift him up to the surface of the sea of life for a time, and with her he had floated on the surface of the sea, under the sky, in the sunlight. The woman's warm body—given to him in love—had been as a boat in which he had floated on the surface of the sea, and now the boat had been wrecked and he was sinking again, back into the sea.

All of this had happened and he did not know—that is to say he did not know and at the same time he did know.

He was a poet, I presume, and perhaps at the moment a new poem was forming itself in his mind.

At any rate he stood for a time, as I have said, and then he must have had a feeling that he should make some move, that he should if possible save himself from some disaster about to overtake him.

He had an impulse to go to the door and, by way of the stairway, to go downstairs and into the street—but the body of the woman was between him and the door.

What he did and what, when he later told of it, sounded so terribly cruel to others, was to treat the woman's dead body as one might treat a fallen tree in the darkness in a forest. First he tried to push the body aside with his foot and then, as that seemed impossible, he stepped awkwardly over it.

He stepped directly on the woman's arm. The discolored mark where his heel landed was afterward found on the body.

He almost fell, and then his body righted itself and he went walking, marched down the rickety stairs and went walking in the streets.

By chance the night had cleared. It had grown colder and a cold wind had driven the fog away. He walked along very nonchalantly for several blocks. He walked along as calmly as you, the reader, might walk after having had lunch with a friend.

As a matter of fact he even stopped to make a purchase at a store. I remember that the place was called The Whip. He went in, bought himself a package of cigarettes, lighted one and stood a moment, apparently listening to a conversation going on among several idlers in the place.

And then he strolled again, going along smoking the cigarette and thinking of his poem no doubt. Then he came to a moving-picture theatre.

That perhaps touched him off. He also was an old fireplace, stuffed with old thoughts, scraps of unwritten poems—God knows what rubbish. Often he had gone at night to the theatre, where the woman was employed, to walk home with her, and now the people were coming out of a small moving-picture house. They had been in there seeing a play called "The Light of the World."

Wilson walked into the midst of the crowd, lost himself in the crowd, smoking his cigarette, and then he took off his hat, looked anxiously about for a moment, and suddenly began shouting in a loud voice.

He stood there shouting and trying to tell the story of what had happened in a loud voice, and with the uncertain air of one trying to remember a dream. He did that for a moment and then, after running a little way along the pavement, stopped and began his story again. It was only after he had gone thus, in short rushes, back along the street to the house and up the rickety stairway to where the woman was lying—the crowd following curiously at his heels—that a policeman came up and arrested him.

He seemed excited at first but was quiet afterwards, and he laughed at the notion of insanity when the lawyer who had been retained for him tried to set up the plea in court.

As I have said, his action during his trial was confusing to us all, as he seemed wholly uninterested in the murder and in his own fate. After the confession of the man who had fired the shot he seemed to feel no resentment toward him either. There was something he wanted, having nothing to do with what had happened.

There he had been, you see, before he found the woman, wandering about in the world, digging himself deeper and deeper into the deep wells he talked about in his poetry, building the wall between himself and all us others constantly higher and higher.

He knew what he was doing but he could not stop. That's what he kept talking about, pleading with people about. The man had come up out of the sea of doubt, had grasped for a time the hand of the woman, and with her hand in his had floated for a time upon the surface of life—but now he felt himself again sinking down into the sea.

His talking and talking, stopping people in the street and talking, going into people's houses and talking, was I presume but an effort he was always afterward making not to sink back forever into the sea; it was the struggle of a drowning man I dare say.

At any rate I have told you the man's story—have been compelled to try to tell you his story. There was a kind of power in him, and the power has been exerted over me as it was exerted over the woman from Kansas and the unknown hunchback girl kneeling on the floor in the dust and peering through a keyhole.

Ever since the woman died we have all been trying and trying to drag the man Wilson back out of the sea of doubt and dumbness into which we feel him sinking deeper and deeper—and to no avail.

It may be I have been impelled to tell his story in the hope that by writing of him I may myself understand. Is there not a possibility that with understanding would come also the strength to thrust an arm down into the sea and drag the man Wilson back to the surface again?

AN OHIO PAGAN

CHAPTER I

Tom Edwards was a Welshman, born in Northern Ohio, and a descendant of that Thomas Edwards, the Welsh poet, who was called, in his own time and country, Twm O'r Nant—which in our own tongue means "Tom of the dingle or vale."

The first Thomas Edwards was a gigantic figure in the history of the spiritual life of the Welsh. Not only did he write many stirring interludes concerning life, death, earth, fire and water but as a man he was a true brother to the elements and to all the passions of his sturdy and musical race. He sang beautifully but he also played stoutly and beautifully the part of a man. There is a wonderful tale, told in Wales and written into a book by the poet himself, of how he, with a team of horses, once moved a great ship out of the land into the sea, after three hundred Welshmen had failed at the task. Also he taught Welsh woodsmen the secret of the crane and pulley for lifting great logs in the forests, and once he fought to the point of death the bully of the countryside, a man known over a great part of Wales as The Cruel Fighter. Tom Edwards, the descendant of this man, was born in Ohio near my own native town of Bidwell. His name was not Edwards, but as his father was dead when he was born, his mother gave him the old poet's name out of pride in having such blood in her veins. Then when the boy was six his mother died also and the man for whom both his mother and father had worked, a sporting farmer named Harry Whitehead, took the boy into his own house to live.

They were gigantic people, the Whiteheads. Harry himself weighed two hundred and seventy pounds and his wife twenty pounds more. About the time he took young Tom to live with him the farmer became interested in the racing of horses, moved off his farms, of which he had three, and came to live in our town.

In the town of Bidwell there was an old frame building, that had once been a factory for the making of barrel staves but that had stood for years vacant, staring with windowless eyes into the streets, and Harry bought it at a low price and transformed it into a splendid stable with a board floor and two long rows of box stalls. At a sale of blooded horses held in the city of Cleveland he bought twenty young colts, all of the trotting strain, and set up as a trainer of race horses.

Among the colts thus brought to our town was one great black fellow named Bucephalus. Harry got the name from John Telfer, our town poetry lover. "It was the name of the mighty horse of a mighty man," Telfer said, and that satisfied Harry.

Young Tom was told off to be the special guardian and caretaker of Bucephalus, and the black stallion, who had in him the mighty blood of the Tennessee Patchens, quickly became the pride of the stables. He was in his nature a great ugly-tempered beast, as given to whims and notions as an opera star, and from the very first began to make trouble. Within a year no one but Harry Whitehead himself and the boy Tom dared go into his stall. The methods of the two people with the great horse were entirely different but equally effective. Once big Harry turned the stallion loose on the floor of the stable, closed all the doors, and with a cruel long whip in his hand, went in to conquer or to be conquered. He came out victorious and ever after the horse behaved when he was about.

The boy's method was different. He loved Bucephalus and the wicked animal loved him. Tom slept on a cot in the barn and day or night, even when there were mares about, walked into Bucephalus' box stall without fear. When the stallion was in a temper he sometimes turned at the boy's entrance and with a snort sent his iron-shod heels banging against the sides of the stall, but Tom laughed and, putting a simple rope halter over the horse's head, led him forth to be cleaned or hitched to a cart for his morning's jog on our town's half-mile race track. A sight it was to see the boy with the blood of Twm O'r Nant in his veins leading by the nose Bucephalus of the royal blood of the Patchens.

When he was six years old the horse Bucephalus went forth to race and conquer at the great spring race meeting at Columbus, Ohio. He won two heats of the trotting free-for-all—the great race of the meeting—with heavy Harry in the sulky and then faltered. A gelding named Light o' the Orient beat him in the next heat. Tom, then a lad of sixteen, was put into the sulky and the two of them, horse and boy, fought out a royal battle with the gelding and a little bay mare, that hadn't been heard from before but that suddenly developed a whirlwind burst of speed.

The big stallion and the slender boy won. From amid a mob of cursing, shouting, whip-slashing men a black horse shot out and a pale boy, leaning far forward, called and murmured to him. "Go on, boy! Go boy! Go boy!" the lad's voice had called over and over all through the race. Bucephalus got a record of 2.06 $1/4$ and Tom Edwards became a newspaper hero. His picture was in the Cleveland *Leader* and the Cincinnati *Enquirer,* and when he came back to Bidwell we other boys fairly wept in our envy of him.

Then it was, however, that Tom Edwards fell down from his high place. There he was, a tall boy, almost of man's stature and, except for a few months during the winters when he lived on the Whitehead farms, and between his sixth and thirteenth years, when he had attended a country school and had learned to read and write and do sums, he was without education. And now, during that very fall of the year of his triumph at Columbus, the Bidwell truant officer, a thin man with white hair, who was also superintendent of the Baptist Sunday School, came one afternoon to the Whitehead stables and told him that if he did not begin going to school both he and his employer would get into serious trouble.

Harry Whitehead was furious and so was Tom. There he was, a great tall slender fellow who had been with race horses to the fairs all over Northern Ohio and Indiana, during that very fall, and who had just come home from the journey during which he had driven the winner in the free-for-all trot at a Grand Circuit meeting and had given Bucephalus a mark of 2.06 $1/4$.

Was such a fellow to go sit in a schoolroom, with a silly school book in his hand, reading of the affairs of the men who dealt in butter, eggs, potatoes and apples, and whose unnecessarily complicated business life the children were asked to unravel—was such a fellow to go sit in a room, under the eyes of a woman teacher, and in the company of boys half his age and with none of his wide experience of life?

It was a hard thought and Tom took it hard. The law was all right, Harry Whitehead said, and was intended to keep no-account kids off the streets but what it had to do with himself Tom couldn't make out. When the truant officer had gone and Tom was left alone in the stable with his employer, the man and boy stood for a long time glumly staring at each other. It was all right to be educated but Tom felt he had book education enough. He could read, write and do sums, and what other book-training did a horseman need? As for books, they were all right for rainy evenings when there were no men sitting by the stable door and talking of horses and races. And also when one went to the races in a strange town and arrived, perhaps on Sunday, and the races did not begin until the following Wednesday—it was all right then to have a book in the chest with the horse blankets. When the weather was fine and the work was all done on a fine fall afternoon, and the other swipes, both niggers and whites, had gone off to town, one could take a book out under a tree and read of life in far away places that was as strange and almost as fascinating as one's own life. Tom had read *Robinson Crusoe, Uncle Tom's Cabin* and *Tales from the Bible*, all of which he had found in the Whitehead house, and Jacob Friedman, the school superintendent at Bidwell, who had a fancy for horses, had loaned him other books that he intended reading during the coming winter. They were in his chest—one called *Gulliver's Travels* and the other *Moll Flanders*.

And now the law said he must give up being a horseman and go every day to a school and do little foolish sums, he who had already proven himself a man. What other schoolboy knew what he did about life? Had he not seen and spoken to several of the greatest men of this world, men who had driven horses to beat world records, and did they not respect him? When he became a driver of race horses, such men as Pop Geers, Walter Cox, John Splan, Murphy and the others would not ask him what books he had read, or how many feet make a rod and how many rods in a mile. In the race at Columbus, where he had won his spurs as a driver, he had already proven that life had given him the kind of education he needed. The driver of the gelding Light o' the Orient had tried to bluff him in that third heat and had not succeeded. He was a big man with a black mustache and had lost one eye so that he looked fierce and ugly, and when the two horses were fighting it out, neck and neck, up the back stretch, and when Tom was tooling Bucephalus smoothly and surely to the front, the older man turned in his sulky to glare at him. "You damned little whipper-snapper," he yelled, "I'll knock you out of your sulky if you don't take back."

He had yelled that at Tom and then had struck at the boy with the butt of his whip—not intending actually to hit him perhaps but just missing the boy's head, and Tom had kept his eyes steadily on his own horse, had held him smoothly in his stride and at the upper turn, at just the right moment, had begun to pull out in front.

Later he hadn't even told Harry Whitehead of the incident, and that fact too, he felt vaguely, had something to do with his qualifications as a man.

And now they were going to put him into a school with the kids. He was at work on the stable floor, rubbing the legs of a trim-looking colt, and Bucephalus was in his stall waiting to be taken to a late fall meeting at Indianapolis on the following Monday, when the blow fell. Harry Whitehead walked back and forth swearing at the two men who were loafing in chairs at the stable door. "Do you call that law, eh, robbing a kid of the chance Tom's got?" he asked, shaking a riding whip under their noses. "I never see such a law. What I say is Dod blast such a law."

Tom took the colt back to its place and went into Bucephalus' box stall. The stallion was in one of his gentle moods and turned to have his nose rubbed, but Tom went and buried his face against the great black neck and for a long time stood thus, trembling. He had thought perhaps Harry would let him drive Bucephalus in all his races another season and now that was all to come to an end and he was to be pitched back into childhood, to be made just a kid in school. "I won't do it," he decided suddenly and a dogged light came into his eyes. His future as a driver of race horses might have to be sacrificed but that didn't matter so much as the humiliation of this other, and he decided he would say nothing to Harry Whitehead or his wife but would make his own move.

"I'll get out of here. Before they get me into that school I'll skip out of town," he told himself as his hand crept up and fondled the soft nose of Bucephalus, the son royal of the Patchens.

Tom left Bidwell during the night, going east on a freight train, and no one there ever saw him again. During that winter he lived in the city of Cleveland, where he got work driving a milk wagon in a district where factory workers lived.

Then spring came again and with it the memory of other springs—of thundershowers rolling over fields of wheat, just appearing, green and vivid, out of the black ground—of the sweet smell of new plowed fields, and most of all the smell and sound of animals about barns at the Whitehead farms north of Bidwell. How sharply he remembered those days on the farms and the days later when he lived in Bidwell, slept in the stables and went each morning to jog race horses and young colts round and round the half-mile race track at the fairgrounds at Bidwell.

That was a life! Round and round the track they went, young colthood and young manhood together, not thinking but carrying life very keenly within themselves and feeling tremendously. The colts' legs were to be hardened and their wind made sound and for the boy long hours were to be spent in a kind of dream world, and life lived in the company of something fine, courageous, filled with a terrible, waiting surge of life. At the fairground, away at the town's edge, tall grass grew in the enclosure inside the track and there were trees from which came the voices of squirrels, chattering and scolding, accompanied by the call of nesting birds and, down below on the ground, by the song of bees visiting early blossoms and of insects hidden away in the grass.

How different the life of the city streets in the springtime! To Tom it was in a way fetid and foul. For months he had been living in a boardinghouse with some six, and often eight or ten, other young fellows, in narrow rooms above a foul street. The young fellows were unmarried and made good wages, and on the winter evenings and on Sundays they dressed in good clothes and went forth, to return later, half drunk, to sit for long hours boasting and talking loudly in the rooms. Because he was shy, often lonely and sometimes startled and frightened by what he saw and heard in the city, the others would have nothing to do with Tom. They felt a kind of contempt for him, looked upon him as a "rube" and in the late afternoon when his work was done he often went for long walks alone in grim streets of workingmen's houses, breathing the smoke-laden air and listening to the roar and clatter of machinery in great factories. At other times and immediately after the evening meal he went off to his room and to bed, half sick with fear and with some strange nameless dread of the life about him.

And so in the early summer of his seventeenth year Tom left the city and, going back into his own Northern Ohio lake country, found work with a man named John Bottsford who owned a

threshing outfit and worked among the farmers of Erie County,
Ohio. The slender boy, who had urged Bucephalus to his greatest
victory and had driven him the fastest mile of his career, had
become a tall strong fellow with heavy features, brown eyes, and
big nerveless hands—but in spite of his apparent heaviness there
was something tremendously alive in him. He now drove a team
of plodding grey farm horses and it was his job to keep the threshing
engine supplied with water and fuel and to haul the threshed
grain out of the fields and into farmers' barns.

The thresherman Bottsford was a broad-shouldered, powerful
old man of sixty and had, besides Tom, three grown sons in his
employ. He had been a farmer, working on rented land, all his
life and had saved some money, with which he had bought the
threshing outfit, and all day the five men worked like driven slaves
and at night slept in the hay in the farmers' barns. It was rainy
that season in the lake country and at the beginning of the time
of threshing things did not go very well for Bottsford.

The old thresherman was worried. The threshing venture had
taken all of his money and he had a dread of going into debt and,
as he was a deeply religious man, at night when he thought the
others asleep, he crawled out of the hayloft and went down onto
the barn floor to pray.

Something happened to Tom and for the first time in his life
he began to think about life and its meaning. He was in the country
that he loved, in the yellow sunwashed fields, far from the dreaded
noises and dirt of city life, and here was a man of his own type, in
some deep way a brother to himself, who was continuously crying
out to some power outside himself, some power that was in the
sun, in the clouds, in the roaring thunder that accompanied the
summer rains—that was in these things and that at the same
time controlled all these things.

The young threshing apprentice was impressed. Throughout
the rainy days, when no work could be done, he wandered about
and waited for night, and then, when they all had gone into the
barn loft and the others prepared to sleep, he stayed awake to
think and listen. He thought of God and of the possibilities of

God's part in the affairs of men. The thresherman's youngest son, a fat jolly fellow, lay beside him and, for a time after they had crawled into the hay, the two boys whispered and laughed together. The fat boy's skin was sensitive and the dry broken ends of grass stalks crept down under his clothes and tickled him. He giggled and twisted about, wriggling and kicking, and Tom looked at him and laughed also. The thoughts of God went out of his mind.

In the barn all became quiet and when it rained a low drumming sound went on overhead. Tom could hear the horses and cattle, down below, moving about. The smells were all delicious smells. The smell of the cows in particular awoke something heady in him. It was as though he had been drinking strong wine. Every part of his body seemed alive. The two older boys, who like their father had serious natures, lay with their feet buried in the hay. They lay very still and a warm musty smell arose from their clothes, that were full of the sweat of toil. Presently the bearded old thresherman, who slept off by himself, arose cautiously and walked across the hay in his stockinged feet. He went down a ladder to the floor below, and Tom listened eagerly. The fat boy snored but he was quite sure that the older boys were awake like himself. Every sound from below was magnified. He heard a horse stamp on the barn floor and a cow rub her horns against a feed box. The old thresherman prayed fervently, calling on the name of Jesus to help him out of his difficulty. Tom could not hear all his words but some of them came to him quite clearly and one group of words ran like a refrain through the thresherman's prayer. "Gentle Jesus," he cried, "send the good days. Let the good days come quickly. Look out over the land. Send us the fair warm days."

Came the warm fair days and Tom wondered. Late every morning, after the sun had marched far up into the sky and after the machines were set by a great pile of wheat bundles, he drove his tank wagon off to be filled at some distant creek or at a pond. Sometimes he was compelled to drive two or three miles to the lake. Dust gathered in the roads and the horses plodded along. He passed through a grove of trees and went down a lane and into a small valley where there was a spring and he thought of the old man's words, uttered in the silence and the darkness of the barns. He made himself a figure of Jesus as a young god walking about over the land. The young god went through the lanes and through the shaded covered places. The feet of the horses came down with a thump in the dust of the road and there was an echoing thump far away in the wood. Tom leaned forward and listened and his cheeks became a little pale. He was no longer the growing man but had become again the fine and sensitive boy who had driven Bucephalus through a mob of angry, determined men to victory. For the first time the blood of the old poet Twm O'r Nant awoke in him.

The water boy for the threshing crew rode the horse Pegasus down through the lanes back of the farmhouses in Erie County, Ohio, to the creeks where the threshing tanks must be filled. Beside him on the soft earth in the forest walked the young god Jesus. At the creek Pegasus, born of the springs of Ocean, stamped on the ground. The plodding farm horses stopped. With a dazed look in his eyes Tom Edwards arose from the wagon seat and prepared his hose and pump for filling the tank. The god Jesus walked away over the land and with a wave of his hand summoned the smiling days.

A light came into Tom Edwards' eyes and grace seemed to come also into his heavy maturing body. New impulses came to him. As the threshing crew went about, over the roads and through the villages from farm to farm, women and young girls looked at the young man and smiled. Sometimes as he came from the fields to a farmer's barn with a load of wheat in bags on his wagon, the daughter of the farmer stepped out of the farmhouse and stood looking at him. Tom looked at the woman and hunger crept into his heart and, in the evenings while the thresherman and his sons sat on the ground by the barns and talked of their affairs, he walked nervously about. Making a motion to the fat boy, who was not really interested in the talk of his father and brothers, the two younger men went to walk in the nearby fields and on the roads. Sometimes they stumbled along a country road in the dusk of the evening and came into the lighted streets of a town. Under the store-lights young girls walked about. The two boys stood in the shadows by a building and watched and later, as they went homeward in the darkness, the fat boy expressed what they both felt. They passed through a dark place where the road wound through a wood. In silence the frogs croaked, and birds roosting in the trees were disturbed by their presence and fluttered about. The fat boy wore heavy overalls and his fat legs rubbed against each other. The rough cloth made a queer creaking sound. He spoke passionately. "I would like to hold a woman, tight, tight, tight," he said.

One Sunday the thresherman took his entire crew with him to a church. They had been working near a village called Castalia, but did not go into the town but to a small white frame church that stood amid trees and by a stream at the side of a road, a mile north of the village. They went on Tom's water wagon, from which they had lifted the tank and placed boards for seats. The boy drove the horses.

Many teams were tied in the shade under the trees in a little grove near the church, and strange men—farmers and their sons— stood about in little groups and talked of the season's crops. Although it was hot, a breeze played among the leaves of the trees under which they stood, and back of the church and the grove the stream ran over stones and made a persistent soft murmuring noise that arose above the hum of voices.

In the church Tom sat beside the fat boy who stared at the country girls as they came in and who, after the sermon began, went to sleep while Tom listened eagerly to the sermon. The minister, an old man with a beard and a strong sturdy body, looked, he thought, not unlike his employer Bottsford the thresherman.

The minister in the country church talked of that time when Mary Magdalene, the woman who had been taken in adultery, was being stoned by the crowd of men who had forgotten their own sins and when, in the tale the minister told, Jesus approached and rescued the woman, Tom's heart thumped with excitement.

Then later the minister talked of how Jesus was tempted by the devil, as he stood on a high place in the mountain, but the boy did not listen. He leaned forward and looked out through a window across fields and the minister's words came to him but in broken sentences. Tom took what was said concerning the temptation on the mountain to mean that Mary had followed Jesus and had offered her body to him, and that afternoon, when he had returned with the others to the farm where they were to begin threshing on the next morning, he called the fat boy aside and asked his opinion.

The two boys walked across a field of wheat stubble and sat down on a log in a grove of trees. It had never occurred to Tom that a man could be tempted by a woman. It had always seemed to him that it must be the other way, that women must always be tempted by men. "I thought men always asked," he said, "and now it seems that women sometimes do the asking. That would be a fine thing if it could happen to us. Don't you think so?"

The two boys arose and walked under the trees and dark shadows began to form on the ground underfoot. Tom burst into words and continually asked questions and the fat boy, who had been often to church and for whom the figure of Jesus had lost most of its reality, felt a little embarrassed. He did not think the subject should be thus freely discussed and when Tom's mind kept playing with the notion of Jesus, pursued and tempted by a woman, he grunted his disapproval. "Do you think he really refused?" Tom asked over and over. The fat boy tried to explain. "He had twelve disciples," he said. "It couldn't have happened. They were always about. Well, you see, she wouldn't ever have had no chance. Wherever he went they went with him. They were men he was teaching to preach. One of them later betrayed him to soldiers who killed him."

Tom wondered. "How did that come about? How could a man like that be betrayed?" he asked. "By a kiss," the fat boy replied.

On the evening of the day when Tom Edwards—for the first and last time in his life—went into a church, there was a light shower, the only one that fell upon John Bottsford's threshing crew during the last three months the Welsh boy was with them, and the shower in no way interfered with their work. The shower came up suddenly and in a few minutes was gone. As it was Sunday and as there was no work, the men had all gathered in the barn and were looking out through the open barn doors. Two or three men from the farmhouse came and sat with them on boxes and barrels on the barn floor and, as is customary with country people, very little was said. The men took knives out of their pockets and, finding little sticks among the rubbish on the barn floor, began to whittle, while the old thresherman went restlessly about with his hands in his trouser pockets. Tom, who sat near the door, where an occasional drop of rain was blown against his cheek, alternately looked from his employer to the open country where the rain played over the fields. One of the farmers remarked that a rainy time had come on and that there would be no good threshing weather for several days and, while the thresherman did not answer, Tom saw his lips move and his grey beard bob up and down. He thought the thresherman was protesting but did not want to protest in words.

As they had gone about the country many rains had passed to the north, south and east of the threshing crew and on some days the clouds hung over them all day, but no rain fell and when they had got to a new place they were told it had rained there three days before. Sometimes when they left a farm Tom stood up on the seat of his water wagon and looked back. He looked across fields to where they had been at work and then looked up into the sky. "The rain may come now. The threshing is done and the wheat is all in the barn. The rain can now do no harm to our labor," he thought.

On the Sunday evening when he sat with the men on the floor of the barn, Tom was sure that the shower that had now come would be but a passing affair. He thought his employer must be very close to Jesus, who controlled the affairs of the heavens, and that a long rain would not come because the thresherman did not want it. He fell into a deep reverie and John Bottsford came and stood close beside him. The thresherman put his hand against the door jamb and looked out and Tom could still see the grey beard moving. The man was praying and was so close to himself that his trouser leg touched Tom's hand. Into the boy's mind came the remembrance of how John Bottsford had prayed at night on the barn floor. On that very morning he had prayed. It was just as daylight came and the boy was awakened because, as he crept across the hay to descend the ladder, the old man's foot had touched his hand.

As always Tom had been excited and wanted to hear every word said in the older man's prayers. He lay tense, listening to every sound that came up from below. A faint glow of light came into the hayloft through a crack in the side of the barn, a rooster crowed, and some pigs, housed in a pen near the barn, grunted loudly. They had heard the thresherman moving about and wanted to be fed, and their grunting, and the occasional restless movement of a horse or a cow in the stable below, prevented Tom's hearing very distinctly. He, however, made out that his employer was thanking Jesus for the fine weather that had attended them and was protesting that he did not want to be selfish in asking it to continue. "Jesus," he said, "send, if you wish, a little shower on this day when, because of our love for you, we do not work in the fields. Let it be fine tomorrow but today, after we have come back from the house of worship, let a shower freshen the land."

As Tom sat on a box near the door of the barn and saw how aptly the words of his employer had been answered by Jesus, he knew that the rain would not last. The man for whom he worked seemed to him so close to the throne of God that he raised the hand that had been touched by John Bottsford's trouser leg to his lips and secretly kissed it—and when he looked again out over the fields, the clouds were being blown away by a wind and the evening sun was coming out. It seemed to him that the young and beautiful god Jesus must be right at hand, within hearing of his voice. "He is," Tom told himself, "standing behind a tree in the orchard." The rain stopped and he went silently out of the barn towards a small apple orchard that lay beside the farmhouse, but when he came to a fence and was about to climb over he stopped. "If Jesus is there he will not want me to find him," he thought. As he turned again toward the barn he could see, across a field, a low grass-covered hill. He decided that Jesus was not after all in the orchard. The long slanting rays of the evening sun fell on the crest of the hill and touched with light the grass stalks, heavy with drops of rain, and for a moment the hill was crowned as with a crown of jewels. A million tiny drops of water, reflecting the light, made the hilltop sparkle as though set with gems. "Jesus is there," muttered the boy. "He lies on his belly in the grass. He is looking at me over the edge of the hill."

CHAPTER II

John Bottsford went with his threshing crew to work for a large farmer named Barton near the town of Sandusky. The threshing season was drawing near an end and the days remained clear, cool and beautiful. The country into which he now came made a deep impression on Tom's mind and he never forgot the thoughts and experiences that came to him during the last weeks of that summer on the Barton farms.

The traction engine, puffing forth smoke and attracting the excited attention of dogs and children as it rumbled along and pulled the heavy red grain separator, had trailed slowly over miles of road and had come down almost to Lake Erie. Tom, with the fat Bottsford boy sitting beside him on the water wagon, followed the rumbling puffing engine, and when they came to the new place, where they were to stay for several days, he could see, from the wagon seat, the smoke of the factories in the town of Sandusky rising into the clear morning air.

The man for whom John Bottsford was threshing owned three farms, one on an island in the bay, where he lived, and two on the mainland, and the larger of the mainland farms had great stacks of wheat standing in a field near the barns. The farm was in a wide basin of land, very fertile, through which a creek flowed northward into Sandusky Bay and, besides the stacks of wheat in the basin, other stacks had been made in the upland fields beyond the creek, where a country of low hills began. From these latter fields the waters of the bay could be seen glistening in the bright fall sunlight and steamers went from Sandusky to a pleasure resort called Cedar Point. When the wind blew from the north or west and when the threshing machinery had been stopped at the noon hour, the men, resting with their backs against a strawstack, could hear a band playing on one of the steamers.

Fall came on early that year and the leaves on the trees in the forests that grew along the roads that ran down through the low creek bottom lands began to turn yellow and red. In the afternoons when Tom went to the creek for water he walked beside his horses and the dry leaves crackled and snapped underfoot.

As the season had been a prosperous one, Bottsford decided that his youngest son should attend school in town during the fall and winter. He had bought himself a machine for cutting firewood and with his two older sons intended to take up that work. "The logs will have to be hauled out of the wood lots to where we set up the saws," he said to Tom. "You can come with us if you wish."

The thresherman began to talk to Tom of the value of learning. "You'd better go to some town yourself this winter. It would be better for you to get into a school," he said sharply. He grew excited and walked up and down beside the water wagon, on the seat of which Tom sat listening, and said that God had given men both minds and bodies and it was wicked to let either decay because of neglect. "I have watched you," he said. "You don't talk very much but you do plenty of thinking, I guess. Go into the schools. Find out what the books have to say. You don't have to believe when they say things that are lies."

The Bottsford family lived in a rented house facing a stone road near the town of Bellevue, and the fat boy was to go to that town—a distance of some eighteen miles from where the men were at work—afoot, and on the evening before he set out he and Tom went out of the barns intending to have a last walk and talk together on the roads.

They went along in the dusk of the fall evening, each thinking his own thoughts, and, coming to a bridge that led over the creek in the valley, sat on the bridge rail. Tom had little to say but his companion wanted to talk about women and, when darkness came on, the embarrassment he felt regarding the subject went quite away and he talked boldly and freely. He said that in the town of Bellevue, where he was to live and attend school during the coming winter, he would be sure to get in with a woman. "I'm not going to be cheated out of that chance," he declared. He explained that as his father would be away from home when he moved into town he would be free to pick his own place to board.

The fat boy's imagination became inflamed and he told Tom his plans. "I won't try to get in with any young girl," he declared shrewdly. "That only gets a fellow in a fix. He might have to marry her. I'll go live in a house with a widow, that's what I'll do. And in the evening the two of us will be there alone. We'll begin to talk and I'll keep touching her with my hands. That will get her excited."

The fat boy jumped to his feet and walked back and forth on the bridge. He was nervous and a little ashamed and wanted to justify what he had said. The thing for which he hungered had he thought become a possibility—an act half achieved. Coming to stand before Tom he put a hand on his shoulder. "I'll go into her room at night," he declared. "I'll not tell her I'm coming but will creep in when she is asleep. Then I'll get down on my knees by her bed and I'll kiss her, hard, hard. I'll hold her tight, so she can't get away and I'll kiss her mouth till she wants what I want. Then I'll stay in her house all winter. No one will know. Even if she won't have me I'll only have to move, I'm sure, to be safe. No one will believe what she says, if she tells on me. I'm not going to be like a boy anymore, I'll tell you what—I'm as big as a man and I'm going to do like men do, that's what I am."

The two young men went back to the barn where they were to sleep on the hay. The rich farmer for whom they were now at work had a large house and provided beds for the thresherman and his two older sons but the two younger men slept in the barn

loft and on the night before had lain under one blanket. After the
talk by the bridge, however, Tom did not feel very comfortable
and that stout exponent of manhood, the younger Bottsford, was
also embarrassed. In the road the young man, whose name was
Paul, walked a little ahead of his companion and when they got
to the barn each sought a separate place in the loft. Each wanted
to have thoughts into which he did not want the presence of the
other to intrude.

For the first time Tom's body burned with eager desire for a
female. He lay where he could see out through a crack in the side
of the barn, and at first his thoughts were all about animals. He
had brought a horse blanket up from the stable below and crawling under it lay on his side with his eyes close to the crack and
thought about the love-making of horses and cattle. Things he
had seen in the stables when he worked for Whitehead, the racing
man, came back to his mind and a queer animal hunger ran through
him so that his legs stiffened. He rolled restlessly about on the
hay and, for some reason he did not understand, his lust took the
form of anger and he hated the fat boy. He thought he would like
to crawl over the hay and pound his companion's face with his
fists. Although he had not seen Paul Bottsford's face when he
talked of the widow, he had sensed in him a flavor of triumph.
"He thinks he has got the better of me," young Edwards thought.

He rolled again to the crack and stared out into the night.
There was a new moon and the fields were dimly outlined and
clumps of trees, along the road that led into the town of Sandusky,
looked like black clouds that had settled down over the land. For
some reason the sight of the land, lying dim and quiet under the
moon, took all of his anger away and he began to think, not of
Paul Bottsford, with hot eager lust in his eyes, creeping into the
room of the widow at Bellevue, but of the god Jesus, going up
into a mountain with his woman, Mary.

His companion's notion of going into a room where a woman
lay sleeping and taking her, as it were, unawares, now seemed to
him entirely mean and the hot jealous feeling that had turned
into anger and hatred went entirely away. He tried to think what

the god, who had brought the beautiful days for the threshing, would do with a woman.

Tom's body still burned with desire and his mind wanted to think lascivious thoughts. The moon that had been hidden behind clouds emerged and a wind began to blow. It was still early evening and in the town of Sandusky pleasure seekers were taking the boat to the resort over the bay and the wind brought to Tom's ears the sound of music, blown over the waters of the bay and down the creek basin. In a grove near the barn the wind swayed gently the branches of young trees, and black shadows ran here and there on the ground.

The younger Bottsford had gone to sleep in a distant part of the barn loft and now began to snore loudly. The tenseness went out of Tom's legs and he prepared to sleep but before sleeping he muttered, half timidly, certain words that were half a prayer, half an appeal to some spirit of the night. "Jesus, bring me a woman," he whispered.

Outside the barn, in the fields, the wind, becoming a little stronger, picked up bits of straw and blew them about among the hard up-standing stubble and there was a low gentle whispering sound as though the god were answering his appeal.

Tom went to sleep with his arm under his head and with his eye close to the crack that gave him a view of the moonlit fields, and in his dream the cry from within repeated itself over and over. The mysterious god Jesus had heard and answered the needs of his employer John Bottsford and his own need would, he was quite sure, be understood and attended to. "Bring me a woman. I need her. Jesus, bring me a woman," he kept whispering into the night, as consciousness left him and he slipped away into dreams.

After the youngest of the Bottsfords had departed, a change took place in the nature of Tom's work. The threshing crew had got now into a country of large farms where the wheat had all been brought in from the fields and stacked near the barns and where there was always plenty of water near at hand. Everything was simplified. The separator was pulled in close by the barn door and the threshed grain was carried directly to the bins from the separator. As it was not a part of Tom's work to feed the bundles of grain into the whirling teeth of the separator—this work being done by John Bottsford's two elder sons—there was little for the crew's teamster to do. Sometimes John Bottsford, who was the engineer, departed, going to make arrangements for the next stop, and was gone for a half day, and at such times Tom, who had picked up some knowledge of the art, ran the engine.

On other days, however, there was nothing at all for him to do and his mind, unoccupied for long hours, began to play him tricks. In the morning, after his team had been fed and cleaned until the grey coats of the old farm horses shone like racers, he went out of the barn and into an orchard. Filling his pockets with ripe apples he went to a fence and leaned over. In a field young colts played about. As he held the apples and called softly, they came timidly forward, stopping in alarm and then running a little forward, until one of them, bolder than the others, ate one of the apples out of his hand.

All through those bright warm clear fall days a restless feeling, it seemed to Tom, ran through everything in nature. In the clumps of woodland still standing on the farms, flaming red spread itself out along the limbs of trees and there was one grove of young maple trees, near a barn, that was like a troop of girls, young girls who had walked together down a sloping field, to stop in alarm at seeing the men at work in the barnyard. Tom stood looking at the trees. A slight breeze made them sway gently from side to side. Two horses standing among the trees drew near each other. One nipped the other's neck. They rubbed their heads together.

The crew stopped at another large farm and it was to be their last stop for the season. "When we have finished this job we'll go home and get our own fall work done," Bottsford said. Saturday evening came and the thresherman and his sons took the horses and drove away, going to their own home for the Sunday, and leaving Tom alone. "We'll be back early on Monday morning," the thresherman said as they drove away. Sunday alone among the strange farm people brought a sharp experience to Tom and

when it had passed he decided he would not wait for the end of
the threshing season—but a few days off now—but would quit
his job and go into the city and surrender to the schools. He
remembered his employer's words, "Find out what the books have
to say. You don't have to believe when they say things that are
lies."

As he walked in lanes, across meadows and upon the hillsides
of the farm, also on the shores of Sandusky Bay that Sunday morning,
Tom thought almost constantly of his friend the fat fellow, young
Paul Bottsford, who had gone to spend the fall and winter at
Bellevue, and wondered what his life there might be like. He had
himself lived in such a town, in Bidwell, but had rarely left Harry
Whitehead's stable. What went on in such a town? What happened
at night in the houses of the towns? He remembered Paul's plan
for getting into a house alone with a widow and how he was to
creep into her room at night, holding her tightly in his arms until
she wanted what he wanted. "I wonder if he will have the nerve.
Gee, I wonder if he will have the nerve," he muttered.

For a long time, ever since Paul had gone away and he had no
one with whom he could talk, things had taken on a new aspect
in Tom's mind. The rustle of dry leaves underfoot as he walked in
a forest—the playing of shadows over the open face of a field—
the murmuring song of insects in the dry grass beside the fences
in the lanes—and at night the hushed contented sounds made by
the animals in the barns, were no longer so sweet to him. For him
no more did the young god Jesus walk beside him, just out of
sight behind low hills or down the dry beds of streams. Something
within himself that had been sleeping was now awakening. When
he returned from walking in the fields on the fall evenings and,
thinking of Paul Bottsford alone in the house with the widow at
Bellevue, half wishing he were in the same position, he felt ashamed
in the presence of the gentle old thresherman, and afterward did
not lie awake listening to the older man's prayers. The men who
had come from nearby farms to help with the threshing laughed
and shouted to each other as they pitched the straw into great
stacks or carried the filled bags of grain to the bins, and they had

wives and daughters who had come with them and who were
now at work in the farmhouse kitchen, from which also laughter
came. Girls and women kept coming out at the kitchen door
into the barnyard, tall awkward girls, plump red-cheeked girls,
women with worn thin faces and sagging breasts. All men and
women seemed made for each other.

They all laughed and talked together, understood one another.
Only he was alone. He only had no one to whom he could feel
warm and close, to whom he could draw close.

On the Sunday when the Bottsfords had all gone away, Tom
came in from walking all morning in the fields and ate his dinner
with many other people in a big farmhouse dining room. In
preparation for the threshing days ahead and the feeding of many
people, several women had come to spend the day and to help in
preparing food. The farmer's daughter, who was married and lived
in Sandusky, came with her husband, and three other women,
neighbors, came from farms in the neighborhood. Tom did not
look at them but ate his dinner in silence and as soon as he could
manage got out of the house and went to the barns. Going into a
long shed he sat on the tongue of a wagon that from long disuse
was covered with dust. Swallows flew back and forth among the
rafters overhead and, in an upper corner of the shed where they
evidently had a nest, wasps buzzed in the semi-darkness.

The daughter of the farmer, who had come from town, came
from the house with a babe in her arms. It was nursing time, she
wanted to escape from the crowded house and, without having
seen Tom, she sat on a box near the shed door and opened her
dress. Embarrassed and at the same time fascinated by the sight
of a woman's breasts, seen through cracks of the wagon box, Tom
drew his legs up and his head down and remained concealed until the woman had gone back to the house. Then he went again
to the fields and did not go back to the house for the evening
meal.

As he walked on that Sunday afternoon the grandson of the
Welsh poet experienced many new sensations. In a way he came
to understand that the things Paul had talked of doing and that

had, but a short time before, filled him with disgust were now possible to himself also. In the past when he had thought about women there had always been something healthy and animal-like in his lusts but now they took a new form. The passion that could not find expression through his body went up into his mind and he began to see visions. Women became to him something different than anything else in nature, more desirable than anything else in nature, and at the same time everything in nature became woman. The trees in the apple orchard by the barn were like the arms of women. The apples on the trees were round like the breasts of women. They were the breasts of women—and when he had got onto a low hill the contour of the fences that marked the confines of the fields fell into the forms of women's bodies. Even the clouds in the sky did the same thing.

He walked down along a lane to a stream and crossed the stream by a wooden bridge. Then he climbed another hill, the highest place in all that part of the country, and there the fever that possessed him became more active. An odd lassitude crept over him and he lay down in the grass on the hilltop and closed his eyes. For a long time he remained in a hushed, half-sleeping, dreamless state and then opened his eyes again.

Again the forms of women floated before him. To his left the bay was ruffled by a gentle breeze and far over towards the city of Sandusky two sailboats were apparently engaged in a race. The masts of the boats were fully dressed but on the great stretch of water they seemed to stand still. The bay itself, in Tom's eyes, had taken on the form and shape of a woman's head and body, and the two sailboats were the woman's eyes looking at him.

The bay was a woman with her head lying where lay the city of Sandusky. Smoke arose from the stacks of steamers docked at the city's wharves and the smoke formed itself into masses of black hair. Through the farm, where he had come to thresh, ran a stream. It swept down past the foot of the hill on which he lay. The stream was an arm of the woman. Her hand was thrust into the land and the lower part of her body was lost—far down to the north, where the bay became a part of Lake Erie—but her other arm could be seen. It was outlined in the further shore of the bay. Her other arm was drawn up and her hand was pressing against her face. Her form was distorted by pain but at the same time the giant woman smiled at the boy on the hill. There was something in the smile that was like the smile that had come unconsciously to the lips of the woman who had nursed her child in the shed.

Turning his face away from the bay Tom looked at the sky. A great white cloud that lay along the southern horizon formed itself into the giant head of a man. Tom watched as the cloud crept slowly across the sky. There was something noble and quieting about the giant's face, and his hair, pure white and as thick as wheat in a rich field in June, added to its nobility. Only the face appeared. Below the shoulders there was just a white shapeless mass of clouds.

And then this formless mass began also to change. The face of a giant woman appeared. It pressed upward toward the face of the man. Two arms formed themselves on the man's shoulders and pressed the woman closely. The two faces merged. Something seemed to snap in Tom's brain.

He sat upright and looked neither at the bay nor at the sky. Evening was coming on and soft shadows began to play over the land. Below him lay the farm with its barns and houses and, in the field below the hill on which he was lying, there were two smaller hills that became at once in his eyes the two full breasts of a woman. Two white sheep appeared and stood nibbling the grass on the woman's breasts. They were like babes being suckled. The trees in the orchards near the barns were the woman's hair. An arm of the stream that ran down to the bay, the stream he had crossed on the wooden bridge when he came to the hill, cut across a meadow beyond the two low hills. It widened into a pond and the pond made a mouth for the woman. Her eyes were two black hollows—low spots in a field where hogs had rooted the grass away, looking for roots. Black puddles of water lay in the hollows and they seemed eyes shining invitingly up at him.

This woman also smiled and her smile was now an invitation.

Tom got to his feet and hurried away down the hill and, going stealthily past the barns and the house, got into a road. All night he walked under the stars thinking new thoughts. "I am obsessed with this idea of having a woman. I'd better go to the city and go to school and see if I can make myself fit to have a woman of my own," he thought. "I won't sleep tonight but will wait until tomorrow when Bottsford comes back and then I'll quit and go into the city." He walked, trying to make plans. Even a good man like John Bottsford had a woman for himself. Could he do that?

The thought was exciting. At the moment it seemed to him that he had only to go into the city, and go to the schools for a time, to become beautiful and to have beautiful women love him. In his half ecstatic state he forgot the winter months he had spent in the city of Cleveland, and forgot also the grim streets, the long rows of dark prison-like factories, and the loneliness of his life in the city. For the moment and as he walked in the dusty roads under the moon, he thought of American towns and cities as places for beautifully satisfying adventures for all such fellows as himself.

DEATH IN
THE WOODS

SHE WAS AN OLD WOMAN AND LIVED ON A FARM NEAR THE TOWN IN
which I lived. All country and small-town people have seen such
old women, but no one knows much about them. Such an old
woman comes into town driving an old worn-out horse or she
comes afoot carrying a basket. She may own a few hens and have
eggs to sell. She brings them in a basket and takes them to a
grocer. There she trades them in. She gets some salt pork and
some beans. Then she gets a pound or two of sugar and some
flour.

Afterwards she goes to the butcher's and asks for some dog-
meat. She may spend ten or fifteen cents, but when she does she
asks for something. Formerly the butchers gave liver to anyone
who wanted to carry it away. In our family we were always having
it. Once one of my brothers got a whole cow's liver at the slaugh-
terhouse near the fairgrounds in our town. We had it until we
were sick of it. It never cost a cent. I have hated the thought of it
ever since.

The old farm woman got some liver and a soupbone. She never
visited with anyone, and as soon as she got what she wanted she
lit out for home. It made quite a load for such an old body. No
one gave her a lift. People drive right down a road and never
notice an old woman like that.

There was such an old woman who used to come into town past our house one summer and fall when I was a young boy and was sick with what was called inflammatory rheumatism. She went home later carrying a heavy pack on her back. Two or three large gaunt-looking dogs followed at her heels.

The old woman was nothing special. She was one of the nameless ones that hardly anyone knows, but she got into my thoughts. I have just suddenly now, after all these years, remembered her and what happened. It is a story. Her name was Grimes, and she lived with her husband and son in a small unpainted house on the bank of a small creek four miles from town.

The husband and son were a tough lot. Although the son was but twenty-one, he had already served a term in jail. It was whispered about that the woman's husband stole horses and ran them off to some other county. Now and then, when a horse turned up missing, the man had also disappeared. No one ever caught him. Once, when I was loafing at Tom Whitehead's livery barn, the man came there and sat on the bench in front. Two or three other men were there, but no one spoke to him. He sat for a few minutes and then got up and went away. When he was leaving he turned around and stared at the men. There was a look of defiance in his eyes. "Well, I have tried to be friendly. You don't want to talk to me. It has been so wherever I have gone in this town. If, some day, one of your fine horses turns up missing, well, then what?" He did not say anything actually. "I'd like to bust one of you on the jaw," was about what his eyes said. I remember how the look in his eyes made me shiver.

The old man belonged to a family that had had money once. His name was Jake Grimes. It all comes back clearly now. His father, John Grimes, had owned a sawmill when the country was new, and had made money. Then he got to drinking and running after women. When he died there wasn't much left.

Jake blew in the rest. Pretty soon there wasn't any more lumber to cut and his land was nearly all gone.

He got his wife off a German farmer, for whom he went to work one June day in the wheat harvest. She was a young thing then and scared to death. You see, the farmer was up to something with the girl—she was, I think, a bound girl and his wife had her suspicions. She took it out on the girl when the man wasn't around. Then, when the wife had to go off to town for supplies, the farmer got after her. She told young Jake that nothing really ever happened, but he didn't know whether to believe it or not.

He got her pretty easy himself, the first time he was out with her. He wouldn't have married her if the German farmer hadn't tried to tell him where to get off. He got her to go riding with him in his buggy one night when he was threshing on the place, and then he came for her the next Sunday night.

She managed to get out of the house without her employer's seeing, but when she was getting into the buggy he showed up. It was almost dark, and he just popped up suddenly at the horse's head. He grabbed the horse by the bridle and Jake got out his buggy-whip.

They had it out all right! The German was a tough one. Maybe he didn't care whether his wife knew or not. Jake hit him over the face and shoulders with the buggy-whip, but the horse got to acting up and he had to get out.

Then the two men went for it. The girl didn't see it. The horse started to run away and went nearly a mile down the road before the girl got him stopped. Then she managed to tie him to a tree beside the road. (I wonder how I know all this. It must have stuck in my mind from small-town tales when I was a boy.) Jake found her there after he got through with the German. She was huddled up in the buggy seat, crying, scared to death. She told Jake a lot of stuff, how the German had tried to get her, how he chased her once into the barn, how another time, when they happened to be alone in the house together, he tore her dress open clear down the front. The German, she said, might have got her that time if he hadn't heard his old woman drive in at the gate. She had been off to town for supplies. Well, she would be putting the horse in the barn. The German managed to sneak off to the fields without his wife seeing. He told the girl he would

kill her if she told. What could she do? She told a lie about rip-
ping her dress in the barn when she was feeding the stock. I remember now that she was a bound girl and did not know where
her father and mother were. Maybe she did not have any father.
You know what I mean.

Such bound children were often enough cruelly treated. They
were children who had no parents, slaves really. There were very
few orphan homes then. They were legally bound into some home.
It was a matter of pure luck how it came out.

II

She married Jake and had a son and daughter, but the daughter
died.

Then she settled down to feed stock. That was her job. At the
German's place she had cooked the food for the German and his
wife. The wife was a strong woman with big hips and worked
most of the time in the fields with her husband. She fed them
and fed the cows in the barn, fed the pigs, the horses and the
chickens. Every moment of every day, as a young girl, was spent
feeding something.

Then she married Jake Grimes and he had to be fed. She was a
slight thing, and when she had been married for three or four
years, and after the two children were born, her slender shoulders
became stooped.

Jake always had a lot of big dogs around the house, that stood
near the unused sawmill near the creek. He was always trading
horses when he wasn't stealing something and had a lot of poor
bony ones about. Also he kept three or four pigs and a cow. They
were all pastured in the few acres left of the Grimes place and
Jake did little enough work.

He went into debt for a threshing outfit and ran it for several
years, but it did not pay. People did not trust him. They were
afraid he would steal the grain at night. He had to go a long way
off to get work and it cost too much to get there. In the winter he
hunted and cut a little firewood, to be sold in some nearby town.
When the son grew up he was just like the father. They got

drunk together. If there wasn't anything to eat in the house when they came home the old man gave his old woman a cut over the head. She had a few chickens of her own and had to kill one of them in a hurry. When they were all killed she wouldn't have any eggs to sell when she went to town, and then what would she do?

She had to scheme all her life about getting things fed, getting the pigs fed so they would grow fat and could be butchered in the fall. When they were butchered her husband took most of the meat off to town and sold it. If he did not do it first the boy did. They fought sometimes and when they fought the old woman stood aside trembling.

She had got the habit of silence anyway—that was fixed. Sometimes, when she began to look old—she wasn't forty yet—and when the husband and son were both off trading horses or drinking or hunting or stealing, she went around the house and the barnyard muttering to herself.

How was she going to get everything fed?—that was her problem. The dogs had to be fed. There wasn't enough hay in the barn for the horses and the cow. If she didn't feed the chickens how could they lay eggs? Without eggs to sell how could she get things in town, things she had to have to keep the life of the farm going? Thank heaven, she did not have to feed her husband—in a certain way. That hadn't lasted long after their marriage and after the babies came. Where he went on his long trips she did not know. Sometimes he was gone from home for weeks, and after the boy grew up they went off together.

They left everything at home for her to manage and she had no money. She knew no one. No one ever talked to her in town. When it was winter she had to gather sticks of wood for her fire, had to try to keep the stock fed with very little grain.

The stock in the barn cried to her hungrily, the dogs followed her about. In the winter the hens laid few enough eggs. They huddled in the corners of the barn and she kept watching them. If a hen lays an egg in the barn in the winter and you do not find it, it freezes and breaks.

One day in winter the old woman went off to town with a few

eggs and the dogs followed her. She did not get started until nearly three o'clock and the snow was heavy. She hadn't been feeling very well for several days and so she went muttering along, scantily clad, her shoulders stooped. She had an old grain bag in which she carried her eggs, tucked away down in the bottom. There weren't many of them, but in winter the price of eggs is up. She would get a little meat in exchange for the eggs, some salt pork, a little sugar, and some coffee perhaps. It might be the butcher would give her a piece of liver.

When she had got to town and was trading in her eggs, the dogs lay by the door outside. She did pretty well, got the things she needed, more than she had hoped. Then she went to the butcher and he gave her some liver and some dog-meat.

It was the first time anyone had spoken to her in a friendly way for a long time. The butcher was alone in his shop when she came in and was annoyed by the thought of such a sick-looking old woman out on such a day. It was bitter cold and the snow, that had let up during the afternoon, was falling again. The butcher said something about her husband and her son, swore at them, and the old woman stared at him, a look of mild surprise in her eyes as he talked. He said that if either the husband or the son were going to get any of the liver or the heavy bones with scraps of meat hanging to them that he had put into the grain bag, he'd see him starve first.

Starve, eh? Well, things had to be fed. Men had to be fed, and the horses that weren't any good but maybe could be traded off, and the poor thin cow that hadn't given any milk for three months.

Horses, cows, pigs, dogs, men.

III

The old woman had to get back before darkness came if she could. The dogs followed at her heels, sniffing at the heavy grain bag she had fastened on her back. When she got to the edge of town she stopped by a fence and tied the bag on her back with a piece of rope she had carried in her dress-pocket for just that purpose. That was an easier way to carry it. Her arms ached. It was hard when she had to crawl over fences and once she fell over and landed in the snow. The dogs went frisking about. She had to struggle to get to her feet again, but she made it. The point of climbing over the fences was that there was a shortcut over a hill and through a woods. She might have gone around by the road, but it was a mile farther that way. She was afraid she couldn't make it. And then, besides, the stock had to be fed. There was a little hay left and a little corn. Perhaps her husband and son would bring some home when they came. They had driven off in the only buggy the Grimes family had, a rickety thing, a rickety horse hitched to the buggy, two other rickety horses led by halters. They were going to trade horses, get a little money if they could. They might come home drunk. It would be well to have something in the house when they came back.

The son had an affair on with a woman at the county seat, fifteen miles away. She was a rough enough woman, a tough one. Once in the summer the son had brought her to the house. Both she and the son had been drinking. Jake Grimes was away and the son and his woman ordered the old woman about like a servant. She didn't mind much; she was used to it. Whatever happened she never said anything. That was her way of getting along. She had managed that way when she was a young girl at the German's and ever since she had married Jake. That time her son brought his woman to the house they stayed all night, sleeping together just as though they were married. It hadn't shocked the old woman, not much. She had got past being shocked early in life.

With the pack on her back she went painfully along across an open field, wading in the deep snow, and got into the woods.

There was a path, but it was hard to follow. Just beyond the top of the hill, where the woods was thickest, there was a small clearing. Had someone once thought of building a house there? The clearing was as large as a building lot in town, large enough for a house and a garden. The path ran along the side of the clearing, and when she got there the old woman sat down to rest at the foot of a tree.

It was a foolish thing to do. When she got herself placed, the pack against the tree's trunk, it was nice, but what about getting up again? She worried about that for a moment and then quietly closed her eyes.

She must have slept for a time. When you are about so cold you can't get any colder. The afternoon grew a little warmer and the snow came thicker than ever. Then after a time the weather cleared. The moon even came out.

There were four Grimes dogs that had followed Mrs. Grimes into town, all tall gaunt fellows. Such men as Jake Grimes and his son always keep just such dogs. They kick and abuse them, but they stay. The Grimes dogs, in order to keep from starving, had to do a lot of foraging for themselves, and they had been at it while the old woman slept with her back to the tree at the side of the clearing. They had been chasing rabbits in the woods and in adjoining fields and in their ranging had picked up three other farm dogs.

After a time all the dogs came back to the clearing. They were excited about something. Such nights, cold and clear and with a moon, do things to dogs. It may be that some old instinct, come down from the time when they were wolves and ranged the woods in packs on winter nights, comes back into them.

The dogs in the clearing, before the old woman, had caught two or three rabbits and their immediate hunger had been satisfied. They began to play, running in circles in the clearing. Round and round they ran, each dog's nose at the tail of the next dog. In the clearing, under the snow-laden trees and under the wintry moon, they made a strange picture, running thus silently, in a circle their running had beaten in the soft snow. The dogs made no sound. They ran around and around in the circle.

It may have been that the old woman saw them doing that before she died. She may have awakened once or twice and looked at the strange sight with dim old eyes.

She wouldn't be very cold now, just drowsy. Life hangs on a long time. Perhaps the old woman was out of her head. She may have dreamed of her girlhood, at the German's, and before that, when she was a child and before her mother lit out and left her.

Her dreams couldn't have been very pleasant. Not many pleasant things had happened to her. Now and then one of the Grimes dogs left the running circle and came to stand before her. The dog thrust his face close to her face. His red tongue was hanging out.

The running of the dogs may have been a kind of death ceremony. It may have been that the primitive instinct of the wolf, having been aroused in the dogs by the night and the running, made them somehow afraid.

"Now we are no longer wolves. We are dogs, the servants of men. Keep alive, man! When man dies we become wolves again."

When one of the dogs came to where the old woman sat with her back against the tree and thrust his nose close to her face, he seemed satisfied and went back to run with the pack. All the Grimes dogs did it at some time during the evening, before she died. I knew all about it afterward, when I grew to be a man, because once in a woods in Illinois, on another winter night, I saw a pack of dogs act just like that. The dogs were waiting for me to die as they had waited for the old woman that night when I was a child, but when it happened to me I was a young man and had no intention whatever of dying.

The old woman died softly and quietly. When she was dead and when one of the Grimes dogs had come to her and had found her dead, all the dogs stopped running.

They gathered about her.

Well, she was dead now. She had fed the Grimes dogs when she was alive, what about now?

There was the pack on her back, the grain bag containing the piece of salt pork, the liver the butcher had given her, the dog-meat, the soup bones. The butcher in town, having been suddenly overcome with a feeling of pity, had loaded her grain bag heavily. It had been a big haul for the old woman.

It was a big haul for the dogs now.

IV

One of the Grimes dogs sprang suddenly out from among the

others and began worrying the pack on the old woman's back. Had the dogs really been wolves, that one would have been the leader of the pack. What he did, all the others did.

All of them sank their teeth into the grain bag the old woman had fastened with ropes to her back.

They dragged the old woman's body out into the open clearing. The worn-out dress was quickly torn from her shoulders. When she was found a day or two later, the dress had been torn from her body clear to the hips, but the dogs had not touched her body. They had got the meat out of the grain bag, that was all. Her body was frozen stiff when it was found, and the shoulders were so narrow and the body so slight that in death it looked like the body of some charming young girl.

Such things happened in towns of the Middle West, on farms near town, when I was a boy. A hunter out after rabbits found the old woman's body and did not touch it. Something, the beaten round path in the little snow-covered clearing, the silence of the place, the place where the dogs had worried the body trying to pull the grain bag away or tear it open—something startled the man and he hurried off to town.

I was in Main Street with one of my brothers who was town newsboy and who was taking the afternoon papers to the stores. It was almost night.

The hunter came into a grocery and told his story. Then he went to a hardware shop and into a drugstore. Men began to gather on the sidewalks. Then they started out along the road to the place in the woods.

My brother should have gone on about his business of distributing papers but he didn't. Everyone was going to the woods. The undertaker went and the town marshal. Several men got on a dray and rode out to where the path left the road and went into the woods, but the horses weren't very sharply shod and slid about on the slippery roads. They made no better time than those of us who walked.

The town marshal was a large man whose leg had been injured in the Civil War. He carried a heavy cane and limped rapidly along the road. My brother and I followed at his heels, and as we went other men and boys joined the crowd.

It had grown dark by the time we got to where the old woman had left the road but the moon had come out. The marshal was thinking there might have been a murder. He kept asking the hunter questions. The hunter went along with his gun across his shoulders, a dog following at his heels. It isn't often a rabbit hunter has a chance to be so conspicuous. He was taking full advantage of it, leading the procession with the town marshal. "I didn't see any wounds. She was a beautiful young girl. Her face was buried in the snow. No, I didn't know her." As a matter of fact, the hunter had not looked closely at the body. He had been frightened. She might have been murdered and someone might spring out from behind a tree and murder him. In a woods in the late afternoon, when the trees are all bare and there is white snow on the ground, when all is silent, something creepy steals over the mind and body. If something strange or uncanny has happened in the neighborhood all you think about is getting away from there as fast as you can.

The crowd of men and boys had got to where the old woman had crossed the field and went, following the marshal and the hunter, up the slight incline and into the woods.

My brother and I were silent. He had his bundle of papers in a bag slung across his shoulder. When he got back to town he would have to go on distributing his papers before he went home to supper. If I went along, as he had no doubt already determined I should, we would both be late. Either mother or our older sister would have to warm our supper.

Well, we would have something to tell. A boy did not get such a chance very often. It was lucky we just happened to go into the grocery when the hunter came in. The hunter was a country fellow. Neither of us had ever seen him before.

Now the crowd of men and boys had got to the clearing. Darkness comes quickly on such winter nights, but the full moon made everything clear. My brother and I stood near the tree beneath which the old woman had died.

She did not look old, lying there in that light, frozen and still. One of the men turned her over in the snow and I saw everything. My body trembled with some strange mystical feeling and so did my brother's. It might have been the cold.

Neither of us had ever seen a woman's body before. It may have been the snow, clinging to the frozen flesh, that made it look so white and lovely, so like marble. No woman had come with the party from town; but one of the men, he was the town blacksmith, took off his overcoat and spread it over her. Then he gathered her into his arms and started off to town, all the others following silently. At that time no one knew who she was.

V

I had seen everything, had seen the oval in the snow, like a miniature race track, where the dogs had run, had seen how the men were mystified, had seen the white bare young-looking shoulders, had heard the whispered comments of the men.

The men were simply mystified. They took the body to the undertaker's, and when the blacksmith, the hunter, the marshal and several others had got inside they closed the door. If father had been there perhaps he could have got in, but we boys couldn't.

I went with my brother to distribute the rest of his papers and when we got home it was my brother who told the story.

I kept silent and went to bed early. It may have been I was not satisfied with the way he told it.

Later, in the town, I must have heard other fragments of the old woman's story. She was recognized the next day and there was an investigation.

The husband and son were found somewhere and brought to town and there was an attempt to connect them with the woman's death, but it did not work. They had perfect enough alibis.

However, the town was against them. They had to get out. Where they went I never heard.

I remember only the picture there in the forest, the men standing about, the naked girlish-looking figure face down in the snow, the tracks made by the running dogs and the clear cold winter sky above. White fragments of clouds were drifting across the sky. They went racing across the little open space among the trees.

The scene in the forest had become for me, without my knowing it, the foundation for the real story I am now trying to tell. The fragments, you see, had to be picked up slowly, long afterwards.

Things happened. When I was a young man I worked on the farm of a German. The hired girl was afraid of her employer. The farmer's wife hated her.

I saw things at that place. Once later, I had a half-uncanny, mystical adventure with dogs in an Illinois forest on a clear, moon-lit winter night. When I was a schoolboy, and on a summer day, I went with a boy friend out along a creek some miles from town and came to the house where the old woman had lived. No one had lived in the house since her death. The doors were broken from the hinges; the window lights were all broken. As the boy and I stood in the road outside, two dogs, just roving farm dogs no doubt, came running around the corner of the house. The dogs were tall, gaunt fellows and came down to the fence and glared through at us, standing in the road.

The whole thing, the story of the old woman's death, was to me as I grew older like music heard from far off. The notes had to be picked up slowly one at a time. Something had to be understood.

The woman who died was one destined to feed animal life. Anyway, that is all she ever did. She was feeding animal life before she was born, as a child, as a young woman working on the farm of the German, after she married, when she grew old and when she died. She fed animal life in cows, in chickens, in pigs, in horses, in dogs, in men. Her daughter had died in childhood and with her one son she had no articulate relations. On the night when she died she was hurrying homeward, bearing on her body food for animal life.

She died in the clearing in the woods and even after her death continued feeding animal life.

You see it is likely that, when my brother told the story that night when we got home and my mother and sister sat listening, I did not think he got the point. He was too young and so was I.

A thing so complete has its own beauty.

I shall not try to emphasize the point. I am only explaining why I was dissatisfied then and have been ever since. I speak of that only that you may understand why I have been impelled to try to tell the simple story over again.

THE RETURN

EIGHTEEN YEARS. WELL, HE WAS DRIVING A GOOD CAR, AN EXPENSIVE roadster. He was well clad, a rather solid, fine-looking man, not too heavy. When he had left the Middle-Western town to go live in New York City he was twenty-two and now, on his way back, he was forty. He drove toward the town from the east, stopping for lunch at another town ten miles away.

When he went away from Caxton, after his mother died, he used to write letters to friends at home, but after several months the replies began to come with less and less frequency. On the day when he sat eating his lunch at a small hotel in the town ten miles east of Caxton he suddenly thought of the reason and was ashamed. "Am I going back there on this visit for the same reason I wrote the letters?" he asked himself. For a moment he thought he might not go on. There was still time to turn back.

Outside, in the principal business street of the neighboring town, people were walking about. The sun shone warmly. Although he had lived for so many years in New York, he had always kept, buried away in him somewhere, a hankering for his own country. All the day before he had been driving through the eastern Ohio country, crossing many small streams, running down through small valleys, seeing the white farmhouses set back from the road and the big red barns.

The elders were still in bloom along the fences, boys were swimming in a creek, the wheat had been cut, and now the corn was shoulder-high. Everywhere the drone of bees; in patches of woodland along the road, a heavy, mysterious silence.

Now, however, he began thinking of something else. Shame crept over him. "When I first left Caxton, I wrote letters back to my boyhood friends there, but I wrote always of myself. When I had written a letter telling what I was doing in the city, what friends I was making, what my prospects were, I put, at the very end of the letter perhaps, a little inquiry: 'I hope you are well. How are things going with you?' Something of that sort."

The returning native—his name was John Holden—had grown very uneasy. After eighteen years it seemed to him he could see, lying before him, one of the letters written eighteen years before, when he had first come into the strange Eastern city. His mother's brother, a successful architect in the city, had given him such and such an opportunity; he had been at the theater to see Mansfield as Brutus; he had taken the night boat upriver to Albany with his aunt; there were two very handsome girls on the boat.

Everything must have been in the same tone. His uncle had given him a rare opportunity, and he had taken advantage of it. In time he had also become a successful architect. In New York City there were certain great buildings, two or three skyscrapers, several huge industrial plants, any number of handsome and expensive residences, that were the products of his brain.

When it came down to scratch, John Holden had to admit that his uncle had not been excessively fond of him. It had just happened that his aunt and uncle had no children of their own. He did his work in the office well and carefully, had developed a certain rather striking knack for design. The aunt had liked him better. She had always tried to think of him as her own son, had treated him as a son. Sometimes she called him son. Once or twice, after his uncle died, he had a notion. His aunt was a good woman, but sometimes he thought she would rather have enjoyed having him, John Holden, go in a bit more for wickedness, go a little on the loose, now and then. He never did anything she had to forgive him for. Perhaps she hungered for the opportunity to forgive.

Odd thoughts, eh? Well, what was a fellow to do? You had but the one life to live. You had to think of yourself.

Botheration! John Holden had rather counted on the trip back to Caxton, had really counted on it more than he realized. It was a bright summer day. He had been driving over the mountains of Pennsylvania, through New York State, through eastern Ohio. Gertrude, his wife, had died during the summer before, and his one son, a lad of twelve, had gone away for the summer to a boys' camp in Vermont.

The idea had just come to him. "I'll drive the car along slowly through the country, drinking it in. I need a rest, time to think. What I really need is to renew old acquaintances. I'll go back to Caxton and stay several days. I'll see Herman and Frank and Joe. Then I'll go call on Lillian and Kate. What a lot of fun, really!" It might just be that when he got to Caxton, the Caxton ball team would be playing a game, say with a team from Yerington. Lillian might go to the game with him. It was in his mind faintly that Lillian had never married. How did he know that? He had heard nothing from Caxton for many years. The ball game would be in Heffler's field, and he and Lillian would go out there, walking under the maple trees along Turner Street, past the old stave factory, then in the dust of the road, past where the sawmill used to stand, and on into the field itself. He would be carrying a sunshade over Lillian's head, and Bob French would be standing at the gate where you went into the field and charging the people twenty-five cents to see the game.

Well, it would not be Bob; his son perhaps. There would be something very nice in the notion of Lillian's going off to a ball game that way with an old sweetheart. A crowd of boys, women and men, going through a cattle gate into Heffler's field, tramping through the dust, young men with their sweethearts, a few gray-haired women, mothers of boys who belonged to the team, Lillian and he sitting in the rickety grandstand in the hot sun.

Once it had been—how they had felt, he and Lillian, sitting

there together! It had been rather hard to keep the attention centered on the players in the field. One couldn't ask a neighbor,
"Who's ahead now, Caxton or Yerington?" Lillian's hands lay in
her lap. What white, delicate, expressive hands they were! Once—
that was just before he went away to live in the city with his uncle
and but a month after his mother died—he and Lillian went to
the ball field together at night. His father had died when he was a
young lad, and he had no relatives left in the town. Going off to
the ball field at night was maybe a risky thing for Lillian to do—
risky for her reputation if anyone found it out—but she had seemed
willing enough. You know how small-town girls of that age are.

Her father owned a retail shoe store in Caxton and was a good,
respectable man; but the Holdens—John's father had been a lawyer.

After they got back from the ball field that night—it must
have been after midnight—they went to sit on the front porch
before her father's house. He must have known. A daughter cavorting
about half the night with a young man that way! They had clung
to each other with a sort of queer, desperate feeling neither understood. She did not go into the house until after three o'clock,
and went then only because he insisted. He hadn't wanted to
ruin her reputation. Why, he might have... She was like a little
frightened child at the thought of his going away. He was twenty-
two then, and she must have been about eighteen.

Eighteen and twenty-two make forty. John Holden was forty
on the day when he sat at lunch at the hotel in the town ten miles
from Caxton.

Now, he thought, he might be able to walk through the streets
of Caxton to the ball park with Lillian with a certain effect. You
know how it is. One has to accept the fact that youth is gone. If
there should turn out to be such a ball game and Lillian would go
with him, he would leave the car in the garage and ask her to
walk. One saw pictures of that sort of thing in the movies—a
man coming back to his native village after twenty years; a new
beauty taking the place of the beauty of youth—something like
that. In the spring the leaves on maple trees are lovely, but they
are even more lovely in the fall—a flame of color—manhood and

womanhood.

After he had finished his lunch John did not feel very comfortable. The road to Caxton—it used to take nearly three hours to travel the distance with a horse and buggy, but now, and without any effort, the distance might be made in twenty minutes.

He lit a cigar and went for a walk, not in the streets of Caxton, but in the streets of the town ten miles away. If he got to Caxton in the evening, just at dusk, say, now ...

With an inward pang John realized that he wanted darkness, the kindliness of soft evening lights. Lillian, Joe, Herman and the rest. It had been eighteen years for the others as well as for himself. Now he had succeeded, a little, in twisting his fear of Caxton into fear for the others, and it made him feel somewhat better; but at once he realized what he was doing and again felt uncomfortable. One had to look out for changes, new people, new buildings, middle-aged people grown old, youth grown middle-aged. At any rate, he was thinking of the other now. He wasn't, as when he wrote letters home eighteen years before, thinking only of himself. "Am I?" It *was* a question.

An absurd situation, really. He had sailed along so gayly through upper New York State, through western Pennsylvania, through eastern Ohio. Men were at work in the fields and in the towns, farmers drove into towns in their cars, clouds of dust rose on some distant road seen across a valley. Once he had stopped his car near a bridge and had gone for a walk along the banks of a creek where it wound through a wood.

He was liking people. Well, he had never before given much time to people, to thinking of them and their affairs. "I hadn't time," he told himself. He had always realized that, while he was a good enough architect, things move fast in America. New men were coming on. He couldn't take chances of going on forever on his uncle's reputation. A man had to be always on the alert. Fortunately, his marriage had been a help. It had made valuable connections for him.

Twice he had picked up people on the road. There was a lad of sixteen from some town of eastern Pennsylvania, working his way westward toward the Pacific coast by picking up rides in cars—a summer's adventure. John had carried him all of one day and had listened to his talk with keen pleasure. And so this was the younger generation. The boy had nice eyes and an eager, friendly manner. He smoked cigarettes, and once, when they had a puncture, he was very quick and eager about changing the tire. "Now, don't you soil your hands, mister, I can do it like a flash," he said, and he did. The boy said he intended working his way overland to the Pacific coast, where he would try to get a job of some kind on an ocean freighter, and that, if he did, he would go on around the world. "But do you speak any foreign languages?" The boy did not. Across John Holden's mind flashed pictures of hot Eastern deserts, crowded Asiatic towns, wild half-savage mountain countries. As a young architect, and before his uncle died, he had spent two years in foreign travel, studying buildings in many countries; but he said nothing of this thought to the boy. Vast plans entered into with eager, boyish abandon, a world tour undertaken as he, when a young man, might have undertaken to find his way from his uncle's house in East Eighty-first Street downtown to the Battery. "How do I know—perhaps he will do it," John thought. The day in company with the boy had been very pleasant, and he had been on the alert to pick him up again the next morning; but the boy had gone on his way, had caught a ride with some earlier riser. Why hadn't John invited him to his hotel for the night? The notion hadn't come to him until too late.

"Youth, rather wild and undisciplined, running wild, eh? I wonder why I never did it, never wanted to do it."

If he had been a bit wilder, more reckless that night, that time when he and Lillian ... "It's all right being reckless with yourself, but when someone else is involved, a young girl in a small town, you yourself lighting out..." He remembered sharply that on the night long before, as he sat with Lillian on the porch before her father's house, his hand... It had seemed as though Lillian, on that evening, might not have objected to anything he wanted to do. He had thought—well, he had thought of the consequences. Women must be protected by men, all that sort of thing. Lillian had seemed rather stunned when he walked away, even though it was three o'clock in the morning. She had been rather like a person waiting at a railroad station for the coming of a train. There is a blackboard, and a strange man comes out and writes on it, "Train Number 287 has been discontinued"—something like that.

Well, it had been all right.

Later, four years later, he had married a New York woman of good family. Even in a city like New York, where there are so many people, her family had been well known. They had connections.

After marriage, sometimes, it is true, he had wondered. Gertrude used to look at him sometimes with an odd light in her eyes. That boy he picked up in the road—once during the day when he said something to the boy, the same queer look came into his eyes. It would be rather upsetting if you knew that the boy had purposely avoided you next morning. There had been Gertrude's cousin. Once after his marriage, John heard a rumor that Gertrude had wanted to marry that cousin, but of course he had said nothing to her. Why should he have? She was his wife. There had been, he had heard, a good deal of family objection to the cousin. He was reputed to be wild, a gambler and drinker.

Once the cousin came to the Holden apartment at two in the morning, drunk and demanding that he be allowed to see Gertrude, and she slipped on a dressing-gown and went down to him. That was in the hallway of the apartment, downstairs, where almost anyone might have come in and seen her. As a matter of fact, the elevator boy and janitor did see her. She had stood in the hallway below talking for nearly an hour. What about? He had never asked Gertrude directly, and she had never told him anything. When she came upstairs again and had got into her bed, he lay in his own bed trembling but remained silent. He had been afraid that if he spoke he might say something rude; better keep still. The cousin had disappeared. John had a suspicion that Gertrude later supplied him with money. He went out West somewhere.

Now Gertrude was dead. She had always seemed very well, but suddenly she was attacked by a baffling kind of slow fever that lasted nearly a year. Sometimes she seemed about to get better, and then suddenly the fever grew worse. It might be that she did not want to live. What a notion! John had been at the bedside with the doctor when she died. There was something of the same feeling he had that night of his youth when he went with Lillian to the ball field, an odd sense of inadequacy. There was no doubt that in some subtle way both women had accused him.

Of what? There had always been, in some vague, indefinable way, a kind of accusation in the attitude toward him of his uncle, the architect, and of his aunt. They had left him their money, but... It was as though the uncle had said, as though Lillian during that night long ago had said...

Had they all said the same thing, and was Gertrude his wife saying it as she lay dying? A smile. "You have always taken such good care of yourself, haven't you, John dear? You have observed the rules. You have taken no chances for yourself or the others." She had actually said something of that sort to him once in a moment of anger.

II

In the small town ten miles from Caxton there wasn't any park to which a man could go to sit. If one stayed about the hotel, someone from Caxton might come in. "Hello, what are you doing here?"

It would be inconvenient to explain. He had wanted the kindliness of soft evening light, both for himself and the old friends he was to see again.

He began thinking of his son, now a boy of twelve. "Well," he said to himself, "his character has not begun to form yet." There was as yet in the son an unconsciousness of other people, a rather casual selfishness, an unawareness of others, an unhealthy sharpness about getting the best of others. It was a thing that should be corrected in him and at once. John Holden had got himself into a small panic. "I must write him a letter at once. Such a habit gets fixed in a boy and then in the man, and it cannot later be shaken off. There are such a lot of people living in the world! Every man and woman has his own point of view. To be civilized, really, is to be aware of the others, their hopes, their gladnesses, their illusions about life."

John Holden was now walking along a residence street of a small Ohio town, composing in fancy a letter to his son in the boys' camp in Vermont. He was a man who wrote to his son every day. "I think a man should," he told himself. "He should remember that now the boy has no mother."

He had come to an outlying railroad station. It was neat with grass and flowers growing in a round bed in the very center of a lawn. Some man, the station agent and telegraph operator perhaps, passed him and went inside the station. John followed him in. On the wall of the waiting room there was a framed copy of the timetable, and he stood studying it. A train went to Caxton at five. Another train came from Caxton and passed through the town he was now in at seven forty-three, the seven-nineteen out of Caxton. The man in the small business section of the station opened a sliding panel and looked at him. The two men just stared at each other without speaking, and then the panel was slid shut again.

John looked at his watch. Two twenty-eight. At about six he could drive over to Caxton and dine at the hotel there. After he had dined, it would be evening and people would be coming into the main street. The seven-nineteen would come in. When John was a lad, sometimes, he, Joe, Herman, and often several other lads had climbed on the front of the baggage or mail car and had stolen a ride to the very town he was now in. What a thrill, crouched down in the gathering darkness on the platform as the train ran the ten miles, the car rocking from side to side! When it got a little dark in the fall or spring, the fields beside the track were lighted up when the fireman opened his fire box to throw in coal. Once John saw a rabbit running along in the glare of light beside the track. He could have reached down and caught it with his hand. In the neighboring town the boys went into saloons and played pool and drank beer. They could depend upon catching a ride back home on the local freight that got to Caxton at about ten-thirty. On one of the adventures John and Herman got drunk and Joe had to help them into an empty coal car and later get them out at Caxton. Herman got sick, and when they were getting off the freight at Caxton, he stumbled and came very near falling under the wheels of the moving train. John wasn't as drunk as Herman. When the others weren't looking, he had poured several of the glasses of beer into a spittoon. In Caxton he and Joe had to walk about with Herman for several hours, and when John finally got home, his mother was still awake and was worried. He had to lie to her. "I drove out into the country with Herman, and a wheel broke. We had to walk home." The reason Joe could carry his beer so well was because he was German. His father owned the town meat market and the family had beer on the table at home. No wonder it did not knock him out as it did Herman and John.

There was a bench at the side of the railroad station in the shade, and John sat there for a long time—two hours, three hours. Why hadn't he brought a book? In fancy he composed a letter to his son and in it he spoke of the fields lying beside the road outside the town of Caxton, of his greeting old friends there, of things that had happened when he was a boy. He even spoke of his former sweetheart, of Lillian. If he now thought out just what he was going to say in the letter, he could write it in his room at the hotel over in Caxton in a few minutes without having to stop and think what he was going to say. You can't always be too fussy about what you say to a young boy. Really, sometimes, you should take him into your confidence, into your life, make him a part of your life.

It was six-twenty when John drove into Caxton and went to the hotel, where he registered and was shown to a room. On the street as he drove into town he saw Billy Baker, who, when he was a young man, had a paralyzed leg that dragged along the sidewalk when he walked. Now he was getting old; his face seemed wrinkled and faded like a dried lemon, and his clothes had spots down the front. People, even sick people, live a long time in small Ohio towns. It is surprising how they hang on.

John had put his car, of a rather expensive make, into a garage beside the hotel. Formerly, in his day, the building had been used as a livery barn. There used to be pictures of famous trotting and pacing horses on the walls of the little office at the front. Old Dave Grey, who owned race horses of his own, ran the livery barn then, and John occasionally hired a rig there. He hired a rig and took Lillian for a ride into the country along moonlit roads. By a lonely farmhouse a dog barked. Sometimes they drove along a little dirt road lined with elders and stopped the horse. How still everything was! What a queer feeling they had! They couldn't talk. Sometimes they sat in silence thus, very near each other, for a long, long time. Once they got out of the buggy, having tied the horse to the fence, and walked in a newly cut hay field. The cut hay lay all about in little cocks. John wanted to lie on one of the haycocks with Lillian but did not dare suggest it.

At the hotel John ate his dinner in silence. There wasn't even a traveling salesman in the dining room, and presently the proprietor's wife came and stood by his table to talk with him. The hotel had a good many tourists, but this just happened to be a quiet day. Dull days came that way in the hotel business. The woman's husband was a traveling man and had bought the hotel to give his wife something to keep her interested while he was on the road. He was away from home so much! They had come to Caxton from Pittsburgh.

After he had dined, John went up to his room, and presently the woman followed. The door leading into the hall had been left open, and she came and stood in the doorway. Really, she was rather handsome. She only wanted to be sure that everything was all right, that he had towels and soap and everything he needed.

For a time she lingered by the door talking of the town.

"It's a good little town. General Hurst is buried here. You should drive out to the cemetery and see the statue." He wondered who General Hurst was. In what war had he fought? Odd that he hadn't remembered about him. The town had a piano factory, and there was a watch company from Cincinnati talking of putting up a plant. "They figure there is less chance of labor trouble in a small town like this."

The woman went reluctantly away. As she was going along the hallway she stopped once and looked back. There was something a little queer. They were both self-conscious. "I hope you'll be comfortable," she said. At forty a man did not come home to his own home town to start... A traveling man's wife, eh? Well, well!

At seven forty-five John went out for a walk on Main Street and almost at once he met Tom Ballard, who at once recognized him, a fact that pleased Tom. He bragged about it. "Once I see a face, I never forget. Well, well!" When John was twenty-two, Tom must have been about fifteen. His father was the leading doctor of the town. He took John in tow, walked back with him toward the hotel. He kept exclaiming: "I knew you at once. You haven't changed much, really."

Tom was in his turn a doctor, and there was about him something... Right away John guessed what it was. They went up into John's room, and John, having in his bag a bottle of whisky, poured Tom a drink, which he took somewhat too eagerly, John thought. There was talk. After Tom had taken the drink he sat on the edge of the bed, still holding the bottle John had passed to him. Herman was running a dray now. He had married Kit Small and had five kids. Joe was working for the International Harvester Company. "I don't know whether he's in town now or not. He's a trouble-shooter, a swell mechanic, a good fellow," Tom said. He drank again.

As for Lillian, mentioned with an air of being casual by John, he, John, knew of course the she had been married and divorced. There was some sort of trouble about another man. Her husband married again later, and now she lived with her mother, her father, the shoe merchant, having died. Tom spoke somewhat guardedly, as though protecting a friend.

"I guess she's all right now, going straight and all. Good thing she never had any kids. She's a little nervous and queer; has lost her looks a good deal."

The two men went downstairs and, walking along Main Street, got into a car belonging to the doctor.

"I'll take you for a little ride," Tom said; but as he was about to pull away from the curb where the car had been parked, he turned and smiled at his passenger. "We ought to celebrate a little, account of your coming back here," he said. "What do you say to a quart?"

John handed him a ten-dollar bill, and he disappeared into a nearby drugstore. When he came back he laughed.

"I used your name, all right. They didn't recognize it. In the prescription I wrote out I said you had a general breakdown, that you needed to be built up. I recommended that you take a tea-spoonful three times a day. Lord! my prescription book is getting almost empty." The drugstore belonged to a man named Will Bennett. "You remember him, maybe. He's Ed Bennett's son; married Carrie Wyatt." The names were but dim things in John's mind. "This man is going to get drunk. He is going to try to get me drunk too," he thought.

When they had turned out of Main Street and into Walnut Street they stopped midway between two street lights and had another drink, John holding the bottle to his lips but putting his tongue over the opening. He remembered the evenings with Joe and Herman when he had secretly poured his beer into a spittoon. He felt cold and lonely. Walnut Street was one along which he used to walk, coming home late at night from Lillian's house. He remembered people who then lived along the street, and a list of names began running through his head. Often the names remained but did not call up images of people. They were just names. He hoped the doctor would not turn the car into the street in which the Holdens had lived. Lillian had lived over in another part of town, in what was called "the Red House District." Just why it had been called that John did not know.

III

They drove silently along, up a small hill, and came to the edge of town, going south. Stopping before a house that had evidently been built since John's time, Tom sounded his horn.

"Didn't the fairgrounds used to stand about here?" John asked.

The doctor turned and nodded his head.

"Yes, just here," he said. He kept on sounding his horn, and a man and woman came out of the house and stood in the road beside the car.

"Let's get Maud and Alf and all go over to Lylse's Point," Tom said. John had indeed been taken into tow. For a time he wondered if he was to be introduced. "We got some hooch. Meet John Holden; used to live here years ago." At the fairgrounds, when John was a lad, Dave Grey, the livery man, used to work out his race horses in the early morning. Herman, who was a horse enthusiast, dreaming of someday becoming a horseman, came often to John's house in the early morning and the two boys went off to the fairgrounds without breakfast. Herman had got some sandwiches made of slices of bread and cold meat out of his mother's pantry. They went 'cross-lots, climbing fences and eating the sandwiches. In a meadow they had to cross there was heavy dew on the grass, and meadowlarks flew up before them. Herman had at least come somewhere near expressing in his life his youthful passion: he still lived about horses; he owned a dray. With a little inward qualm John wondered. Perhaps Herman ran a motor-truck.

The man and woman got into the car, the woman on the back seat with John, the husband in front with Tom, and they drove away to another house. John could not keep track of the streets they passed through. Occasionally he asked the woman, "What street are we in now?" They were joined by Maud and Alf, who also crowded into the back seat. Maud was a slender woman of twenty-eight or thirty, with yellow hair and blue eyes, and at once she seemed determined to make up to John. "I don't take more than an inch of room," she said, laughing and squeezing herself in between John and the first woman, whose name he could not later remember.

He had rather liked Maud. When the car had been driven some eighteen miles along a gravel road, they came to Lylse's farmhouse, which had been converted into a roadhouse, and got out. Maud had been silent most of the way, but she sat very close to John and as he felt cold and lonely, he was grateful for the warmth of her slender body. Occasionally she spoke to him in a half-whisper: "Ain't the night swell! Gee! I like it out in the dark this way."

Lylse's Point was at a bend of the Samson River, a small stream to which John as a lad had occasionally gone on fishing excursions with his father. Later he went out there several times with crowds of young fellows and their girls. They drove out then in Grey's old bus, and the trip out and back took several hours. On the way home at night they had great fun singing at the top of their voices and waking the sleeping farmers along the road. Occasionally some of the party got out and walked for a ways. It was a chance for a fellow to kiss his girl when the others could not see. By hurrying a little, they could easily enough catch up with the bus.

A rather heavy-faced Italian named Francisco owned Lylse's, and it had a dance hall and dining room. Drinks could be had if you knew the ropes, and it was evident the doctor and his friends were old acquaintances. At once they declared John should not buy anything, the declaration, in fact, being made before he had offered. "You're our guest now; don't you forget that. When we come sometime to your town, then it will be all right," Tom said. He laughed. "And that makes me think. I forgot your change," he said, handing John a five-dollar bill. The whisky got at the drugstore had been consumed on the way out, all except John and Maud drinking heartily. "I don't like the stuff. Do you, Mr. Holden?" Maud said and giggled. Twice during the trip out her fingers had crept over and touched lightly his fingers, and each time she had apologized. "Oh, do excuse me!" she said. John felt a little as he had felt earlier in the evening when the woman of the hotel had come to stand at the door of his room and had seemed reluctant about going away.

After they got out of the car at Lylse's, he felt uncomfortably old and queer. "What am I doing here with these people?" he kept asking himself. When they had got into the light, he stole a look at his watch. It was not yet nine o'clock. Several other cars, most of them, the doctor explained, from Yerington, stood before the door, and when they had taken several drinks of rather mild Italian red wine, all of the party except Maud and John went into the dance hall to dance. The doctor took John aside and whispered to him: "Lay off Maud," he said. He explained hurriedly that Alf and Maud had been having a row and that for several days they had not spoken to each other, although they lived in the same house, ate at the same table, and slept in the same bed. "He thinks she gets too gay with men," Tom explained. "You better look out a little."

The woman and man sat on a bench under a tree on the lawn before the house, and when the others had danced, they came out, bringing more drinks. Tom had got some more whisky. "It's moon but pretty good stuff," he declared. In the clear sky overhead stars were shining, and when the others were dancing, John turned his head and saw across the road and between the trees that lined its banks the stars reflected in the waters of the Samson. A light from the house fell on Maud's face, a strikingly lovely face in that light but, when looked at closely, rather petulant. "A good deal of the spoiled child in her," John thought.

She began asking him about life in the city of New York.

"I was there once, but for only three days. It was when I went to school in the East. A girl I knew lived there. She married a lawyer named Trigan, or something like that. You didn't know him, I guess."

And now there was a hungry, dissatisfied look on her face.

"God! I'd like to live in a place like that, not in this hole! There hadn't no man better tempt me." When she said that she giggled again. Once during the evening they walked across the dusty road and stood for a time by the river's edge but got back to the bench before the others finished their dance. Maud persistently refused to dance.

At ten-thirty, all of the others having got a little drunk, they drove back to town, Maud again sitting beside John. On the drive Alf went to sleep. Maud pressed her slender body against John's, and after two or three futile moves to which he made no special response, she boldly put her hand into his. The second woman and her husband talked with Tom of people they had seen at

Lylse's. "Do you think there's anything up between Fanny and Joe?" "No; I think she's on the square."

They got to John's hotel at eleven-thirty, and, bidding them all good night, he went upstairs. Alf had awakened. When they were parting, he leaned out of the car and looked closely at John. "What did you say your name was?" he asked.

John went up a dark stairway and sat on the bed in his room. Lillian had lost her looks. She had married, and her husband had divorced her. Joe was a trouble-shooter. He worked for the International Harvester Company, a swell mechanic. Herman was a drayman. He had five kids.

Three men in a room next to John's were playing poker. They laughed and talked, and their voices came clearly to John. "You think so, do you? Well, I'll prove you're wrong." A mild quarrel began. As it was summer, the windows of John's room were open, and he went to one to stand, looking out. A moon had come up, and he could see down into an alleyway. Two men came out of a street and stood in the alleyway, whispering. After they left, two cats crept along a roof and began a love-making scene. The game in the next room broke up. John could hear voices in the hallway.

"Now, forget it. I tell you, you're both wrong." John thought of his son at the camp up in Vermont. "I haven't written him a letter today." He felt guilty.

Opening his bag, he took out paper and sat down to write but after two or three attempts gave it up and put the paper away again. How fine the night had been as he sat on the bench beside the woman at Lylse's! Now the woman was in bed with her husband. They were not speaking to each other.

"Could I do it?" John asked himself, and then, for the first time that evening, a smile came to his lips.

"Why not?" he asked himself.

With his bag in his hand he went down the dark hallway and into the hotel office and began pounding on a desk. A fat old man with thin red hair and sleep-heavy eyes appeared from somewhere. John explained.

"I can't sleep. I think I'll drive on. I want to get to Pittsburgh and as I can't sleep, I might as well be driving." He paid his bill.

Then he asked the clerk to go and arouse the man in the garage, and gave him an extra dollar. "If I need gas, is there any place open?" he asked, but evidently the man did not hear. Perhaps he thought the question absurd.

He stood in the moonlight on the sidewalk before the door of the hotel and heard the clerk pounding on a door. Presently voices were heard, and the headlights of his car shone. The car appeared, driven by a boy. He seemed very alive and alert.

"I saw you out to Lylse's," he said, and, without being asked, went to look at the tank. "You're all right; you got 'most eight gallons," he assured John, who had climbed into the driver's seat.

How friendly the car, how friendly the night! John was not one who enjoyed fast driving, but he went out of the town at very high speed. "You go down two blocks, turn to your right, and go three. There you hit the cement. Go right straight to the east. You can't miss it."

John was taking the turns at racing speed. At the edge of town someone shouted to him from the darkness, but he did not stop. He hungered to get into the road going east.

"I'll let her out," he thought. "Lord! It will be fun! I'll let her out."

THERE SHE IS— SHE IS TAKING HER BATH

ANOTHER DAY WHEN I HAVE DONE NO WORK. IT IS MADDENING. I went to the office this morning as usual and tonight came home at the regular time. My wife and I live in an apartment in the Bronx, here in New York City, and we have no children. I am ten years older than she. Our apartment is on the second floor and there is a little hallway downstairs used by all the people in the building.

If I could only decide whether or not I am a fool, a man turned suddenly a little mad or a man whose honor has really been tampered with, I should be quite all right. Tonight I went home, after something most unusual had happened at the office, determined to tell everything to my wife. "I will tell her and then watch her face. If she blanches, then I will know all I suspect is true," I said to myself. Within the last two weeks everything about me has changed. I am no longer the same man. For example, I never in my life before used the word "blanched." What does it mean? How am I to tell whether my wife blanches or not when I do not know what the word means? It must be a word I saw in a book when I was a boy, perhaps a book of detective stories. But wait, I know how that happened to pop into my head.

But that is not what I started to tell you about. Tonight, as I have already said, I came home and climbed the stairs to our apartment.

When I got inside the house I spoke in a loud voice to my wife. "My dear, what are you doing?" I asked. My voice sounded strange.

"I am taking a bath," my wife answered.

And so you see she was at home taking a bath. There she was.

She is always pretending she loves me, but look at her now. Am I in her thoughts? Is there a tender look in her eyes? Is she dreaming of me as she walks along the streets?

You see she is smiling. There is a young man who has just passed her. He is a tall fellow with a little mustache and is smoking a cigarette. Now I ask you—is he one of the men who, like myself, does, in a way, keep the world going?

Once I knew a man who was president of a whist club. Well, he was something. People wanted to know how to play whist. They wrote to him. "If it turns out that after three cards are played the man to my right still has three cards while I have only two, etc., etc."

My friend, the man of whom I am now speaking, looks the matter up. "In rule four hundred and six you will see, etc., etc.," he writes.

My point is that he is of some account in the world. He helps keep things going and I respect him. Often we used to have lunch together.

But I am a little off the point. The fellows of whom I am now thinking, these young squirts who go through the streets ogling women—what do they do? They twirl their mustaches. They carry canes. Some honest man is supporting them too. Some fool is their father.

And such a fellow is walking in the street. He meets a woman like my wife, an honest woman without too much experience of life. He smiles. A tender look comes into his eyes. Such deceit. Such callow nonsense.

And how are the women to know? They are children. They know nothing. There is a man, working somewhere in an office, keeping things moving, but do they think of him?

The truth is the woman is flattered. A tender look, that should be saved and bestowed only upon her husband, is thrown away. One never knows what will happen.

But pshaw, if I am to tell you the story, let me begin. There are men everywhere who talk and talk, saying nothing. I am afraid I am becoming one of that kind. As I have already told you, I have come home from the office at evening and am standing in the hallway of our apartment, just inside the door. I have asked my wife what she is doing and she has told me she is taking a bath.

Very well, I am then a fool. I shall go out for a walk in the park. There is no use my not facing everything frankly. By facing everything frankly one gets everything quite cleared up.

Aha! The very devil has got into me now. I said I would remain cool and collected, but I am not cool. The truth is I am growing angry.

I am a small man but I tell you that, once aroused, I will fight. Once when I was a boy I fought another boy in the school yard. He gave me a black eye but I loosened one of his teeth. "There, take that and that. Now I have got you against a wall. I will muss your mustache. Give me that cane. I will break it over your head. I do not intend to kill you, young man. I intend to vindicate my honor. No, I will not let you go. Take that and that. When next you see a respectable married woman on the street, going to the store, behaving herself, do not look at her with a tender light in your eyes. What you had better do is to go to work. Get a job in a bank. Work your way up. You said I was an old goat but I will show you an old goat can butt. Take that and that."

Very well, you who read also think me a fool. You laugh. You smile. Look at me. You are walking along here in the park. You are leading a dog.

Where is your wife? What is she doing?

Well, suppose she is at home taking a bath. What is she thinking? If she is dreaming as she takes her bath, of whom is she dreaming?

I will tell you what, you who go along leading that dog, you may have no reason to suspect your wife, but you are in the same position as myself.

She was at home taking a bath and all day I had been sitting at my desk and thinking such thoughts. Under the circumstances I would never have had the temerity to go calmly off and take a bath. I admire my wife. Ha, ha. If she is innocent I admire her, of course, as a husband should, and if she is guilty I admire her even more. What nerve, what insouciance. There is something noble, something almost heroic, in her attitude toward me just at this time.

With me this day is like every day now. Well, you see, I have been sitting all day with my head in my hand thinking and thinking and while I have been doing that she has been going about leading her regular life.

She has got up in the morning and has had her breakfast sitting opposite her husband; that is, myself. Her husband has gone off to his office. Now she is speaking to our maid. She is going to the stores. She is sewing, perhaps making new curtains for the windows of our apartment.

There is the woman for you. Nero fiddled while Rome was burning. There was something of the woman in him.

A wife has been unfaithful to her husband. She has gone gayly off, let us say on the arm of a young blade. Who is he? He dances. He smokes cigarettes. When he is with his companions, his own kind of fellows, he laughs. "I have got me a woman," he says. "She is not very young but she is terrifically in love with me. It is very convenient." I have heard such fellows talk in the smoking cars on trains and in other places.

And there is the husband, a fellow like myself. Is he calm? Is he collected? Is he cool? His honor is perhaps being tampered with. He sits at his desk. He smokes a cigar. People come and go. He is thinking, thinking.

And what are his thoughts? They concern her. "Now she is still at home, in our apartment," he thinks. "Now she is walking along a street." What do you know of the secret life led by your wife? What do you know of her thoughts? Well, hello! You smoke a pipe. You put your hands in your pockets. For you, your life is all very well. You are gay and happy. "What does it matter, my wife is at home taking a bath," you are telling yourself. In your daily life you are, let us say, a useful man. You publish books, you run a store, you write advertisements. Sometimes you say to yourself, "I am lifting the burden off the shoulders of others." That makes you feel good. I sympathize with you. If you let me, or rather I should say, if we had met in the formal transactions of our regular occupations, I dare say we would be great friends. Well, we would have lunch together, not too often, but now and then. I would tell you of some real-estate deal and you would tell me what you had been doing. "I am glad we met! Call me up. Before you go away, have a cigar."

With me it is quite different. All today, for example, I have been in my office, but I have not worked. A man came in, a Mr. Albright. "Well, are you going to let that property go or are you going to hold on?" he said.

What property did he mean? What was he talking about?

You can see for yourself what a state I am in.

And now I must be going home. My wife will have finished taking her bath. We will sit down to dinner. Nothing of all this I have been speaking about will be mentioned at all. "John, what is the matter with you?" "Aha. There is nothing the matter. I am worried about business a little. A Mr. Albright came in. Shall I sell or shall I hold on?" The real thing that is on my mind shall not be mentioned at all. I will grow a little nervous. The coffee will be spilled on the tablecloth or I will upset my dessert.

"John, what is the matter with you?" What coolness. As I have already said, what insouciance.

What is the matter? Matter enough.

A week, two weeks, to be exact, just seventeen days ago, I was a happy man. I went about my affairs. In the morning I rode to my office in the subway, but, had I wished to do so, I could long ago have bought an automobile.

But no, long ago, my wife and I had agreed there should be no such silly extravagance. To tell the truth, just ten years ago I failed in business and had to put some property in my wife's name. I bring the papers home to her and she signs. That is the way it is done.

"Well, John," said my wife, "we will not get us any automobile." That was before the thing happened that so upset me. We were walking together in the park. "Mabel, shall we get us an automobile?" I asked. "No," she said, "we will not get us an automobile." "Our money," she has said more than a thousand times, "will be a comfort to us later."

A comfort indeed. What can be a comfort now that this thing has happened?

It was just two weeks, more than that, just seventeen days ago, that I went home from the office just as I came home tonight. Well, I walked in the same streets, passed the same stores.

I am puzzled as to what that Mr. Albright meant when he asked me if I intended to sell the property or hold on to it. I answered in a noncommittal way. "We'll see," I said. To what property did he refer? We must have had some previous conversation regarding the matter. A mere acquaintance does not come into your office and speak of property in that careless, one might say familiar, way without having previous conversation on the same subject.

As you see I am still a little confused. Even though I am facing things now, I am still, as you have guessed, somewhat confused. This morning I was in the bathroom, shaving as usual. I always shave in the morning, not in the evening, unless my wife and I are going out. I was shaving and my shaving brush dropped to the floor. I stooped to pick it up and struck my head on the bathtub. I only tell you this to show what a state I am in. It made a large bump on my head. My wife heard me groan and asked me what was the matter. "I struck my head," I said. Of course, one quite in control of his faculties does not hit his head on a bathtub when he knows it is there, and what man does not know where the bathtub stands in his own house?

But now I am thinking again of what happened, of what has upset me this way. I was going home on that evening just seventeen days ago. Well, I walked along, thinking nothing. When I reached our apartment building I went in, and there, lying on the floor in the little hallway in front, was a pink envelope with my wife's name, Mabel Smith, written on it. I picked it up thinking, "This is strange." It had perfume on it and there was no address, just the name Mabel Smith, written in a bold man's hand.

I quite automatically opened it and read.

Since I first met her twelve years ago at a party at Mr. Westley's house, there have never been any secrets between me and my wife; at least until that moment in the hallway seventeen days ago this evening, I had never thought there were any secrets between us. I have always opened her letters and she had always opened mine. I think it should be that way between a man and his wife. I know there are some who do not agree with me but what I have always argued is I am right.

I went to the party with Harry Selfridge and afterward took my wife home. I offered to get a cab. "Shall we have a cab?" I asked her. "No," she said, "let's walk." She was the daughter of a man in the furniture business and he has died since. Everyone thought he would leave her some money but he didn't. It turned out he owed almost all he was worth to a firm in Grand Rapids. Some would have been upset, but I wasn't. "I married you for love, my dear," I said to her on the night when her father died. We were walking home from his house, also in the Bronx, and it was raining a little, but we did not get very wet. "I married you for love," I said, and I meant what I said.

But to return to the note. "Dear Mabel," it said, "come to the park on Wednesday when the old goat has gone away. Wait for me on the bench near the animal cages where I met you before."

It was signed Bill. I put it in my pocket and went upstairs.

When I got into my apartment, I heard a man's voice. The voice was urging something upon my wife. Did the voice change when I came in? I walked boldly into our front room where my wife sat facing a young man who sat in another chair. He was tall and had a little mustache.

The man was pretending to be trying to sell my wife a patent carpet-sweeper, but just the same, when I sat down in a chair in the corner and remained there, keeping silent, they both became self-conscious. My wife, in fact, became positively excited. She got up out of her chair and said in a loud voice, "I tell you I do not want any carpet-sweeper."

The young man got up and went to the door and I followed. "Well, I had better be getting out of here," he was saying to himself. And so he had been intending to leave a note telling my wife to meet him in the park on Wednesday but at the last moment he had decided to take the risk of coming to our house. What he had probably thought was something like this: "Her husband may come and get the note out of the mail box." Then he decided to come and see her and had quite accidentally dropped the note in the hallway. Now he was frightened. One could see that. Such men as myself are small but we will fight sometimes.

He hurried to the door and I followed him into the hallway. There was another young man coming from the floor above, also with a carpet-sweeper in his hand. It is a pretty slick scheme, this carrying carpet-sweepers with them, the young men of this generation have worked out, but we older men are not to have the wool pulled over our eyes. I saw through everything at once. The second young man was a confederate and had been concealed in the hallway in order to warn the first young man of my approach. When I got upstairs, of course, the first young man was pretending to sell my wife a carpet-sweeper. Perhaps the second young man had tapped with the handle of the carpet-sweeper on the floor above. Now that I think of that I remember there was a tapping sound.

At the time, however, I did not think everything out as I have since done. I stood in the hallway with my back against the wall and watched them go down the stairs. One of them turned and laughed at me, but I did not say anything. I suppose I might have gone down the stairs after them and challenged them both to fight but what I thought was, "I won't."

And sure enough, just as I suspected from the first, it was the young man pretending to sell carpet-sweepers I had found sitting in my apartment with my wife, who had lost the note. When they got down to the hallway at the front of the house the man I had caught with my wife began to feel in his pocket. Then, as I leaned over the railing above, I saw him looking about the hallway. He laughed. "Say, Tom, I had a note to Mabel in my pocket. I intended to get a stamp at the post office and mail it. I had forgotten the street number. 'Oh, well,' I thought, 'I'll go see her!' I didn't want to bump into that old goat, her husband."

"You have bumped into him," I said to myself; "now we will see who will come out victorious."

I went into our apartment and closed the door.

For a long time, perhaps for ten minutes, I stood just inside the door of our apartment thinking and thinking, just as I have been doing ever since. Two or three times I tried to speak, to call out to my wife, to question her and find out the bitter truth at once but my voice failed me.

What was I to do? Was I to go to her, seize her by the wrists, force her down into a chair, make her confess at the risk of personal violence? I asked myself that question.

"No," I said to myself, "I will not do that. I will use finesse."

For a long time I stood there thinking. My world had tumbled down about my ears. When I tried to speak, the words would not come out of my mouth.

At last I did speak, quite calmly. There is something of the man of the world about me. When I am compelled to meet a situation I do it. "What are you doing?" I said to my wife, speaking in a calm voice. "I am taking a bath," she answered.

And so I left the house and came out here to the park to think, just as I have done tonight. On that night, and just as I came out at our front door, I did something I have not done since I was a boy. I am a deeply religious man but I swore. My wife and I have had a good many arguments as to whether or not a man in business should have dealings with those who do such things; that is to say, with men who swear. "I cannot refuse to sell a man a piece of property because he swears," I have always said. "Yes, you can," my wife says.

It only shows how little women know about business. What I have always maintained is I am right.

And I maintain too that we men must protect the integrity of our homes and our firesides. On that first night I walked about until dinner time and then went home. I had decided not to say anything for the present but to remain quiet and use finesse, but at dinner my hand trembled and I spilled the dessert on the tablecloth.

And a week later I went to see a detective.

But first something else happened. On Wednesday—I had found the note on Monday evening—I could not beat sitting in my office and thinking perhaps that that young squirt was meeting my wife in the park, so I went to the park myself.

Sure enough there was my wife sitting on a bench near the animal cages and knitting a sweater.

At first I thought I would conceal myself in some bushes but instead I went to where she was seated and sat down beside her. "How nice! What brings you here?" my wife said smiling. She looked at me with surprise in her eyes.

Was I to tell her or was I not to tell her? It was a moot question with me. "No," I said to myself. "I will not. I will go see a detective. My honor has no doubt already been tampered with and I shall find out." My naturally quick wits came to my rescue. Looking directly into my wife's eyes I said: "There was a paper to be signed and I had my own reasons for thinking you might be here, in the park."

As soon as I had spoken I could have torn out my tongue. However, she had noticed nothing and I took a paper out of my pocket and, handing her my fountain pen, asked her to sign; and when she had done so I hurried away. At first I thought perhaps I would linger about, in the distance, that is to say, but no, I decided not to do that. He will no doubt have his confederate on the watchout for me, I told myself.

And so on the next afternoon, I went to the office of the detective. He was a large man, and when I told him what I wanted he smiled. "I understand," he said, "we have many such cases. We'll track the guy down."

And so, you see, there it was. Everything was arranged. It was to cost me a pretty penny but my house was to be watched and I was to have a report on everything. To tell the truth, when everything was arranged I felt ashamed of myself. The man in the detective place—there were several men standing about—followed me to the door and put his hand on my shoulder. For some reason I don't understand, that made me mad. He kept patting me on the shoulder as though I were a little boy. "Don't worry. We'll manage everything," was what he said. It was all right. Business is business but for some reason I wanted to bang him in the face with my fist.

That's the way I am, you see. I can't make myself out. "Am I a fool, or am I a man among men?" I keep asking myself, and I can't get an answer.

After I had arranged with the detective I went home and didn't sleep all night long.

To tell the truth I began to wish I had never found that note. I suppose that is wrong of me. It makes me less a man perhaps, but it's the truth.

Well, you see, I couldn't sleep. "No matter what my wife was up to I could sleep now if I hadn't found that note," was what I said to myself. It was dreadful. I was ashamed of what I had done and at the same time ashamed of myself for being ashamed. I had done what any American man, who is a man at all, would have done, and there I was. I couldn't sleep. Every time I came home in the evening I kept thinking: "There is that man standing over there by a tree—I'll bet he is a detective." I kept thinking of the fellow who had patted me on the shoulders in the detective office, and every time I thought of him I grew madder and madder. Pretty soon I hated him more than I did the young man who had pretended to sell the carpet-sweeper to Mabel.

And then I did the most foolish thing of all. One afternoon— it was just a week ago—I thought of something. When I had been in the detective office I had seen several men standing about but had not been introduced to any of them. "And so," I thought, "I'll go there pretending to get my reports. If the man I engaged is not there I'll engage someone else."

So I did it. I went to the detective office, and sure enough my man was out. There was another fellow sitting by a desk and I made a sign to him. We went into an inner office. "Look here," I whispered; you see I had made up my mind to pretend I was the man who was ruining my own fireside, wrecking my own honor. "Do I make clear what I mean?"

It was like this, you see—well, I had to have some sleep, didn't I? Only the night before my wife had said to me, "John, I think you had better run away for a little vacation. Run away by yourself for a time and forget about business."

At another time her saying that would have been nice, you see, but now it only upset me worse than ever. "She wants me out of the way," I thought, and for just a moment I felt like jumping up and telling her everything I knew. Still I didn't. "I'll just keep quiet. I'll use finesse," I thought.

A pretty kind of finesse. There I was in that detective office again hiring a second detective. I came right out and pretended I was my wife's paramour. The man kept nodding his head and I kept whispering like a fool. Well, I told him that a man named Smith had hired a detective from that office to watch his wife. "I have my own reasons for wanting him to get a report that his wife is all right," I said, pushing some money across a table toward him. I had become utterly reckless about money. "Here is fifty dollars and when he gets such a report from your office you come to me and you may have two hundred more," I said.

I had thought everything out. I told the second man my name was Jones and that I worked in the same office with Smith. "I'm in business with him," I said, "a silent partner, you see."

Then I went out and, of course, he, like the first one, followed me to the door and patted me on the shoulder. That was the hardest thing of all to stand, but I stood it. A man has to have sleep.

And, of course, today both men had to come to my office within five minutes of each other. The first one came, of course, and told me my wife was innocent. "She is as innocent as a little lamb," he said. "I congratulate you upon having such an innocent wife."

Then I paid him, backing away so he couldn't pat me on the shoulders, and he had only just closed the door when in came the other man, asking for Jones.

And I had to see him too and give him two hundred dollars.

Then I decided to come on home, and I did, walking along the same street I have walked on every afternoon since my wife and I married. I went home and climbed the stairs to our apartment just as I described everything to you a little while ago. I could not decide whether I was a fool, a man who has gone a little mad, or a man whose honor has been tampered with, but anyway I knew there would be no detectives about.

What I thought was that I would go home and have everything out with my wife, tell her of my suspicions and then watch her face. As I have said before, I intended to watch her face and see if she blanched when I told her of the note I had found in the hallway downstairs. The word "blanched" got into my mind because I once read it in a detective story when I was a boy and I had been dealing with detectives.

And so I intended to face my wife down, force a confession from her, but you see how it turned out. When I got home the apartment was silent and at first I thought it was empty. "Has she run away with him?" I asked myself, and maybe my own face blanched a little.

"Where are you, dear, what are you doing?" I shouted in a loud voice and she told me she was taking a bath.

And so I came out here in the park.

But now I must be going home. Dinner will be waiting. I am wondering what property that Mr. Albright had in his mind. When I sit at dinner with my wife my hands will shake. I will spill the dessert. A man does not come in and speak of property in that offhand manner unless there has been conversation about it before.

IN A STRANGE TOWN

A MORNING IN A COUNTRY TOWN IN A STRANGE PLACE. EVERYTHING is quiet. No, there are sounds. Sounds assert themselves. A boy whistles. I can hear the sound here, where I stand, at a railroad station. I have come away from home. I am in a strange place. There is no such thing as silence. Once I was in the country. I was at the house of a friend. "You see, there is not a sound here. It is absolutely silent." My friend said that because he was used to the little sounds of the place, the humming of insects, the sound of falling water—far-off—the faint clattering sound of a man with a machine in the distance, cutting hay. He was accustomed to the sounds and did not hear them. Here, where I am now, I hear a beating sound. Someone has hung a carpet on a clothes-line and is beating it. Another boy shouts, far off—"A-ho, a-ho."

It is good to go and come. You arrive in a strange place. There is a street facing a railroad track. You get off a train with your bags. Two porters fight for possession of you and the bags as you have seen porters do with strangers in your own town.

As you stand at the station there are things to be seen. You see the open doors of the stores on the street that faces the station. People go in and out. An old man stops and looks. "Why, there is the morning train," his mind is saying to him.

The mind is always saying such things to people. "Look, be

aware," it says. The fancy wants to float free of the body. We put a stop to that.

Most of us live our lives like toads, sitting perfectly still under a plantain leaf. We are waiting for a fly to come our way. When it comes out darts the tongue. We nab it.

That is all. We eat it.

But how many questions to be asked that are never asked. Whence came the fly? Where was he going?

The fly might have been going to meet his sweetheart. He was stopped; a spider ate him.

The train on which I have been riding, a slow one, pauses for a time. All right, I'll go to the Empire House. As though I cared.

It is a small town—this one—to which I have come. In any event I'll be uncomfortable here. There will be the same kind of cheap brass beds as at the last place to which I went unexpectedly like this—with bugs in the bed perhaps. A traveling salesman will talk in a loud voice in the next room. He will be talking to a friend, another traveling salesman. "Trade is bad," one of them will say. "Yes, it's rotten."

There will be confidences about women picked up—some words heard, others missed. That is always annoying.

But why did I get off the train here at this particular town? I remember that I had been told there was a lake here—that there was fishing. I thought I would go fishing.

Perhaps I expected to swim. I remember now.

"Porter, where is the Empire House? Oh, the brick one. All right, go ahead. I'll be along pretty soon. You tell the clerk to save me a room, with a bath, if they have one."

I remember what I was thinking about. All my life, since that happened, I have gone off on adventures like this. A man likes to be alone sometimes.

Being alone doesn't mean being where there are no people. It means being where people are all strangers to you.

There is a woman crying there. She is getting old, that woman.

Well, I am myself no longer young. See how tired her eyes are. There is a younger woman with her. In time that younger woman will look exactly like her mother.

She will have the same patient, resigned look. The skin will sag on her cheeks that are plump now. The mother has a large nose and so has the daughter.

There is a man with them. He is fat and has red veins in his face. For some reason I think he must be a butcher.

He has that kind of hands, that kind of eyes.

I am pretty sure he is the woman's brother. Her husband is dead. They are putting a coffin on the train.

They are people of no importance. People pass them casually. No one has come to the station to be with them in their hour of trouble. I wonder if they live here. Yes, of course they do. They live somewhere, in a rather mean little house, at the edge of town, or perhaps outside the town. You see the brother is not going away with the mother and daughter. He has just come down to see them off.

They are going, with the body, to another town where the husband, who is dead, formerly lived.

The butcher-like man has taken his sister's arm. That is a gesture of tenderness. Such people make such gestures only when someone in the family is dead.

The sun shines. The conductor of the train is walking along the station platform and talking to the station-master. They have been laughing loudly, having their little joke.

That conductor is one of the jolly sort. His eyes twinkle, as the saying is. He has his little joke with every station-master, every telegraph operator, baggage man, express man, along the way. There are all kinds of conductors of passenger trains.

There, you see, they are passing the woman whose husband has died and is being taken away somewhere to be buried. They drop their jokes, their laugher. They become silent.

A little path of silence made by that woman in black and her daughter and the fat brother. The little path of silence has started with them at their house, has gone with them along streets to the railroad station, will be with them on the train and in the town to which they are going. They are people of no importance, but they have suddenly become important.

They are symbols of Death. Death is an important, a majestic thing, eh?

How easily you can comprehend a whole life, when you are in a place like this, in a strange place, among strange people. Everything is so much like other towns you have been in. Lives are made up of little series of circumstances. They repeat themselves, over and over, in towns everywhere, in cities, in all countries.

They are of infinite variety. In Paris, when I was there last year, I went into the Louvre. There were men and women there, making copies of the works of the old masters that were hung on the walls. They were professional copyists.

They worked painstakingly, were trained to do just that kind of work, very exactly.

And yet no one of them could make a copy. There were no copies made.

The little circumstances of no two lives anywhere in the world are just alike.

You see I have come over into a hotel room now, in this strange town. It is a country-town hotel. There are flies in here. A fly has just alighted on this paper on which I have been writing these impressions. I stopped writing and looked at the fly. There must be billions of flies in the world and yet, I dare say, no two of them are alike.

The circumstances of their lives are not just alike.

I think I must come away from my own place on trips, such as I am on now, for a specific reason.

At home I live in a certain house. There is my own household, the servants, the people of my household. I am a professor of philosophy in a college in my town, hold a certain definite position there, in the town life and in the college life.

Conversations in the evening, music, people coming into our house.

Myself going to a certain office, then to a classroom where I lecture, seeing people there.

I know some things about these people. That is the trouble with me perhaps. I know something but not enough.

My mind, my fancy, becomes dulled looking at them.

I know too much and not enough.

It is like a house in the street in which I live. There is a particular house in that street—in my home town—I was formerly very curious about. For some reason the people who lived in it were recluses. They seldom came out of their house and hardly ever out of the yard, into the street.

Well, what of all that?

My curiosity was aroused. That is all.

I used to walk past the house with something strangely alive in me. I had figured out this much. An old man with a beard and a white-faced woman lived there. There was a tall hedge and once I looked through. I saw the man walking nervously up and down on a bit of lawn under a tree. He was clasping and unclasping his hands and muttering words. The doors and shutters of the mysterious house were all closed. As I looked, the old woman with the white face opened the door a little and looked out at the man. Then the door closed again. She said nothing to him. Did she look at him with love or with fear in her eyes? How do I know? I could not see.

Another time I heard a young woman's voice, although I never saw a young woman about the place. It was evening and the woman was singing—a rather sweet young woman's voice it was.

There you are. That is all. Life is more like that than people suppose. Little odd fragmentary ends of things. That is about all we get. I used to walk past that place all alive, curious. I enjoyed it. My heart thumped a little.

I heard sounds more distinctly, felt more.

I was curious enough to ask my friends along the street about the people.

"They're queer," people said.

Well, who is not queer?

The point is that my curiosity gradually died. I accepted the queerness of the life of that house. It became a part of the life of my street. I became dulled to it.

I have become dulled to the life of my own house or my street, to the lives of my pupils.

"Where am I? Who am I? Whence came I?" Who asks himself these questions any more?

There is that woman I saw taking her dead husband away on the train. I saw her only for a moment before I walked over to this hotel and came up to this room (an entirely commonplace hotel room it is) but here I sit, thinking of her. I reconstruct her life, go on living the rest of her life with her.

Often I do things like this, come off alone to a strange place like this. "Where are you going?" my wife says to me. "I am going to take a bath," I say.

My wife thinks I am a bit queer too, but she has grown used to me. Thank God, she is a patient and a good-natured woman.

"I am going to bathe myself in the lives of people about whom I know nothing."

I will sit in this hotel until I am tired of it and then I will walk in strange streets, see strange houses, strange faces. People will see me.

Who is he?

He is a stranger.

That is nice. I like that. To be a stranger sometimes, going about in a strange place, having no business there, just walking, thinking, bathing myself.

To give others, the people here in this strange place, a little jump at the heart too—because I am something strange.

Once, when I was a young man I would have tried to pick up a girl. Being in a strange place, I would have tried to get my jump at the heart out of trying to be with her.

Now I do not do that. It is not because I am especially faithful—as the saying goes—to my wife, or that I am not interested in strange and attractive women.

It is because of something else. It may be that I am a bit dirty with life and have come here, to this strange place, to bathe myself in strange life and get clean and fresh again.

And so I walk in such a strange place. I dream. I let myself have fancies. Already I have been out into the street, into several streets of this town, and have walked about. I have aroused in myself a little stream of fresh fancies, clustered about strange lives, and as I walked, being a stranger, going along slowly, carrying a cane, stopping to look into stores, stopping to look into the windows of houses and into gardens, I have, you see, aroused in others something of the same feeling that has been in me.

I have liked that. Tonight, in the houses of this town, there will be something to speak of.

"There was a strange man about. He acted queerly. I wonder who he was."

"What did he look like?"

An attempt to delve into me too, to describe me. Pictures being made in other minds. A little current of thoughts, fancies, started in others, in me too.

I sit here in this room in this strange town, in this hotel, feeling oddly refreshed. Already I have slept here. My sleep was sweet. Now it is morning and everything is still. I dare say that, some time today, I shall get on another train and go home.

But now I am remembering things.

Yesterday, in this town, I was in a barber shop. I got my hair cut. I hate getting my hair cut.

"I am in a strange town with nothing to do, so I'll get my hair cut," I said to myself as I went in.

A man cut my hair. "It rained a week ago," he said. "Yes," I said. That is all the conversation there was between us.

However, there was other talk in that barber shop, plenty of it.

A man had been here in this town and had passed some bad checks. One of them was for ten dollars and was made out in the name of one of the barbers in the shop.

The man who passed the checks was a stranger, like myself. There was talk of that.

A man came in who looked like President Coolidge and had his hair cut.

Then there was another man who came for a shave. He was an old man with sunken cheeks and for some reason looked like a sailor. I dare say he was just a farmer. This town is not by the sea.

There was talk enough in there, a whirl of talk.

I came out thinking.

Well, with me it is like this. A while ago I was speaking of a habit I have formed of going suddenly off like this to some strange place. "I have been doing it ever since it happened," I said. I used the expression "it happened."

Well, what happened?

Not so very much.

A girl got killed. She was struck by an automobile. She was a girl in one of my classes.

She was nothing special to me. She was just a girl—a woman, really—in one of my classes. When she was killed I was already married.

She used to come into my room, into my office. We used to sit in there and talk.

We used to sit and talk about something I had said in my lecture.

"Did you mean this?"

"No, that is not exactly it. It is rather like this."

I suppose you know how we philosophers talk. We have almost a language of our own. Sometimes I think it is largely nonsense.

I would begin talking to that girl—that woman—and on and on I would go. She had gray eyes. There was a sweet serious look on her face.

Do you know, sometimes, when I talked to her like that (it is, I am pretty sure, all nonsense), well, I thought ...

Her eyes seemed to me sometimes to grow a little larger as I talked to her. I had a notion she did not hear what I said.

I did not care much.

I talked so that I would have something to say.

Sometimes, when we were together that way, in my office in the college building, there would come odd times of silence.

No, it was not silence. There were sounds.

There was a man walking in a hallway, in the college building outside my door. Once when this happened I counted the man's footsteps. Twenty-six, twenty-seven, twenty-eight.

I was looking at the girl—the woman—and she was looking at me.

You see I was an older man. I was married.

I am not such an attractive man. I did, however, think she was very beautiful. There were plenty of young fellows about.

I remember now that when she had been with me like that—after she had left—I used to sit sometimes for hours alone in my office, as I have been sitting here, in this hotel room, in a strange town.

I sat thinking of nothing. Sounds came in to me. I remembered things of my boyhood.

I remembered things about my courtship and my marriage. I sat like that dumbly, a long time.

I was dumb, but I was at the same time more aware than I had ever been in my life.

It was at that time I got the reputation with my wife of being a little queer. I used to go home, after sitting dumbly like that, with that girl, that woman, and I was even more dumb and silent when I got home.

"Why don't you talk?" my wife said.

"I'm thinking," I said.

I wanted her to believe that I was thinking of my work, my studies. Perhaps I was.

Well, the girl, the woman, was killed. An automobile struck her when she was crossing a street. They said she was absent-minded—that she walked right in front of a car. I was in my office, sitting there, when a man, another professor, came in and told me. "She is quite dead, was quite dead when they picked her up," he said.

"Yes." I dare say he thought I was pretty cold and unsympathetic—a scholar, eh, having no heart.

"It was not the driver's fault. He was quite blameless."

"She walked right out in front of the car?"

"Yes."

I remember that at the moment I was fingering a pencil. I did not move. I must have been sitting like that for two or three hours.

I got out and walked. I was walking when I saw a train. So I got on.

Afterward I telephoned to my wife. I don't remember what I told her at that time.

It was all right with her. I made some excuse. She is a patient and a good-natured woman. We have four children. I dare say she is absorbed in the children.

I came to a strange town and I walked about there. I forced myself to observe the little details of life. That time I stayed three or four days and then I went home.

At intervals I have been doing the same thing ever since. It is because at home I grow dull to little things. Being in a strange place like this makes me more aware. I like it. It makes me more alive.

So you see, it is morning and I have been in a strange town, where I know no one and where no one knows me.

As it was yesterday morning, when I came here, to this hotel room, there are sounds. A boy whistles in the street. Another boy, far off, shouts "A-ho."

There are voices in the street, below my window, strange voices. Someone, somewhere in this town, is beating a carpet. I hear the sound of the arrival of a train. The sun is shining.

I may stay here in this town another day or I may go on to another town. No one knows where I am. I am taking this bath in life, as you see, and when I have had enough of it I shall go home feeling refreshed.

THESE
MOUNTAINEERS

WHEN I HAD LIVED IN THE SOUTHWEST VIRGINIA MOUNTAINS FOR
some time, people of the North, when I went up there, used to
ask me many questions about the mountain people. They did it
whenever I went to the city. You know how people are. They like
to have everything ticketed.

The rich are so and so, the poor are so and so, the politicians,
the people of the western coast. As though you could draw one
figure and say—"There it is. That's it."

The men and women of the mountains were what they were.
They were people. They were poor whites. That certainly meant
that they were white and poor. Also they were mountaineers.

After the factories began to come down into this country, into
Virginia, Tennessee and North Carolina, a lot of them went, with
their families, to work in the factories and to live in mill towns.
For a time all was peace and quiet, and then strikes broke out.
Everyone who reads newspapers knows about that. There was a
lot of writing in newspapers about these mountain people. Some
of it was pretty keen.

But there had been a lot of romancing about them before that.
That sort of thing never did anyone much good.

So I was walking alone in the mountains and had got down
into what in the mountain country is called "a hollow." I was

lost. I had been fishing for trout in mountain streams and was tired and hungry. There was a road of a sort I had got into. It would have been difficult to get a car over that road. "This ought to be a good whisky-making country," I thought.

In the hollow along which the road went I came to a little town. Well now, you would hardly call it a town. There were six or eight little unpainted frame houses and, at a crossroads, a general store.

The mountains stretched away, above the poor little houses. On both sides of the road were the magnificent hills. You understand, when you have been down there, why they are called the "Blue Ridge." They are always blue, a glorious blue. What a country it must have been before the lumber men came! Over near my place in the mountains men were always talking of the spruce forests of former days. Many of them worked in the lumber camps. They speak of soft moss into which a man sank almost to the knees, the silence of the forest, the great trees.

The great forest is gone now, but the young trees are growing. Much of the country will grow nothing but timber.

The store before which I stood that day was closed, but an old man sat on a little porch in front. He said that the storekeeper also carried the mail and was out on his route but that he would be back and open his store in an hour or two.

I had thought I might at least get some cheese and crackers or a can of sardines.

The man on the porch was old. He was an evil-looking old man. He had gray hair and a gray beard and might have been seventy, but I could see that he was a tough-bodied old fellow.

I asked my way back over the mountain to the main road and had started to move off up the hollow when he called to me. "Are you the man who has moved in here from the North and has built a house in here?"

There is no use my trying to reproduce the mountain speech. I am not skilled at it.

The old man invited me to his house to eat. "You don't mind eating beans, do you?" he asked.

I was hungry and would be glad to have beans. I would have eaten anything at the moment. He said he hadn't any woman, that his old woman was dead. "Come on," he said, "I think I can fix you up."

We went up a path, over a half mountain and into another hollow, perhaps a mile away. It was amazing. The man was old. The skin on his face and neck was wrinkled like an old man's skin and his legs and body were thin, but he walked at such a pace that to follow him kept me panting.

It was a hot, still day in the hills. Not a breath of air stirred. That old man was the only being I saw that day in that town. If anyone else lived there he had kept out of sight.

The old man's house was on the bank of another mountain stream. That afternoon, after eating with him, I got some fine trout out of the stream.

But this isn't a fishing story. We went to his house.

It was dirty and small and seemed about to fall down. The old man was dirty. There were layers of dirt on his old hands and on his wrinkled neck. When we were in the house, which had but one room on the ground floor, he went to a small stove. "The fire is out," he said. "Do you care if the beans are cold?"

"No," I said. By this time I did not want any beans and wished I had not come. There was something evil about this old mountain man. Surely the romancers could not have made much out of him.

Unless they played on the Southern hospitality chord. He had invited me there. I had been hungry. The beans were all he had.

He put some of them on a plate and put them on a table before me. The table was a home-made one covered with a red oil cloth, now quite worn. There were large holes in it. Dirt and grease clung about the edges of the holes. He had wiped the plate, on which he had put the beans, on the sleeve of his coat.

But perhaps you have not eaten beans prepared in the mountains, in the mountain way. They are the staff of life down there. Without beans there would be no life in some of the hills. The beans are, when prepared by a mountain woman and served hot, often delicious. I do not know what they put in them or how they cook them, but they are unlike any beans you will find anywhere else in the world.

As Smithfield ham, when it is real Smithfield ham, is unlike any other ham.

But beans cold, beans dirty, beans served on a plate wiped on the sleeve of that coat ...

I sat looking about. There was a dirty bed in the room in which we sat and an open stairway, leading up to the room above.

Someone moved up there. Someone walked barefooted across the floor. There was silence for a time and then it happened again.

You must get the picture of a very hot still place between hills. It was June. The old man had become silent. He was watching me. Perhaps he wanted to see whether or not I was going to scorn his hospitality. I began eating the beans with a dirty spoon. I was many miles away from any place I had ever been before.

And then there was that sound again. I had got the impression that the old man had told me his wife was dead, that he lived alone.

How did I know it was a woman upstairs? I did know.

"Have you got a woman up there?" I asked. He grinned, a toothless malicious grin, as though to say, "Oh, you're curious, eh?"

And then he laughed, a queer cackle.

"She ain't mine," he said.

We sat in silence after that and then there was the sound again. I heard bare feet walking across a plank floor.

Now the feet were descending the crude open stairs. Two legs appeared, two thin young girl's legs.

She didn't look to be over twelve or thirteen.

She came down, almost to the foot of the stairs, and then stopped and sat down.

How dirty she was, how thin, what a wild look she had! I have never seen a wilder-looking creature. Her eyes were bright. They were like the eyes of a wild animal.

And, at that, there was something about her face. In many of

these young mountain faces there is a look it is difficult to explain—
it is a look of breeding, of aristocracy. I know no other word for
the look.

And she had it.

And now the two were sitting there, and I was trying to eat.
Suppose I rose and threw the dirty beans out at the open door. I
might have said, "Thank you, I have enough." I didn't dare.

But perhaps they weren't thinking of the beans. The old man
began to speak of the girl, sitting ten feet from him, as though
she were not there.

"She ain't mine," he said. "She came here. Her pop died. She
ain't got anyone."

I am making a bad job of trying to reproduce his speech.

He was giggling now, a toothless old man's giggle. "Ha, she
won't eat."

"She's a hellcat," he said.

He reached over and touched me on the arm. "You know what.
She's a hellcat. You couldn't satisfy her. She had to have her a
man.

"And she got one too."

"Is she married?" I asked, half whispering the words, not wanting
her to hear.

He laughed at the idea. "Ha. Married, eh?"

He said it was a young man from farther down the hollow.
"He lives here with us," the old man said laughing, and as he said
it the girl rose and started back up the stairs. She had said nothing,
but her young eyes had looked at us, filled with hatred. As she
went up the stairs the old man kept laughing at her, his queer,
high-pitched, old man's laugh. It was really a giggle. "Ha, she
can't eat. When she tries to eat she can't keep it down. She thinks
I don't know why. She's a hellcat. She would have a man and
now she's got one.

"Now she can't eat."

I fished in the creek in the hollow during the afternoon and
toward evening began to get trout. They were fine ones. I got
fourteen of them and got back over a mountain and into the

main road before dark.

What took me back into the hollow I don't know. The face of the girl possessed me.

And then there was good trout fishing there. That stream at least had not been fished out.

When I went back I put a twenty-dollar bill in my pocket. "Well," I thought—I hardly know what I did think. There were notions in my head, of course.

The girl was very, very young.

"She might have been kept there by that old man," I thought, "and by some young mountain rough. There might be a chance for her."

I thought I would give her the twenty dollars. "If she wants to get out perhaps she can," I thought. Twenty dollars is a lot of money in the hills.

It was just another hot day when I got in there again and the old man was not at home. At first I thought there was no one there. The house stood alone by a hardly discernible road and near the creek. The creek was clear and had a swift current. It made a chattering sound.

I stood on the bank of the creek before the house and tried to think.

"If I interfere ..."

Well, let's admit it. I was a bit afraid. I thought I had been a fool to come back.

And then the girl suddenly came out of the house and came toward me. There was no doubt about it. She was that way. And unmarried, of course.

At least my money, if I could give it to her, would serve to buy her some clothes. The ones she had on were very ragged and dirty. Her feet and legs were bare. It would be winter by the time the child was born.

A man came out of the house. He was a tall young mountain man. He looked rough. "That's him," I thought. He said nothing.

He was dirty and unkempt as the old man had been and as the child was.

At any rate she was not afraid of me. "Hello, you are back here," she said. Her voice was clear.

Just the same I saw the hatred in her eyes. I asked about the fishing. "Are the trout biting?" I asked. She had come nearer me now, and the young man had slouched back into the house.

Again I am at a loss about how to reproduce her mountain speech. It is peculiar. So much is in the voice.

Hers was cold and clear and filled with hatred.

"How should I know? He" (indicating with a gesture of her hand the tall slouching figure who had gone into the house) "is too damn lazy to fish.

"He's too damn lazy for anything on earth."

She was glaring at me.

"Well," I thought, "I will at least try to give her the money." I took the bill in my hand and held it toward her. "You will need some clothes," I said. "Take it and buy yourself some clothes."

It may have been that I had touched her mountain pride. How am I to know? The look of hatred in her eyes seemed to grow more intense.

"You go to hell," she said. "You get out of here. And don't you come back in here again."

She was looking hard at me when she said this. If you have never known such people who live like that, "on the outer fringe of life," as we writers say (you may see them sometimes in the tenement districts of cities as well as in the lonely and lovely hills)— such a queer look of maturity in the eyes of a child...

It sends a shiver through you. Such a child knows too much and not enough. Before she went back into the house she turned and spoke to me again. It was about my money.

She told me to put it somewhere, I won't say where. The most modern of modern writers has to use some discretion.

Then she went into the house. That was all. I left. What was I to do? After all, a man looks after his hide. In spite of the trout I did not go fishing in that hollow again.

A MEETING SOUTH

HE TOLD ME THE STORY OF HIS ILL FORTUNE—A CRACK-UP IN AN airplane—with a very gentlemanly little smile on his very sensitive, rather thin lips. Such things happened. He might well have been speaking of another. I liked his tone and I liked him.

This happened in New Orleans, where I had gone to live. When he came, my friend, Fred, for whom he was looking, had gone away, but immediately I felt a strong desire to know him better and so suggested we spend the evening together. When we went down the stairs from my apartment I noticed that he was a cripple. The slight limp, the look of pain that occasionally drifted across his face, the little laugh that was intended to be jolly but did not quite achieve its purpose, all these things began at once to tell me the story I have now set myself to write.

"I shall take him to see Aunt Sally," I thought. One does not take every caller to Aunt Sally. However, when she is in fine feather, when she has taken a fancy to her visitor, there is no one like her. Although she has lived in New Orleans for thirty years, Aunt Sally is Middle Western, born and bred.

However I am plunging a bit too abruptly into my story.

First of all I must speak more of my guest, and for convenience's sake I shall call him David. I felt at once that he would be wanting a drink and in New Orleans—dear city of Latins and hot night1ws—

even in Prohibition times such things can be managed. We achieved several and my own head became somewhat shaky but I could see that what we had taken had not affected him. Evening was coming, the abrupt waning of the day and the quick smoky soft-footed coming of night, characteristic of the semi-tropic city, when he produced a bottle from his hip pocket. It was so large that I was amazed. How had it happened that the carrying of so large a bottle had not made him look deformed? His body was very small and delicately built. "Perhaps, like the kangaroo, his body has developed some kind of a natural pouch for taking care of supplies," I thought. Really he walked as one might fancy a kangaroo would walk when out for a quiet evening stroll. I went along thinking of Darwin and the marvels of Prohibition. "We are a wonderful people, we Americans," I thought. We were both in fine humor and had begun to like each other immensely.

He explained the bottle. The stuff, he said, was made by a Negro man on his father's plantation somewhere over in Alabama. We sat on the steps of a vacant house deep down in the old French Quarter of New Orleans — the Vieux Carré — while he explained that his father had no intention of breaking the law— that is to say, in so far as the law remained reasonable. "Our nigger just makes whisky for us," he said. "We keep him for that purpose. He doesn't have anything else to do, just makes the family whisky, that's all. If he went selling any, we'd raise hell with him. I dare say Dad would shoot him if he caught him up to any such unlawful trick, and you bet, Jim, our nigger I'm telling you of, knows it too.

"He's a good whisky-maker, though, don't you think?" David added. He talked of Jim in a warm friendly way. "Lord, he's been with us always, was born with us. His wife cooks for us and Jim makes our whisky. It's a race to see which is best at his job, but I think Jim will win. He's getting a little better all the time and all of our family—well, I reckon we just like and need our whisky more than we do our food."

Do you know New Orleans? Have you lived there in the summer

when it is hot, in the winter when it rains, and through the glorious
late fall days? Some of its own, more progressive, people scorn it
now. In New Orleans there is a sense of shame because the city is
not more like Chicago or Pittsburgh.

It, however, suited David and me. We walked slowly, on account
of his bad leg, through many streets of the Old Town, Negro
women laughing all around us in the dusk, shadows playing over
old buildings, children with their shrill cries dodging in and out
of old hallways. The old city was once almost altogether French,
but now it is becoming more and more Italian. It however remains
Latin. People live out of doors. Families were sitting down to
dinner within full sight of the street—all doors and windows open.
A man and his wife quarreled in Italian. In a patio back of an old
building a Negress sang a French song.

We came out of the narrow little streets and had a drink in
front of the dark cathedral and another in a little square in front.
There is a statue of General Jackson, always taking off his hat to
Northern tourists who in winter come down to see the city. At
his horse's feet an inscription—"The Union must and will be
preserved." We drank solemnly to that declaration and the general
seemed to bow a bit lower. "He was sure a proud man," David
said, as we went over toward the docks to sit in the darkness and
look at the Mississippi. All good New Orleanians go to look at
the Mississippi at least once a day. At night it is like creeping into
a dark bedroom to look at a sleeping child—something of that
sort—gives you the same warm nice feeling, I mean. David is a
poet and so in the darkness by the river we spoke of Keats and
Shelley, the two English poets all good Southern men love.

All of this, you are to understand, was before I took him to
see Aunt Sally.

Both Aunt Sally and myself are Middle Westerners. We are
but guests down here, but perhaps we both in some queer way
belong to this city. Something of the sort is in the wind. I don't
quite know how it has happened.

A great many Northern men and women come down our
way and, when they go back North, write things about the South.

The trick is to write nigger stories. The North likes them. They are so amusing. One of the best-known writers of nigger stories was down here recently and a man I know, a Southern man, went to call on him. The writer seemed a bit nervous. "I don't know much about the South or Southerners," he said. "But you have your reputation," my friend said. "You are so widely known as a writer about the South and about Negro life." The writer had a notion he was being made sport of. "Now look here," he said, "I don't claim to be a highbrow. I'm a businessman myself. At home, up North, I associate mostly with businessmen and when I am not at work I go out to the country club. I want you to understand I am not setting myself up as a highbrow.

"I give them what they want," he said. My friend said he appeared angry. "About what now, do you fancy?" he asked innocently.

However, I am not thinking of the Northern writer of Negro stories. I am thinking of the Southern poet, with the bottle clasped firmly in his hands, sitting in the darkness beside me on the docks facing the Mississippi.

He spoke at some length of his gift for drinking. "I didn't always have it. It is a thing built up," he said. The story of how he chanced to be a cripple came out slowly. You are to remember that my own head was a bit unsteady. In the darkness the river, very deep and very powerful off New Orleans, was creeping away to the gulf. The whole river seemed to move away from us and then to slip noiselessly into the darkness like a vast moving sidewalk.

When he had first come to me in the late afternoon, and when we had started for our walk together, I had noticed that one of his legs dragged as we went along and that he kept putting a thin hand to an equally thin cheek.

Sitting over by the river, he explained as a boy would explain when he has stubbed his toe running down a hill.

When the World War broke out he went over to England and managed to get himself enrolled as an aviator, very much, I gathered, in the spirit in which a countryman, in a city for a night, might take in a show.

The English had been glad enough to take him on. He was

one more man. They were glad enough to take anyone on just then. He was small and delicately built but after he got in he turned out to be a first-rate flyer, serving all through the war with a British flying squadron, but at the last got into a crash and fell.

Both legs were broken, one of them in three places, the scalp was badly torn and some of the bones of the face had been splintered.

They had put him into a field hospital and had patched him up. "It was my fault if the job was rather bungled," he said. "You see it was a field hospital, a hell of a place. Men were torn all to pieces, groaning and dying. Then they moved me back to a base hospital and it wasn't much better. The fellow who had the bed next to mine had shot himself in the foot to avoid going into a battle. A lot of them did that, but why they picked on their own feet that way is beyond me. It's a nasty place, full of small bones. If you're ever going to shoot yourself don't pick on a spot like that. Don't pick on your feet. I tell you it's a bad idea.

"Anyway, the man in the hospital was always making a fuss and I got sick of him and the place too. When I got better I faked, said the nerves of my leg didn't hurt. It was a lie, of course. The nerves of my leg and of my face have never quit hurting. I reckon maybe, if I had told the truth, they might have fixed me up all right."

I got it. No wonder he carried his drinks so well. When I understood, I wanted to keep on drinking with him, wanted to stay with him until he got tired of me as he had of the man who lay beside him in the base hospital over there somewhere in France.

The point was that he never slept, could not sleep, except when he was a little drunk. "I'm a nut," he said smiling.

It was after we got over to Aunt Sally's that he talked most. Aunt Sally had gone to bed when we got there, but she got up when we rang the bell and we all went to sit together in the little patio back of her house. She is a large woman with great arms and rather a paunch, and she had put on nothing but a light flowered dressing-gown over a thin, ridiculously girlish, nightgown. By this time the moon had come up and, outside, in the narrow

street of the Vieux Carré, three drunken sailors from a ship in the
river were sitting on a curb and singing a song,

> *"I've got to get it,*
> *You've got to get it,*
> *We've all got to get it*
> *In our own good time."*

They had rather nice boyish voices and every time they sang a
verse and had done the chorus they all laughed together heartily.

In Aunt Sally's patio there are many broad-leafed banana plants
and a Chinaberry tree throwing its soft purple shadows on a brick
floor.

As for Aunt Sally, she is as strange to me as he was. When we
came and when we were all seated at a little table in the patio, she
ran into her house and presently came back with a bottle of whisky.
She, it seemed, had understood him at once, had understood
without unnecessary words that the little Southern man lived always in the black house of pain, that whisky was good to him,
that it quieted his throbbing nerves, temporarily at least. "Everything is temporary, when you come to that," I can fancy Aunt
Sally saying.

We sat for a time in silence, David having shifted his allegiance
and taken two drinks out of Aunt Sally's bottle. Presently he rose
and walked up and down the patio floor, crossing and re-crossing
the network of delicately outlined shadows on the bricks. "It's
really all right, the leg," he said, "something just presses on the
nerves, that's all." In me there was a self-satisfied feeling. I had
done the right thing. I had brought him to Aunt Sally. "I have
brought him to a mother." She has always made me feel that way
since I have known her.

And now I shall have to explain her a little. It will not be so
easy. That whole neighborhood in New Orleans is alive with tales
concerning her.

Aunt Sally came to New Orleans in the old days, when the
town was wild, in the wide-open days. What she had been before

she came no one knew, but anyway she opened a place. That was very, very long ago when I was myself but a lad, up in Ohio. As I have already said Aunt Sally came from somewhere up in the Middle-Western country. In some obscure subtle way it would flatter me to think she came from my state.

The house she had opened was one of the older places in the French Quarter down here, and when she had got her hands on it, Aunt Sally had a hunch. Instead of making the place modern, cutting it up into small rooms, all that sort of thing, she left it just as it was and spent her money rebuilding falling old walls, mending winding broad old stairways, repairing dim high-ceilinged old rooms, soft-colored old marble mantels. After all, we do seem attached to sin and there are so many people busy making sin unattractive. It is good to find someone who takes the other road. It would have been so very much to Aunt Sally's advantage to have made the place modern, that is to say, in the business she was in at that time. If a few old rooms, wide old stairways, old cooking ovens built into the walls, if all these things did not facilitate the stealing in of couples on dark nights, they at least did something else. She had opened a gambling and drinking house, but one can have no doubt about the ladies stealing in. "I was on the make all right," Aunt Sally told me once.

She ran the place and took in money, and the money she spent on the place itself. A falling wall was made to stand up straight and fine again, the banana plants were made to grow in the patio, the Chinaberry tree got started and was helped through the years of adolescence. On the wall the lovely Rose of Montana bloomed madly. The fragrant Lantana grew in a dense mass at a corner of the wall.

When the Chinaberry tree, planted at the very center of the patio, began to get up into the light it filled the whole neighborhood with fragrance in the spring.

Fifteen, twenty years of that, with Mississippi River gamblers and race-horse men sitting at tales by windows in the huge rooms upstairs in the house that had once, no doubt, been the town house of some rich planter's family—in the boom days of the forties. Women stealing in too in the dusk of evenings. Drinks being sold. Aunt Sally raking down the kitty from the game, raking in her share, quite ruthlessly.

At night, getting a good price too from the lovers. No questions asked, a good price for drinks. Moll Flanders might have lived with Aunt Sally. What a pair they would have made! The Chinaberry tree beginning to be lusty. The Lantana blossoming—in the fall the Rose of Montana.

Aunt Sally getting hers. Using the money to keep the old house in fine shape. Salting some away all the time.

A motherly soul, good, sensible Middle-Western woman, eh? Once a racehorse man left twenty-four thousand dollars with her and disappeared. No one knew she had it. There was a report the man was dead. He had killed a gambler in a place down by the French Market and while they were looking for him he managed to slip in to Aunt Sally's and leave his swag. Some time later a body was found floating in the river and it was identified as the horseman but in reality he had been picked up in a wire-tapping haul in New York City and did not get out of his Northern prison for six years.

When he did get out, naturally he skipped for New Orleans. No doubt he was somewhat shaky. She had him. If he squealed there was a murder charge to be brought up and held over his head. It was night when he arrived and Aunt Sally went at once to an old brick oven built into the wall of the kitchen and took out a bag. "There it is," she said. The whole affair was part of the day's work for her in those days.

Gamblers at the tables in some of the rooms upstairs, lurking couples, from the old patio below the fragrance of growing things.

When she was fifty, Aunt Sally had got enough and had put them all out. She did not stay in the way of sin too long and she never went in too deep, like that Moll Flanders, and so she was all right and sitting pretty. "They wanted to gamble and drink and play with the ladies. The ladies liked it all right. I never saw none of them come in protesting too much. The worst was in the morning when they went away. They looked so sheepish and guilty. If they felt that way, what made them come? If I took a man, you bet I'd want him and no monkey-business or nothing doing.

"I got a little tired of all of them, that's the truth." Aunt Sally laughed. "But that wasn't until I had got what I went after. Oh pshaw, they took up too much of my time after I got enough to be safe."

Aunt Sally is now sixty-five. If you like her and she likes you she will let you sit with her in her patio gossiping of the old times, of the old river days. Perhaps—well, you see there is still something of the French influence at work in New Orleans, a sort of matter-of-factness about life—what I started to say is that if you know Aunt Sally and she likes you, and if, by chance, your lady likes the smell of flowers growing in a patio at night—really, I am going a bit too far. I only meant to suggest that Aunt Sally at sixty-five is not harsh. She is a motherly soul.

We sat in the garden talking, the little Southern poet, Aunt Sally and myself—or rather they talked and I listened. The Southerner's great-grandfather was English, a younger son, and he came over here to make his fortune as a planter, and did it. Once he and his sons owned several great plantations with slaves, but now his father had but a few hundred acres left, about one of the old houses—somewhere over in Alabama. The land is heavily mortgaged and most of it has not been under cultivation for years. Negro labor is growing more and more expensive and unsatisfactory since so many Negroes have run off to Chicago, and the poet's father and the one brother at home are not much good at working the land. "We aren't strong enough and we don't know how," the poet said.

The Southerner had come to New Orleans to see Fred, to talk with Fred about poetry, but Fred was out of town. I could only walk about with him, help him drink his home-made whisky. Already I had taken nearly a dozen drinks. In the morning I would have a headache.

I drew within myself, listening while David and Aunt Sally talked. The Chinaberry tree had been so and so many years growing—she spoke of it as she might have spoken of a daughter.

"It had a lot of different sicknesses when it was young, but it pulled through." Someone had built a high wall on one side of her patio so that the climbing plants did not get as much sunlight as they needed. The banana plants, however, did very well and now the Chinaberry tree was big and strong enough to take care of itself. She kept giving David drinks of whisky and he talked.

He told her of the place in his leg where something, a bone perhaps, pressed on the nerve, and of the place on his left cheek. A silver plate had been set under the skin. She touched the spot with her fat old fingers. The moonlight fell softly down on the patio floor. "I can't sleep except somewhere out of doors," David said.

He explained how that, at home on his father's plantation, he had to be thinking all day whether or not he would be able to sleep at night.

"I go to bed and then I get up. There is always a bottle of whisky on the table downstairs and I take three or four drinks. Then I go out doors." Often very nice things happened.

"In the fall it's best," he said. "You see the niggers are making molasses." Every Negro cabin on the place had a little clump of ground back of it where cane grew and in the fall the Negroes were making their 'lasses. "I take the bottle in my hand and go into the fields, unseen by the niggers. Having the bottle with me that way, I drink a good deal and then lie down on the ground. The mosquitoes bite me some, but I don't mind much. I reckon I get drunk enough not to mind. The little pain makes a kind of rhythm for the great pain—like poetry.

"In a kind of shed the niggers are making the 'lasses, that is to say, pressing the juice out of the cane and boiling it down. They keep singing as they work. In a few years now I reckon our family won't have any land. The banks could take it now if they wanted it. They don't want it. It would be too much trouble for them to manage, I reckon.

"In the fall, at night, the niggers are pressing the cane. Our niggers live pretty much on 'lasses and grits.

"They like working at night and I'm glad they do. There is an old mule going round and round in a circle and beside the press a pile of the dry cane. Niggers come, men and women, old and young. They build a fire outside the shed. The old mule goes round and round.

"The niggers sing. They laugh and shout. Sometimes the young niggers with their gals make love on the dry cane pile. I can hear it rattle.

"I have come out of the big house, me and my bottle, and I creep along, low on the ground, till I get up close. There I lie. I'm a little drunk. It all makes me happy. I can sleep some on the ground like that when the niggers are singing, when no one knows I'm there.

"I could sleep here, on these bricks here," David said, pointing to where the shadows cast by the broad leaves of the banana plants were broadest and deepest.

He got up from his chair and went limping, dragging one foot after the other, across the patio and lay down on the bricks.

For a long time Aunt Sally and I sat looking at each other, saying nothing, and presently she made a sign with her fat finger and we crept away into the house. "I'll let you out at the front door. You let him sleep, right where he is," she said. In spite of her huge bulk and her age she walked across the patio floor as softly as a kitten. Beside her I felt awkward and uncertain. When we had got inside she whispered to me. She had some champagne left from the old days, hidden away somewhere in the old house. "I'm going to send a magnum up to his dad when he goes home," she explained.

She, it seemed, was very happy having him there, drunk and asleep on the brick floor of the patio. "We used to have some good men come here in the old days too," she said. As we went into the house through the kitchen door I had looked back at David, asleep now in the heavy shadows at a corner of the wall. There was no doubt he also was happy, had been happy ever since I had brought him into the presence of Aunt Sally. What a small huddled figure of a man he looked, lying thus on the brick, under the night sky, in the deep shadows of the banana plants.

I went into the house and out at the front door and into a dark narrow street, thinking. Well, I was, after all, a Northern man. It was possible Aunt Sally had become completely Southern, being down here so long.

I remembered that it was the chief boast of her life that once she had shaken hands with John L. Sullivan and that she had known P. T. Barnum.

"I knew Dave Gears. You mean to tell me you don't know who Dave Gears was? Why, he was one of the biggest gamblers we ever had in this city."

As for David and his poetry—it is in the manner of Shelley. "If I could write like Shelley I would be happy. I wouldn't care what happened to me," he had said during our walk of the early part of the evening.

I went along enjoying my thoughts. The street was dark and occasionally I laughed. A notion had come to me. It kept dancing in my head and I thought it very delicious. It had something to do with aristocrats, with such people as Aunt Sally and David. "Lordy," I thought, "maybe I do understand them a little. I'm from the Middle West myself and it seems we can produce our aristocrats too." I kept thinking of Aunt Sally and of my native state, Ohio. "Lordy, I hope she comes from up there, but I don't think I had better inquire too closely into her past," I said to myself, as I went smiling away into the soft smoky night.

THE FLOOD

IT CAME ABOUT WHILE HE WAS TRYING TO DO A VERY DIFFICULT THING. He was a college professor and was trying to write a book on the subject of values.

A good many men had written on the subject, but now he was trying his hand.

He had read, he said, everything he could find that had been written on the subject.

There had been books consumed, months spent sitting and reading books.

The man had a house of his own at the edge of the town where stood the college in which he taught, but he was not teaching that year. It was his sabbatical year. There was a whole year to be spent just on his book.

"I thought," he said, "I would go to Europe." He thought of some quiet place, say in a little Normandy town. He remembered such a town he had once visited.

It would have to be very quiet, a place where no one would know him, where he would be undisturbed.

He had got a world of notes down into little books, piled neatly on a long work table in his room. He was a small alert almost bald man and had been married, but his wife was dead. He told me that for years he had been a very lonely man.

He had lived alone in his house for several years, having no children. There was an old housekeeper. There was a walled garden.

The old housekeeper did not sleep in the house. She came there early in the morning and went to her own home at night.

Nothing had happened to the man for months at a time through several years, he said.

He had been lonely, had felt his loneliness a good deal. He hadn't much of a way with people.

He had, I gathered, before that summer, been rather hungry for people. "My wife was a cheerful soul, when she was here," he said, speaking of his loneliness. I got from him and others—I had never known his wife—the sense of her as a rather frivolous-seeming woman.

She had been a light-hearted little woman, fond of frills, one of the kind whose blond hair is always flying in the wind. They are always chattering, that kind. They love everyone. My friend, the scholar, had adored his wife.

And then she had died, and there he was. He was one of the sort who hurry along through streets with books under their arms. You are always seeing such men about college towns. They go along staring at people with their impersonal eyes. If you speak to such a one he answers you absent-mindedly. "Don't bother me, please," he seems to be saying, while all the time, within himself, he is cursing himself that he cannot be more outgoing toward people.

He told me that, when his wife was alive and he was in his study, absorbed in his books, taking notes, lost in thought as one might say, preparing to write his book on values that was to be his magnum opus, she used to come in there.

She would come in, put one arm about his neck, lean over him, kiss him, and with the other hand would punch him in the stomach.

He said she used to drag him out and make him play croquet on the lawn or help with the garden. It was her money, he said, that had built the house.

He said she always called him an old stick.

"Come on, you old stick, kiss me, make love to me," she said to him sometimes. "You aren't much good to me or anyone, but you're all I've got." She would have people in, worlds of people, just anyone. When the house was full of people and the scholar, that little wide-eyed man, was standing about among them, rather confused, trying, in the midst of the hubbub, to hang onto his thoughts on the subject of values, remembering the far dim reaches of thought that occasionally came to him when he was alone ... In him a feeling that all of man's notions of values, particularly in America, had got distorted, "perverted," he said, and that, when he was alone, when his wife and the people she was always dragging into the house did not disturb him—he had a feeling sometimes, at moments when he was undisturbed thus, that persistent mind of his reaching out, himself impersonal, untouched ... "I almost thought sometimes," he said, "that I had got something."

"There was," he said, "a kind of divine balance to all values to be found."

You got, to be sure, the crude sense of values that everyone understands, values in land, money, possessions.

Then you got more subtle values, feeling coming in.

You got a painting, let us say by Rembrandt, selling to a rich man for fifty thousand dollars.

That is enough money to raise a dozen poor families, add some fifty or sixty citizens to the State.

The citizens being, let us say, all worthy men and women, without question of value to the State, producers, let us say.

Then you got the Rembrandt painting, hanging on a wall, say in some rich man's house, he having people into his house. He would stand before the painting.

He would brag about it as though he had himself painted it.

"I was pretty shrewd to get it at all," he would say. He would tell how he got it. Another rich man had been after it.

He talked about it as he might have talked about getting control of some industry by a skillful maneuver in the stock market.

Just the same it, the painting, was, in some way, adding a kind of value to that rich man's life.

It, the painting, was hanging on his wall, producing by hanging there nothing he could put his fingers on, producing no food, no clothes, nothing at all in the material world.

He himself being essentially a man of the material world. He had got rich being that.

Just the same ...

My acquaintance, the scholar, wanted to be very just. No, that wasn't it. He said he wanted truth.

His mind reached out. He got hold of things a little sometimes, or thought he did. He took notes, he prepared to write his book.

He adored his wife and sometimes, often, he said he hated her. She used to laugh at him. "Your old values," she said. It seems he had been on that subject for years. He used to read papers before philosophical societies and afterward they were printed in little pamphlets by the societies. No one understood them, not even perhaps his fellow philosophers, but he read them aloud to his wife.

"Kiss me, kiss me hard," she would say. "Do it now. Don't wait."

He wanted to kill her sometimes, he said. He said he adored her.

She died. He was alone. He was bitterly lonely sometimes.

People, remembering his wife, came for a time to see him, but he was cold with them. It was because he was absorbed in thought. They talked to him and he replied absent-mindedly. "Yes, that's so. Perhaps you're right." Remarks of that kind.

Wanting them just the same, he said.

Then, he said, the flood came. He said you couldn't account for floods.

"What's the use talking of balance?" he asked. "There is no balance."

He couldn't account for what happened during the summer of
that sabbatical year. He had a theory about life. I had heard it
before.

"Everything in life comes in surges, floods, really. There is a
whole city, thousands, even millions of people in it," he said.

"They are all, let us say, dull; they are all stupid; they are coarse
and crude.

"All of them have become bored with life; they are full of hatreds
for each other.

"It is not only cities. Whole nations are like that sometimes.

"How else are you to account for wars?

"And then there are other times when whole neighborhoods,
whole cities, whole nations become something else. They are all
irreligious, and then suddenly, without any cause anyone has ever
understood, ever perhaps can understand, they become religious.
They are proud and they become humble, full of hatred and then
suddenly filled with love.

"The individual, trying to assert himself against the mass, always
without success, is drowned in a flood.

"There is a lifetime of work and thought washed away thus.

"There are these little tragedies. Are they tragedies or are they
merely amusing?"

He, my friend the scholar, was seeking, as I have said, a kind
of impersonal delicate balance on the subject of values.

That, in solitude, to be transcribed into words. His book, that
was to be his magnum opus, the work of a lifetime justified.

There was no wife to bother him now by dragging people into
the house.

There was no wife to say, "Come on, old stick, kiss me quick,
now, while I want your kisses.

"Get this, get what I have to offer you while I have it to offer."

That sort of thing, of course, pitching him down off his mountain
top of thought, thump.

He having to struggle for days afterwards, trying to get back
up there again.

In his thinking he had, alone that summer in his house, almost achieved the thing, the perfect balance of thought.

He said he struggled all through the winter, spring and early summer. For years no one had come to see him.

Then suddenly his wife's sister, a younger sister, came. She hadn't even written him for a year, and then she telegraphed she was coming that way. It seems she was driving in a car, going to some place; he couldn't remember where.

She brought a young woman, a cousin, with her. The cousin, like his wife's sister, was another frivolous one.

And then the scholar's brother came. He was a big boastful youngish man who was in business.

He only came to stay a day or two, but, like the scholar, he had lost his wife. He was attracted to the two young women.

He stayed on and on because of them. They may have stayed on and on because of him.

He was a man who had a big car. He brought other men into the house.

Suddenly the scholar's house was filled with men and women. There was a good deal of gin-drinking.

There was a flood of people. The scholar's brother brought in a phonograph and wanted to install a radio.

There were dances in the evening.

Even the old housekeeper caught it. She had always been rather quiet, a staid, sad old woman. One evening the scholar said, after a day, during the afternoon of which he had struggle and struggled, alone in his room, the door shut, sound coming in nevertheless, coarse sounds, he said, sound of women's laughter, men's voices.

He said the two young women who had come there and who he believed had stayed because of his brother—he having stayed because of them—the two had met other people of the town. They filled his house with people.

He had, however, almost got something he was after in spite of them.

"I swear I almost had it."

"Had what?"

"Why, my definition of values. There had to be something, you see, at the very core of my book."

"Yes, of course."

"I mean one place in my book where everything was defined. In simple words, so that everyone could understand."

"Of course."

I shall never forget the scholar when he was telling me all this, the puzzled, half-hurt look in his eyes.

He said they had even got his housekeeper going. "What do you think of it—she also drinking gin?"

There was a crash of sounds that afternoon in his house.

He was alone in his room upstairs in his house, in his study.

They had got the sad, staid old housekeeper going. He said his brother was very efficient. They had her dancing to the music of the phonograph. The scholar's brother, that big blustering bragging man—he was a manufacturer of some sort—was dancing with the housekeeper—with that staid, sad old woman.

The others had got into a circle.

The phonograph was going.

What happened was that the scholar's sister—just, I imagine from all he said and from what others afterward said of her, a miniature edition, a new printing one might say, of his dead wife...

She, it seems, came running upstairs and burst into his room, her blond hair flying. She was laughing.

"I had almost got it," he said.

"What? Oh, yes. Your definition."

"Yes, just the definition I had been after for years.

"I was about to write it down. It embraced all, everything I had to say."

She burst in.

I gather the sister must have been at least a little in love with the man and that he, after all, did not want the bragging, blustering brother to have her. He admitted that.

She rushed in.

"Come on, you old stick," she said to him.

He said he tried to explain to her. "I made a fight," he said.

He got up from his desk and tried to reason with her. She had fairly taken possession of his house.

He tried to tell her what he was up to. He spoke of standing there, beside his desk, where he sat when he told me all this, trying to explain all this to her.

I thought the scholar got a bit vulgar when he told me of that moment.

"There was nothing doing," he said. He had got that expression from the young woman, his wife's sister.

She was laughing at him as his wife had formerly done; she wouldn't have kissed him.

She wouldn't have said, "Kiss me quick, you old stick, while I feel that way."

I gathered she merely dragged him downstairs. He said he went with her, couldn't help himself, couldn't, of course, be rude to her, his wife's sister.

He went with her and saw his staid, sad old housekeeper acting like that.

The housekeeper didn't seem to care whether he saw or not. She had broken loose. The whole house had broken loose.

And so, in the end, my acquaintance, the scholar, didn't care either.

"I was in the flood," he said. "What was the use?"

He was a little afraid that, if he didn't do something about it, his bragging brother, or some man like him, might get his wife's sister.

He didn't quite want that to happen. So that evening, when he was alone with her, he proposed to her.

He said she called him an old stick. "It must have been a family expression," he said. Something of the scholar came back into him when he said that.

He had been caught in a flood. He had let go.

He had proposed to his wife's sister, in the garden back of his

house, under an apple tree, near the croquet grounds, and she
had said...

He didn't tell me what she said. I imagine she said, "Yes, you
old stick."

"Kiss me quick while I feel that way," she said.

That, at least, gets a certain balance to my tale.

The scholar, however, says there is no balance.

"There are only floods, one flood following another," he says.
When I talked to him of all this he was a bit discouraged.

However, he seemed cheerful enough.

BROTHER DEATH

THERE WERE THE TWO OAK STUMPS, KNEE HIGH TO A NOT-TOO-TALL man and cut quite squarely across. They became to the two children objects of wonder. They had seen the two trees cut but had run away just as the trees fell. They hadn't thought of the two stumps to be left standing there, hadn't even looked at them. Afterwards Ted said to his sister Mary, speaking of the stumps: "I wonder if they bled like legs when a surgeon cuts a man's leg off." He had been hearing war stories. A man came to the farm one day to visit one of the farmhands, a man who had been in the World War and had lost an arm. He stood in one of the barns talking. When Ted said that Mary spoke up at once. She hadn't been lucky enough to be at the barn when the one-armed man was there talking, and was jealous. "Why not a woman or a girl's leg?" she said, but Ted said the idea was silly. "Women and girls don't get their legs and arms cut off," he declared. "Why not? I'd just like to know why not," Mary kept saying.

It would have been something if they had stayed, that day the trees were cut. "We might have gone and touched the places," Ted said. He meant the stumps. Would they have been warm? Would they have bled? They did go and touch the places afterwards, but it was a cold day and the stumps were cold. Ted stuck to his point that only men's arms and legs were cut off, but Mary thought of automobile accidents. "You can't think just about wars. There might be an automobile accident," she declared, but Ted wouldn't be convinced.

They were both children, but something had made them both in an odd way old. Mary was fourteen and Ted eleven, but Ted wasn't strong and that rather evened things up. They were the children of a well-to-do Virginia farmer named John Grey in the Blue Ridge country in Southwestern Virginia. There was a wide valley called the "Rich Valley," with a railroad and a small river running through it and high mountains in sight to the north and south. Ted had some kind of heart disease, a lesion, something of the sort, the result of a severe attack of diphtheria when he was a child of eight. He was thin and not strong but curiously alive. The doctor said he might die at any moment, might just drop down dead. The fact had drawn him peculiarly close to his sister Mary. It had awakened a strong and determined maternalism in her.

The whole family, the neighbors on neighboring farms in the valley, and even the other children at the schoolhouse where they went to school recognized something as existing between the two children. "Look at them going along there," people said. "They do seem to have good times together, but they are so serious. For such young children they are too serious. Still, I suppose, under the circumstances, it's natural." Of course, everyone knew about Ted. It had done something to Mary. At fourteen she was both a child and a grown woman. The woman side of her kept popping out at unexpected moments.

She had sensed something concerning her brother Ted. It was because he was as he was, having that kind of a heart, a heart likely at any moment to stop beating, leaving him dead, cut down like a young tree. The others in the Grey family, that is to say, the older ones, the mother and father and an older brother, Don, who was eighteen now, recognized something as belonging to the two children, being, as it were, between them, but the recognition wasn't very definite. People in your own family are likely at any moment to do strange, sometimes hurtful things to you. You have to watch them. Ted and Mary had both found that out.

The brother Don was like the father, already at eighteen almost a grown man. He was that sort, the kind people speak of, saying: "He's a good man. He'll make a good solid dependable man." The father, when he was a young man, never drank, never went chasing the girls, was never wild. There had been enough wild young ones in the Rich Valley when he was a lad. Some of them had inherited big farms and had lost them, gambling, drinking, fooling with fast horses and chasing after the women. It had been almost a Virginia tradition, but John Grey was a land man. All the Greys were. There were other large cattle farms owned by Greys up and down the valley.

John Grey, everyone said, was a natural cattle man. He knew beef cattle, of the big so-called export type, how to pick and feed them to make beef. He knew how and where to get the right kind of young stock to turn into his fields. It was bluegrass country. Big beef cattle went directly off the pastures to market. The Grey farm contained over twelve hundred acres, most of it in bluegrass.

The father was a land man, land hungry. He had begun as a cattle farmer with a small place inherited from his father, some two hundred acres, lying next to what was then the big Aspinwahl place and, after he began, he never stopped getting more land. He kept cutting in on the Aspinwahls who were a rather horsey, fast lot. They thought of themselves as Virginia aristocrats, having, as they weren't so modest about pointing out, a family going back and back, family tradition, guests always being entertained, fast horses kept, money being bet on fast horses. John Grey getting their land, now twenty acres, then thirty, then fifty, until at last he got the old Aspinwahl house, with one of the Aspinwahl girls, not a young one, not one of the best-looking ones, as wife. The Aspinwahl place was down, by that time, to less than a hundred acres, but he went on, year after year, always being careful and shrewd, making every penny count, never wasting a cent, adding and adding to what was now the Grey place. The former Aspinwahl house was a large old brick house with fireplaces in all the rooms and was very comfortable.

People wondered why Louise Aspinwahl had married John Grey, but when they were wondering they smiled. The Aspinwahl girls were all well educated, had all been away to college, but Louise wasn't so pretty. She got nicer after marriage, suddenly almost beautiful. The Aspinwahls were, as everyone knew, naturally sensitive, really first class but the men couldn't hang onto land and the Greys could. In all that section of Virginia, people gave John Grey credit for being what he was. They respected him. "He's on the level," they said, "as honest as a horse. He has cattle sense, that's it." He could run his big hand down over the flank of a steer and say, almost to the pound, what he would weigh on the scales or he could look at a calf or a yearling and say, "He'll do," and he would do. A steer is a steer. He isn't supposed to do anything but make beef.

There was Don, the oldest son of the Grey family. He was so evidently destined to be a Grey, to be another like his father. He had long been a star in the 4H Club of the Virginia county and, even as a lad of nine and ten, had won prizes at steer judging. At twelve he had produced, no one helping him, doing all the work himself, more bushels of corn on an acre of land than any other boy in the state.

It was all a little amazing, even a bit queer to Mary Grey, being as she was a girl peculiarly conscious, so old and young, so aware. There was Don, the older brother, big and strong of body, like the father, and there was the young brother Ted. Ordinarily, in the ordinary course of life, she being what she was—female—it would have been quite natural and right for her to have given her young girl's admiration to Don but she didn't. For some reason, Don barely existed for her. He was outside, not in it, while for her Ted, the seemingly weak one of the family, was everything.

Still there Don was, so big of body, so quiet, so apparently sure of himself. The father had begun, as a young cattle man, with the two hundred acres, and now he had the twelve hundred. What would Don Grey do when he started? Already he knew, although he didn't say anything, that he wanted to start. He wanted to run things, be his own boss. His father had offered to send him away to college, to an agricultural college, but he wouldn't go. "No. I can learn more here," he said.

Already there was a contest, always kept under the surface, between the father and son. It concerned ways of doing things, decisions to be made. As yet the son always surrendered.

It is like that in a family, little isolated groups formed within the larger group, jealousies, concealed hatreds, silent battles secretly going on—among the Greys, Mary and Ted, Don and his father, the mother and the two younger children, Gladys, a girl child of six now, who adored her brother Don, and Harry, a boy child of two.

As for Mary and Ted, they lived within their own world, but their own world had not been established without a struggle. The point was that Ted, having the heart that might at any moment stop beating, was always being treated tenderly by the others. Only Mary understood that—how it infuriated and hurt him.

"No, Ted, I wouldn't do that."

"Now, Ted, do be careful."

Sometimes Ted went white and trembling with anger, Don, the father, the mother, all keeping at him like that. It didn't matter what he wanted to do, learn to drive one of the two family cars, climb a tree to find a bird's nest, run a race with Mary. Naturally, being on a farm, he wanted to try his hand at breaking a colt, beginning with him, getting a saddle on, having it out with him. "No, Ted. You can't." He had learned to swear, picking it up from the farmhands and from boys at the country school. "Hell! Goddam!" he said to Mary. Only Mary understood how he felt, and she had not put the matter very definitely into words, not even to herself. It was one of the things that made her old when she was so young. It made her stand aside from the others of the family, aroused in her a curious determination. "They shall not." She caught herself saying the words to herself. "They shall not.

"If he is to have but a few years of life, they shall not spoil what he is to have. Why should they make him die, over and over, day after day?" The thoughts in her did not become so definite. She had resentment against the others. She was like a soldier, standing guard over Ted.

The two children drew more and more away into their own world and only once did what Mary felt come to the surface. That was with the mother.

It was on an early summer day and Ted and Mary were playing in the rain. They were on a side porch of the house, where the water came pouring down from the eaves. At a corner of the porch there was a great stream, and first Ted and then Mary dashed through it, returning to the porch with clothes soaked and water running in streams from soaked hair. There was something joyous, the feel of the cold water on the body, under clothes, and they were shrieking with laughter when the mother came to the door. She looked at Ted. There was fear and anxiety in her voice. "Oh, Ted, you know you mustn't, you mustn't." Just that. All the rest implied. Nothing said to Mary. There it was. "Oh, Ted, you mustn't. You mustn't run hard, climb trees, ride horses. The least shock to you may do it." It was the old story again, and, of course, Ted understood. He went white and trembled. Why couldn't the rest understand that was a hundred times worse for him? On that day, without answering his mother, he ran off the porch and through the rain toward the barns. He wanted to go hide himself from everyone. Mary knew how he felt.

She got suddenly very old and very angry. The mother and daughter stood looking at each other, the woman nearing fifty and the child of fourteen. It was getting everything in the family reversed. Mary felt that but felt she had to do something. "You should have more sense, Mother," she said seriously. She also had gone white. Her lips trembled. "You mustn't do it any more. Don't you ever do it again."

"What, child?" There was astonishment and half anger in the mother's voice. "Always making him think of it," Mary said. She wanted to cry but didn't.

The mother understood. There was a queer tense moment before Mary also walked off toward the barns in the rain. It wasn't all so clear. The mother wanted to fly at the child, perhaps shake her for daring to be so impudent. A child like that to decide things—

to dare to reprove her mother. There was so much implied—even that Ted be allowed to die quickly, suddenly, rather than that death, danger of sudden death, be brought again and again to his attention. There were values in life, implied by a child's words: "Life, what is it worth? Is death the most terrible thing?" The mother turned and went silently into the house while Mary, going to the barns, presently found Ted. He was in an empty horse stall, standing with his back to the wall, staring. There were no explanations. "Well," Ted said presently, and, "Come on, Ted," Mary replied. It was necessary to do something, even perhaps more risky than playing in the rain. The rain was already passing. "Let's take off our shoes," Mary said. Going barefoot was one of the things forbidden Ted. They took their shoes off and, leaving them in the barn, went into an orchard. There was a small creek below the orchard, a creek that went down to the river and now it would be in flood. They went into it and once Mary got swept off her feet so that Ted had to pull her out. She spoke then. "I told Mother," she said, looking serious.

"What?" Ted said. "Gee, I guess maybe I saved you from drowning," he added.

"Sure you did," said Mary. "I told her to let you alone." She grew suddenly fierce. "They've all got to—they've got to let you alone," she said.

There was a bond. Ted did his share. He was imaginative and could think of plenty of risky things to do. Perhaps the mother spoke to the father and to Don, the older brother. There was a new inclination in the family to keep hands off the pair, and the fact seemed to give the two children new room in life. Something seemed to open out. There was a little inner world created, always, every day, being re-created, and in it there was a kind of new security. It seemed to the two children—they could not have put their feeling into words—that, being in their own created world, feeling a new security there, they could suddenly look out at the outside world and see, in a new way, what was going on out there in the world that belonged also to others.

It was a world to be thought about, looked at, a world of drama too, the drama of human relations, outside their own world, in a family, on a farm, in a farmhouse... On a farm, calves and yearling steers arriving to be fattened, great heavy steers going off to market, colts being broken to work or to saddle, lambs born in the late winter. The human side of life was more difficult, to a child often incomprehensible, but after the speech to the mother on the porch of the house that day when it rained, it seemed to Mary almost as though she and Ted had set up a new family. Everything about the farm, the house and the barns got nicer. There was a new freedom. The two children walked along a country road, returning to the farm from school in the late afternoon. There were other children in the road but they managed to fall behind or they got ahead. There were plans made. "I'm going to be a nurse when I grow up," Mary said. She may have remembered dimly the woman nurse from the county-seat town, who had come to stay in the house when Ted was so ill. Ted said that as soon as he could—it would be when he was younger yet than Don was now—he intended to leave and go out West...far out, he said. He wanted to be a cowboy or a bronco-buster or something, and, that failing, he thought he would be a railroad engineer. The railroad that went down through the Rich Valley crossed a corner of the Grey farm, and, from the road in the afternoon, they could sometimes see trains quite far away, the smoke rolling up. There was a faint rumbling noise, and on clear days they could see the flying piston rods of the engines.

As for the two stumps in the field near the house, they were what was left of two oak trees. The children had known the trees. They were cut one day in the early fall.

There was a back porch to the Grey house—the house that had once been the seat of the Aspinwahl family—and from the porch steps a path led down to a stone springhouse. A spring came out of the ground just there, and there was a tiny stream that went along the edge of a field, past two large barns and out across a meadow to a creek—called a "branch" in Virginia, and the two trees stood close together beyond the springhouse and the fence.

They were lusty trees, their roots down in the rich, always damp soil, and one of them had a great limb that came down near the ground, so that Ted and Mary could climb into it and out another limb into its brother tree, and in the fall, when other trees, at the front and side of the house, had shed their leaves, blood-red leaves still clung to the two oaks. They were like dry blood on gray days, but on other days, when the sun came out, the trees flamed against distant hills. The leaves clung, whispering and talking when the wind blew, so that the trees themselves seemed carrying on a conversation.

John Grey had decided he would have the trees cut. At first it was not a very definite decision. "I think I'll have them cut," he announced.

"But why?" his wife asked. The trees meant a good deal to her. They had been planted, just in that spot, by her grandfather, she said, having in mind just a certain effect. "You see how, in the fall, when you stand on the back porch, they are so nice against the hills." She spoke of the trees, already quite large, having been brought from a distant woods. Her mother had often spoken of it. The man, her grandfather, had a special feeling for trees. "An Aspinwahl would do that," John Grey said. "There is enough yard here about the house and enough trees. They do not shade the house or the yard. An Aspinwahl would go to all that trouble for trees and then plant them where grass might be growing." He had suddenly determined, a half-formed determination in him suddenly hardening. He had perhaps heard too much of the Aspinwahls and their ways. The conversation regarding the trees took place at the table at the noon hour, and Mary and Ted heard it all.

It began at the table and was carried on afterwards out of doors, in the yard back of the house. The wife had followed her husband out. He always left the table suddenly and silently, getting quickly up and going out heavily, shutting doors with a bang as he went. "Don't, John," the wife said, standing on the porch and calling to her husband. It was a cold day but the sun was out and the trees were like great bonfires against gray distant fields and hills. The older son of the family, young Don, the one so physically like the father and apparently so like him in every way, had come out of the house with the mother, followed by the two children, Ted and Mary, and at first Don said nothing, but, when the father did not answer the mother's protest but started toward the barn, he also spoke. What he said was obviously the determining thing, hardening the father.

To the two other children—they had walked a little aside and stood together watching and listening—there was something. There was their own child's world. "Let us alone and we'll let you alone." It wasn't as definite as that. Most of the definite thoughts about what happened in the yard that afternoon came to Mary Grey long afterwards, when she was a grown woman. At the moment there was merely a sudden sharpening of the feeling of isolation, a wall between herself and Ted and the others. The father, even then perhaps, seen in a new light, Don and the mother seen in a new light.

There was something, a driving destructive thing in life, in all relationships between people. All of this felt dimly that day—she always believed both by herself and Ted—but only thought out long afterwards, after Ted was dead. There was the farm her father had won from the Aspinwahls—greater persistence, greater shrewdness. In a family, little remarks dropped from time to time, an impression slowly built up. The father, John Grey, was a successful man. He had acquired. He owned. He was the commander, the one having power to do his will. And the power had run out and covered not only other human lives, impulses in others, wishes, hungers in others...he himself might not have, might not even understand...but it went far out beyond that. It was, curiously, the power also of life and death. Did Mary Grey think such thoughts at that moment? She couldn't have... Still there was her own peculiar situation, her relationship with her brother Ted, who was to die.

Ownership that gave curious rights, dominances—fathers over children, men and women over lands, houses, factories in cities, fields. "I will have the trees in that orchard cut. They produce apples but not of the right sort. There is no money in apples of that sort anymore."

"But, sir...you see...look...the trees there against that hill, against the sky."

"Nonsense. Sentimentality."

Confusion.

It would have been such nonsense to think of the father of Mary Grey as a man without feeling. He had struggled hard all his life, perhaps, as a young man, gone without things wanted, deeply hungered for. Someone has to manage things in this life. Possessions mean power, the right to say, "Do this" or "Do that." If you struggle long and hard for a thing it becomes infinitely sweet to you.

Was there a kind of hatred between the father and the older son of the Grey family? "You are one also who has this thing— the impulse to power, so like my own. Now you are young and I am growing old." Admiration mixed with fear. If you would retain power it will not do to admit fear.

The young Don was so curiously like the father. There were the same lines about the jaws, the same eyes. They were both heavy men. Already the young man walked like the father, slammed doors as did the father. There was the same curious lack of delicacy of thought and touch—the heaviness that plows through, gets things done. When John Grey had married Louise Aspinwahl he was already a mature man, on his way to success. Such men do not marry young and recklessly. Now he was nearing sixty and there was the son—so like himself, having the same kind of strength.

Both land lovers, possession lovers. "It is my farm, my house, my horses, cattle, sheep." Soon now, another ten years, fifteen at the most, and the father would be ready for death. "See, already my hand slips a little. All of this to go out of my grasp." He, John Grey, had not got all of these possessions so easily. It had taken much patience, much persistence. No one but himself would ever quite know. Five, ten, fifteen years of work and saving, getting the Aspinwahl farm piece by piece. "The fools!" They had liked to think of themselves as aristocrats, throwing the land away, now twenty acres, now thirty, now fifty.

Raising horses that could never plow an acre of land.

And they had robbed the land too, had never put anything back, doing nothing to enrich it, build it up. Such a one thinking: "I'm an Aspinwahl, a gentleman. I do not soil my hands at the plow."

"Fools who do not know the meaning of land owned, possessions, money—responsibility. It is they who are second-rate men."

He had got an Aspinwahl for a wife and, as it had turned out, she was the best, the smartest and, in the end, the best-looking one of the lot.

And now there was his son, standing at the moment near the mother. They had both come down off the porch. It would be natural and right for this one—he being what he already was, what he would become—for him, in his turn, to come into possession, to take command.

There would be, of course, the rights of the other children. If you have the stuff in you (John Grey felt that his son Don had) there is a way to manage. You buy the others out, make arrangements. There was Ted—he wouldn't be alive—and Mary and the two younger children. "The better for you if you have to struggle."

All of this, the implication of the moment of sudden struggle between a father and son, coming slowly afterwards to the man's daughter, as yet little more than a child. Does the drama take place when the seed is put into the ground or afterwards when the plant has pushed out of the ground and the bud breaks open, or still later, when the fruit ripens? There were the Greys with their ability—slow, saving, able, determined, patient. Why had they superseded the Aspinwahls in the Rich Valley? Aspinwahl blood also in the two children, Mary and Ted.

There was an Aspinwahl man—called "Uncle Fred," a brother to Louise Grey—who came sometimes to the farm. He was a rather striking-looking, tall old man with a gray Vandyke beard and a mustache, somewhat shabbily dressed but always with an indefinable air of class. He came from the county-seat town, where he lived now with a daughter who had married a merchant, a polite courtly old man who always froze into a queer silence in the presence of his sister's husband.

The son Don was standing near the mother on the day in the fall, and the two children, Mary and Ted, stood apart.

"Don't, John," Louise Grey said again. The father, who had started away toward the barns, stopped.

"Well, I guess I will."

"No, you won't," said young Don, speaking suddenly. There was a queer fixed look in his eyes. It had flashed into life—something that was between the two men: "I possess"..."I will possess." The father wheeled and looked sharply at the son and then ignored him.

For a moment the mother continued pleading.

"But why, why?"

"They make too much shade. The grass does not grow."

"But there is so much grass, so many acres of grass."

John Grey was answering his wife, but now again he looked at his son. There were unspoken words flying back and forth.

"I possess. I am in command here. What do you mean by telling me that I won't?"

"Ha! So! You possess now but soon I will possess."

"I'll see you in hell first."

"You fool! Not yet! Not yet!"

None of the words set down above was spoken at the moment, and afterwards the daughter Mary never did remember the exact words that had passed between the two men. There was a sudden quick flash of determination in Don—even perhaps sudden determination to stand by the mother—even perhaps something else—a feeling in the young Don out of the Aspinwahl blood in him—for the moment tree love superseding grass love—grass that would fatten steers...

Winner of 4H Club prizes, champion young corn-raiser, judge of steers, land lover, possession lover.

"You won't," Don said again.

"Won't what?"

"Won't cut those trees."

The father said nothing more at the moment but walked away from the little group toward the barns. The sun was still shining brightly. There was a sharp cold little wind. The two trees were like bonfires lighted against distant hills.

It was the noon hour and there were two men, both young, employees on the farm, who lived in a small tenant house beyond the barns. One of them, a man with a harelip, was married and the other, a rather handsome silent young man, boarded with him. They had just come from the midday meal and were going toward one of the barns. It was the beginning of the fall corn-cutting time and they would be going together to a distant field to cut corn.

The father went to the barn and returned with the two men. They brought axes and a long crosscut saw. "I want you to cut those two trees." There was something, a blind, even stupid determination in the man, John Grey. And at that moment his wife, the mother of his children... There was no way any of the children could ever know how many moments of the sort she had been through. She had married John Grey. He was her man.

"If you do, Father..." Don Grey said coldly.

"Do as I tell you! Cut those two trees!" This addressed to the two workmen. The one who had a harelip laughed. His laughter was like the bray of a donkey.

"Don't," said Louise Grey, but she was not addressing her husband this time. She stepped to her son and put a hand on his arm.

"Don't.

"Don't cross him. Don't cross my man." Could a child like Mary Grey comprehend? It takes time to understand things that happen in life. Life unfolds slowly to the mind. Mary was standing with Ted, whose young face was white and tense. Death at his elbow. At any moment. At any moment.

"I have been through this a hundred times. That is the way this man I married has succeeded. Nothing stops him. I married him; I have had my children by him.

"We women choose to submit.

"This is my affair more than yours, Don, my son."

A woman hanging onto her thing—the family—created about her.

The son not seeing things with her eyes. He shook off his mother's hand, lying on his arm. Louise Grey was younger than her husband, but, if he was now nearing sixty, she was drawing near fifty. At the moment she looked very delicate and fragile. There was something, at the moment, in her bearing... Was there, after all, something in blood, the Aspinwahl blood?

In a dim way perhaps, at the moment, the child Mary did comprehend. Women and their men. For her then, at that time, there was but one male, the child Ted. Afterwards she remembered how he looked at that moment, the curiously serious old look on his young face. There was even, she thought later, a kind of contempt for both the father and brother, as though he might have been saying to himself—he couldn't really have been saying it—he was too young: "Well, we'll see. This is something. These foolish ones—my father and my brother. I myself haven't long to live. I'll see what I can, while I do live."

The brother Don stepped over near to where his father stood.

"If you do, Father..." he said again.

"Well?"

"I'll walk off this farm and I'll never come back."

"All right. Go then."

The father began directing the two men who had begun cutting the trees, each man taking a tree. The young man with the harelip kept laughing, the laughter like the bray of a donkey. "Stop that," the father said sharply, and the sound ceased abruptly. The son Don walked away, going rather aimlessly toward the barn. He approached one of the barns and then stopped. The mother, white now, half ran into the house.

The son returned toward the house, passing the two younger children without looking at them, but did not enter. The father did not look at him. He went hesitatingly along a path at the front of the house and through a gate and into a road. The road ran for several miles down through the valley and then, turning, went over a mountain to the county-seat town.

As it happened, only Mary saw the son Don when he returned to the farm. There were three or four tense days. Perhaps all the time the mother and son had been secretly in touch. There was a telephone in the house. The father stayed all day in the fields and, when he was in the house, was silent.

Mary was in one of the barns on the day when Don came back and when the father and son met. It was an odd meeting.

The son came, Mary always afterwards thought, rather sheepishly. The father came out of a horse's stall. He had been throwing corn to work horses. Neither the father nor son saw Mary. There was a car parked in the barn and she had crawled into the driver's seat, her hands on the steering wheel, pretending she was driving.

"Well," the father said. If he felt triumphant, he did not show his feeling.

"Well," said the son, "I have come back."

"Yes, I see," the father said. "They are cutting corn." He walked toward the barn door and then stopped. "It will be yours soon now," he said. "You can be boss then."

He said no more and both men went away, the father toward the distant fields and the son toward the house. Mary was afterwards quite sure that nothing more was ever said.

What had the father meant?

"When it is yours you can be boss." It was too much for the child. Knowledge comes slowly. It meant:

"You will be in command, and for you, in your turn, it will be necessary to assert.

"Such men as we are cannot fool with delicate stuff. Some men are meant to command and others must obey. You can make them obey in your turn.

"There is a kind of death.

"Something in you must die before you can possess and command."

There was, so obviously, more than one kind of death. For Don Grey one kind and for the younger brother Ted, soon now perhaps, another.

Mary ran out of the barn that day wanting eagerly to get out into the light, and afterwards, for a long time, she did not try to think her way through what had happened. She and her brother Ted did, however, afterwards, before he died, discuss quite often the two trees. They went on a cold day and put their fingers on the stumps, but the stumps were cold. Ted kept asserting that only men got their legs and arms cut off, and she protested. They continued doing things that had been forbidden Ted to do, but no one protested, and, a year or two later, when he died, he died during the night in his bed.

But while he lived, there was always, Mary afterwards thought, a curious sense of freedom, something that belonged to him that made it good, a great happiness, to be with him. It was, she finally thought, because having to die his kind of death, he never had to make the surrender his brother had made—to be sure of possessions, success, his time to command—would never have to face the more subtle and terrible death that had come to his older brother.

IN A FIELD

ONE NIGHT, YEARS AGO, WHEN I WAS A YOUNG LABORER AND WAS beating my way westward on a freight train, a brakeman succeeded in throwing me off the train in an Indiana town. I remembered the place long afterward because of my embarrassment—walking about among people in dirty torn clothes and with dirty hands and face. However, I had a little money and after I had walked through the town to a country road I found a creek and bathed. Then I went back to town to a restaurant and bought food.

It was a Saturday evening and the streets of the town were filled with people. After it grew dark my torn clothes were not so much in evidence and by a street light near a church on a side street a girl smiled at me. Half undecided as to whether or not I had better try to follow and pick up an acquaintance, I stood for some moments by a tree staring after her. Then I bethought me that when she had seen me more closely and had seen the condition of my clothes she would in any event have nothing to do with me.

As is natural to man under such circumstances, I told myself I did not want her anyway and went off down another street.

I came to a bridge and stood for a time looking down into the water and then went on across the bridge along a road and into a field where long grass grew. It was a summer night and I was sleepy but after I had slept, perhaps for several hours, I was awakened by something going on in the field and within a few feet of me.

The field was small and two houses stood facing it, the one near where I lay in a fence corner and the other a few hundred yards away. When I had come into the field lights were lighted in both houses but now they were both dark, and before me—some ten paces away—three men were struggling silently while near them stood a woman who held her hands over her face and who sobbed, not loudly but with a kind of low wailing cry. There was something, dimly seen, something white, lying on the ground near the woman and suddenly by a kind of flash of intuition I understood what had happened. The white thing on the ground was a woman's garment.

The three men were struggling desperately and even in the dim light it was evident that two of them were trying to overcome the third. He was the woman's lover and lived in the house at the end of the path that crossed the field and the two others were her brothers. They had gone into the town for the evening and had come home late and as they were walking silently across the grass in the field they had stumbled upon the love-makers and in a flash there was the impulse to kill their sister's lover. Perhaps they felt the honor of their house had been destroyed.

And now one of them had got a knife out of his pocket and had slashed at the lover, laying his cheek open, and they might have killed the man as the woman and I watched trembling but at that moment he got away and ran across the field toward his own house followed by the others.

I was left alone in the field with the woman—we were within a few feet of each other—and for a long time she did not move. "After all I am not a man of action. I am a recorder of things, a teller of tales." It was somewhat thus I excused myself for not coming to the lover's aid, as I lay perfectly still in the fence corner, looking and listening. The woman continued to sob and now, from across the dark field, there was a shout. The lover had not succeeded in getting into his own house, was really but a step ahead of his pursuers, and perhaps did not dare risk trying to open a door. He ran back across the field, dodging here and there, and, passing near us, crossed the bridge into the road that led to town. The woman in the field began calling, evidently to her two brothers, but they paid no attention. "John! Fred!" she called between her sobs. "Stop! Stop!"

And now again all was silent in the field and I could hear the rapid steps of the three running men in the dusty road in the distance.

Then lights appeared in both the houses facing the field and the woman went into the house near me, still sobbing bitterly, and presently there were voices to be heard. Then the woman—now fully clad—came out and went across the field to the second house and presently came back with another woman. Their skirts almost brushed my face as they passed me.

The two sat on the steps of the house on my side of the field, both crying, and above the sound of their crying I could still hear, far off, the sound of running feet. The lover had got into the town, which was but half a mile away, and was evidently dodging through streets. Was the town aroused? Now and then shouts came from the distance. I had no watch and did not know how long I had slept in the field.

Now all became silent again and there were just the three people, myself lying trembling in the grass and the two women on the steps of the house near me, and both crying softly. Time passed. What had happened? What would happen? In fancy I was the running man caught and perhaps killed in some dark little side street of an Indiana farming town into which I had been thrown by the accident that a railroad brakeman had seen me standing on the bumpers between two cars of his train and had ordered me off. "Well, get off or give me a dollar," he had said, and I had not wanted to give him a dollar. I had only had three dollars in my pocket. Why should I give one to him? "There will be other freight trains," I had said to myself, "and perhaps I shall see something of interest here in this town."

Interest indeed! Now I lay in the grass trembling with fear. In fancy I had become the lover of the younger of the women sitting on the steps of the house and my sweetheart's brothers with open knives in their hands were pursuing me in a dark street. I felt the knives slashing my body and knew that what I felt the women also felt. Every few minutes the younger of the two cried out. It was as though a knife had gone into her body. All three of us trembled with fear.

And then, as we waited and shook with dread, there was a stir in the silence. Feet, not running but walking steadily, were heard on the bridge that led into the road that passed the field and four men appeared. Somewhere in the town, in the dark night streets of the town, the two brothers had caught the lover but it was evident there had been an explanation. The three had gone together to a doctor, the cut cheek had been patched, they had got a marriage license and a preacher and were now coming home for a marriage.

The marriage took place at once, there before me on the steps of the house, and after the marriage, and after some sort of heavy joke on the part of the preacher, a joke at which no one laughed, the lover with his sweetheart, accompanied by the second woman, the one from the house across the field and who was evidently the lover's mother, went off across the field. Presently the field where I lay was all dark and silent again.

A CRIMINAL'S
CHRISTMAS

EVERY MAN'S HAND AGAINST ME. THERE I WAS IN THE DARKNESS OF
the empty house. It was cold outside and snow was falling. I crept
to a window and raising a curtain peered out. A man walked in
the street. Now he had stopped at a corner and was looking about.
He was looking toward the house I was in. I drew back into the
darkness.

Two o'clock, four o'clock. The night before Christmas.

Yesterday I had walked freely in the streets. Then temptation
came. I committed a crime. The manhunt was on.

Always men creeping in darkness in cities, in towns, in alleyways
in cities, on dark country roads.

Man wanted. The manhunt. Who was my friend? Who could
I trust? Where should I go?

It was my own fault. I had brought it on myself. We were hard
up that year and I had got a job in Willmott's grocery and general
store. I was twelve years old and was to have fifty cents a day.

During the afternoon of the day before Christmas there was a
runaway on Main Street. Everyone rushed out. I was tying a package
and there—right at my hand—was an open cash drawer.

I did not think. I grabbed. There was so much silver. Would
anyone know? Afterward I found I had got six dollars, all in quarters,
nickels and dimes. It made a handful. How heavy it felt. When I

put it in my pocket what a noise it made.

No one knew. Yes they did. Now wait. Don't be nervous.

You know what such a boy—twelve years of age—would tell himself. I wanted presents for the other kids of our family—wanted something for mother. Mother had been ill. She was just able to sit up.

When I got out of the store that evening it was for a time all right. I spent a dollar seventy-five. Fifty cents of it was for mother—a lacy-looking kind of thing to put around her neck. There were five other children. I spent a quarter on each.

Then I spent a quarter on myself. That left four dollars. I bought a kite. That was silly. You don't fly kites in the winter. When I got home and before I went into the house I hid it in a shed. There were some old boxes in a corner. I put it in behind the boxes.

It was grand going in with the presents in my arms. Toys, candy, the lace for mother.

Mother never said a word. She never asked me where I got the money to buy so many things.

I got away as soon as I could. There was a boy named Bob Mann giving a party and I went to it.

I had come too early. I looked through a window and saw I had come long before the party was to start so I went for a walk.

It had begun to snow. I had told mother I might stay at Bob Mann's all night.

That was what raised the devil—just walking about. When I had grabbed the money out of the cash drawer I did not think there was a soul in the store. There wasn't. But just as I was slipping it into my pocket a man came in.

The man was a stranger. What a noise the silver made. Even when I was walking in the street that night, thinking about the man, it made a noise. Every step I took it jingled in my pockets.

A fine thing to go to a party making a noise like that. Suppose they played some game. In lots of games you chase each other.

I was frightened now. I might have thrown the money away, buried it in the snow, but I thought . . .

I was full of remorse. If they did not find me out I could go back to the store next day and slip the four dollars back into the drawer.

"They won't send me to jail for two dollars," I thought, but there was that man.

I mean the one who came into the store just when I had got the money all safe and was putting it into my pocket.

He was such a strange-acting man. He just came into the store and then went right out. I was confused of course. I must have acted rather strangely. No doubt I looked scared.

He may have been just a man who had got into a wrong place. Perhaps he was a man looking for his wife.

When he had gone all the others came back. There had been a rush before the runaway happened and there was a rush again. No one paid any attention to me. I never even asked whose horse ran away.

The man might, however, have been a detective. That thought did not come until I went to Bob Mann's party and got there too early. It came when I was walking in the street waiting for the party to begin.

I never did go to the party. Like any other boy I had read a lot of dime novels. There was a boy in our town named Roxie Williams who had been in a reform school. What I did not know about crime and detectives he had told me.

I was walking in the street thinking of that man who came into the store just as I stole the money and then, when I began to think of detectives, I began to be afraid of every man I met.

In a snow like that, in a small town where there aren't many lights, you can't tell who anyone is.

There was a man started to go into a house. He went right up to the front door and seemed about to knock and then he didn't. He stood by the front door a minute and then started away.

It was the Musgraves' house. I could see Lucy Musgrave inside through a window. She was putting coal in a stove. All the houses I saw that evening, while I was walking around, getting more and more afraid all the time, seemed the most cheerful and comfortable places.

There was Lucy Musgrave inside a house and that man outside by the front door, only a few feet away and she never knowing it. It might have been the detective and he might have thought the Musgrave house was our house.

After that thought came I did not dare go home and did not know where I could go. Fortunately the man at the Musgraves' front door hadn't seen me. I had crouched behind a fence. When he went away along the street I started to run but had to stop.

The loose silver in my pocket made too much racket. I did not dare go and hide it anywhere because I thought, "If they find and arrest me and I have four dollars to give back maybe they'll let me go."

Then I thought of a house where a boy named Jim Moore lived. It was right near Buckeye Street—a good place. Mrs. Moore was a widow and only had Jim and one daughter and they had gone away for Christmas.

I made it there all right, creeping along the streets. I knew the Moores hid their key in a woodshed, under a brick near the door. I had seen Jim Moore get it dozens of times.

It was there all right and I got in. Such a night! I got some clothes out of a closet to put on and keep me warm. They belonged to Mrs. Moore and her grown-up daughter. Afterward they found them all scattered around the house and it was a town wonder. I would get a coat and skirt and wrap them around me. Then I'd put them down somewhere and as I did not dare light a match would have to get some more. I took some spreads off beds.

It was all like being crazy or dead or something. Whenever anyone went along the street outside I was so scared I trembled all over. Pretty soon I had got the notion the whole town was on the hunt.

Then I began thinking of mother. Perhaps by this time they had been to our house. I could not make up my mind what to do.

Sometimes I thought—well, in stories I was always at that time reading—boys about my own age were always beginning life as bootblacks and rising to affluence and power. I thought I would slide out of town before daylight and get me a bootblack's outfit somehow. Then I'd be all right.

I remember that I thought I'd start my career at a place called Cairo, Illinois. Why Cairo I do not know.

I thought that all out, crouching by a window in the Moores' house that Christmas eve, and then, when no one came along the street for a half hour and I began to be brave again, I thought that if I had a pistol I would let myself out of the house and go boldly home. If, as I supposed, detectives were hid in front of the house, I'd shoot my way through.

I would get desperately wounded of course. I was pretty sure I would get a mortal wound but before I died I would stagger in at the door and fall at mother's feet.

There I would lie dying, covered with blood. I made up some dandy speeches. "I stole the money, mother, to bring a moment of happiness into your life. It was because it was Christmas eve." I remember that was one of the speeches. When I thought of it— of my getting it off and then dying — I cried.

Well, I was cold and frightened enough to cry anyway.

What really happened was that I stayed in the Moores' house until daylight came. After midnight it got so quiet in the street outside that I risked a fire in the kitchen stove but I went to sleep for a moment in a chair beside the stove and falling forward made a terrible burned place on my forehead.

The mark of Cain. I am only telling this story to show that I know just how a criminal feels.

I got out of the Moore house at daylight and went home and got into our house without anyone knowing. I had to crawl into bed with a brother but he was asleep. Next morning, in the excitement of getting all the presents they did not expect, no one asked me where I had been. When mother asked me where I had got the burn I said, "At the party," and she put some soda on it and did not say anything more.

And on the day after Christmas I went back to the store and sure enough got the four dollars back into the drawer. Mr. Willmott gave me a dollar. He said I had hurried away so fast on Christmas eve that he hadn't got a chance to give me a present.

They did not need me any more after that week and I was all right and knew the man that came in such an odd way into the store wasn't a detective at all.

As for the kite—in the spring I traded it off. I got me a pup but the pup got distemper and died.

VIRGINIA JUSTICE

FRED'S PLACE, AT THE EDGE OF OUR TOWN, IS IN A LITTLE VALLEY IN the hills. Fred is a small, quiet man. I am not putting down his real name. He is a well-known writer. A good many writers who go into the country to live are seeking what they call local color, but I do not believe Fred is up to anything of the sort. Once I asked him: "Did you come here just to live among us, or did you build your house and settle down here to write us up?"

He smiled. "I haven't run short of things to write about," he said. "Every man and woman I ever saw is a story. There are too many stories. A man is a fool who seeks materials. The thing is to know how to handle materials. That's something."

When Fred settled here in our hills among our Blue Ridge mountain people, "hillbillies" I guess you'd call them, he was misunderstood. For one thing, everyone thought he was rich. These mountain people of ours aren't much like the mountain moonshiners you read about in magazine stories. It's true a good many of them can't read or write, but if you think they are stupid, just try to trade horses with one of them.

When Fred built his house in his upland valley a few miles out of town, half the mountain men for miles about worked for him. Old Jim Salt was boss on the job when he wasn't drunk. Fred paid good wages, the best ever paid about here. That may have been a mistake. Folks thought he was easy.

They began laying for him, robbing him a little here, a little there. They thought he didn't know it, but the truth is that he didn't much mind. He isn't a man who has much money sense, and once when I spoke to him of the matter, he said: "Pshaw! They haven't enough imagination to rob me much."

The little sharp tricks some of our mountain men worked on him only amused the man.

Once he talked to me a long time about money. It seemed to puzzle him. I guess he talked to me more openly than others in town because I've been a college professor. He may have thought I was more at home in his book world. He had a mountain man named Felix working for him. Felix was building a stone wall, and he is a great talker. Fred told me that he went and sat for an hour on the wall near where Felix was at work, and that Felix began spinning yarns. What Felix was really doing was loafing, but he told Fred a tale and Fred went into the house and wrote it down, "word for word as Felix told it," he said. "I got $300 for it and I was paying Felix $2 a day. I guess if a man understood about money, he'd understand a lot."

Fred had a neighbor named Tom Case, a one-eyed man. Tom's queer. He is both mean and generous. Catch him in one mood and he'll steal the fillings out of your teeth, but the next day, when you meet him, he'll give you his shirt.

Tom's farm is on the hillside above the valley where Fred built his house, and, after Fred moved in, Tom laid for him. Fred had bought himself an old saddle horse to ride about the country, and one day the horse got through a fence into Tom's corn field. It was an accident the first time, but Tom got roaring mad, or pretended to be mad, and went down to Fred's house, raving and swearing and demanding $10 damage. The horse hadn't done fifty cents worth of damage to the corn, but Fred gave him the ten.

So it happened again, and then a third time. We all thought Tom was letting the horse into the corn. It was a small hillside field, and there wasn't $5 worth of corn in it. Thirty dollars for

Tom. "Pretty good, eh?" everyone said. We all knew well enough what Tom was doing, but in all of us there was something of the same feeling. "Well, he's a city man. He makes money easy." We might even have been a little jealous of Tom's easy picking.

And then Tom spoiled it. He went whole-hog on Fred. The horse got in the corn a fourth time and he wanted $25. Jake Wilson told me he wanted to get his roof fixed. "Roof fixed?" said Hardy Davidson. "He's after a new house and a new farm."

But he overreached that time. He raved and swore and declared he'd kill Fred, and he took Fred's horse and locked it in his barn. I've noticed that when a man is being dirty, mean and crooked with another, he begins to hate the other. Fred kept quiet when all this happened, and came into town and got the sheriff to go get his horse. He had decided to go to law with Tom and put up a $100 bond to cover any possible damage Tom might get in court.

Tom was so sore he even threatened to shoot the sheriff when he went for the horse. Fred told me that, in the mood he was in, he was afraid Tom might starve the beast. The business about shooting the sheriff was bluff, of course. The sheriff just laughed and made Tom unlock the barn and took the horse home.

"You're a fool. You've spoiled your own racket," he said, and Tom, who was standing in the barnyard with a shotgun in his hand, danced with rage. Our sheriff, Sam Hopkins, says that when a man is going to shoot he don't talk. "He just shoots," he says.

So there was to be a trial in a Virginia squire's court, and half the town and all the farmers and hill men for miles around turned out. It was a nice day, a Saturday in the fall after the corn was cut. The trial was on the Burleson road at Squire Wills' house. Squire Wills sat with Squire Grey from the Flat Ridge. These Virginia squires don't pretend to know much law, and they don't like lawyers around telling them what's what. Get a lawyer and you lose your case every time. That's why neither Fred nor Tom got one. The squires are elected, and there may be as many as a dozen in one county. They get $3 each for sitting in a case, and you can have as many as three sitting, if you want.

So we were all fixed for a big day, and we all went. These country courts are our theater here in the hills. The two squires, both old men, sat solemnly on the front porch of Squire Wills' house, and we all gathered on the lawn in front or in the road.

There was a good deal going on. It was a rare day in the fall, and the horse traders were out. Men and women had come in cars, and the mountain men on horses. There was a good deal of shouting and laughing, some at Tom, some at Fred.

Tom didn't speak to anyone but his brother from Floyd County, who had come over for the trial. The brother stood in the road, and Tom rode up and down on a big black horse. He had his shotgun with him, and he had been drinking a good deal of "mountain moon," and he was trying to intimidate both Fred and the judges.

It didn't work. So Tom stopped his horse near his brother and leaned over to whisper to him. We were all watching. After all, we thought, although Tom Case never had shot anyone, he might begin.

And then, after Tom had whispered to another man, and he to a third, and the third man had gone to whisper to Fred, who was sitting on the edge of the porch, and Fred shook his head, we all knew that, anyway, the trial wasn't going to be settled out of court. Fred told me afterwards that Tom offered to settle for $12. "I wouldn't have settled for ten cents," Fred said.

He was beginning to get the spirit of the country all right.

So then the trial began, and Fred got up and told how he had given Tom $10 three times, and he said he might have done it this time but that Tom had been a hog. "I suggest," he said, "that the judges, or Tom and me, select three men and let them go down to Tom's place and look at that corn field. I'll still pay whatever they say is right."

So that, of course, brought on something new. The two squires put their heads together and whispered and nodded, and finally said that Fred could choose a man, Tom another, and that the judges would choose a third.

Of course Tom objected. He swore, he raved, he rode his big horse up and down the road, he waved his gun, he whispered with his brother, and once one of the judges warned him.

"We could have you up for contempt of court, Tom," Squire Wills yelled, and everyone, even Tom and the other judge, had to laugh at that. They figured some lawyer must have been talking to Squire Wills.

Finally, anyway, Tom selected his Floyd County brother, and Fred chose me, and the judges named Jim Wilson, and we drove down to Tom's field. Tom's wife came out while we were looking over the corn. We couldn't see where there had been any damage done that you could notice . . . it's pretty hard to damage a hillside corn field much . . . and the wife said she was fair ashamed of Tom and had argued with him but for us not to tell him what she said. We decided on $2 because we all thought Fred could spare it, but Tom's brother spoke up and said, "No, let's make it $3."

He laughed when he said it, and I said $3 would be all right. "Fred'll maybe write all this up and get his money back anyway," I said.

Then we came back and gave in our decision, and you should have heard Tom roar. He threw his gun on the ground and rode around and shook his fist under first his brother's nose, then Jim's and then mine, but, as we say in the hills, we didn't pay him no mind, and the judges gave out their decision and stuck Fred for the costs.

So then Fred got a little sore, the first time I ever saw him bothered much. He got up and protested. "Look here," he said, "I tendered this man $10. You all know I've got $30 invested in that corn field now, and you all know he was after $25 from me, and the judges you sent down there only found $3 damage." He turned to us referees. "Men," he said, "how much would the whole crop of corn in the field have been worth if my horse had never got in there? If he got in and wasn't put in."

"About $7," Jim Wilson said, and the whole crowd had to laugh.

What was wrong, of course, was with the judges. There was a little shed beside Squire Wills' house, and he and Squire Grey went in there. They stayed for a while, conferring, I guess, and then Squire Grey came to the door and motioned for Fred to come in. He told me afterwards how it was. He said the squires told him that the costs of the trial would be $6. "Three dollars apiece," they said. "We don't want to stick you, Fred, but Tom's mad. He won't pay," they said. They told Fred they thought it wouldn't be fair for them not to get their regular fees for such an important trial, and Fred told them he thought so too. "Only I don't want that Tom to get the best of me in this," he said.

Then Fred did some fast thinking. He told me afterwards that he was prouder of that moment than of any other in his whole life.

"Look here," he said to the two Virginia squires, "I'll tell you what let's do. You go out there on the porch and announce that the cost of the trial is to be divided, fifty-fifty. I'll pay the $3 damage, and half the costs, and that makes $6. You two keep it all. Tom won't get a red cent."

And so it was done, and I don't believe Tom quite understands it yet. He got some damage, and he didn't get it. He was madder than ever, not at Fred now, but at the squires, and he swore he'd run them both out of the country.

So he got his gun off the ground where he had thrown it and rode off swearing and we all went on home. Afterwards, Fred told me of something else that happened. He said he didn't see Tom again for as much as two months and that then, one day in the early winter when it was raining, he was out for a walk in the rain and met Tom on his black horse on a narrow mountain road. He said Tom stopped, and he stopped, and they both stared at each other a while, and then they both began to laugh and Tom got down off his horse.

Fred said they must have talked for two hours, friendly as the devil, about crops and weather and Democrats and Republicans and horses and who'd be a good man for county assessor, old Sylvester Sullivan being dead, but they never mentioned the trial at all.

And after that, Fred had Tom on his hands. He'd come down once a week looking for some work to do, and when Fred let him do a few chores now and then, he wouldn't take a cent.

"I'm only doing this work because I believe in neighbors being good neighbors," Tom said.

THE CORN PLANTING

THE FARMERS WHO COME TO OUR TOWN TO TRADE ARE A PART OF THE town life. Saturday is the big day. Often the children come to the high school in town.

It is so with Hatch Hutchenson. Although his farm, some three miles from town, is small, it is known to be one of the best-kept and best-worked places in all our section. Hatch is a little gnarled old figure of a man. His place is on the Scratch Gravel Road and there are plenty of poorly kept places out that way.

Hatch's place stands out. The little frame house is always kept painted, the trees in his orchard are whitened with lime halfway up the trunks, and the barn and sheds are in repair, and his fields are always clean-looking.

Hatch is nearly seventy. He got a rather late start in life. His father, who owned the same farm, was a Civil War man and came home badly wounded, so that, although he lived a long time after the war, he couldn't work much. Hatch was the only son and stayed at home, working the place until his father died. Then, when he was nearing fifty, he married a school teacher of forty and they had a son. The school teacher was a small one like Hatch. After they married they both stuck close to the land. They seemed to fit into their farm life as certain people fit into the clothes they wear. I have noticed something about people who make a go of marriage. They grow more and more alike. They even grow to look alike.

Their one son, Will Hutchenson, was a small but remarkably strong boy. He came to our high school in town and pitched on our town baseball team. He was a fellow always cheerful, bright and alert, and a great favorite with all of us.

For one thing, he began as a young boy to make amusing little drawings. It was a talent. He made drawings of fish and pigs and cows and they looked like people you knew. I never did know before that people could look so much like cows and horses and pigs and fish.

When he had finished in the town high school, Will went to Chicago, where his mother had a cousin living, and he became a student in the Art Institute out there. Another young fellow from our town was also in Chicago. He really went two years before Will did. His name was Hal Weyman and he was a student at the University of Chicago. After he graduated, he came home and got a job as principal of our high school.

Hal and Will Hutchenson hadn't been close friends before, Hal being several years older than Will, but in Chicago they got together, went together to see plays, and, as Hal later told me, they had a good many long talks.

I got it from Hal that, in Chicago, as at home here when he was a young boy, Will was immediately popular. He was good looking, so the girls in the art school liked him, and he had a straightforwardness that made him popular with all the young fellows.

Hal told me that Will was out to some party nearly every night, and right away he began to sell some of his amusing little drawings and to make money. The drawings were used in advertisements and he was well paid.

He even began to send some money home. You see, after Hal came back here, he used to go quite often out to the Hutchenson place to see Will's father and mother. He would walk or drive out there in the afternoon or on summer evenings and sit with them. The talk was always of Will.

Hal said it was touching how much the father and mother depended on their one son, how much they talked about him and dreamed of his future. They had never been people who went about much with the town folks or even with their neighbors. They were of the sort who work all the time, from early morning till late in the evenings, and on moonlight nights, Hal said, and after the little old wife had got the supper, they often went out into the fields and worked again.

You see, by this time old Hatch was nearing seventy and his wife would have been ten years younger. Hal said that whenever he went out to the farm they quit work and came to sit with him. They might be in one of the fields, working together, but when they saw him in the road, they came running. They had got a letter from Will. He wrote every week.

The little old mother would come running following the father. "We got another letter, Mr. Weyman," Hatch would cry, and then his wife, quite breathless, would say the same thing, "Mr. Weyman, we got a letter."

The letter would be brought out at once and read aloud. Hal said the letters were always delicious. Will larded them with little sketches. There were humorous drawings of people he had seen or been with, rivers of automobiles on Michigan Avenue in Chicago, a policeman at a street crossing, young stenographers hurrying into office buildings. Neither of the old people had ever been to the city and they were curious and eager. They wanted the drawings explained, and Hal said they were like two children wanting to know every little detail Hal could remember about their son's life in the big city. He was always at them to come there on a visit and they would spend hours talking of that.

"Of course," Hatch said, "we couldn't go."

"How could we?" he said. He had been on that one little farm since he was a boy. When he was a young fellow, his father was an invalid and so Hatch had to run things. A farm, if you run it right, is very exacting. You have to fight weeds all the time. There are the farm animals to take care of. "Who would milk our cows?" Hatch said. The idea of anyone but him or his wife touching one of the Hutchenson cows seemed to hurt him. While he was alive, he didn't want anyone else plowing one of his fields, tending his corn, looking after things about the barn. He felt that way about his farm. It was a thing you couldn't explain, Hal said. He seemed to understand the two old people.

It was a spring night, past midnight, when Hal came to my house and told me the news. In our town we have a night telegraph operator at the railroad station and Hal got a wire. It was really addressed to Hatch Hutchenson, but the operator brought it to Hal. Will Hutchenson was dead, had been killed. It turned out later that he was at a party with some other young fellows and there might have been some drinking. Anyway, the car was wrecked and Will Hutchenson was killed. The operator wanted Hal to go out and take the message to Hatch and his wife, and Hal wanted me to go along.

I offered to take my car but Hal said no. "Let's walk out," he said. He wanted to put off the moment, I could see that. So we did walk. It was early spring and I remember every moment of the silent walk we took, the little leaves just coming on the trees, the little streams we crossed, how the moonlight made the water seem alive. We loitered and loitered, not talking, hating to go on.

Then we got out there, and Hal went to the front door of the farmhouse while I stayed in the road. I heard a dog bark, away off somewhere. I heard a child crying in some distant house. I think that Hal, after he got to the front door of the house, must have stood there for ten minutes, hating to knock.

Then he did knock and the sound his fist made on the door seemed terrible. It seemed like guns going off. Old Hatch came to the door and I heard Hal tell him. I know what happened. Hal had been trying, all the way out from town, to think up words to tell the old couple in some gentle way, but when it came to the scratch, he couldn't. He blurted everything right out, right into old Hatch's face.

That was all. Old Hatch didn't say a word. The door was opened, he stood there in the moonlight, wearing a funny long white nightgown, Hal told him, and the door went shut again with a bang, and Hal was left standing there.

He stood for a time and then came back out into the road to me. "Well," he said, and "Well," I said. We stood in the road looking and listening. There wasn't a sound from the house.

And then...it might have been ten minutes or it might have been a half-hour...we stood silently, listening and watching, not knowing what to do...we couldn't go away..."I guess they are trying to get so they can believe it," Hal whispered to me. I got his notion all right. The two old people must have thought of their son Will always only in terms of life, never of death.

We stood watching and listening and then, suddenly, after a long time, Hal touched me on the arm. "Look," he whispered. There were two white-clad figures going from the house to the barn. It turned out, you see, that old Hatch had been plowing that day. He had finished plowing and harrowing a field near the barn.

The two figures went into the barn and presently came out. They went into the field, and Hal and I crept across the farmyard to the barn and got to where we could see what was going on without being seen.

It was an incredible thing. The old man had got a hand corn planter out of the barn and his wife had got a bag of seed corn, and there, in the moonlight, that night, after they got that news, they were planting corn.

It was a thing to curl your hair—it was so ghostly. They were both in their nightgowns. They would do a row across the field, coming quite close to us as we stood in the shadow of the barn, and then, at the end of each row, they would kneel side by side by the fence and stay silent for a time. The whole thing went on in silence. It was the first time in my life I ever understood something, and I am far from sure now that I can put down what I understood and felt that night...I mean something about the connection between certain people and the earth...a kind of silent cry, down into the earth, of these two old people, putting corn down into the earth. It was as though they were putting death down into the ground that life might grow again, something like that.

They must have been asking something of the earth too. But what's the use? What they were up to in connection with the life in their field and the lost life in their son is something you can't very well make clear in words. All I know is that Hal and I stood the sight as long as we could, and then we crept away and went back to town, but Hatch Hutchenson and his wife must have got what they were after that night because Hal told me that when he went out in the morning to see them and to make the arrangements for bringing their dead son home, they were both curiously quiet and Hal thought in command of themselves. Hal said he thought they had got something. "They have their farm and they have still got Will's letters to read," Hal said.

MRS. WIFE

THE DOCTOR TOLD THE STORY. HE GOT VERY QUIET, VERY SERIOUS in speaking of it. I knew him well, knew his wife and his daughter. He said that I must know of course that in his practice he came into intimate contact with a good many women. We had been speaking of the relations of men and women. He had been living through an experience that must come to a great many men.

In the first place I should say, in speaking of the doctor, that he is a rather large, very strong and very handsome man. He had always lived in the country where I knew him. He was a doctor and his father had been a doctor in that country before him. I spent only one summer there but we became great friends. I went with him in his car to visit his patients, living here and there over a wide countryside, valleys, hills and plains. We were both fond of fishing and there were good trout streams in that country.

And then besides there was something else we had in common. The doctor was a great reader and, as with all true book lovers, there were certain books, certain tales, he read over and over.

"Do you know," he said laughing, "I one time thought seriously of trying to become a writer. I couldn't make it, found that when I took pen in hand I became dumb and self-conscious. I knew

that Chekhov the Russian was a doctor." He looked at me smiling. He had steady grey eyes and a big head on which grew thick
curly hair, now turning a little grey.

"You see, we doctors find out a good many things." That I, of
course, knew. What writer does not envy these country doctors
the opportunity they have to enter houses, hear stories, stand
with people in times of trouble? Oh the stories buried away in
the houses, in lonely farm houses, in the houses of town people,
the rich, the well-to-do, the poor, tales of love, of sacrifice and of
envy, hatred too. There is, however, this consolation: the problem
is never to find and know a little the people whose stories are
interesting. There are too many stories. The great difficulty is to
tell them.

"When I got my pen in hand I became dumb." How foolish.
After I had left the country the doctor used to write me long
letters. He still does it sometimes, but not often enough. The
letters are wonderful little stories of the doctor's moods on certain
days as he drives about in the country, descriptions of days, of fall
days and spring days...how full of true feeling the man is...what a
deep and true culture he has...little tales of people, his patients.
He has forgotten he is writing. The letters are like his talk.

But I must say something of the doctor's wife and of his daughter.
The daughter was a cripple, like President Roosevelt a victim of
infantile paralysis, moving about with great difficulty. She would
have been, but for this misfortune, a very beautiful woman. She
died some four years after the summer when her father and I
were so much together. And there was the wife. Her name was, I
remember, Martha.

I did not know well either the wife or the daughter. Sometimes
there are such friendships formed between two men. "Now you
look here...I have a certain life inside my own house. I have, let
me say, a certain loyalty to that life but it is not the whole of my
life. It isn't that I don't want to share that intimate life with you
but...I am sure you will understand...we have chanced upon each
other...you are in one field of work and I in another."

There is a life that goes on between men too...something almost

like love can be born and grow steadily...what an absurd word
that "love"...it does not at all describe what I mean.

Common experience, feelings a man sometimes has, his own
kind of male flights of fancy as it were...we men you see...I wonder
if it is peculiarly true of Americans? I often think so. We men
here, I often think, depend too much upon women. It is due to
our intense hunger, half shy, for each other.

I wonder if two men, in the whole history of man, were ever
much together that they did not begin to speak presently of their
experiences with women. I dare say that the same thing goes on
between women and women. Not that the doctor ever spoke much
of his wife. She was rather small and dark, a woman very beautiful
in her own way...the way I should say of a good deal of suffering.

In the first place, the doctor, that man, so very male, virile,
was naturally quick and even affectionate in all his relations with
people and particularly with women. He was a man needing more
than one outlet for his feelings. He needed dozens. If he had let
himself go in that direction he could have had his office always
full of women patients of the neurotic sort. There are that sort,
plenty of them, on farms and in country towns as well as in the
cities. He could not stand them. "I won't have it, will not be that
sort of doctor." They were the only sort of people he ever treated
rudely. "Now you get out of here and don't come back. There is
nothing wrong with you that I can cure."

I knew from little tales he told of what a struggle it had been.
Some of the women were very persistent, were determined not to
be put off. It happened that his practice was in a hill country to
which in the summer a good many city people came. There would
be wives without husbands, the husbands coming from a distant
city for the weekend or for a short vacation in the hot
months...women with money, with husbands who had money.
There was one such woman with a husband who was an insurance
man in a city some two hundred miles away. I think he was president
of the company, a small rather mouse-like man but with eyes that
were like the eyes of a ferret, sharp, quick-moving little eyes, missing
nothing. The woman, his wife, had money, plenty of it from him,

and she had inherited money.

She wanted the doctor to come to the city. "You could be a great success. You could get rich." When he would not see her in his office she wrote him letters and every day sent flowers for his office, to the office of a country doctor. "I don't mind selling her out to you," he said. "There are women and women." There were roses ordered for him from the city. They came in big boxes and he used to throw them out of his office window and into an alleyway. "The whole town, including my wife, knew of it. You can't conceal anything of this sort in a small town. At any rate my wife has a head. She knew well enough I was not to be caught by one of that sort."

He showed me a letter she had written him. It may sound fantastic but she actually offered, in the letter, to place at his disposal a hundred thousand dollars. She said she did not feel disloyal to her husband in making the offer. It was her own money. She said she was sure he had in him the making of a great doctor. Her husband need know nothing at all of the transaction. She did not ask him to give himself to her, to be her lover. There was but one string to the offer, intended to give him the great opportunity, to move to the city, set up offices in a fashionable quarter, become a doctor to rich women. He was to take her as a patient, see her daily.

"The hell," he said. "I am in no way a student and never have been. By much practice I have become a fairly good country doctor. It is what I am."

"There is but one other thing I ask. If you are not to be my lover, you must promise that you will not become the lover of some other woman." He was, I gathered, to keep himself, as she said, pure.

The doctor had very little money. His daughter was the only living child of his marriage. There had been two sons born but they had both died in the outbreak of infantile paralysis that had crippled the daughter.

The daughter, then a young woman of seventeen, had to spend most of her life in a wheel chair. It was possible that, with plenty of money to send her off to some famous physician, perhaps to Europe...the woman in her letter suggested something of the sort...she might be cured.

"Oho!" The doctor was one of the men who throw money about, cannot save it, cannot accumulate. He was very careless about sending bills. His wife had undertaken that job but there were many calls he did not report to her. He forgot them, often purposely.

"My husband need know nothing of all this."

"Is that so? What, that little ferret-eyed man? Why, he has never missed a money bet in his life."

The doctor took the letter to his wife who read it and smiled. I have already said that his wife was in her own way beautiful. Her beauty was certainly not very obvious. She had been through too much, had been too badly hurt in the loss of her sons. She had grown thin and, in repose, there was a seeming hardness about her mouth and about her eyes that were of a curious greenish grey. The great beauty of the doctor's wife only came to life when she smiled. There was then a curious, a quite wonderful transformation. "By this woman, hard or soft, hurt or unhurt, I will stand until I die.

"It is not always, however, so easy," said the doctor. He spoke of something. We had gone for an afternoon fishing and were sitting and resting on a flat rock, under a small tree by a mountain brook. We had brought some beer packed in ice in a hamper. "It is not a story you may care to use." I have already said that the doctor is a great reader. "Nowadays, it seems there is not much interest in human relations. Human relations are out of style. You must write now of the capitalists and of the proletariat. You must give things an economic slant. Hurrah for economics! Economics forever!"

I have spoken of his wife's smile. The doctor seldom smiled. He laughed heartily, with a great roar of laughter that could frighten the trout for a mile along a stream. His big body and his big head shook. He enjoyed his own laughter.

"And so it shall be an old fashioned story of love, eh, what?"

Another woman had come to him. It had all happened some two or three years before the summer when I knew him and when I spent so much time in his company. There was a well-to-do family, he said, that came into that country for the summer and they had an only child, a daughter, crippled as was his own daughter. They were not, he said, extremely rich but they had money enough or at first he thought they had. He said that the father, the head of that family, was some sort of manufacturer. "I never saw him but twice and then we did not have much talk, although I think we liked each other. He let me know that he was very busy and I saw that he was a little worried. It was because things at his factory were not going so well.

"There was the man's wife and daughter and a servant and they had brought for the daughter a nurse. She was a very strong woman, a Pole. They engaged me to come on my regular rounds to their house. They had taken a house in the country, some three miles out of town. There were certain instructions from their city doctor. There was the wish to have within call a doctor, to be at hand in case of an emergency.

"And so I went there." I have already spoken of sitting with the doctor at the end of an afternoon's fishing. Moments and hours with such people as the doctor are always afterward remembered. There is something...shall I call it inner laughter...to speak in the terms of fighters, "They can take it." They have something...it may be knowledge, or better yet maturity...surely a rare enough quality, that last, that maturity. You get the feeling from all sorts of people.

There is a little farmer who has worked for years. For no fault of his own...as everyone knows, nature can be very whimsical and cruel...long droughts coming, corn withering, hail in the young crops, or sudden pests of insects coming suddenly, destroying all. And so everything goes. You imagine such a one, struggling on into late middle life, trying, let us say, to get money to educate his children, to give them a chance he did not have, a man not afraid of work, an upstanding straight-going man.

And so all is gone. Let us think of him thus, say on a fall day.

His little place, fields he has learned to love, as all real workers love the materials in which they work, to be sold over his head. You imagine him, the sun shining. He takes a walk alone over the fields. His old wife, who has also worked as he has, with rough hands and careworn face...she is in the house, has been trying to brace him up. "Never mind, John. We'll start over again. We'll make it yet." The children with solemn faces. The wife would really like to go alone into a room and cry. "We'll make it yet, eh."

"The hell we will. Not us."

He says nothing of the sort. He walks across his fields, goes into a wood. He stands for a while there, perhaps at the edge of the wood, looking over the fields.

And then the laughter, down inside him...laughter not bitter. "It has happened to others. I am not alone in this. All over the world men are getting it in the neck as I am now...men are being forced into wars in which they do not believe...there is a Jew, an upright man, cultured, a man of fine feeling, suddenly insulted in a hotel or in the street...the bitter necessity of standing and taking it...a Negro scholar spat upon by some ignorant white.

"Well, men, here we are. Life is like this.

"But I do not go back on life. I have learned to laugh, not loudly, boisterously, bitterly, because it happens that I, by some strange chance, have been picked upon by fate. I laugh quietly.

"Why?

"Why, because I laugh."

There must be thousands of men and women...they may be the finest flowers of humanity...who will understand the above. It is the secret of America's veneration for Abraham Lincoln. He was that sort of man.

"And so.

"So I went to that house." It was my friend, the country doctor, telling his tale. "There was the woman, the mother of the crippled girl, a very gentle-looking woman, in some odd way like my wife. I have told you that I had a talk with the girl's father, the manufacturer.

"There was the crippled girl herself, destined perhaps to spend her life in bed, or going laboriously about in a wheel chair. Surely she had done nothing, this girl, that God, or nature, call it what you will, should have done this to her. Would it not be wonderful to have some of these cock-sure people explain the mystery of such things in the world? There is a job for your thinker, eh what?"

And then there was the woman, the Polish woman. The doctor, with a queer smile, began to speak of something that often happens suddenly to men and women. He was a man at that time forty-seven years old and the Polish woman...he never told me her name...might have been thirty. I have already said that the doctor was physically very strong, have tried to give the suggestion of a fine animal. There are men like that who are sometimes subject to very direct and powerful sex calls. The calls descend on them as storms descend on peaceful fields. It happened to him with the Polish woman the moment he saw her and as it turned out it also happened to her.

He said that she was in the room with the crippled girl when he went in. She was sitting in a chair near the bed. She arose and they faced each other. It all happened, I gather, at once. "I am the doctor."

"Yes," she said. There was something slightly foreign in her pronunciation of even the one simple English word, a slight shade of something he thought colored the word, made it extraordinarily nice. For a moment he just stood, looking at her as she did at him. She was a rather large woman, strong in the shoulders, big breasted, in every way, he said, physically full and rich. She had, he said, something very full and strong about her head. He spoke particularly of the upper part of her face, the way the eyes were set in the head, the broad white forehead, the shape of the head. "It is odd," he said, "now that she is gone, that I do not remember the lower part of her face." He began to speak of woman's beauty. "All this nonsense you writers write, concerning beauty in women," he said. "You know yourself that the extraordinary beauty of my own wife is not in the color of her eyes, the shape of her mouth...this rosebud mouth business, Cupid's bow, eyes of blue, or, damn it

man, of red or pink or lavender for that matter." I remember
thinking, as the man talked, that he might have made a fine sculptor.
He was emphasizing form, what he felt in the Polish woman as
great beauty of line. "In my wife beauty comes at rare intervals
but then how glorious it is. It comes, as I think you may have
noted, with her rare and significant smile."

He was standing in that room, with the little crippled girl and
the Polish woman.

"For a time, I do not know how long, I couldn't move, could
not take my eyes from her.

"My God, how crazy it now seems," the doctor said.

"There she was. Voices I had never heard before were calling
in me and, as I later found out, in her also. The strangeness of it.
'Why there you are, at last, at last, there you are.'

"You have to keep it all in mind," said the doctor, "my love of
my wife, what my wife and I had been through, our suffering
together over the loss of our two sons, our one child, our daughter,
a cripple as you know.

"And then our daily life together for years. My wife had done
something very fine for me. You know how I am. But for her I
might have starved. I could not remember to send bills, was always
getting into debt, spending too freely. She had taken my affairs in
hand. She attended to everything for me.

"And there I was, you see, suddenly stricken like that...by love,
ha! What does any sensible man know of this love?

"Why, it was pure lust in me and nothing else. I did not know
that woman, had never seen her until that moment, did not know
her name. As it was with me so it turned out it was with her. In
some way I knew that. Afterwards she told me, and I believed
her, that, as the Bible likes to put it, she had never known man.

"I stood there, you understand, looking at her and she at me."
He spoke of all this happening, as he presently realized, when
with an effort he got himself in hand, in the presence of the little
crippled girl in her bed. "It was almost as though I had, in that
moment, in the child's presence, actually taken the woman. It
seemed to me that she was something I had all of my life been

wanting with a kind of terrible force, you understand, with my entire being."

The doctor's mind went off at a tangent. The reader is not to think that he told me all this in a high excited voice. Quite the contrary. His voice was very low and quiet and I remember the scene before us as we sat on the flat rock above the mountain stream...we had driven a hundred miles to get to that stream...the soft hills in the distance beyond the stream, which just there went dashing down over the rocks, the deepening light over distant hills and distant forests. Later we got some very nice trout out of a pool below the rapids above which we sat.

It may have been the stream that sent him off into a side tale of a fishing trip taken alone, on a moonlight night, in a very wild mountain stream, on the night after he had buried his second son, the strangeness of that night, himself wading in a rushing stream, feeling his way sometimes in the half darkness, touches of moonlight on occasional pools, the casts made into such pools, often dark forests coming down to the stream's edge, the cast and, now and then, the strike, himself standing in the swift running water.

Himself fighting, all that night, not to be overcome by the loss of the second and last of his sons, the utter strangeness of what seemed to him that night a perfectly primitive world. "As though," he said, "I had stepped off into a world never before known to man, untouched by any man."

And then the strike, perhaps of a fine big trout...the sudden sharp feeling of life out there at the end of a slender cord running between it and him...the fight for life out there and, at the other end of the cord, in him.

The fight to save himself from despair.

Was it the same thing between him and the Polish woman? He said he did manage at last to free himself from the immediate thing. The city doctor had written him a letter. "I am told you have yourself a daughter, a sufferer from infantile paralysis." My friend had thought of the city doctor. "He must have been a man of sense."

"We know so very little," the city doctor had said. "There is perhaps nothing we can do. I do not quite know why it is but the foolish people seem to like to have one of us about, within call." My friend, the country doctor, made on that day of his first visit a passing examination of the child and went on his way.

"So she is the nurse they have brought here," he thought that time when he first saw her. He said he had a terrible week, a time of intense jealousy. "Would you believe it, it did not seem possible to me that any man could resist that woman," he said. He suspected the child's father. "That man, that manufacturer...he is her lover. It cannot be otherwise." The doctor laughed. "As for my wife, she was, for the time, utterly out of my life.

"Why, I do not mean to say I did not respect her. What a word, eh, that respect. I even told myself that I loved her. For the rest of the week I was in a muddle, could not remember what patients needed my services. I kept missing calls, and of course my wife, who, as I have told you, attends to all the details of my life, was disturbed.

"And, at that, she may well have been deeply aware. I do not think that people ever successfully lie to each other."

It was during that week he saw and talked briefly to the manufacturer from the city, the father of the crippled child, going there, to that house, he said, hoping again to see the woman. He did not see her and as for the man..."I had been having such silly suspicions...I wonder yet whether or not, at the time, I knew how silly they were.

"The manufacturer was a man in terrible trouble. Afterwards I learned that at just that time his affairs were going to pieces. He stood to lose all he had gained by a lifetime of work. He was thinking of his wife and of his crippled daughter. He might have to begin life again, perhaps as a workman, with a workman's pay. His daughter would perhaps, all her life, be needing the care of physicians."

I gathered that the city man had tried to take the country doctor into his confidence. They had gone into the yard of the country house and had stood together, the doctor's heart beating heavily. "I am near her. She is there in the house. If I were a real man I would go to her at once, tell her how I feel. In some way I know that this terrible hunger in me is in her also." The man, the manufacturer, was trying to tell him.

"Yes, yes, of course, it is all right."

There were certain words said. The man in trouble was trying to explain to him.

"Doctor, I will be very grateful if you can feel that you can come here, that we can depend upon you. I am a stranger to you. It may be you will get no pay for your trouble."

"Aha! What, in God's name, could keep me away?"

He did not say the words. "It is all right. I understand. It is all right."

The doctor waited a few days and then he went again. He said he was asleep in his own house, or rather was lying in his bed. Of a sudden he determined upon something. He arose. To leave the house he had to pass through his wife's room. "It is," he said, "a great mistake for a man and wife to give up sleeping together. There is something in the perfectly natural and healthy fact of being nightly so close physically to the other, your sworn companion in life. It should not be given up." The doctor and his wife had, however, I gathered, given it up. He went through her room and she was awake. "It is you, Harry?" she asked.

Yes, it was he.

"And you are going out? I have not heard any call. I have been wide awake."

It was a white moonlit night, just such a night as the one when he went in his desperation over the loss of his second son to wade in the mountain stream.

It was a moonlit night and the moonlight was streaming into his wife's room and fell upon her face. It was one of the times when she was, for some perverse reason, most beautiful to him.

"And I had got out of bed to go to that woman, had thought out a plan."

He would go to that house, would arouse and speak to the mistress of the house. "There has been an accident. I need a nurse for the night. There is no one available."

He would get the Polish woman into his car.

"I was sure...I don't know why...that she felt as I did. As I had been lying so profoundly disturbed in my bed, so she in her bed had been lying."

She was almost a stranger to him. "She wants me. I know she does."

He had got into his wife's room. "Well, you see, when at night I had to go out, to answer a call, it was my custom to go to her, to kiss her before I left. It was a simple enough thing. I could not do it.

"I know that the Polish woman is waiting for me, that she also aches, that she hungers for me. I will take her into my car. We will turn into a wood, and there, in the moonlight...

"A man cannot help what he is. When I have been with her this one time it may be that things will get clear."

He was hurrying thus through his wife's room.

"No, my dear, I have had no call.

"There is a feeling has come to me," he said. "It is that girl, the crippled one, crippled as is our Katie." Katie was the name of his daughter. "I have told you of her. It is, my dear, as though a voice has been calling me.

"And what a lie, what a terrible lie, and to that woman, my own wife.

"All right. I accepted that. There was a voice calling to me. It was the voice of that strange woman, the woman I scarcely knew, who had never spoken but the one word to me."

The doctor was hurrying through his wife's room. There was a stairway that led directly down out of the room. His crippled daughter slept in another room on the same floor and a servant, a colored woman who had been in the household for years, slept in the daughter's room on a cot. The doctor had got through his wife's room and was on the stairs when his wife spoke to him.

"But Harry!" she said. "You have forgotten something. You have not kissed me."

"Why, of course," he said. His feet were on the stairs but he came back up into her room. She was lying there, wide awake. "I am going to that woman. I do not know what will happen. I must, I must. She will surrender.

"It may all end in some sort of a scandal. I do not know but I cannot help doing what I am about to do. There are times when a man is in the grip of forces stronger than himself.

"What is this thing about women, about men? Why does all of this thing, this force, so powerful, so little understood, why with the male does it all become suddenly directed upon one woman and not upon another? Why is it sometimes true also of the female?

"There is this force, so powerful. I have suddenly, at forty-seven, a man established in life, fallen into its grip. I am powerless.

"There is this woman, my wife, in bed here, in this room. The moonlight is falling upon her upturned face. How beautiful she is. I do not want her, do not want to kiss her. She is looking up expectantly at me." The doctor was by his wife's bed. He leaned over her.

"I am going to this woman. I am going. I am going."

He was leaning over his wife, about to kiss her, but suddenly turned away.

"Martha," he said, "I cannot explain. This is a strange night for me. I will perhaps explain it all later. I cannot kiss you now."

"Wait. Wait."

He was hurrying away from her down the stairs. He got into his car. He went to that house. He got the woman, the Polish woman. "When I explained to her she was quite willing." He thought afterwards that she had been on the whole rather fine, telling him quite plainly that as he had felt when he saw her so she had felt.

She was definite enough. "I am not a weak woman. Although I am thirty I am still a virgin. However I am in no way virginal."

She had been, the doctor said, half a mystic, saying that she had always known that the man who would answer some powerful call in her would some day come. "He has come. It is you."

They went, I gathered, to walk. She told him that since she

had first seen him she had made some inquiries. She had found out about the loss of his two sons, about his crippled daughter, about his wife. "I do not want you to be unfaithful to her."

All this, the doctor explained, said to him by the woman, as, having left his car by the roadside, they walked in country roads. It was a very beautiful night and they had got into a road lined with trees. There were splashes of moonlight falling down through the leaves in the road before them as they walked. For an hour, two hours, they walked, not, as it turned out, ever touching each other. Sometimes they stopped and stood for long silent times. He said that several times he put out his hand to touch her but each time he drew it back.

"Why?"

It was the doctor himself who asked the question. He tried to explain. "There she was. She was mine to possess." He said that he thought she was to him the most beautiful woman he had ever known or ever would know.

"But that is not true," he said. "It is both true and untrue.

"It may be that if I had touched her, even with my finger ends, there would have been quite a different story to tell. She was beautiful, with her own beauty, so appealing, oh so very appealing to me, but there was also, at home, lying as I knew awake in her bed, my own wife."

He said that in the end, after he had been with the Polish woman for perhaps an hour, she understood. He thought she must have been extremely intelligent. They had stopped in the road and she turned to him and again, as in the room with the cripple, there was a long silence. "You are not going to take me," she said.

"I am a woman of thirty and have never been taken by a man. I had never wanted to be until I saw you.

"It may be that now I never shall be."

The doctor said he did not answer. What was to be said? "I couldn't," he explained. He thought that it was the great moment of his life. He used the word I have also used in speaking of him. "I think, a little, I have been, since that moment, a mature man."

The doctor had stopped talking but I could not resist questioning him.

"And you ended by not touching her?" I asked.

"Yes. I took her back to her place and when I next went there to see the crippled girl she was gone and another woman had taken her place.

"I think that man, that manufacturer, did not fail after all."

There was another time of silence. "After all," I thought, "this man has, from his own impulse, told me this tale. I have not asked for it. There is a question I think now that I may dare ask." I ventured. "And your wife?" There was that laugh that I so liked. It is my theory that it can come only from the men and women who have got their maturity.

"I returned to her. I gave her the kiss I had denied earlier that night."

I was of course not satisfied. "But," I said. Again the laugh. "If I had not wanted to tell you I should not have begun this tale," he said. We got up from the flat stone on which we had been sitting and prepared for the great moment of trout fishing, as every trout fisherman knows, the quivering time, so short a time between the last of the day and the beginning of the night. The doctor preceded me down across a flat sloping rock to the pool where we each got two fine trout. "I was in love with her as I had never really been with the Polish woman and in the same way. In a way until after that time I never had been.

"And there was all the rest, our life together, what we had gone through together."

The doctor stopped talking but did not look at me. He was selecting a fly. "You know my wife's name is Martha.

"When I returned to her that night and when I had kissed her, she for a moment held my face in her hands. She said something. "We have been through it again, haven't we?" she said. She took her hands away and turned her face from me. "I have been thinking for the last week or two that we had lost each other," she said. "I do not know why," she added and then she laughed. "It was the nicest laugh I ever heard from her lips. It seemed to come from so far down inside. I guess all men and women who have got something know that it might be easily lost," the doctor said as he finished his tale. He had hooked a trout and was absorbed in playing his fish.

PASTORAL

THE MOST UNFORGETTABLE MAN I THINK I HAVE EVER KNOWN WAS A country doctor, a little, quiet-seeming man, going busily from house to house in his middlewestern town and through the nearby country. He had parked his car, an old Ford, beside a country road and had found a new variety of mushroom in a wood. There was a book on mushrooms in the car, another on birds, one on trees, others on insects and wild flowers. I had a job as an advertising writer and went often to his town. I wrote catalogs, booklets and pamphlets for a manufacturer of the town and often stayed for a week or two at a time.

I became ill and the doctor was sent for. He was a fat, under-sized man of forty-five, a man with a big head, thin yellow hair that had begun to turn grey, and pale blue eyes. I was in the town's one hotel and the doctor had been sent to me by the manufacturer. I had been told that he was the best doctor in town, that he had an immense practice.

"But don't think you can get anything out of him. He won't talk much," the manufacturer had said.

The doctor came. There was a certain book by an old and little-read author lying on a table by my bed.

The doctor had examined me. He had said little or nothing and his silence had begun to annoy me. I was about to break forth, demand that he tell me something definite concerning my illness, when he suddenly picked up the book.

He became excited. An exclamation burst from his lips. He began walking up and down the room. The author of the book was the one author whose books he read. I had by chance hit upon his one venture into the field of imaginative literature. It created a bond between us.

The little doctor was one of the silent men you sometimes meet who, once they begin to talk, let out a flood of words. He explained that when he was a young man in college another young man had given him one of the author's books and that since he had become a doctor he had found little time for reading. "I do go back to his books," he said. "On many nights I cannot sleep and I have one of his books with me by my bed.

"Or I am with a patient who is very ill. I can't go away. There is nothing I can do. I have one of the books in my car. I read it as I wait for death to come."

My own illness amounted to nothing, but the doctor and I became friends. I often drove with him. He had an office on the second floor of an old two-storied brick building on the main street of his town, a place of some four thousand people, the office got to by climbing an outside stairway. During the hours he had set aside for his office practice, the large waiting room, poorly furnished, was always filled with people. There was the large waiting room and, facing the street, an inner office where he saw his patients.

The doctor had a large country practice and, except for the hours spent seeing people in his office, was seldom in town, and I got the habit of riding about with him.

I began seeing the doctor more and more, often when I visited his town doing my own work in my room at the hotel at night so that I could be free to ride with him during the day. He was one of the small, outwardly quiet but inwardly intensely active men you sometimes meet who constantly amaze you by the amount of work they can do. He never seemed to tire. He was in his office seeing people, one after another. He seemed always to go direct to the point. He was with all of his patients as he had been with me in the hotel room. He took the patient's pulse, his blood pressure, his temperature. He sat for a moment in silence looking at the patient. He had got, in the town and in all the country about, the reputation of being infinitely wise. There was the little stretch of time, often three or four minutes, when he sat thus, staring directly at the patient. If the patient spoke, began to ask questions, he did not answer. He could give, more than any other man I have ever known, the impression of being alone with his own thoughts in the presence of others. If he was seeing a patient in the country he took some medicine from his medicine case or if in town wrote a prescription.

"It is all nonsense," he once said to me. "All I know is that most people who are sick want to be sick. You humor them, take them seriously for a time. Why not? It helps." At times, without ever saying so, he gave the impression of being very contemptuous of people. He was going along the street and when people spoke to him he did not answer. He would look directly at the one addressing him as he looked at his patients, as though absorbed in his own thoughts, not answering the salutations; and when I first knew him I was surprised that he was not disliked.

He wasn't. He was admired. "He is a great student," people said. The town was full of stories of his wide reading in the literature of his profession. Whether or not he did much of such reading, I never knew. The people knew also of his intense interest in nature. They seemed to have decided that this too was a part of the wide knowledge that enabled him at times to make what seemed to them quite marvelous cures. They looked admiringly at him going along the street. "I wish I had that man's education," one man said to another.

Our talks, when on rare occasions we did talk, were always of the life of the author whose book he had found in my room. It seemed at times as though the only reason the man had for wanting my company was to speak of the life and adventures of the writer. He told me nothing of his own life and did not seem curious about mine. There was this one point of contact, the adventures of another written into a book. I kept trying to break into the doctor's long periods of silence, occasionally asking him questions about his work or his patients, but got no answers. Sometimes I was amused and at times when I was with him I grew impatient and irritated.

"If he did not want me with him, why did he come to my hotel for me?" I asked myself. We were driving on a country road when he suddenly stopped the car. He went into a wood and did not ask me to go with him. I sat waiting in the car when he had left me thus, and when he presently returned, he maintained his silence.

There were times he did talk, breaking into eager speech. He had discovered in the woods the nest of a bird he had long been seeking, or he had found a new kind of mushroom.

He got his bird or his mushroom book from the back of his car. The pages of the books were dirty with much handling. The doctor's clothes were shabby from long wear, and the car in which we rode seemed about to fall to pieces.

When he did talk thus, I had always the feeling that he was not addressing me. He knew all of the long scientific names of the birds, the trees, the wild flowers, the insects. He had perhaps captured a tiny insect with delicately colored, almost transparent wings. He had identified it and spoke of it at length and with a kind of eager enthusiasm; but, as he spoke thus, he did not look at me, did not seem to be addressing me.

One day we were at the door of a farmhouse and, after seeing his patient, he had gone into the vegetable garden back of the house, while I had got out of the car and stood in the yard before the house.

A farm woman had come out of the house and had entered into conversation with me. When the doctor returned to where we stood, he held a toad in his hand. He began speaking of the habits of the toad but again did not seem to be addressing either me or the woman. He held the toad in the palm of one of his little fat hands and caressed it with the fingers of the other. He looked away from us and talked and, when the woman addressed

292 CERTAIN THINGS LAST

a remark to him, he was with her as he so often was with me.

He turned and stared at her. "So you are here?" his eyes seemed to be saying. "And why do you need to be bothering me?"

As he talked thus, he stood looking off as though into some distant place, and the farm woman, thus so obviously snubbed, looked over his head and smiled at me. "He has always been like that," one such woman once remarked to me. She said that people were used to him and that they did not mind. "We all know what a good doctor he is," she said.

There was a man plowing in a field near the road at a place where the doctor had stopped his car. He sat absorbed, apparently watching the farmer's team as they came toward us, the ground curling away from the plow, the heavy muscles playing across the horses' breasts.

The plowman also spoke to the doctor but got no answer and, as he turned his horses and started back across the field, he winked at me. He did not seem offended. When he had gone back across the field, the doctor sat for a time, still staring apparently at the man and his team, and then, before starting his car, he did begin to speak.

He never seemed to be speaking to me. For a moment he sat, looking directly into my eyes, as I had often seen him look into the eyes of his patients, and then he turned and spoke as though to another. I had sharply at such times the feeling of being in the presence of something like an invisible third. It was a little startling.

At such times, when he spoke thus, there was an odd gentleness in his voice. There was never much said, some little comment made on the scene before us, on a bird that had just flown across the road or on a flowering bush growing at the edge of a wood, and then again the silence. Sometimes when I had been with him for hours, he turned and looked at me as though surprised to discover my presence.

The doctor had married soon after setting up his practice in the town, and on two or three occasions I went to his house. I did not go there with the doctor. The manufacturer and his wife took me there.

There were two handsome daughters and a very handsome although somewhat overpowering wife. There was a huge frame house of many rooms, beautifully furnished, on the best residence street of the town. My little doctor must have been making a good deal of money. He had built the big house with a wide and deep lawn, there was an expensive car the doctor never drove, and the older of the daughters was a student in one of the better known women's colleges of the East. As it turned out, after the doctor died, as he did suddenly of heart disease, there was an insurance policy that enabled his family to go on living rather in affluence.

The wife, a large woman of striking appearance, was a leader in all the civic affairs of the town. She was everything the doctor wasn't, an organizer, a joiner, the best woman golf player in the town, once having been runner-up in a women's state tournament, the president of a women's political club, a leader in the Parent-Teacher Association, a member of the book club and the music club. It was a little difficult to figure how and why she had married the doctor.

There was the doctor in his office that during the late morning hours was filled with waiting patients. He was in his old Ford going from house to house in the town or driving in the country. He was delivering babies, setting broken legs and arms, sitting in a farmhouse with a book on insects in his hand while he waited for some old man to die. He had come back into town after one of his country drives and it was early evening. Soon it would be dark. He had parked his car on a street near his house and sat waiting, studying one of his nature books until darkness came. Many people of the town saw him sitting thus. They smiled and spoke to him but he did not answer. When darkness came, he crept near and looked through a window of his house. If there was company for dinner or young men had come to call on his daughters, he went quietly away. Often he ate in a cheap restaurant in the lower end of the town. He went up into his inner office, locked the door, and pulled the shades at the windows. At such times if his telephone rang he did not answer. When he was found dead, sitting in his car beside a country road, several specimens of wood mushrooms on the seat beside him, his big mushroom book fallen to the floor of the car at his feet, there was a lawyer of the town who took charge of his affairs.

The lawyer found, in a small locked safe in the doctor's office, a great batch of letters. The doctor must have been writing them for years. The lawyer took them to his office and, as I happened to be in town, he called me in. The letters were all addressed to a woman. There was a small and a seemingly rather colorless woman who worked as a clerk in a drugstore on the main street of the town, a store just opposite the doctor's office, and the letters were all addressed to her. The man must have been sitting alone in his office, I always fancied, on a summer evening some years before I came to know him. He would long since have got himself married and he had the two daughters. I am very sure that, when he was newly married, he had tried for a time to interest his wife in his study of nature.

He had this passion for amateur research into the mysteries of nature and would have been bringing the specimens he collected home to his wife; and she, I am sure, would have tried to be interested in his interests but there would have come a stalemate. She couldn't make it. All that was alive to him was dead to her. A mushroom was to her a toadstool, a bird was a bird. He hadn't blamed her for her lack of interest. "She is herself and I am myself," he would have thought. He had remained all the rest of his life what is called loyal to her, had worked hard to provide for the wife and the two daughters what he thought they wanted in life.

He was a man who, all his life, had found it difficult to make a direct contact with people. He must have been sitting alone in his office on a certain evening (I have always thought of him on that occasion as sitting in darkness and looking down into the lighted main street of his town), when he saw, coming along the street to go into the drugstore, the little woman clerk.

He got up from his chair by the window. He pulled the shades and turned on the lights. He began a letter to her. The lawyer thought the letters had not been destroyed because the doctor was like many men about making a will. He would always have intended to do it tomorrow. He had begun writing the letters and immediately had found for himself a way to pour himself out. After an investigation carefully made by the lawyer after his death, it was quite certain that the woman to whom the letters were addressed had known nothing of the doctor's passion. On the few occasions when, having to go to the drugstore, he had been fairly compelled to speak to her, he had been rude and once had made her cry. He spoke of that in one of the letters. After it happened, he returned to his office and also cried.

The letters written by the little doctor were very tender. As they have all been destroyed, I shall not try to quote from them. There were many little stories of his discoveries in nature. For all his seeming indifference, the letters revealed that he had been a close observer of others. There were tales of people and how they acted at the moment of death, of men and women among his patients and their relations to each other. Although in all the letters he addressed his woman clerk as his darling, there was never any direct mention of love, nor did he ever in any way criticize his wife; but there was this continued going out of himself into what he saw and felt in nature and in people. There was even a kind of hidden poetry; and the lawyer and myself, as we sat in his office at night reading the letters, were both deeply moved.

There was this man and his life, as I and all the others who had known him had seen it, as it was understood by his wife and daughters, and there was this other and secret life he had led. The lawyer, a dignified looking man with greying hair, read the letters. There must have been at least two hundred of them. We had begun reading in the late afternoon and finished quite late at night. We went to the lawyer's house and into the cellar. We burned the letters in a furnace. We went then for a walk together and presently, as though pulled by some force outside ourselves, found ourselves in the drugstore.

Although it was late, the little woman clerk was still there and busy at her job. The store was one of the modern drugstores that is also half a restaurant and a place of soft drinks. It was filled with people, for the most part young, and there were booths in which they sat and many little tables. The lawyer and I seated ourselves at one of the tables.

On that particular night the little clerk must have been very tired, but she kept trying to smile. She made gay little remarks. The lawyer told me that she was the daughter of a workman in a factory of the town and that her father had died some years before. He said that there was a half-invalid mother whom she no doubt supported. As the lawyer and I sat at the table at the back of the store, I saw her go behind a counter piled high with goods and stand for a moment hidden from the customers.

As she stood thus, her shoulders seemed to droop and she put her hand to her head. For just a moment she was a figure expressing infinite weariness, and then she began again running back and forth delivering drinks. Again she smiled. Again she made gay little remarks.

The lawyer and I went out of the store and for a moment stood in the empty street of the town looking into each other's eyes. There was nothing to be said. I remember to have thought that we looked at each other much as the little doctor had always looked at people. We said good night to each other.

NOT SIXTEEN

SHE KEPT INSISTING ON IT. SHE WHISPERED IT IN THE BARN AT NIGHT, after the day in the cornfield. Her father was milking a cow. John could hear the milk strike against the side of the pail. When the sound stopped, they had to dodge into an empty horse stall.

He was pressing her body against a board wall. She was limp, relaxed in his arms. Was he in love? He didn't know. He thought he was.

There had been moments during the weeks he was there on her father's farm, working there—he was helping with the fall corn cutting —when he had wanted her to marry him. He spoke of it.

"Shall we get married?" he asked.

"No," she said. "I am not sixteen."

"Well," he said.

"No, and not that either," she said. "Not yet," she said. "I am not sixteen."

He thought about it at night in bed.

"It would be too stupid to get married now," he thought. He had no money and he didn't want to go on, perhaps all of his life, being a farmhand.

She had a baffling attitude about it all. They had spoken of it, John pressing the question.

"Let's," he said.

"There won't nobody know," he said.

"Let's! Just once! Let's!" he pleaded.

He talked and talked, exaggerated his suffering, his pain, his sleeplessness. He threatened to go away.

"Please don't," she said. "You stay here. It won't be long. I'll be sixteen in a year."

She kept insisting. She was slender, with bright red spots on her pale cheeks. Her mouth was inviting, her eyes inviting.

She was curiously frank, had not been shocked by John's words, when he began to plead with her. She knew what he meant. She wanted to.

She came down into the field to work with John and her father.

John had got the job on the farm. It was in the fall, after the spring when he came home from the World War.

"I'll work," he had thought, "for, say, a year. I'll take any job I can get. I'll save my money." He had brought some money home from the war—had hidden it away. It wasn't much.

The war, the traveling about, the seeing strange places, mountains, the sea, the being in a foreign land—all of these things had made him restless. He didn't know what he wanted.

"I want her, but I don't want to settle down, not yet."

He had come home to his Michigan town with other soldiers, and there had been parades. There had been a banquet in the town hall. He and other soldiers had been called heroes again. He thought it was the bunk. He had been lucky, hadn't been in any battles. He was only nineteen, and that girl Lillian, on the farm, was only fifteen. When he came home from the war and was called a hero, he spoke to other men who had been soldiers.

"All this talk. It's bushwa," he said.

"They are handing us the lousy bunk," he said.

There was no work to be had. When he had gone off to war, he had chucked a job. That was in Detroit in an automobile plant. He didn't want to go back. He had been on the line in the plant.

The job had got his goat. He said so. "This hero bunk," he said. "I didn't go to be no hero. The job had got me. I didn't sleep good at night."

"All right," he said to himself. "I'll go take a look." He thought he would go on the bum for a time. There was an old man in the Michigan town who had a deformed hip. The Michigan town was near the larger town, Kalamazoo, where grand circuit trotting meetings are held and the old man had been a race-horse driver. Now he owned a garage, but he still kept two or three good ones.

He had been thrown from a sulky during a race and his hip had been broken. It had never properly mended. He walked in a curious way, swinging his body from side to side.

He stopped John in a street. Before the war and before John went away to Detroit, he had worked for the man, whose name was Yardley. It was when John was sixteen. He had been a swipe. He had got the race-horse bug.

"If you want to work for me again, you can," the man said.

He said that he already had two men in his barn.

"I don't need another, not now, not till the races begin, but if you want to come, you can.

"I can't pay you anything. You can take care of What Chance," he said.

What Chance was a trotter. He was a bay gelding, a three-year-old. He was fast.

"You take care of him this winter and jog him on the roads. It won't be much work. I can't pay you anything, but you can come up and live at my house. You can sleep there, get your meals there."

The man Yardley said he was making John the offer because he admired the boys who had the guts to go out and fight for their country. They walked over to the barn, the man Yardley swaying along beside John. He was chewing tobacco. He kept spitting. They went into the box stall to the horse.

It had been a temptation to John. He went to caress the horse. He ran his hand along his back and down his legs. "He's a good one," he thought.

He thought of the drifting from town to town. In time he might become a driver. It was an old dream come back. Yardley would be doing the half-mile tracks. With a good one like What Chance they might clean up.

John had a little money. He'd be on the inside. He could lay some bets.

He thought of nights in strange towns with the other swipes. There'd be drinking, there'd be some whoring done. He stood looking at the horse.

"Naw," he thought. "I got to cut that out."

"These race-horse men," he thought, "where do they ever get?"

"I'll see. I'll let you know," he said to Yardley. He took a walk.

"I can't," he told himself. He had brought a little money home from the war. When he had been a kid around the tracks, he had learned to juggle dice. He had got into crap games in the camp, in France, on the boats, going and coming.

He wanted to go with Yardley, but he felt guilty. There was his sister. John's mother was dead and his sister was running the house.

His father was out of work, and John's sister, three years older than John, was wanting to get John's two younger brothers through school.

"I ought to tell her about the money, give it to her," he thought.

"I can't," he thought.

It seemed to him that if he gave up the money he had won at craps, he would be sunk.

"If I could go to school now, just for two or three years," he thought.

He could maybe get into business, become a prosperous man. John had a picture in mind of himself, a man risen in the world, money in pocket, good clothes to wear.

"If I can pull it off I can do ten times as much for the kids," he thought.

It seemed to him that everything depended upon his getting an education. "If I don't do it now I'm gone." If he did not get an education he would remain as he was—sunk, a worker, a man going through life with his feet in the mud.

There was a ladder up which you climbed. Education was the thing that did it.

"O.K.," John had said to himself, "but I'll give up going to school this year. I'll give up what I want to be, a horseman." John had been through grade school. He had an idea that presently he would take the money put secretly away, and would go somewhere, perhaps to a business college.

There was a young man he knew who was going to a dental college. John thought he might do that. There was another who was away from home at a school where you learned to fix watches.

"That might be better," he thought.

You begin by repairing watches. You save your money. Then presently you own a store where jewelry is sold. You sell rings and watches. You dress well. Very likely you marry—say now, a rich girl.

It might be that her father would be the one that would set you up in your own business. When you had such a business of your own, you could, if you chose, own some horses of your own.

So you get a clerk to take care of your store. You go away to the races. You drive your own horses.

John had got on a freight train at night and had begun beating his way from town to town, looking for work. He thought he would earn some money and send it home. Pretty soon what little money he had in his pockets was gone, and he had to take what he could get. He had got down into Ohio, was in a town in Ohio. He had hired out to the farmer. He was cutting corn. It was a new kind of work for John. He thought it was a pretty hard job, but he could stand it all right.

Her name was Lillian, and her father and mother were old. They seemed old to John. The man, her father, was a renter. Once he had owned a farm of his own, but, he told John, he had had hard luck and had lost it.

His wife was a small woman, with bright eyes, like Lillian's, John thought. The mother had a curiously bent back. "They must have been married a long time," he thought. He was always doing things like that, wondering about people, thinking of them. "I wonder if, when you get old and live with your wife, you have

any fun," he thought. There had been four children, three of
them grown now, and all married except Lillian. The others were
gone. Lillian told John about it all when she came down into the
field where he was cutting the corn.

She got him at once. "Oh, Lord, she's got me," he thought.
She was small, but she could cut corn like a man. She was shy
and at the same time bold. She looked weak but she was strong.
The work was new to John and she kept showing him how. There
was a certain swing you got. You learned to ease yourself.

You have to cut the tall corn and carry it to the shock. You
hold it in one arm and swing the knife with the other. There is a
way you handle your body, easing it to the load. When you know
how, it's twice as easy. She showed John how.

They talked and talked. When her father was there working
with them, they worked in silence, he continually looking at her
and she at him, but when her father had gone to the barn or the
house, they talked. It was something new to John. He talked and
talked. He looked at her. "I wonder whether she will," he thought.

"She doesn't seem so young," he thought. Right away he knew
she liked to be with him.

They talked at night. There were moonlight nights.

"Come. Let's go and work awhile," she said. It wasn't in the
agreement that John was to work at night, but he went. He was
glad to go.

Her father, the farmer, did not come at night. He said he was
tired. He said he was getting too old. She told John of a sister
who was married and lived with her husband, a railroad brakeman
in another town. The sister had been fifteen years old before Lillian
was born. "She got married when she was fifteen, but I'm not
going to," she said. John wanted to ask if it was a shot-gun marriage.
He didn't.

"How do you reckon I came to come so late?" she asked. She
asked John that and laughed.

"I'd a-thought they'd got so old they couldn't," she said.

She kept saying bold things to John.

When they were working together thus, in the evening, in the cornfield, in the moonlight, they kept talking. She didn't seem young to John. "It may be because she came so late," he thought. He thought she had a figure, nice, like a woman's. She seemed curiously old for her years.

They were at work in a big field and there was the part of the field where the corn was already cut. They could look across the open place. There were the shocks of corn they had cut standing out there. There were yellow pumpkins on the ground. Beyond the open place where the corn shocks stood, there was a wood. There was a strange feeling John had, as though he were alone with her in a place where no man had ever been before. "Like maybe in the Garden of Eden," he thought. Out there in the field with her like that at night, quite far from the farmhouse, there were always strange sounds and sometimes there was a wind. The leaves were turning on the trees in the wood. They were falling. The wind made them race across the open place. They seemed like little living things running along. "I wonder why they let her come," he thought. He thought maybe they wanted to get her married. "Then maybe I'd have to stay here and work for them for nothing, like with Yardley," he thought. She had told him about her sister. "I'll bet that's the way she got that brakeman," he thought.

He talked to her of the leaves, running along the ground. "Look," he said. The shocked corn standing in the open place made him think of his life in the army. They could look off across the open place, where the corn was cut, to other fields on other farms. It was a flat country. They could see other corn already cut and in its shocks in other fields.

John kept talking to her. He never talked so before. He spoke of the shocks standing in the moonlight. They were like armies of soldiers standing, he said. He grew bolder as he talked. He couldn't touch her until he began to talk and then he could.

They didn't cut much corn at night. He went to her and put an arm about her shoulders. He was quite tall and she was short. Standing thus, he could say things about the dry leaves running along the ground and the little sound they made. He could pretend there was another world, besides the one they lived in, a world of little living things, men and women like themselves, but small, he said. "No bigger than that," he said. He put his thumb at the first joint of a finger. He began inventing. He told her that the little people lived, in the daytime, in the wood, that they hid in there.

"Now see, they've come out to play," he said.

"They are men and women like us," he said, "but they don't get married." Two dry leaves went skipping along. "Look," he said, "he's going to get her." He told her of his thought about the shocked corn, like armies standing, he said. "Look," he said. "They stand in silence.".

They quit working and went to stand by the fence. He had an arm about her. He made her put her head down on his shoulder. It could just reach. Their corn knives fell on the ground.

He talked and talked. He told her about his life in the army, about things he'd seen.

Then he told her about a girl he'd been with once. "It was when I was younger than you are," he said. He said it was a little town girl. "It was when I was at the races. A man older than me, who worked with our outfit, got me the girl." He said that she with another one had come at night to a fairground where they were. The man had given one of the girls to John to go with him into an empty horse stall.

He told of it and how he felt, how he couldn't speak to the girl, how excited he was. "It was my first," he said. A quiver ran through her body and he held her close.

He went on talking, holding her, not feeling at all as he had with the girl in the horse stall.

"I was afraid of her, but I'm not of you," he said.

"Was it nice?" she asked, and he said it was.

She was like that. She seemed to come right up to him, with her mind, with all of herself, not afraid or ashamed.

"I'm going to when I'm sixteen," she said.

"I won't wait any longer," she said.

It had begun between them and it went on. It was in the

moonlight, when they were in the cornfield at night. It was in the barn. It was upstairs, in the house, at night. He went up to her. He went up in his bare feet. Her father snored and her mother snored. He waited until he heard it and then he went up to her.

She had a room up there.

Her father and mother were asleep downstairs. She said it would be all right for him to come. He had been given a room downstairs. "You come up. I want you to," she said.

It seemed to John that he was near to being insane. He was very strong. Now the work didn't tire him at all.

"I'll ask her to marry me," he thought.

Then he thought, "No. I won't," but he did, and she laughed. "No. We won't do that," she said. He was glad because her people were poor. They were too much like his own people, he thought. He kept thinking that, if they got married, he couldn't ever go to school and rise in the world.

He did not speak to her of that. When he wasn't with her, alone with her, he got half frantic, but when he was with her, in the barn—while her father was milking—holding her tight, or in the field, or when he went up to her at night, he got strangely quiet.

She had fixed a blanket on the floor by her bed. She said he could lie there for a time. "There's no harm in that," she said. She said that if there was, she didn't care. She would be lying on the edge of her bed. The bed was low. She leaned down. She had hard little hands.

"You talk," she said, and sometimes he did.

"Like out there, with the leaves running like that," she said.

He would lie thus and whisper to her and sometimes she would lean down and they'd kiss. He wanted to pull her down, make her come to him, struggle with her until she surrendered, but for some obscure reason he didn't.

He talked and talked. He had never talked so before. When he was talking, he could not tell what, of all he told her, was real and what invented.

Sometimes he'd beg her, growing a little frantic, but she could quiet him.

"I can't. I'm not sixteen," she said.

She said it would be almost a year before she could. She laughed softly.

"You can stay and wait or you can go away and come back," she said.

"If you go away and you're not here on time—" She laughed.

She had a laugh that made him grow quiet. There was something in her, he thought, like a wall. "There's no use pounding against a wall," he thought.

At times, on some nights when he had crept up there and had talked for a long time, he grew suddenly sad. Tears came to his eyes.

"Please, please," he said.

"Be quiet," she said.

"When I am sixteen," she said.

She kept saying it. It was like a song in his head. He had to give it up. He stood it as long as he could, and then he ran away. He had come down from her room. It was on one of the moonlight nights and cold. He'd been lying up there on the blanket by her bed.

"When I'm sixteen.

"When I'm sixteen."

He was a young man and a year seemed infinitely long. If he could have been with her all the time, day and night, near her, he thought he could have stood it.

He came down to his own room at night and suddenly knew.

"It's because I'm not like her," he thought.

"She can wait and I can't."

He dressed and slipped silently out of the house. He walked in a moonlit road.

There was something in her as strong as iron, but it wasn't in him. Her father owed him some money he never got, but he didn't care. When he had got into the road, he was suddenly proud. "I have controlled myself," he thought. He began to walk proudly along.

"After all, she is not sixteen," he thought.

NOBODY LAUGHED

IT WASN'T, MORE THAN OTHERS OF ITS SIZE, A DULL TOWN. BUZZ McCleary got drunk regularly once a month and got arrested, and for two summers there was a semi-professional baseball team. Sol Grey managed the promoting of the ball team. He went about town to the druggist, the banker, the local Standard Oil manager and others, and got them to put up money. Some of the players were hired outright. They were college boys having a little fun during their vacation time, getting board and cigarette money, playing under assumed names, not to hurt their amateur standing. Then there were two fellows from the coal mining country a hundred miles to the north in a neighboring state. The handle factory gave these men jobs. Bugs Calloway was one of these. He was a home run hitter and afterwards got into one of the big leagues. That made the town pretty proud. "It puts us on the map," Sol Grey said.

However, the baseball team couldn't carry on. It had been in a small league and the league went to pieces. Things got dull after that. In such an emergency the town had to give attention to Hallie and Pinhead Perry.

The Perrys had been in Greenhope since the town was very small. Greenhope was a town of the upper South, and there had been Perrys there ever since long before the Civil War. There were rich Perrys, well-to-do Perrys, a Perry who was a preacher, and one who had been a brigadier general in the Northern army in the Civil War. That didn't go so well with the other well-to-do Perrys. They liked to keep reminding people that the Perrys were of the old South. "The Perrys are one of the oldest and best families of the old South," they said. They kept pretty quiet about Brigadier General Perry who went over to the damned Yanks.

As for Pinhead Perry, he, to be sure, belonged to the no-account branch of the Perrys. The tree of even the best Southern family must have some such branches. Look at the Pinametters. But let's not drag in names.

Pinhead Perry was poor. He was born poor, and he was simple-minded. He was undersized. A girl named Mag Hunter got into trouble with a Perry named Robert, also of the no-account Perrys, and Mag's father went over to Robert's father's house one night with a shotgun. After Robert married Mag he lit out. No one knew where he went, but everyone said he went over into a neighboring state, into the coal mining country. He was a big man with a big nose and hard fists. "What the hell'd I want a wife for? Why keep a cow when milk's so cheap?" he said before he went away.

They called his son Pinhead, began calling him that when he was a little thing. His mother worked in the kitchen of several well-to-do families in Greenhope but it was a little hard for her to get a job, what with Negro help so cheap and her having Pinhead. Pinhead was a little off in the head from the first, but not so much.

His father was a big man but the only thing big about Pinhead was his nose. It was gigantic. It was a mountain of a nose. It was very red. It looked very strange, even grotesque, sticking on Pinhead. He was such a little scrawny thing, sitting often for a half day at a time on the kitchen step at the back of the house of some well-to-do citizen. He was a very quiet child and his mother, in spite of the rather hard life she had, always dressed him neatly. Other kitchen help, the white kitchen help, what there was of it in Greenhope, wouldn't have much to do with Mag Perry, and all the other Perrys were indignant at the very idea of her calling herself a Perry. It was confusing, they said. The other white kitchen help whispered. "She was only married to Bob Perry a month when the kid was born," they said. They avoided Mag.

There was a philosopher in the town, a sharp-tongued lawyer who hadn't much practice. He explained. "The sex morals of America have to be upheld by the working classes," he said. "The financial morals are in the hands of the middle-class.

"That keeps them busy," he said.

Pinhead Perry grew up and his mother Mag died and Pinhead got married. He married one of the Albright girls . . . her name was Hallie . . . from out by Albright's Creek. She was the youngest one of eight children and was a cripple. She was a little pale thing and had a twisted foot. "It oughten to be allowed," people said. They said such bad blood ought not to be allowed to breed. They said, "Look at them Albrights." The Albrights were always getting into jail. They were horse traders and chicken thieves. They were moon-liquor makers.

But just the same the Albrights were a proud and a defiant lot. Old Will Albright, the father, had land of his own. And he had money. If it came to paying a fine to get one of his boys out of jail, he could do it. He was the kind of man who, although he had less than a hundred acres of land . . . most of it hillside land and not much good, and a big family, mostly boys . . . always getting drunk, always fighting, always getting into jail for chicken stealing or liquor making, in spite, as they said in Greenhope, of hell and high water . . . in spite of everything as, you see, he had money. He didn't put it in a bank. He carried it. "Old Will's always got a roll," people in town said. "It's big enough to choke a cow," they said. The town people were impressed. It gave Will Albright a kind of distinction. That family also had big noses and old Will had a big walrus mustache.

They were rather a dirty and a disorderly lot, the Albrights, and they were sometimes sullen and defiant, but just the same, like the Perrys and other big families of that country, they had

family pride. They stuck together. Suppose you had a few drinks
in town on a Saturday night, and you felt a little quarrelsome and
not averse to a fight yourself, and you met one of the Albright
boys, say down in the lower end of town, down by the Greek
restaurant, and he got gay and gave you a little of his lip, and you
said to him, "Come on, you big stiff, let's see what you've got."

And you got ready to sock him.

Better not to do that. God only knows how many other Albrights
you'd have on your hands. They'd be like Stonewall Jackson at
the battle of Chancellorsville. They came down on you suddenly,
seemingly out of nowhere, out of the woods, as it were.

"Now, you take one of that crew. You can't trust 'em. One of
them'll stick a knife into you. That's what he'll do."

And think of it, little, quiet Pinhead Perry, marrying into that
crew. He had grown up. But that's no way to put it. He was still
small and rather sick looking. God knows how he had lived since
his mother died.

He had become a beggar. That was it. He'd stand before one of
the grocery stores when people were coming out with packages
in their hands. "Hello!" He called all the other Perrys "cousin"
and that was bad. "Hello, Cousin John," or "Cousin Mary," or
Kate or Harry. He smiled in that rather nice little way he had.
His mouth looked very tiny under his big nose and his teeth had
got black. He was crazy about bananas. "Hello, Cousin Kate.
Give me a dime please. I got to get me some bananas."

And there were men, the smart-alecks of the town, taking up
with him too, men who should have known better, encouraging
him.

That lawyer . . . his father was a Yank from Ohio . . . the
philosophic one, always making wisecracks about decent people
. . .getting Pinhead to sweep out his office . . . he let him sleep up
there . . . and Burt McHugh, the plumber, and Ed Cabe, who ran
the poolroom down by the tracks.

"Pinhead, I think you'd better go up and see your Cousin Tom.
He was asking for you. I think he'll give you a quarter." Cousin

Tom Perry was cashier of the biggest bank in town. One of those fellows, damn smart-alecks, had seen Judge Buchanan...the Perrys and the Buchanans were the two big families of the county...they'd seen Judge Buchanan go into the bank. He was a director. There was going to be a directors' meeting. There were other men going in. You could depend on Pinhead walking right into the directors' room where they had the big mahogany table and the mahogany chairs. The Buchanans sure liked to take down the Perrys.

"You go in there, Pinhead. Cousin Tom has been asking for you. He wants to give you a quarter."

"Lordy," said Burt McHugh, the plumber, "Cousin Tom give him a quarter, eh? Why, he'd as soon give him an automobile."

Pinhead took up with the Albrights. They liked him. He'd go out there and stay for weeks. The Albright place was three miles out of town. On a Saturday night, and sometimes all day on Sundays, there'd be a party out there.

There'd be moon whiskey, plenty of that, and sometimes some of the men from town, even sometimes men who should have known better, men like Ed Cabe and that smarty lawyer, or even maybe Willy Buchanan, the judge's youngest son, the one who drank so hard and they said had a cancer.

And all kinds of rough people.

There were two older Albright girls, unmarried, Sally and Katherine, and it was said they were "putting out."

Drinking and sometimes dancing and singing and general hell-raising and maybe a fight or two.

"What the hell?" old Will Albright said . . . his wife was dead and Sally and Katherine did the housework . . . "What the hell? It's my farm. It's my house. A man's king in his own house, ain't he?"

Pinhead grew fond of the little crippled Albright girl, little twisted-footed Hallie, and he'd sit out there in that house, dancing and all that kind of a jamboree going on . . . in a corner of the big untidy bare room at the front of the house, two of the Albright boys playing guitars and singing rough songs at the tops of their voices.

If the Albright boys were sullen and looking for a fight when they came to town, they weren't so much like that at home. They'd be singing some song like "Hand Me Down My Bottle of Moon" and that one about the warden and the prisoners in the prison, you know, on a Christmas morning, the warden trying to be Santa Claus to the boys and what the old hardboiled prisoner said to him, the two older Albright girls dancing maybe with a couple of the men from town—old Will Albright . . . he was sure boss in his own family . . . sitting over near the fireplace, chewing tobacco and keeping time with his feet. He'd spit clean and sharp right through his walrus mustache and never leave a trace. That lawyer said he could keep perfect time with his feet and his jaws. "Look at it," he said, "there ain't another man in the state can spit like old Will."

Pinhead sitting quietly over in a corner with his Hallie. They both smiled softly. Pinhead didn't drink. He wouldn't. "You let him alone," Will Albright said to his boys. Pinhead and Hallie got married one Saturday night and there was a big party, everyone howling drunk. Two of the guests wrecked a car trying to get back to town and one of them, Henry Haem . . . a nice young fellow, a clerk in Williamson's drygoods store . . . you wouldn't think he'd want to associate with such people . . . he got his arm broke. Will Albright gave Pinhead and Hallie ten acres of land. . . good enough land . . . not too good . . . down by the creek at the foot of a hill and he and the boys built them a house. It wasn't much of a house but you could live in it if you were hardy enough.

Neither Pinhead nor Hallie was so very hardy.

They lived. They had children. People said there had been ten of the children. Pinhead and Hallie were getting pretty old. It was after the Albrights were all gone. Pinhead was nearly seventy and Hallie was even older. Women in town said, "How could she ever have had all of those children?

"I'd like to know," they said.

The children were nearly all gone. Some had died. An officer had descended on the family and four of the children had been carried off to a state institution.

There were left only Pinhead and Hallie and one daughter. They had managed to cling to her and the little strip of land given them by Will Albright, but the house, a mere shed in the beginning, was now in ruins. Every day the three people struck out for town where now, the philosophic lawyer being dead, a new one had taken his place. There will always be at least one such smarty in every town. This one was a tall, slender young man who had inherited money and was fond of race horses.

He was also passionately fond of practical jokes.

The plumber, Burt McHugh, was also gone, but there were new men, Ed Hollman the sheriff, Frank Collins, another young lawyer, Joe Walker, who owned the hotel, and Bob Cairn, who ran the weekly newspaper in Greenhope.

These were the men who with Sol Grey and others had helped organize the baseball team. They went to every game. When the team disbanded they were heartbroken.

And there was Pinhead coming into town followed by Hallie and the one daughter. Mabel was her name. Mabel was tall and gaunt and cross-eyed. She was habitually silent and had an odd habit. Let some man or woman stop on the sidewalk and look steadily at her for a moment and she would begin to cry. When she did it, Pinhead and Hallie both ran to her. She was so tall that they had to stand on tiptoes and reach up, but they both began patting her thin cheeks and her gaunt shoulders. "There, there," they said. It didn't turn out so badly. When someone had made Mabel cry, it usually ended by Pinhead collecting a nickel or a dime. He went up to the guilty one and smiled softly. "Give her a little something and she'll quit," he said. "She wants a banana."

He had kept to his plea for bananas. It was the best way to get money. He, Hallie and Mabel always walked into town single-file, Pinhead walking in front . . . although he was old now, he was still very alive . . . then came Hallie . . . her hair hanging down in strings about her pinched face . . . and then Mabel, very tall and in the summer barelegged. Summer or winter she wore the same dress.

It had been black. It had been given her by a widow. There was a little black hat that perched oddly on her head. The dress had been black but it had been patched with cloth of many colors. The colors blended. There was a good deal of discussion of the dress in town. No two people agreed as to its color. Everything depended on the angle at which she approached you.

These people came into town every day to beg. They begged food at the back doors of houses. The town had grown and many new people had come in. Formerly the Perrys came into town along a dirt road, passing town people who, when there had been a shower and the road was not too dusty, were out for a drive in buggies and phaetons, but now the road was paved and they, the Perrys, passed automobiles. It was too bad for the other Perrys. The family was still prosperous and had increased in numbers and standing. None of the other Perrys took their afternoon drives out of town by that road.

It was the lack of a baseball team. It was because of a dull summer. It was Sol Grey, the man who had the notion of organizing the baseball team, who got the big idea.

He told the others. He told the two young lawyers and Ed Hollman the sheriff. He told Joe Walker the hotel man and Bob Cairn who was editor of the newspaper. He explained. He said that he was standing in front of a store.

"I was in front of Herd's grocery," he said. He had just been standing there when the three Perrys had come along. He thought that Pinhead had intended to ask him for a nickel or a dime. Anyway Pinhead had stopped before Sol and then Hallie and Mabel had stopped. Sol thought he must have been thinking of something else. Perhaps he was trying to think of some new way to break the monotony of life in Greenhope that summer. He found himself staring hard and long, not at Mabel but at Hallie Perry.

He did it unconsciously like that and didn't know how long he had kept it up, but suddenly there had come a queer change over Pinhead.

"Why, you all know Pinhead," Sol said. The men were all gathered that day before Doc Foreman's drugstore. Sol kept bending over and slapping his knees with his hands as he told of what had happened. He had been staring at Hallie that way, not thinking of what he was doing, and Pinhead had got suddenly and furiously jealous.

Pinhead had no doubt intended to ask Sol for a nickel or a dime to buy bananas. Up to that moment no one in town had ever seen Pinhead angry.

"Well, did he get sore," Sol Grey cried. He shook with laughter. Pinhead had begun to berate him. "You let my woman alone!

"What do you mean staring at my woman?

"I won't have any man fooling with my woman."

It was pretty rich. Pinhead had got the idea into his head that Sol . . . he was a lumber and coal dealer . . . a man who took pride in his clothes . . . a married man . . . the crazy loon had thought Sol was trying to make up to Pinhead's wife.

It was something gaudy. It was something to talk and to laugh about. It was something to work on. Sol said that Pinhead had offered to fight him. "My God," cried Joe Walker. Pinhead Perry was past seventy by that time and there was Hallie with her lame foot and her goiter—

And all three of the Perrys so hopelessly dirty.

"My God! Oh my Lord! He thinks she's beautiful," Joe Walker cried.

"Swell," said Bob Cairn. The newspaper man, who was always looking for ideas, had one at once.

It sure had innumerable funny angles and all the men went to work. They began stopping Pinhead on the street. He would be coming along followed by the two women, but the man who had stopped the little procession would draw Pinhead aside. "It's like this," he'd say. He'd declare he hated to bring the matter up but he thought he should. "A man's a man," he'd say. "He can't have other men fooling around with his woman." It was so much fun to see the serious, baffled, hurt look in Pinhead's eyes.

There would be dark hints cast out.

The man who had taken Pinhead aside spoke of an evening, a night in fact, of the past. He said he had been out at night and had come into town past Pinhead's house. There was no road out that way and Pinhead and his two women, when they made their daily trip into town, had to follow a cow path along Albright Creek to get into the main road, but the man did not bother to take that into account.

"I was going along the road past your house."

There had been various men of the town seen creeping away from the house at night.

No doubt Pinhead was asleep. Certain very respectable men of the town were named. There was Hal Pawsey. He kept the jewelry store in Greenhope and was a very shy modest man. Pinhead rushed into his store and began to shout. There was a woman, the wife of the Baptist minister, in the store at that time. She was seeing about getting her watch fixed. Hallie and Mabel were outside on the sidewalk and they were both crying. Pinhead began beating with his fists on the glass showcase in the store. He broke the case. He used such language that he frightened the Baptist minister's wife so that she ran out of the store.

That was one incident of the summer but there were many others. The hotel man, the newspaper man, the lawyer, Sol Grey, and several others kept busily at work.

They got Pinhead to tackle a stranger in town, a traveling man, coming out of a store with bags in his hand, and Pinhead got arrested and had to serve a term in jail. It was the first time he'd ever been in jail.

Then when he was let out, they began again. It was swell. It was great fun. There was a story going around town that Pinhead had begun to beat his wife and that she took it stoically. Someone had seen him doing it on the road into town. They said she just stood and took it and didn't cry much.

The men kept it going. It was a dull summer. One evening, when the moon was shining and the corn was getting knee-high, several of the men went in a car out to Pinhead's house. They left the car in the road and crept through bushes until they got quite near to the house. One of them had given Pinhead some money and had advised him to spend it to buy a bag of flour. The men in the bushes could see into the open door of the shack. "My God," said Joe Walker. "Look!" he said. "He's got her tied to a chair.

"Ain't that rich?" he said.

Pinhead had Hallie sitting in the one chair of the one-roomed house . . . the roof was almost gone and when it rained the water poured in . . . and he was tying her to the chair with a piece of rope. Someone of the men had told Pinhead that another man of the town had planned to visit the house that night.

The men from town lay in the bushes watching. The tall daughter Mabel was on the porch outside and she was crying. Pinhead, having got his wife tied to the chair, began to scatter flour on the floor of the room and on the porch outside. He backed away from Hallie, scattering the flour, and she was crying. When he had got to the door and as he was backing across the narrow rickety front porch, he scattered the flour thickly. The idea was that if any one of Hallie's lovers came, he'd leave his footprints in the flour.

He came out into a little yard at the front and got under a bush. He sat on the ground under the bush. In the moonlight the men from town could see him quite plainly. They said afterwards that he also began to cry. For some reason, even to the men of Greenhope, who were trying as best they could to get through a dull summer, the scene from the bushes before Pinhead's house that night wasn't funny. When they had crept out from under the bushes and had got back to their car and into town, one of them went to the drugstore and told the story, but nobody laughed.

FOR WHAT?

THE BIG GERMAN MAN CAME ALONG THE RIVER BANK TO WHERE I was lying on the brown grass at the river's edge. The book I had been reading was on the grass beside me. I had been gazing across the sluggish little river at the distant horizon.

I had hoped to spend the day working. There was a story I wanted to write. This was in a low flat country southwest of the city of Chicago. I had come there that morning by train with the others, Joe and George, and Jerry, the big German.

They all wanted to be painters. They were striving. The Sundays were very precious to the others and to me. We were all working during the week and looking forward to the weekends. There were certain canvases the others wanted to paint. If one of them could get a painting hung in the Chicago Art Institute, it might be a beginning.

We used to speak of it at the lunch hours during the week.

There was a certain story that had been in my mind for weeks, even months. We were all living about in little rooming houses. We were clerks. Jerry, the big German, had been a truck driver. Now he had a job as a shipping clerk in a cold storage warehouse.

I had tried time and again to write the particular story that was in my mind. I told the others about it. I didn't tell them the story. That would bring bad luck. I spoke instead of how I wanted the words and sentences to march.

"Like soldiers marching across a field," I said.

"Like a plow turning up its ribbon of earth across a field."

Fine phrases about work not done. There had been too much of that. You can kill any job so. Just keep talking about the great thing you are to do, some time in the future. That will kill it.

"Yes, and it is so also that paint should go on a canvas."

This would be one of the others, one of the painters speaking.

There was this big talk, plenty of that, words, too many words. Sometimes, after the day's work, in the hot Chicago summers, we all got together to dine in some cheap place. There was a chop suey joint to which we went often, soft-footed, soft-voiced Chinamen trotting up and down. Chop suey and then a couple of bottles of beer each. We lingered long over that. Then a walk together along the lake front on the near North Side. There was a little strip of park up there facing the lake, a bathing beach; working men with wives and children came there to escape the heat, newspapers spread on the grass, whole families huddled together in the heat, even the moon, looking down, seeming to give forth heat.

We would be full of literary phrases, culled out of books. Some one of us had been reading Kipling.

"City of dreadful night," he said.

Only Jerry, the big German, was a little different. He had a wife and children.

"What's it all about? Why do I want to paint? Why can't I be satisfied driving a truck and working in my warehouse?

"Going home at night to the wife and kids.

"What is it keeps stirring in a man, making him want to do something out of just himself?"

He grew profane. He would be describing a scene. He had come to the Chinese place from his warehouse across the Chicago River, this before the river was beautified, in the days of the old wooden bridges over the river.

He had stood for a time on one of the bridges, seeing a lake boat pass, lake sailors standing on the deck of the boat and looking up at him standing there above on the moving bridge, the curiously lovely chrysoprase color of the river, the gulls floating over the river.

He would begin speaking of all that, the beauty of the smoky sky over buildings off to the west. Sometimes he pounded with his fists on the table in the chop suey joint. A string of oaths flowed from his lips. Sometimes tears came into his eyes.

He was, to be sure, ridiculous. There was in him something I knew so well later in another friend, Tom Wolfe—a determination, half physical, all his big body in it, like a man striving to push his way through a stone wall.

Out into what?

He couldn't have said what any more than I could of my own hopes, my own passionate desires, of which I was always half ashamed.

To get it in some way down, something felt.

A man was too much in a cage—in some way trapped.

A man got himself trapped. All this business of making a living. There were Jerry and Joe, both married. They both had children.

Joe had been a farmer boy, on his father's farm, somewhere in Iowa. He had come to Chicago filled with hope.

He was like Jerry, the German. He wanted to paint.

"That's what I want.

"I want something."

And why the hell did a man get married? They spoke of that. They weren't complaining of the particular women they had married. You knew they were both fond of their children.

A man got stuck on some dame. A man was made that way. When it got him, when it gripped him, he thought, he convinced himself, that in her, in that particular one, was the thing he sought.

Then the kids coming.

They trap you that way.

Joe speaking up. He wasn't as intense as Jerry. He said we couldn't blame them, the women, his own or any other man's woman.

How'd we know they weren't trapped too? They were wanting to be beautiful in some man's eyes, that was it. They had, Joe declared, as much right to want their thing as we had to want ours.

But what was it we were all wanting, the little group of us, there in that vast Chicago, who had in some way found each other?

Comradeship in hungers we couldn't express.

Anyway it wasn't really success. We knew that. We had got that far.

George said we ought to be skunks. "A man should be a skunk," he said. George wasn't married but had an old mother and father he was supporting. He was laying down a law he couldn't obey.

"So I'm a clerk, eh?

"And whose fault is it?

"Mine, I tell you.

"I ought to walk out on them, on everyone, let 'em go to hell.

"What I want is to wander up and down for a long time. Look and look.

"People think of it as a virtue, a man like me, sticking to a clerk's job, supporting my old father and mother, when it's just cowardice, that's all.

"If I had the courage to walk out on them, be a skunk."

It was something he couldn't do. We all knew that.

By the river bank, on the Sunday afternoon, after a morning trying to write the story I had for weeks been trying to write, I had torn up what I had written. There were the pages of meaningless words, that refused to march, thrown into the sluggish river, floating slowly away.

White patches on a background of yellow sluggish river.

"Patience, patience."

White clouds floating in a hot sky, over a distant cornfield.

"Oh, to hell with patience."

How many men like me, over the world, everywhere, all over America, in big towns like Chicago and New York, small towns or farms.

Trying for it.

For what?

There was something beyond money to be made, fame got, a big name. I was already past thirty. There were the others, Joe, Jerry, and George, none of them any longer young.

The World War had not yet come. It was to scatter us, shatter us.

The big German, Jerry, came down to where I lay on my back on the dry grass by the sluggish stream. He had with him the canvas on which he had been working all day. Now it was growing late. At noon, when we had together eaten our lunches, he had been hopeful.

"I think I'll get something. By the gods, I think I will."

Now he sat beside me on the grass at the stream's edge. He had thrown his wet canvas aside. Across the stream from us we could see stretched away the vast cornfields.

The corn was ripening now. The stalks grew high, the long ears hanging down. Soon it would be corn cutting time.

It was a fat rich land—the Middle West. At noon Jerry, the German, son of a German immigrant, who had been a city man all his life, had suddenly begun talking.

He had been trying to paint the cornfield. For the time he had forgotten to be profane. We others had all come from farms or from country towns of the Middle West. He had said that he wanted to paint a cornfield in such a way that everyone looking at his painting would begin at once to think of the fatness and richness of all Middle Western America.

It would be something to give men new confidence in life. He had grown serious. He was the son of a German immigrant who had fled to America to escape military service. Germany believed in the army, in the brute power of arms, but he, Jerry, wanted by his painting to make people believe in the land.

I remember that, in his earnestness, he had shaken a big finger under our noses. "You fellows, your fathers and grandfathers were born on the land. You can't see how rich it all is, how gloriously men might live here." He had spoken of his father, the immigrant, now an old man. We others couldn't understand how hard and meagre life had become for the peasants in all the European lands. We didn't know our own richness—what a foundation, the land, on which to build.

But he would show them, through the richness of the fields. The skyscrapers in the cities, money piled in banks, men owning great factories, they were not the significant things.

The real significance was in the tall corn growing. There was the real American poetry.

He'd show them.

He sat beside me on the grass, by the stream. We sat a long time in silence. There was a grim look on his face, and I knew that he had failed as, earlier in the day, I had. I did not want to embarrass him by speaking. I stayed silent, occasionally looking up at him.

He sat staring at the sluggish stream and looking across the stream to where the cornfields began, and I thought I saw tears in his eyes.

He didn't want me to see.

Suddenly he jumped up. Profane words flew from his lips. He began to dance up and down on the canvas lying on the grass. I remember that the sun was going down over the tops of the tall cornstalks, and he shook his fists at it. He cursed the sun, the corn, himself. What was the use? He had wanted to say something he'd never be able to say. "I'm a shipping clerk in a lousy warehouse, and I'll always be just that, nothing else." It was a child's rage in a grown man. He picked up the canvas on which he had been at work all day and threw it far out into the stream.

We were on our way to the suburban station where we would get our train into the city. All the others, Joe, George, and Jerry, had their painting traps, their easels, boxes of color, palettes. They had little canvas stools on which they sat while painting, and Joe and George carried the wet canvases they had done during the day.

We went along in silence. Joe and George ahead while I walked with Jerry. Did he want me to carry some of his traps?

"Oh, to hell with them, and you too."

He was in this grim mood. Fighting back something in himself. We went along a dusty road beside a wood and cut across a field in which tall weeds grew. We were getting near the station where we were to take the train.

Back to the city.

To our clerkships.

To his being a shipping clerk in his warehouse.

To little hot and cold Chicago flats where some of us had wives and children waiting.

To be fed, clothed, housed.

"A man can't just live in his children. He can't, I tell you."

Something rebellious in all of us.

What is it a man wants, to be of some account in the world, in himself, in his own manhood?

The attempts to write, to paint—these efforts only a part of something we wanted.

All of us half knowing all our efforts would end in futility.

I am very sure the same thoughts were in all our minds that evening, in the field of tall weeds, in the half darkness, as we drew near the little prairie railroad station, the lights of the train already seen far off, across the flat prairies.

And then the final explosion from Jerry. He had suddenly put his painting traps down. He began to throw his tubes of paint about, hurling them into the tall weeds in the field.

"You get out of here, damn you. Go on about your business."

He had thrown his easel, his stool, his paintbrushes. He stood there dancing among the tall weeds.

"Go on. Go away. I'll kill you if you don't."

I moved away from him and joined the others on the platform by the station. It was still light enough to see the man out there in the field, where the tall weeds grew waist-high. He was still dancing with rage, his hands raised, no doubt still cursing his fate.

He was expressing something for us all. He was going through something we had all been through and before we died would all go through again and again.

And then the train came and we got silently aboard, but already we could see happening what I think we all knew would happen. We saw Jerry, that brusque, profane German, already down on his knees among the weeds in the field.

We knew what he was doing, but, when our train arrived in the city and we separated at the station, Joe and George still clinging to the canvases they both knew were no good, when the others had gone I hung about the station.

I had been a farm boy, an American small-town boy like Joe and George. I was curious. Jerry, the big German, had spoken of the land. We had, all of us, been thinking of ourselves as rather special human beings, men with a right to that curious happiness that comes sometimes, fleetingly enough, with accomplishment.

Forgetting the millions like us on farms, holding minor jobs in cities.

What old Abe Lincoln meant when he spoke of "the people."

I was remembering bad years when I was a small-town boy, working about on farms, farmers working all through the year, from daylight until dark.

Big Jerry wanted to express something out of the American land.

Droughts coming, hailstorms destroying crops, disease among the cattle, often a long year's work come to nothing.

Something else remembered out of my own boyhood.

Springs coming, after such disastrous years, and the farmers near my own Middle Western town out again in their fields, again plowing the land.

A kind of deep patient heroism in millions of men on the land, in cities too.

The government pensioning men who went out to kill other men but no pensions for men who spent long lives raising food to feed men.

Killers become heroes, the millions of others never thinking of themselves as heroes.

There would be another train in an hour, and I wanted to see what I did see, keeping myself unseen, the arrival of Jerry, most of his painting traps again collected.

Knowing, as I did know, that on another weekend he would be trying again.

THE MASTERPIECE

IT WAS GETTING NEAR THE END OF MY TIME. I LAUGHED AND STRETCHED myself. "Work now, you slave. Well, what shall I do? Shall I go to work in a factory? In me there is no gift for the factories. I work and work but do not rise. You see, I have read all the books. I know that, in a factory, when a man has done his work well he is promoted. At night he takes a course in something—well, let us say in mechanical engineering—and then, some day in the factory, there is a problem to solve and he solves it.

"But I cannot solve any problems. Do you not understand that figures mean nothing to me?" Once I knew a man. He was a sheet writer at the races and his name was Billy. How I envied that man. There he stood on the platform making the odds for a race. There was a blackboard before him on which he wrote down figures. Another man was selling the pools and a crowd surged about. It was my friend's problem to see that his employer did not really bet on the race. He collected money from one man and gave part of it to another, something like that. It sounded pretty slick to hear Billy tell how it was done. From time to time Billy's employer looked at the board on which Billy had put the figures. "10 to 1 Billy McGee. 8 to 5 Harry Hurry. Miss Maud at 2 to 6. Apple Pie at even money, boys." I did not hear the voice of the man. I looked at Billy. What a man! What a captain of modern industry he would have made! When I spoke to him of the matter in the evening, paying him compliments, flattering him, he was unmoved. "Ah, go on. Cut out that bunk," was what he said.

"But my dear man, you will have to work. Go then to a store. Get a job as a clerk. Be honest. There must be a way in which you can rise in the world. You should cultivate respectable people. You cannot be a lazy lout lying in bed and reading books all your life."

What I have been trying to write here is the substance of a lecture I gave myself every morning at twelve when I got out of bed. When, however, I had said the words put down above, I sprang out of bed and dressed myself quickly. I had resolved to go get a job, being nearly broke, but when I had got out of doors the sun was shining. I lived at that time in a room near a park in the city of Chicago and when I had walked in the park and had eaten my breakfast at a nearby lunch counter I stood for a moment on the street. "Shall I go look for work or shall I go call on Harold?" The trouble with me is that I cannot solve problems. As I walked along I became suddenly gloomy. "I'm in for trouble," I said to myself.

But I never had thought it would come as it did. I had not thought it would come from the woman named Mildred.

I shall have to explain. In those days, although I had at that time no notion I would ever practice one of the arts, I had a great fondness for making friends with young art students, students of music and the theater, and young poets, and among all such friends I had made, Harold was my prize, and for months I had been his shadow and, I am afraid, half his servant. He was called the prize student of the Art Institute at that time and the girl students all worshipped him but Mildred had won him. It was even said . . . Well, he had a studio and Mildred went there almost any time. We who were their friends did not use the word but we thought, perhaps we hoped . . . Romance of just that sort is so hard to come at in Chicago.

She was also an art student and very quick and facile at making pleasant little drawings but no one took her art seriously. Harold was, however, a different matter. He was a Modern. A painting of his had once been accepted and hung at a show of young moderns in New York City. I remember it now as a wild thing of red and white perpendicular lines across which went meandering a river of red and it was called, I believe, "The Red Laugh," after something Harold had read by the Russian Andreyev.

At the moment, however, and just at the time when I had become most intimate with him, Harold was up to something else. He was in fact in the act of showing the Chicago art world how a man of talent goes about it to win the prize in the annual fall show.

Again I will have to explain. At the moment I was not working and was consequently happy and contented with life and had been so for a long time but my money was beginning to give out. I was living in a cheap rooming house but was living as best I could the life of leisure. In the evening I went to Harold's room or to the room of some other student and in the morning stayed in my bed. And what joy I had of life. Why get up? I had cigarettes and matches on a chair beside the bed and books piled across the foot. If in the night I kicked some of the books off the bed, others remained, and in the morning I had but to turn them over until I found one to my liking. The books had been borrowed from friends, taken from a branch of the Chicago Public Library or bought at a second-hand store nearby. All morning I could read and smoke and in the afternoon walk about. It was the life for me.

Harold had a studio in what had once been a small store in the neighborhood and slept on a cot at the back. I dare say Mildred grew tired of always having me about but Harold seemed glad of my presence in the afternoons. Perhaps I saved him from her too great ardency.

Until—well, until the great scheme had been hatched.

The great scheme was that Harold should paint a perfectly conventional picture for the fall show and win the prize. It was to be an interior. There was to be a corner of a lady's dressing room

of the old rich days, say of the fifteenth century in Italy, with a
window looking out upon a rolling country, hill after hill getting
smaller and smaller in the distance, such hills as Titian or Raphael
liked to put into the backgrounds of their canvases.

The interior of the room would be somewhat somber, a heavily
carved chair sitting before an equally heavily carved table near
the window.

And across the back of the chair—ah, there was the point—
across the back of the chair would be thrown . . . Harold was so
excited about the whole matter when I went to him early that
afternoon that it took him a long time to talk at all.

Across the back of the chair would be thrown a woman's heavy
yellow velvet gown.

At first I could not understand Harold's excitement concerning
the gown but as he talked I began a little to understand. The
folds of the gown should be made to fall in just a certain way.
Harold had in fact got hold of such a gown as he intended painting into the picture in a second-hand store in lower State Street,
Chicago, in a place where women's dresses, that had once belonged
to members of the fashionable world and later perhaps given to
servants, had now been put on sale. In a place in fact where they
were likely to catch the best trade for such wares, that is to say in
a street much frequented at that time by the women of the town.

It may have been that seeing the gown in the store window
had put the notion of the painting into Harold's head and he had
gone into the store and had bought it at once and now had it in
the studio. Its presence there was, I could see at once, a queer sort
of shock to Mildred. He kept walking across the room and throwing
it across the back of a chair (not the heavily carved chair of the
picture—that he would get out of a book at the institute or the
public library, he explained. It would be, he thought, Spanish
and very rococo—but across a kitchen chair he had bought at a
nearby furniture store.)

He flung the gown over the back of the chair, arranged the
folds a little, picked it up again, walked across the room and again
pitched it at the chair. "The thing may have to be carefully arranged

but there is a chance it may fall just right," he said, while Mildred and I looked on in wonder. The gown, he explained, was to be the central point of his painting. There it would be in the corner of the dark somber room with the dark somber landscape in the distance. Other things in the picture, the chair, the table, the hills, he could paint in quickly enough, saving all the best of himself for the painting of the gown. It was there, in the painting of the gown, he would show the old painters something. He would paint the soft rich velvet lying in folds in such a way that the committee, the men who were to hang and judge the pictures, would be fairly knocked off their feet. Did he not know such fellows? Ah, he would get them. Their feelings, their sensuality, would be worked on without their knowing. There would be brush work, color, the feel for texture. Men who had always painted in the conventional way and whose natures had become dried up and half dead were always saying that men like himself, Gauguin, Cézanne, and the others, were only trying to avoid the real challenge of painting but he would show them. I do not remember that Harold, when he called the roll of the great moderns in his studio that afternoon, put himself among them but at least he implied something of the sort.

He would so paint the woman's dress that the power women were able to exert over all men, because of men's sensual natures, would unconsciously be felt by everyone who looked at the painting. "For the time being, for weeks perhaps, while I am doing the painting, I shall be in love, actually and physically in love with an imagined woman of old times who once wore this dress. I am sitting you see at the back of the room waiting for her. The dress is lying across the back of the chair but, as I sit waiting, it, you see, represents her to me. In it I see the gentle but strong mold of her form, all she is to me, all she is to become to me when I have won her. I have not won her yet. Upon the wonder awakened in her by the way I shall paint depends whether or not I shall make her my own."

Harold had now worked himself into a state and had completely won my own admiration, but Mildred . . . I was not entirely sorry when I looked at Mildred's face. There had been moments when I had thought that—if Harold were not about . . .

And now Harold, having determined to begin blocking in his picture at once, that same evening, ran to prepare his canvas and easel, all the while telling us of his plans. His father was a wholesale merchant at Fort Wayne, Indiana, and had objected to his becoming an artist. It was only the mother's influence that had induced him to support Harold at the school, but after he had painted the canvas he was now about to begin and had won the prize in the fall show, all would be changed. Money would be forthcoming and with the money got from his father and from the painting, which would be sure to sell at a large price, he would take Mildred and me with him to Paris. There we would live, Mildred and he studying painting, while I . . . He had stopped his preparations and turning had looked at me. "Well, you'll be all right whatever turns up," he had said, heartily enough I am sure.

I had walked out of Harold's studio with Mildred and we had gone to dine at a nearby table d'hôte. The money that had paid for the weeks of leisure I had just been enjoying was nearly gone. Soon I would have to go to work. At the table d'hôte we spoke of Harold and what a splendid fellow he was. Mildred I thought was hanging between anger and tears. She had wanted a man when Harold had caught her fancy and she had got an artist. Now that he had started on his great canvas, she would, for weeks, get nothing from him. I looked at her and wondered.

And again let me explain. For days a half-crazy notion for getting money with which to extend my season of leisure had been playing about in my mind and now I began to wonder if Mildred might not be ready to go into it with me. She had told me on the way to the table d'hôte that she was nearly broke. For some time she had been holding a job as secretary to a businessman in the Loop district, but Harold was always phoning her in the afternoon and she was always running off with him and now the man had fired her. She had intended telling Harold about it that afternoon but had found him so absorbed in his grand plans that she had hated to disturb him. As she had talked, the hope in me had flared up and after the table d'hôte and while we were still seated at table I took a deep breath and unfolded my scheme.

For several weeks, I explained, Harold would be absorbed with his painting. He would not want Mildred about and she had lost her job. It might well be that she, like myself, was nearly broke. Such a painting as Harold had in mind could not be done offhand. He would be absorbed in it, thinking of nothing else. Above all he would not want a woman about. Had not Mildred heard what he had said about the feeling he would be having for some mysterious woman of old times? Such feelings, while they lasted, were often stronger than the feeling for living people. It was a part of the artist nature that this be so.

"We will have to be comrades now, Mildred," I said and then I unfolded my scheme. It had been in my head, as I have said, for some time but, until that moment, I had not dreamed that I might be so fortunate as to get Mildred to go in with me.

And she would be the very one. How quick and facile she was with her brush and how pretty as she sat there before me with her troubled eyes.

All of this, as you will understand, was before the days of Prohibition and Chicago had within its borders thousands of small saloons. As I had gone about the city I had noted that saloon keepers had a penchant for pictures painted on the looking glasses back of the bars and these were as a rule very stupidly done. Why not have them better done and by a pretty woman painter?

Mildred and I would set out, I carrying a box of paints and doing the talking. A romantic story would be invented. She, Mildred, would be a young and promising painter earning money with which to go to Paris and study. To the saloon keepers I would explain how, at Barbizon and other places, paintings on the walls of little out-of-the-way cafés had become famous and had made the places where some great painter had stopped, usually in his youth, famous. Rich Americans took voyages out from Paris to see such places and spent money lavishly. I had no doubt that, with the tales I could invent, we could get many jobs at from

twenty to thirty dollars each and of course I would stay with
Mildred in each place to protect her from any annoyance from
the patrons. Several little inviting sketches—a mountain scene, a
hunting scene, a mother rocking a child to sleep, two lovers standing
under trees at the gate of a cottage in the moonlight—would be
prepared and, after making the same painting several times, Mildred
would become adept and could do at least two or three a day. We
would divide our takings on an even basis and, while Harold was
engaged with his great work, we would also be making money. "A
woman wants her independence," I said and Mildred nodded. I
had been somewhat afraid she would break into tears.

And so it had been arranged and, for me at least, the adventure
with Mildred had turned out to be a great success. For weeks,
and while Harold was engaged with his great masterpiece, we
had tramped about the streets of Chicago, I making engagements
for Mildred and she executing them. How charming she was. In
the early morning we met and set out on our own mutual adventure
and, as she stood on a chair behind some bar with laborers and
teamsters standing about, painting on the barroom looking glass
one of the several scenes we had prepared in advance, I moved
among the spectators, speaking in whispers of the great future
before her when she had got to Paris and had attracted the attention of the big world. "The day may come when that looking
glass, because of the painting now being put on it, may be worth
a thousand dollars," I said solemnly, and often some man in the
crowd ordered on the spot a duplicate of the painting to be done
on canvas so that it could be framed and hung up in his house.

What days for me—the presence of Mildred, the dollars rolling
in, a new suit bought, an overcoat against the winter, new linen,
money in my pocket. Occasionally in the evening Mildred went
to see Harold, but he was absorbed and did not ask what she was
doing and she did not tell him. "The matter may go on for months
and it will surely go on until the great canvas is finished," I thought
and saw myself living for months with my books and no more
compelled to go into some factory or to accept a clerkship.

And then one morning it had all come to an end and I shall remember that morning as long as I live. It may be that I had begun to hope I would win Mildred myself.

I had gone to a place on the West Side, near Garfield Park in Chicago, where I was to meet Mildred and where our day's work was to begin, but when she appeared I knew at once something had happened. She was not wearing the gay little smock that had been a part of our stage property and there was a sad serious look on her face. At once and without words she had led the way into the park and we sat down on a bench. She was dressed in black. What a come-down. I perhaps made a mistake. I took her hand.

That may have broken the floodgates. She may have intended only to tell me she could not carry on our scheme anymore. On the evening before she had gone to Harold and the great painting was at last finished. He had wanted her back. "Where have you been and what have you been doing?" he had asked, and it was then the horror of what she had been doing had for the first time dawned upon Mildred. The thought of it had made her half ill and she had cried all night. While he, Harold, had been doing his great painting, making a real and lasting contribution to the arts, she, betrayed by me, by the baseness in my nature, had been going about to low saloons and had been painting such pictures on the looking glasses back of the bars. Now, if she had her own way, she would go about painting them all out. The common people, such people as came into small Chicago saloons, had also been betrayed. One should be engaged in lifting up, not in casting down into greater and greater vulgarities, the common people.

"But Mildred," I said. She had taken her hand from mine and was weeping. A man passing along the path had stopped and seemed about to speak. There was an angry look in his eyes. Perhaps he thought we were married and that I had been beating her. In the far distance, across a flat open green space, some golf players, tiny figures against a sea of green, were passing in and out across an opening between trees. It was early fall and in Chicago early fall days can be lovely.

To think that I had been the one who had betrayed Mildred

and through her had betrayed Harold's art. "There is nothing now you can do except one thing and that you must do. Promise me that I will never see you again and that you will never see Harold again," she said, getting to her feet and preparing to leave me flat there in the park.

Without another word Mildred had left me sitting disconsolate and alone on the bench. I arose and stretched. As I have already pointed out, I am one who cannot solve problems. "Work now, you slave," I had begun saying to myself again when another thought came. My new overcoat was warm and, as I have said, fall days in Chicago can sometimes be quite lovely. I put the paint box on the bench and stared at the man who had been staring at me. "Get out," I thought although I said nothing to him. "Perhaps," I said to myself, "when there is a new masterpiece to be done." I had, you see, not entirely given up the notion of Mildred.

And so I went back again to my room and my books.

As for the masterpiece, as it turned out, I did not see it at all. It was hung in the fall show and, although it did not win the prize, attracted a great deal of attention. It just happened that at that time I had gone off on my travels.

It did not win the fall prize but that was because the jury was fixed. I had that from a friend who had it from Mildred. And had you been with us during the days of our mutual adventure, you also would have been unable to doubt what Mildred had said.

Mildred was, you see, such a masterpiece in herself.

I am very sure she must have been worthy of Harold.

FRED

FRED IS A SMALL TOWN MAN WHO HAS LIVED FIFTEEN YEARS IN NEW York City. He is a magazine illustrator and must make a good deal of money. I knew him first in New York.

Later, once, I went with him on a visit to his home town.

It was in West Virginia, on the Ohio River. We spent two weeks there.

He had a sister still living in his home town. She was married to the superintendent of schools.

The sister had grown rather fat. When I was there she had been having trouble with her teeth. The upper teeth had been taken out. She was going to have a plate, I fancy.

She was very curious about Fred and used to corner me and ask questions.

She had two daughters at that time. One of them has since died. She was killed in an automobile accident.

The girls were slender and tall, like Fred, who has always had the reputation of being a handsome fellow. They were a little leggy, rather smart. They both drove a car well, used a good deal of lipstick, sat in chairs with their legs crossed in such a way as to show half the leg expanse from the knees to the hips.

They were delighted to have Fred in the house, although I could see his sister and her husband were both nervous all the time we were there.

The husband was prematurely bald. Both he and his wife had got old fast. Small-town people often do that. At about thirty-five, almost overnight, they turn old.

Then they go on being just like that for the next twenty-five years.

The school superintendent had a new cheap car and drove it badly. When we all rode together the wife and I sat on the back seat with one of the daughters, and Fred, the husband and the other girl squeezed into the front seat.

The superintendent's wife, Fred's sister, kept giving driving advice and the superintendent got sore. I could see his jaw getting more and more set. Fred had his arm around the girl on the seat beside him. He liked that and the girl liked it.

That one, I have forgotten her name, was learning to play a violin. Fred and I were in two rooms upstairs in the big frame house in which the family lived and the girls were up there too.

They used to go to bed at night and lie whispering and giggling together until Fred stopped them.

He would roar at them, "Stop that racket in there or I'll come and spank you." They didn't always stop. One night Fred went in there, clad in his pajamas. The two girls tackled him. The three of them rolled and tumbled on the bed and on the floor and there were screams of laughter from the girls and curses from Fred.

The superintendent, with his funny old fat face, came upstairs.

Of course he was shocked. The girls had torn Fred's pajamas and he came out into the hallway, where the father was, holding them together.

The trouble about Fred lay in the fact that, when I went up there with him, he had already divorced two wives and had lived with two or three other women.

There was something absolute and cruel about the man when it came to women.

Well, he fell in love, was passionately in love. Both of the women were actresses. When he was in love he gave the women no rest.

I remember seeing him at one of these times. I was living in Chicago then and the actress with whom he was in love was playing out there.

She was married and her husband was in the same company but she had told Fred that she was no longer in love with him.

She was staying at a small outlying hotel and her husband was somewhere else.

I had not known Fred was in Chicago until one night about twelve o'clock, when he called me up. I had gone to bed but he told me that I would have to get up, that he was in trouble.

"You get up and come out here," he said, telling me where he was.

I went of course and found Fred walking up and down a street in front of the hotel. There were tears in his eyes.

He was in love again. How many times had he been in love. This particular woman, he suspected, was up to something. He had thought she had begun to love him a little, but now—

She had told him to wait for her that evening at her hotel but when I got there she was an hour and a half late.

She had perhaps gone off with some other man.

Fred was trying to explain to me. His face was white. He kept walking up and down in the quiet outlying street.

Women were to Fred, he said, the most wonderful and delightful beings in the world, when they were wonderful.

He had been accused of being unfaithful. It was quite true. But, he said, when he got a passion for a woman he was ready to die for her.

He would do anything, go anywhere, take any risk. Several times already in his life he had taken a risk of being shot.

What did that matter? Being shot or even killed was a small matter compared with not having the woman you wanted when you wanted her.

And as for being faithless, Fred said that all people, at bottom, felt as he did but would not admit the fact to themselves. "You see, I started out in life to be an artist and I have not made it," he explained. "I am an illustrator. That, as you know, is a quite secondary art. I have a small talent, which has become, because of the skill I have acquired in developing it, a real talent.

"But a talent is not an art. It does not feed a man as an art does, does not satisfy.

"And so I have tried to make my relationship with women an art. I have made love-making a fine art.

"I have never had a woman quit me, once I have got her. I have always quit them.

"It is because something crude happens. The women themselves spoil things. After it is spoiled I will have nothing to do with one of them.

"But I am frank from the beginning. I tell them all how I feel."

Fred had just told me that about his frankness, that night in Chicago, when the woman we were waiting for arrived.

It was half-past two o'clock. A taxi drove up before the suburban hotel and when the woman got out Fred ran to her.

I did not know what to do but Fred wanted me to stay. The woman looked tired.

She was a thin little blonde and explained that she had been kept at a downtown theatre. The play she was with, she said, wasn't doing very well and so, the producer having come from New York, there was a rehearsal after the performance. Lines and situations had been changed.

Fred, the woman and I had gone into the lobby of the hotel. I was embarrassed and wanted to go away but Fred would not let me. "You stay where you are," he said in a commanding tone. I stayed because I wanted to see what was going to happen.

What happened was that Fred talked and then the actress talked. There was only a dim light in the lobby of the hotel. The night clerk was staring at us. I sat a little to one side. The woman and Fred forgot me.

"Why should you want me?" the woman asked. She was tired and discouraged.

"My God," she said, "I've been ten years now on the stage and have got nowhere.

"I have been married and have had a baby that died.

"There is something about acting I can't get.

"I don't know what it is. I am crazy about acting and tonight that producer told me I wasn't getting half out of my part.

"It was true too. If there had been another actress to take my place he would have fired me."

I was looking at the woman as she talked. Fred was right about her. She was lovely now. Her face was thin and white and her thin white hands lay limply in her lap.

Fred was right about her being lovely and he was telling her so. Regardless of my presence, the late hour and the woman's weariness, he pressed his suit.

He had fallen in love with her and knew that she was not loved by her husband and that she did not love her husband. He said that he wanted to be perfectly frank with her. He had fallen in love many times before. Sometimes he was successful and sometimes he was not.

He said that, as far as the woman being an actress was concerned, he knew about that too.

She had been to the art of acting what he had been to the art of painting, he said. She had been just half what she wanted to be.

It was the queerest courtship I ever heard.

He told her that everything in life that amounted to anything was a matter of surrender to something outside self. He had tried, he said, to surrender himself to art, that is to say to painting, just as she had tried to surrender herself to the parts she was given to play on the stage.

Fred had not quite made it and so he had turned to women.

"I have turned to you just now," he said. I thought he was a little crazy.

"I advise you to do the same thing. I advise you to surrender to me.

"The fact that you are tired just now will make it all the easier for you.

"You may not have this chance again.

"As for your beauty, I think you might leave that to me. If I could not see your beauty I would not be here."

I was edging toward the door. They had begun talking in low tones. When I looked back, the tiredness all seemed gone out of the woman's face and figure.

As a matter of fact, I waited about outside for a half hour and then went and looked into the hotel lobby.

They had disappeared.

As for that time in Fred's sister's house, I have already explained that, at the time I went up there with him, his sister was curious about him.

She kept asking me questions about his life.

Well, she knew about some of his escapades. Could such a man be a good man?

Fred had been very good to both herself and her husband. As an illustrator he made a good deal of money and he had been free with it.

He had, she said, helped them buy the house in which they lived and had done other things.

Both she and her husband, she said, had a great deal of respect for Fred and for his talents, but they had daughters.

The daughters she thought were somewhat too fond of Fred. He would be putting notions into their heads.

There was the one daughter, the one who played the violin.

One evening when I was there she was playing for all of us and did not do it very well.

This is what happened. She had quit playing and had gone to sit with her sister when Fred arose from his chair and went to her.

He put his arm about her and led her from the room. As I have already suggested, she was a slim girl, of perhaps fourteen or fifteen. Fred is tall and rather broad shouldered. His hair is iron grey and he has grey eyes.

truck.

"Nevertheless we sing. We sing of a maiden to whom a great wrong has been done."

I went there and painted that family and what joy I had, but of what use was it? It is my finest work but who will buy it? When I had finished my painting of that family, in that house, they all gathered around me.

"It is fine. You have got us," the little man said. The little fat wife came and kissed me on the cheek. Suddenly I wanted to be as they were, perhaps raise cabbages, have a swarm of ragged, jolly children about me, have a gold tooth of which I was proud.

It is not, however, a man's fate that bothers him. It is the little things that drive him to distraction. There is a screen door that has come loose from its hinges. A man's wife asks him to fix it and he tries. He hits his finger with the hammer.

Or a man has borrowed money at the bank to help pay for his house and there is a payment to be met. It is on his mind and he has no money. He is worried. "I will have to go to that banker, be humble, ask him to wait for the payment, and I do not like him."

I want to shout at him, "Take the house, take the barn that I have made into a studio, take all my equipment for painting."

"I will go and be a tramp," you want to declare. You walk out into your yard. Look down the road. The road is going away to the west, through New Jersey. Cars are running along the road.

Far to the west there are mountains and plains. There are strange towns and cities.

I will chuck everything. I declare I will. How my finger hurts where I hit it with the hammer. The fingernail is black. It will come off.

I am damned if I will go and see that banker.

There is my wife Sue. She is walking along a path toward our chicken yard. She has a tired look on her face. Now she has begun to raise chickens. She imagines herself selling eggs at a high price. She will sell young fowls in the market. She thinks she can help me so.

We are living too well. We should not have bought this house, gone into debt. There she is walking along, a middle-aged woman now, always trying to keep up appearances, help me so, and I am remembering her as a young slender girl, in the Forest of Fontainebleau, as I walked with her along a path in the forest, holding her hand, stopping occasionally in the path to kiss and embrace her.

Speaking of my love.

Am I now capable of love? I am asking myself the question. Am I now capable of love?

You can see that I am an ineffectual man. I am not captain of my soul. It is true that sometimes I paint well but when I do I rarely sell my paintings. I say to myself, "Well, Van Gogh did not sell his paintings. He went to live among potato eaters. He was poor with the poor. Cézanne did not sell his paintings. When he was an old man he went with his son to see an exhibition of his paintings and when he came out of the room where they were hung on a wall there were tears in his eyes.

"Did you see?" he said to his son. "They were all framed."

But where did I get that story? Of what use is it to me to remember such stories? I am not Van Gogh nor am I Cézanne. I am just a man who makes paintings he rarely sells. I have hit my finger with a hammer. It hurts. I have to go and see a banker.

But I sat down here to write the story of the red dog. I did not intend to speak of my woes.

The dog was given to me by the man with the gold tooth. It was a dog that came to his house, a beautiful dog.

It was a stray. It came there. It was lost. It had what is called running fits. It went quietly along and then it began to run. It ran madly with desperate speed for a long way and then it fell down.

It lay on the ground and writhed. Its body jerked and trembled.

It seems there were worms in the dog. It had worms.

The man cured it. He went to town and bought pills, gave them to the dog, and it got well. He gave the dog to me.

That was my first red dog. It was a kind called an Irish setter. It was gentle. It followed me about. It came to me, jumped into my arms. I became attached to it. I loved it.

Such a dog is a thing you can love. It does not, in order to keep up appearances, have to have a new dress. It does not, just as you are preparing to get into your car to take a drive, to get away from your house, to get off by yourself and think, perhaps to see a landscape you want to paint, come to you to tell you the car has a flat.

As I have said it is not a man's fate that bothers him. It is the little things. I had a portrait to paint. It was a rich woman Sue had met through her cousin. She was a tall woman in a black dress and with a long nose.

EDITORIAL NOTES

THE THIRTY SHORT STORIES IN THIS COLLECTION ARE FRESHLY EDITED from Anderson's published editions and manuscripts. In preparing them I have silently corrected punctuation and spelling.

I have tried to present a text that is as close as possible to Anderson's own final intention for each story. He often made revisions of stories between a first publication in a periodical and its inclusion in one of the collected volumes, and, except in unusual circumstances to be described below, I have used the later version but have occasionally corrected errors in it. Some of Anderson's manuscripts survive that are useful in showing the development of the stories and also in revealing the editorial influence of Laura Lu Copenhaver and Paul Rosenfeld on a few of the later texts. I have restored Anderson's own versions whenever possible. However, I have eliminated from the present collection a story that could not be salvaged in the form that Anderson left it. "Daughters," originally published in *The Sherwood Anderson Reader* and reprinted in *Sherwood Anderson: Short Stories*, ed. Maxwell Geismar (New York: Hill and Wang, 1962) and *The Teller's Tales*, ed. Frank Gado (Schenectady, N.Y.: Union College, 1983), is a cut-and-paste assembly by Paul Rosenfeld, along with some rewriting, of sections of a novel abandoned by Anderson.

"I Want to Know Why" appeared in the November 1919 issue

of *Smart Set* two years before it was included in *The Triumph of the Egg*. I have followed the wording of the earlier text in two instances: (1) "in a pocket behind other horses" instead of "in a pocket behind another" (*Triumph* 11), since Anderson must have intended for more than a single horse to form a pocket; (2) "he weaved back and forth" instead of "he waved back and forth" (*Triumph* 19), referring to the drunken actions of Jerry Tillford near the end of the story.

Two texts of "Brothers" appeared in 1921: in the April issue of *Bookman* and in *The Triumph of the Egg*, first printed in October. I have followed the latter text in the present edition, but in three instances I have used the earlier version. First, the *Triumph of the Egg* text (p. 106) omits a sentence in this passage: "After dinner he with his wife went to a picture show. There were two children . and his wife expected another. They came into the apartment and sat down." In the *Bookman* version (p. 111) this sentence follows the first sentence above: "When they came home his wife's mother sat under an electric light reading." In addition to getting the couple home from the picture show, the sentence also introduces the light motif that becomes important as the story proceeds. Second, the husband in the *Triumph of the Egg* text twice states that "there was no light. The janitor has neglected to light the gas" (p. 111), while the *Bookman* version is "had neglected," obviously the correct tense in that context. Finally, at the end of the story the narrator watches the leaves falling, which in *The Triumph of the Egg* reads: "—the yellow, red and golden leaves fall straight down, heavily. The rain beat them brutally down" (115). The *Bookman* text is: "The rain beats them brutally down" (115), which is certainly as Anderson intended.

"The Man's Story" was published in *Dial* in September 1923, just a month before its appearance in *Horses and Men*. I have followed the latter text but have corrected two errors in it with the aid of the *Dial* version. A comma is substituted for the question mark after "all people" on p. 302 of *Horses and Men*, and the "a" is deleted in "in a walking" (*HM* 303). I have also capitalized the brand name "Fordson."

After consulting the typescript of "An Ohio Pagan," I have restored Anderson's version in these instances: (1) spacing breaks at transitional points in the narrative; (2) replacement of a word omitted in the *Horses and Men* version (p. 330): "The shower came up suddenly and [in] a few minutes was gone"; (3) "the gods" changed to "the god" (*HM* 339)—the reference is clearly to Jesus; (4) "and" deleted in "It was nursing time, and she wanted..." (*HM* 344); (5) "The stream was the arm" changed to "an arm" (*HM* 345)—the passage goes on to refer to the other arm.

The texts of some of the later stories were sometimes edited by Anderson's mother-in-law, Laura Lu Copenhaver. She often read through his texts while he was working on them and made corrections, wrote question marks in the margins, or suggested rephrasings. He usually accepted her version, but occasionally he marked out her query or re-wrote the passage his own way. Where there is evidence of such interactivity, resulting in Anderson's approval of the finished text, I have, except in unusual cases to be mentioned later, accepted her changes.

On a few occasions Anderson gave her permission to go through some of his old manuscripts and to revise them on her own. Two stories in this collection were, in their previously published form, the result of this process: "The Masterpiece" and "Mrs. Wife." In these cases I have restored the texts to the form in which Anderson left them.

The typescript of "The Masterpiece" at the Newberry Library shows that Copenhaver made extensive changes, including crossing out Anderson's own title, "The Masterpiece," and writing above it, "The Yellow Gown." Her version was the one published in *Mademoiselle* in 1946 and in subsequent reprintings. But because there is no evidence of any acceptance by Anderson of Copenhaver's changes, I have restored his own more appropriate title and disregarded her other revisions.

Copenhaver's revisions of "Mrs. Wife" were even more significant. She retitled it "A Moonlight Walk," made considerable deletions, and altered—even reversed—the very point of the doctor's story regarding his feelings for his wife. For a detailed discussion of these changes, see Karen Coates, "Reclaiming Mrs. Wife," *Winesburg Eagle* 16 (Summer 1991): 9-12. The text of "Mrs. Wife" in the present collection is based on a typescript that shows both Anderson's latest version and Copenhaver's revisions. It has not been published previously.

Anderson wrote an early version of "Pastoral" in August 1938 entitled "The Writer." When he revised it, with some editorial assistance from Copenhaver, for *Reader's Digest* in April 1939, he called it "The Most Unforgettable Character I Have Ever Known (He Was a Letter Writer)." After they turned it down, *Redbook* accepted it, and it was renamed "Pastoral"—probably not by Anderson although there is no record of his objecting to it. I have used the *Redbook* text, which is almost totally consistent with a typescript containing a few emendations by him and some passages crossed out by an unknown hand—possibly an editor's—that Anderson apparently accepted. In two instances I have restored Anderson's typescript version: "old Ford" instead of *Redbook's* "old model" and "old car" (*Redbook* 38, 59).

"Nobody Laughed" survives in numerous typescripts under three different titles. The first, "Playthings," probably written in 1935 with some editing by Laura Lu Copenhaver, was returned to Anderson by his agent in August 1937. A second version, "The Town's Playthings," was also returned in December 1938, and the third, "Nobody Laughed," was unpublished until Paul Rosenfeld, making some alterations of his own, placed it first in *The Sherwood Anderson Reader.* Several of the surviving typescripts have unique revisions of some parts of the story, suggesting that Anderson worked on it sporadically without settling on a single text. I have used as a copy text the one that appears to be the latest of those he has entitled "Nobody Laughed."

"Not Sixteen" contains various editorial problems arising from the unpolished form in which Anderson left it. A text published in *Tomorrow* in 1946 and the following year in *The Sherwood Anderson Reader* was prepared by Rosenfeld from a typescript (B), a fair copy, which Anderson read and lightly revised, of an earlier, heavily annotated typescript (A). The typist who prepared typescript B made some mistakes and omissions in that text, which Anderson sometimes failed to catch. Rosenfeld later made some additional changes of his own; for example when John after the war refers to "This hero bunk," the Rosenfeld reading is "this here bunk." A more extensive problem arose when the typist of typescript B misread a marginal emendation of part of the scene when John and Lillian are watching the leaves blowing in the wind, and Rosenfeld compounded the error:

Typescript A	*Typescript B*	*Anderson Reader*
"Look," he said, "he's going to get her." He told her of his thought about the shocked corn, like armies standing, he said. "Look," he said. "They stand in silence."	"Look," he said. "They stand in silence."	'Look,' he said. They stood in silence.

The A-text passage has a slight redundancy that Anderson might have eliminated if the passage had been correctly typed: John has already told Lillian his thought about the leaves being like armies. But the completion of the point that "he's going to get her" is an important expression of John's own designs on Lillian.

I have followed the text of typescript A, incorporating Anderson's emendations on typescript B. There are, however, two other problems having to do with Laura Lu Copenhaver's influence on the text. In addition to making a few mechanical corrections, she also had two recommendations. First, she advised him in a note on typescript B to remove "She wanted to" in the paragraph beginning "She was curiously frank," and he complied. Second, she reported to him in a letter on November 30, 1937 (now at the Newberry Library) that she had deleted "I have controlled myself" in the next-to-last paragraph and substituted: "Self-control is a fine thing." She wrote Anderson: "You will change it back & make a mistake." He left in his own sentence but added, "It is a fine thing." Because both changes are clearly an intrusion on

Anderson's own feel for the story, and he made them only to be accommodating to her, I have restored his original versions.

The text of "Certain Things Last" was prepared from an untitled typescript with annotations by Anderson at the Newberry Library. I have supplied the title.

In writing "In a Field," Anderson made a few changes in the version published in *A Story Teller's Story.* For further information on the text, see Charles E. Modlin, "'In a Field': A Story from *A Story Teller's Story*," *Winesburg Eagle* 8 (April 1983): 3-6.

The text of "Fred" is edited from the latest typescript of the story, corrected and signed by Anderson, which is in my possession.

"The Red Dog" is edited from a holograph manuscript at the Newberry Library.

—*C. E. M.*

EARLY PUBLICATIONS
OF STORIES

"Brother Death," *Death in the Woods* (New York: Liveright, 1933), 271-98.

"Brothers," *Bookman* 53 (April 1921): 110-15; *The Triumph of the Egg* (New York: Huebsch, 1921), 102-15.

"Certain Things Last," previously unpublished.

"The Corn Planting," *American Magazine* 118 (November 1934): 47, 149-50; *Penguin Parade* 1 (November 1937): 115-22.

"A Criminal's Christmas," *Vanity Fair* 27 (December 1926): 89, 130; *Hello Towns!* (New York: Liveright, 1929), 79-85.

"Death in the Woods," *American Mercury* 9 (September 1926): 7-13; *Death in the Woods,* 3-24.

"The Egg," originally "The Triumph of the Egg" in *Dial* 68 (March 1920): 295-304; *Triumph of the Egg,* 46-63.

"The Flood," *Death in the Woods,* 243-56.

"For What?" *Yale Review* 30 (June 1941): 750-58.

"Fred," previously unpublished.

"I Want to Know Why," *Smart Set* 60 (November 1919): 35-40; *Triumph of the Egg,* 5-20.

"I'm a Fool," *Dial* 72 (February 1922): 119-29; *London Mercury* 6 (May 1922): 19-27; *Horses and Men,* 3-18.

"In a Field," adapted from *A Story Teller's Story* (New York, Huebsch, 1924), 336-40; *Winesburg Eagle* 8 (April 1983): 3-6.

"In a Strange Town," *Scribner's Magazine* 87 (January 1930): 20-25; *Death in the Woods,* 141-57.

"The Man Who Became a Woman," *Horses and Men,* 185-228.

"The Man's Story," *Dial* 75 (September 1923): 247-64; *Horses and Men,* 287-312.

"The Masterpiece," published as "The Yellow Gown," *Mademoiselle* 15 (September 1942): 94-95, 154-57.

"A Meeting South," *Dial* 78 (April 1925): 269-79; *Sherwood Anderson's Notebook* (New York: Boni & Liveright, 1926), 103-21; *Death in the Woods,* 221-40.

"Milk Bottles," originally "Why There Must Be a Midwestern Literature" in *Vanity Fair* 16 (March 1921): 23-24; *Horses and Men,* 231-42.

"Mrs. Wife," published as "A Moonlight Walk," *Redbook* 70 (December 1937): 43-45.

"Nobody Laughed," *The Sherwood Anderson Reader,* ed. Paul Rosenfeld (Boston: Houghton Mifflin, 1947), 2-11.

"Not Sixteen," *Tomorrow* 5 (March 1946): 28-32; *Sherwood Anderson Reader,* 836-45.

"An Ohio Pagan," *Horses and Men,* 315-47.

"The Other Woman," *Little Review* 7 (May-June 1920): 37-44; *Triumph of the Egg,* 33-45.

"Pastoral," *Redbook* 74 (January 1940): 38-39, 59.

"The Red Dog," previously unpublished.

"The Return," *Century* 110 (May 1925): 3-14; *Death in the Woods,* 27-56.

"There She Is—She Is Taking Her Bath," *The Second American Caravan,* ed. Alfred Kreymborg, Lewis Mumford and Paul Rosenfeld (New York: Macaulay, 1928), 100-11; *Death in the Woods,* 59-80.

"These Mountaineers," *Vanity Fair* 33 (January 1930): 44-45, 94; *Death in the Woods,* 161-71.

"Virginia Justice," *Today* 2 (July 1934): 6-7, 24.

ABOUT
SHERWOOD ANDERSON

BORN IN CAMDEN, OHIO, ON SEPTEMBER 13,1876, SHERWOOD Anderson grew up in Clyde, Ohio, a town that inspired the setting of many of his stories. After serving in the Spanish-American War, he attended Wittenberg Academy in Springfield, Ohio for a year, then took a job in Chicago as a copywriter in an advertising firm. He married Cornelia Lane in 1904, had three children and began a career as president of a mail-order paint company in Elyria, Ohio. Following a difficult period of marital and business problems, he suffered a psychological crisis in November 1912, which led to his leaving his business and family and returning to Chicago to pursue a writing career.

In Chicago he resumed his advertising work to make ends meet and by 1914 began to publish his writings, which in the next eight years included three novels, *Windy McPherson's Son* (1916), *Marching Men* (1917) and *Poor White* (1920); the story cycle *Winesburg, Ohio* (1919); and a story collection, *The Triumph of the Egg* (1921). He married Tennessee Mitchell in 1916, but the marriage was not a success; in 1922 he left Chicago for New York, then Reno, Nevada. After his divorce in 1924, he married Elizabeth Prall, and they moved to New Orleans. His books during this period included two novels, *Many Marriages* (1923), and *Dark Laughter* (1925); an autobiography, *A Story Teller's Story* (1924);

and a new collection of stories, *Horses and Men* (1923).

In the summer of 1925 the Andersons vacationed in Troutdale, Virginia. He liked the area so much that he bought farmland there beside Ripshin creek and built a house that he called Ripshin. In the fall of 1927 he purchased the Marion Publishing Company in Marion, Virginia, twenty-two miles to the north, and became the editor and publisher of two weekly newspapers, articles from which were collected in a 1929 book, *Hello Towns!*. He and Elizabeth Prall separated in late 1928, and in the following year he fell in love with Eleanor Copenhaver, a Marion native and national YWCA official. Under her influence he traveled throughout the South touring factories and studying labor conditions. Their marriage in 1933 proved to be an exceedingly happy one. His publications in these years include two novels: *Beyond Desire* (1932) and *Kit Brandon* (1936); and his last volume of short stories, *Death in the Woods* (1933). The Andersons generally spent their summers at Ripshin and traveled extensively the rest of the year. They were en route to South America when he died of peritonitis in Colón, Panama, on March 8, 1941. Anderson never lost his zest for life and his epitaph in Marion proclaims, as he directed, that "Life, Not Death, Is the Great Adventure."